AF244142

OUTLAWS

Book Three

Mother Trucker Book Series

Outlaws
Copyright ©2016 by CRLE Publishing
Mitchell, Robyn

This is a work of fiction. All names, characters, places, and incidents are the products of the author's imagination or are used ficticiously. Any resemblance to current or local events or to living persons is entirely coincidental.

Library of Congress Cataloging-in –Publication Data

p.   cm

ISBN: 978-0-9972129-2-1   PCN: 2016944571

I. Truckers—Fiction II. Trucking Industry—Fiction III. Adventure Fiction
Fic Mit   PS 3606.A775M46

Editor-in-Chief: Mindy Reed, The Authors' Assistant
Interior Designed by Danielle H. Acee, The Authors' Assistant
Cover Design by Douglas Brown, Album Artist

Printed in the United States

OUTLAWS

a novel by

ROBYN MITCHELL

PUBLISHING
Odessa, TX

CHAPTER ONE

"Look, you imbecile. I pay you to find me drivers for my trucks, and that's what I want done. You find me ten new drivers by the end of the week or else." Pig hung up his cell phone and threw it to the floor. He shifted his four-hundred-pound body in the back seat of his dark SUV with tinted windows. "Head Hunter, take me to the house."

Head Hunter, Pig's driver and lead enforcer, knew that Pig's anger was about to surface, something everyone avoided like the plague. "No problem boss," he said.

Pig wore a three-piece suit custom made from fine Asian silk. His feet were covered with the finest snakeskin, size fourteen boots. He never went anywhere without his black felt fedora—it had become his trademark. There were only two times Pig removed his hats outside his home—when he was making a deal in person, and when someone was going to die.

The leather beneath him moaned under his weight as he looked through the side window. "I am surrounded by idiots," he muttered.

"I know, boss." Head Hunter put the SUV in drive and they pulled away from the restaurant Pig frequented on a regular basis. "I can take care of Black Jack for you if you want, boss."

"Just drive," Pig barked and then wheezed.

He'd been a chain smoker since he was a teenager. He always smelled of sweat and nicotine, even after bathing. His unpleasant aroma was how he had earned the nickname, Pig.

The men who worked for Pig and protected his business had become accustomed to his stench and dreaded the man far more than his smell. Pig was a ruthless protector of what he felt belonged to him.

Pig was strapped with two forty-fives under his coat and two four-ten derringers were hidden in each sleeve of his jacket. He was known to pull a weapon literally at a drop of a hat. He paid his enforcers extremely well for their loyalty and protection, but every one of them knew if they crossed Pig, he would kill them without hesitation. Pig trusted no one and ran much of his operations on his own from a computer that never left his sight. He was only in his early thirties but because of his weight, he used a cane to walk like a man in his eighties.

Although food and cigarettes were unfettered excesses, Pig avoided alcohol; he wanted his mind to remain sharp. He loved beautiful women, but his stench repulsed them, leaving him to pay handsomely for carnal companionship. Seduced by his money, several legitimate women attempted to be his mate, but not even money could make him appealing. Pig had everything he wanted in life…except a woman, and it irked him every time he thought about it.

◊◊◊

Shelby and Jack Mathews had returned from Colorado after much needed time away to recuperate. Shelby had again been traumatized by her former coworker, Betty Burton. Now Betty was dead, and while Shelby had never been one to rejoice over someone else's misfortune, she had to admit she was relieved to have Betty out of the picture for good.

Shelby was glad to be home with Jack, the love of her life. And while she still enjoyed her chosen profession as a trucker, she was not content with her current job. Shelby would always be grateful to Jayne who not only encouraged her to become a trucker, but had also given Shelby her recent position, which allowed her to stay close to home. Shelby, tired of working for other folks, now dreamed of owning her own truck. She knew she couldn't possibly afford one on her own, so kept her wish to herself.

◊◊◊

Shelby had pulled into the Flying J truck stop at exit 277 off I-20 near Tye, Texas for a cup of coffee and to stretch her legs. It was a cool October evening and she put her hands in the pockets of her hoodie and walked briskly to the store.

A man held the door for her as she approached. "Thank you," Shelby said, smiling faintly.

"You're welcome."

Before stopping for coffee, Shelby headed to the restroom. The man who had opened the door for her followed her toward the back of the store and headed for the men's room as she opened the door to the ladies' room.

After using the restroom, Shelby filled a cup with black coffee. The man who had held the door for Shelby was mixing creamer and sugar into his coffee on the counter. "Looks to me like you prefer your coffee black," he said, glancing over at her with a smile. "I used to take mine like that but over the years I guess I've gone soft and like it sweet."

Shelby smiled back at him. "I like my coffee with a little half and half, but I bring it with me and add it when I'm in the truck."

"You aren't taking your husband some coffee?"

Shelby knew the man was fishing for information. She'd gotten the marriage question more times than she could count. "I drive alone," she told him. "Been a solo driver for years. My husband does ride from time to time, though."

The man led the way to the cash register. "Not sure I would let my wife drive a truck alone, especially if she looked like you."

Shelby blushed a little.

"No need to be embarrassed by the truth, my lady."

"Thank you for the compliment."

The man quickly paid for both cups before she could object. "Thank you, but you didn't have to do that for me."

"Nonsense. I never get to buy a beautiful woman a cup of coffee. It was my pleasure."

"Well, thank you. Perhaps I can buy you a cup sometime."

"Perhaps, but this is a big country. We might run into each other again, though. It has been known to happen."

The man escorted Shelby through the doors and walked with her toward her truck. They talked casually about trucking and what each of them was hauling. They discussed their destinations and the amount of time they spent away from their families. When Shelby and the man reached the back of her trailer she stopped. "Well, here I am."

The man put his hand out and Shelby shook it. "It's been great getting to know you."

"Same here."

The man reached into his pocket, pulled out a business card, and handed it to Shelby. "If you ever decide you want to change jobs and make some really good money, give me a call."

Shelby looked at the card and then at the man. "Black Jack? That's your name? Sounds like a handle."

The man chuckled. "Yeah, it is a handle and also what everyone I know calls me."

Shelby looked over the card again and noticed on the back a phone number that had been written by hand.

The man responded before Shelby could ask. "That's my private number in case you can't reach me on my company phone."

Shelby stuffed the card into the pocket of her hoodie and shook the man's hand again. "Okay, I'll keep that in mind." Shelby walked toward her truck, sipping at her coffee. "Thanks again for the coffee, Black Jack."

Shelby could feel Black Jack's eyes on her as she unlocked her truck and started to climb inside. At the last minute, Shelby leaned out of her truck and yelled toward the stranger as he started to walk to his own truck. "They call me Barbie."

The man lifted his coffee and laughed. "I see why."

Shelby smiled and pulled her door closed. Then she pulled the card out of her pocket and examined it. She slapped it a couple times against the steering wheel before placing it on her visor. She looked out her window and saw that the man was driving a beautiful black Peterbilt tractor, chromed to the max. It was attached to an equally chromed out drop deck trailer. The trailer was loaded with what appeared to be a train car box.

I don't see myself calling him for a job, she thought, *but if his company provides that kind of equipment to all its employees, I may just have to think about it.*

◊◊◊

Head Hunter pulled up to the fancy, guarded wrought-iron gate in front of Pig's estate and rolled down his window. The sentry recognized his boss' SUV, gave a cursory glance to ensure his employer was in the vehicle, and quickly opened the gate. Head Hunter closed the window, entered the estate, and moved up the long, winding driveway.

The twelve-thousand-square-foot mansion was isolated and concealed by trees and shrubs, making surveillance of the premises impossible from anywhere but the air. Pig possessed several acres of well-manicured lawn fenced off by white pickets, which separated a smattering of warehouses and other buildings. There was a landing strip for his private plane, which select customers also used. The entire estate was protected and monitored by the best high-tech security money could buy.

Although Pig had cameras everywhere, some of his permanent, dedicated-for-life soldiers had been implanted with microchips in order to assure Pig of their dedication to him as well as granting him access to all of their personal information. As of yet, the microchip implants were not a requirement for employment, but if someone volunteered for the chip, they received a huge bonus with job security for life.

Almost everything Pig owned had microchip locators, from the simplest piece of furniture or electronic device in his home to the many buildings he owned, many with cameras as well. Anything mobile or extremely valuable had a camera. Pig had complete access to and control of everything and everyone from his laptop computer.

Not being a man to take chances, Pig had an off the grid generator and a twenty-four-hour manned surveillance command center.

Pig had layers of politicians and law enforcement officials on his payroll, protecting his lifestyle and theirs. Anyone dealing with Pig was placed on his detection list. Their every movement was tracked in one way or another. All this to protect his warehouses of drugs, guns, and other contraband.

A security guard stationed at his front door quickly met his boss once the vehicle stopped. He opened Pig's door and helped the oversized man exit the back seat. Pig accepted the help, but once he was clear of the door frame he jerked his arms away grumbling, "I can manage. Get my phone from the floor and bring it to me."

Pig waddled up the two steps that led to the front entrance, where his personal attendant opened the front door for him. "I'll be going to the command center and then to my room, Harry. Have Hank, Tazz, and Drifter meet me there."

Harry took Pig's hat. "Yes, sir."

The command center was located just to the left, off the main foyer. Harry opened one of the wide wooden doors that barely allowed his employer to slip sideways through the entrance. The center was manned by a team of eight dispatchers. There were several armed guards, watching every move made in the center. Monitors in the center plastered two complete walls.

In one corner of the huge room, a control panel for the entire operation towered over the cubicles below. Pig made his way up the three steps to the glass-enclosed brain of the operation. Just as he reached the panel, his right-hand man Hank entered the center and hurried over to where his boss was waiting. "Harry said you wanted to see me, boss?"

Pig squinted at him. "Where are Tazz and Drifter?"

"They're taking care of a shipment that just arrived."

Pig nodded and then took a seat in a custom made, oversized chair. He took out his laptop and began punching keys, causing several screens to appear on the main monitors. "I want to know why these warehouse cameras are not giving me wider views of the merchandise, Hank. I pay you to make sure that the items my customers have entrusted me with are safe and secure. You and I both know Bullets and his men will do whatever they have to do to penetrate my operation."

"I was sure we had every inch of that building covered inside, boss."

Pig pointed impatiently to several points of interest on different monitors. "There, there, there, and there, you idiot. If you move from one screen to another you can see the break in security, and I want it fixed at once. I want more camera coverage and listening devices placed in that building immediately!"

"I see what you're talking about, boss, and I'll make sure that it is taken care tonight," Hank said nervously as he scanned the screens.

Pig got slowly out of his chair and waddled toward the exit of the platform. "I'll check in the morning to make sure it has been completed to my satisfaction. Also, check on the building in the M-9 region. I overheard some chatter from a couple of drivers that Time Bomb and some of his flunkies were seen in that area. They may be staking out the area in order to get access to that warehouse."

"Got it, boss. I'll send Parker to the area for a personal inspection and report back."

Gripping the handrails tightly, Pig climbed slowly down the steps. "Parker has done a great job protecting that building, but Bullets is a snake. If his men are snooping around, you know he's up to something."

"I know, boss."

Pig barked out one last command to his lead enforcer before leaving the room. "Check on Black Jack and let me know what he's doing. I gave him an order and I want it followed."

"I'll email you my findings before you wake up in the morning, boss."

Hank breathed a faint sigh of relief once Pig was out of the room. He had no idea what Pig had ordered Black Jack to do other than it had something to do with Texas. Among other things, Black Jack was in charge of recruiting new drivers for Pig. Hank knew Pig was expanding his operation to meet customer requests for "special" storage for their "special" property. He figured Black Jack was being pushed to find several more drivers to transport that property. Whatever it was, Hank knew when Pig wanted someone tracked something was wrong.

He punched up Black Jack's chip and downloaded his activity to Pig's email. Then he switched to the M-9 region and the areas around the warehouses. It took several hours to check the whole area, but there was one specific spot to the back of the area that appeared to be at risk. Hank marked the area and again sent the information to Pig.

Hank put a call into Parker, who had made several verbal threats to Bullets' men. "Parker, you know Pig wants no involvement with any law enforcement agency. Do not confront or make any kind of enforcement movements in the open against any of Bullets' men. Eliminate the leak as quietly and as ghostly as you can."

"Okay, Hank, but without bringing them into the warehouse area and disposing of them in the secrecy of our secured area, I'm not sure how else to keep them from checking out the warehouses."

"INVISIBILITY, PARKER! INVISIBILITY! I have located a possible exposure point to the rear of the warehouse area near the trees. I'll email you the satellite picture of the area and I want it closed. Do not bring anyone into the secured areas without authorization. If you have to eliminate the spies, take it to the border and let Pig's foreign friends have the pleasure of executing them."

"Fine, Hank. But how do you suppose I get those boneheads down there?"

"Figure it out. Just don't draw attention to Pig or his property. That would be a devastating mistake for you."

"Fine," he sighed. "I'll do what I can."

◊◊◊

Pig had a perfect pickup and delivery system. People in particularly sensitive positions were placed along the borders and on docks and ports located on both sides of the country and in customs. He ensured those placements by tapping political clients and business associates that used his services. Products and merchandise that required protection or no detection from honest law abiding politicians and law enforcement were given to Pig for delivery or storage. One thing Pig couldn't control, however, was the DEA. He had been unable to infiltrate that organization. Since he had no idea if they had anything on him, he kept his nose as clean as possible, hoping they wouldn't notice him.

The drivers were hired to pick up sensitive cargo in Texas, California, and border towns near Mexico, as well as ports across the East Coast. They were to deliver their consignments to Pig's secure warehouses. Black Jack, a seasoned truck driver, brought in new drivers straight from the road. The drivers were never given any information about what they were hauling and were forbidden to check out their freight. The pay was fantastic and the work was easy. Of course, there were downsides, too. They were monitored constantly with onboard trackers, cameras, and voice monitors. Any driver who got curious or had run-ins with the law were terminated immediately.

Pig had made it very clear he didn't want or need DOT putting their noses in his business. Trucks and trailers were kept in perfect condition with all mechanical issues attended to immediately. Pig's theory had proven to be correct, if DOT had no reason to watch his trucks, they wouldn't and they didn't. He was allowed to haul his illegal merchandise across the country without problems because he made his company maintain a low profile.

Even with all his precautions and rules, he had a lingering thorn in his side—Bullets. The pain Bullets and his gang had created for Pig was eventually going to lead to an all-out ground war. Pig, however, was doing everything in his power to avoid that confrontation, knowing it would lead to exposure. The inevitability was there regardless. Bullets wanted Pig's business and nothing except death was going to prevent him from going after it.

Pig had even gone as far as inviting Bullets into his organization, willing to make him his lead lieutenant. But Bullets had laughed and let Pig know in no uncertain terms that he would rather take Pig's empire for himself.

◊◊◊

Shelby didn't know why she was so intrigued with Black Jack, but he stuck in her mind as she moved down the highway. She couldn't decide if it was his appearance or his personality. Black Jack was a tall, slender-built man who made a pair of Wrangler jeans fit like a glove. But the black felt cowboy hat that covered most of his forehead hid what Shelby liked best but only caught a glimpse of—dark brown eyes. *Stupid woman. Jack will go crazy if you ask him to buy you a truck*, she thought. *He'll also lose it when you bring up the idea of long hauling again. You just need to put it all out of your mind and live with what you are doing now.*

Shelby reached above the steering wheel and took Black Jack's business card off the visor. She turned on the overhead light and looked at the card again before putting it back in the place she had just taken it from. Then she shook her head and turned the overhead light off again. There was no way Jack would let her change jobs. She let the subject go as she headed home.

Miles away, Black Jack couldn't get Shelby out of his head either. He wished he had gotten her number, but he hadn't wanted to seem too forward, especially after she mentioned her husband. He did think she would have made a great driver. He had recruited only two women since he had been given the assignment, and one of the women—Angelica—had already moved up in the company. In fact, she was one of his best recruits. She was never late for a pickup and was always on time for a delivery.

Shelby seemed to be just what Black Jack was looking for in a recruit. He had liked the results he was getting with his female drivers. The better the drivers did, the better he looked in front of Pig. *I just need to find Barbie again and soon*, he thought.

◊◊◊

After Hank finished sending Pig all the information he'd asked for, he completed his regular scan of properties and then left the command center to the night shift. Hank was met by two of Pig's enforcers in the lobby of Pig's house. "So did you take care of the shipment?"

Tazz and Drifter were always cocky with Hank when Pig wasn't around. They knew he had every inch of his property under cameras and voice monitoring devices but they loved making Hank feel like he had no power over them. "Well, I don't know, Hank sir, is that what we were supposed to do?"

"Shut up, Drifter. You guys had better have done as you were told or Pig will know tomorrow in my report."

"We did, Hank," Tazz said. "Don't get your panties in a bunch."

Hank rolled his eyes. "Good. At least I won't have to have you beheaded by the cartel tonight."

"Ha! Ha! Jackass!"

Hank disappeared in the elevator, leaving Drifter and Tazz to their joking.

◊◊◊

Pig had retired to the comfort of his private quarters. His personal attendant, Harry, helped him undress and get into silk pajamas. He turned down the bed and left a bottle of water on Pig's nightstand. "Will there be anything else this evening, sir?" he asked.

Pig lay in his bed focused on the seventy-two-inch flat screen TV that took up a large portion of the wall. "No, Harry. That's all, thank you."

"Very good, sir." Harry left the room, locking the door as he left. Pig, by habit, had his laptop next to him on the bed. He opened the screen and checked through his warehouses and house and then turned his attention back to the television.

Pig's cell phone rang. He looked at the screen and then answered it. There were no pleasantries with Pig, especially when he was doing business. Pig opened a screen on his computer. "Yes?" The person on the other end of the line said very little but plainly explained what he needed from Pig. "How many?" A response. "Where and what time?" Another response. "Destination and time?" As Pig listened, he typed the information into the computer and then gave confirmation. "Done."

Pig emailed Head Hunter to let him know they'd be going to a warehouse near his property in Louisiana. It was one of the many places not located on his estate He had agreed to meet a client there personally for the pick-up of a very valuable painting that Pig had been protecting for him. The painting had been brought into the States without going through customs. The new owner had obtained this new property through less-than-honest measures and was determined to keep what he had taken no matter the cost.

◊◊◊

Hank reached his room and closed his door. He knew he was still under surveillance, even in his room. Pig, however, had made it clear to his monitors that unless he gave them specific orders, they were to give his top lieutenants their privacy during rest hours. If they violated that small amount of privacy without permission, they would be terminated. Hank liked working for Pig and he was paid well for his loyalty, but sometimes he hated the lack of privacy. He cherished the few hours he had without surveillance. He also hated the fact he had never had time for a family, but this was the life he had chosen. The other stuff would have to wait.

CHAPTER TWO

Rex's cell phone rang and the screen revealed that it was Angelica, his only female driver. She had long brown hair that flowed down her back to her waist and matching deep brown eyes. She was thin, but had well-developed muscles in her arms and legs. She had retired from the Marines several years ago but had managed to stay physically fit.

She missed being a Marine. However, after taking shrapnel from a roadside bomb in Iraq, once she recovered, she decided to try her hand at something she thought might be a little less dangerous. Now Angelica was beginning to realize that her new profession was probably more dangerous than being a soldier. She had taken a position with the DEA. Since her reassignment to the undercover division, Angelica had been shot at, beaten up, and dragged behind a pickup. Fortunately, her current assignment was a little less hazardous; she was driving a truck for a man who the DEA was investigating. So far she had not been put in the line of fire, but she figured the closer she got to the interior of the operation, the more heated things would become.

Angelica was constantly being watched and monitored by both voice and location devices. With those devices in place, the only opportunity Angelica had to use her personal cell phone was when she was outside of her truck. Besides, she could only make contact with her handler at special locations. "Rex, this is Angelica," she said when Rex answered her call. "I'm going to be in Atlanta in a few hours. We need to meet so I can give you my phone downloads. I've got photos and documents for you to analyze. I would have given them to you sooner, but I haven't been alone anywhere until now."

"Okay, Angelica," Rex answered. "Just let me know when you reach the meeting location. How are you doing out there?"

"I'm good. Things are pretty calm really. They're sending me to Mexico tomorrow so I'm sure there will be some interesting information coming from that load. They don't give much information out, but from what some of the other drivers have been saying Pig is pulling a lot of his drivers in for this transport. I guess it's pretty big."

"Have you heard who it's for?"

"No, they never tell us that or what we're hauling. But since it's coming out of Mexico and we're picking it up at night just this side of Mexicali, I'm sure it's cartel."

"Okay. We'll talk more about it when you get here. Be safe."

As a new hire, Angelica had been assigned to a trainer for her first two weeks. He'd been released from his duties just before Angelica was loaded out of California and sent to Atlanta. Angelica was glad to be rid of him. He was a nice guy, but he did not give her any privacy. He didn't follow her into the restroom or the shower but she was sure he would have if he could have. Angelica figured he wasn't a pervert—just lonely and extremely protective of women. When she finally revealed to him that she was a retired Marine, having served in Iraq, his attitude changed. She could take care of herself and didn't need his protection.

◊◊◊

Jack entered the living room where Shelby was curled up on the couch with a throw blanket and glass of wine. He went straight to her and kissed the top of her head. "Hey, baby, glad to see you're home tonight. How was your day?"

"It was okay."

He could tell from his wife's response that there was something on her mind.

He went to the bar and got a beer. "What's up, Shelby? I know something's bothering you."

She wasn't sure how to begin, so she just blurted it out. "Jack, I want my own truck."

"Oh…kay…" he said slowly. "But I didn't think Jayne put on Owner Ops?"

"She doesn't. I like working for her but I'm getting bored with the same old routes. I miss the road, Jack. I mean I really miss the long stuff. And, babe, you should see some of the beautiful trucks out there now. I really want my own, Jack."

Jack listened as Shelby described in great detail several big rigs she had seen on the road. He looked into his wife's vibrant face as she talked about the things that she wanted in her own truck. She was passionate about this and he didn't want to discourage her, even if he wasn't crazy about the idea.

Shelby finally finished telling Jack everything she'd been thinking and waited for him to object.

"Well…I think that sounds great, baby. Have you looked into what we will need to do in order to get our own?"

Shelby was stunned. Jack hadn't given his usual "I'm not sure we can afford it," or "maybe we should wait and see" responses.

"Well, yes," she sputtered. "I've checked them out online and even been to a couple truck dealerships here in town looking around. I've got to say…I'm a little surprised, Jack. Usually when I suggest a change you find a lot of reasons why we shouldn't. Thank you for at least being willing to think about it."

"I can tell from your enthusiasm this is something you are really interested in and I'm willing to explore it with you. Hell, I might even quit my job and we can go trucking together. You know, like a husband and wife team."

Shelby sipped at her wine. "You want to drive a truck? That would be great, but I didn't think you liked driving."

Jack put his beer down and pretended to shift and move a steering wheel. The couple laughed together at Jack's imitation. "Come on, baby, let's make Amarillo by morning."

Shelby laughed so hard tears began to fall. "You're crazy."

Jack stopped pretending and took his wife in his arms. "Crazy for you, baby. I'm willing to do whatever it takes to make you happy."

◊◊◊

Black Jack had spent every waking moment looking for new recruits. He'd been able to sign on eight new drivers, but Pig wanted ten. He knew of a man in Houston who was thinking about signing on but he still had one more truck to fill. His thoughts went back to Shelby. He only knew her by her handle, but he wished now that he had been a little more aggressive with her and gotten her real name. He had until Friday to fill Pig's quota.

When Black Jack arrived in Midland, Texas he stopped at the Warfield Truck Stop for a bite to eat and ate quietly, listening to the buzz of conversation around him. It was his habit to do this in the presence of other truck drivers. He had learned how much information he could get just from listening to their gossip.

His ears perked up when one driver began talking about a little blonde driver he had run into on location. "I don't know where she came from, but she surprised the hell out of me on that mud pit of a location. She was hauling some chemical products that the company man had been waiting on for several hours. He came out of his trailer and started jumping her shit for not having that shit there earlier. I'm not exactly sure what she said to him, but she got back in her truck and started leaving with that stuff still on her trailer. He stopped her. All I saw was her getting out of her truck mad as hell and her finger in his face. Then she pointed to his trailer and he left."

Several men speculated on what she probably said, but the man who witnessed the incident responded, "All I know is I sure wouldn't want to make that Barbie doll pissed at me."

Another man spoke up. "Barbie? You ran into Barbie?"

"Yeah I guess. That was the name on the door of her truck."

"Oh hell man, she's from around here. And yeah, she's a little spitfire."

The man who started the conversation continued, "Well, wherever she's from she sure doesn't look like any truck driver I've ever met. Is she married?"

"Yeah, I think someone said her husband's a boss for one of the oilfield service companies around here."

"Well, if I had that babe for a wife she wouldn't be driving a truck—at least not without me." The crowd of men laughed.

Black Jack was curious now if this might be the same Barbie he had run into at the 277. He decided to press the man who seemed to know who she was for some further information. "So what company does she pull for anyway?" he asked.

"Oh, I can't remember the name exactly, but it's a small local hauling company over off I-20. They run mostly boxes, but they have some drop deck and flatbeds. They haul just about anything, but I think they specialize in hazardous material that doesn't need to be in tanks."

"It's just right over there off the south side of the 20, across from that safety place," another driver chimed in. "Jayne somebody owns it. Rich sugar mama."

The drivers continued laughing about that last comment while Black Jack went back to his meal. *Have I found Barbie?* He planned to check out the business first thing in the morning.

◊◊◊

Angelica arrived in Atlanta and notified Rex. "Hey Rex, I'm at the café and my truck is at the truck stop. I'm not running with anyone and I had a taxi bring me here so if any of the other drivers accidentally spot my truck or see me getting in and out of the taxi I can just tell them I went to town for a good meal."

"Great," said Rex. "I'll be there in a few minutes. We can either talk there in the back or take a walk—whichever you think would be less suspicious."

"I think we need to get a bite to eat here. It smells good and I'm hungry. Then we can take a walk and discuss some important things I've found out."

"Sounds like a plan. Be there soon."

In the restaurant, Angelica ordered a glass of sweet tea and looked over the menu. A short, heavyset black woman came back with Angelica's tea. "Are you ready to order, ma'am?"

Angelica looked up from the menu. "Not yet, but could you bring me some kind of appetizer? I'm starved, but I want to wait until my friend arrives to order my meal."

"Perhaps you would like some sweet potato fries or a cup of gumbo for starters."

Angelica felt her mouth water. "The gumbo sounds perfect, thank you."

The woman smiled and left to retrieve the soup.

Angelica found eating on the road a challenge. She tried to avoid foods that were loaded with lots of carbs or too much red meat. She preferred fruits and vegetables, but those items were difficult to locate in truck stops. She was addicted to coffee and would go days with just coffee and maybe an apple. Today she had consumed several cups of coffee with an orange for breakfast and six crackers for lunch. Her body was letting her know that it was time to put some real fuel into it. She was having trouble deciding; everything looked so good to her.

The waitress returned with her cup of gumbo. Angelica put her nose to the bowl and took a deep whiff of the savory stew. "Oh, this is absolutely divine, thank you."

"Enjoy," said the waitress. "I'll be back in a moment to see if you need anything else."

Angelica had just picked up the saltshaker when she heard a voice say, "I see you started without me."

Angelica looked and saw Rex slide into the booth across from her. She smiled as she stirred her soup and then took a nice spoonful into her mouth. "Oh, you have no idea how long it has been since I have tasted real food. The food on the roads of this country for truck drivers is about as bad as MREs."

Rex laughed as he looked at his menu and ordered a glass of tea from their waitress. "Come on Angelica, you know MREs are good for you."

"Yeah, if you want your ass to become the size of a building. Whoever decided that a carb-saturated, processed food diet was best for a soldier in battle has never been in one."

"That's not true, Angelica. You know the reason they do it."

"Yeah okay, because the carbs break down into sugar in the body and provide the soldier with energy. Plus, it keeps them full longer if that's the only meal of the day."

"Correct."

"Yeah I know, but it still puts fat on soldiers. It did me. I had to work out twice as hard when I returned to base after patrols."

"Your ass looks fine to me." He gave her a wink.

Rex and Angelica talked over dinner about the military and other things they had in common. Rex had also been a Marine but had left the Corps several years before the second entrance by America into Iraq. He had been called up again during the second war, but because of a car accident, resulting in an injury to one of his eyes, he wasn't allowed to deploy. He had been with the DEA since he had left the Marines but because of the accident, he had also been taken out of the field and put in a handler position. He liked being a handler, but he missed the action of being undercover. Angelica had been under his charge since she had signed on with the agency.

Rex was divorced with two grown kids, one of them just ten years younger than Angelica. Angelica had never married and had no children. She told Rex she'd never met the right guy. Rex knew better. He did not let Angelica know that his deep investigation of her past before the DEA hired her had revealed that a man she was going to marry had been killed in Iraq just a few feet from her. She never spoke of it to Rex and he never asked.

The relationship between the two was close—probably too close for the agency if they had gotten wind of it. But Rex and Angelica made sure they kept their feelings for each other in check. Angelica had found herself in Rex's arms several times after close calls and she liked how it felt. But love was something she wasn't about to get into again. The pain from the first time still hung with her.

◊◊◊

Pig met with his customer and released the prized painting to the obsessed collector. The man treated the painting as if it was gold as he yelled and screamed at the two men he had brought with him. The van they arrived in was simple enough from the outside, but the man had the interior in the back of the van extensively modified to protect the painting during transportation to his home. Pig had invested money in art, but he would have never thought to treat a piece of art in such a ridiculous manner. What was even more ridiculous was that the painting was stolen and the man would never be able to show it to anyone but himself for fear of being caught with the stolen property. Pig laughed all the way to the bank and subsequently deposited close to half a million dollars of the man's money into his private security vault.

Pig's distrust of everyone had led him to build a private vault underground on his estate. Only he knew exactly where the vault was located and how to get into the well-fortified container. He knew exactly how much was in there, and he only removed what he needed to make payroll and expenses. He also owned a small bank that he used to move money for customers and keep the government from discovering just how much he was really worth.

Pig knew he was eventually going to have to find someone he could trust to give everything to since he wouldn't live forever. His personal assistant Harry was close to being the only person he truly trusted, but Harry wasn't much of a businessman. Hank was also close, but Pig still had issues with his inability to use a gun when it was needed. Hank was soft, which would definitely interfere with control of the business. Pig wanted a son but he couldn't find a woman who could stand him long enough to create one. Pig had plenty of money and he could afford any kind of surgery to get rid of the excess fat he carried. Two problems interfered with that possible solution. One, he would have to be placed under anesthesia, meaning he wouldn't have any control over his life during the operation. Number two, Pig loved food and he wasn't willing to give it up for anyone. It had become increasingly clear to Pig lately that he was going to have to pay for a son.

◊◊◊

Shelby had arrived a little late to the yard. Since becoming complacent with her job, she'd been less punctual. She drove to her truck and took the things she knew she would need out of her car and put them inside the cab. She routinely but halfheartedly checked the engine fluids, belts, and lines before closing the hood and starting the engine. She hated the feelings she was experiencing toward something she truly loved doing. "What's wrong with you Shelby Mathews?" she muttered to herself. "You love driving a truck. Why are you acting as if you hate it?"

Inside the truck, Shelby turned on all of her lights and took her walk-around to make sure all tires, lights, and truck parts were in their proper functional positions. She casually inspected the truck as she slowly walked the perimeter, all the while daydreaming that someday she would make this same walk around her own truck.

Shelby climbed into her cab and worked on her log. Just as she was about to pull her truck out of its parking space and head for a warehouse in San Antonio, she was interrupted by a knock at her driver's side door. Slightly frightened by the unexpected intrusion into her routine, Shelby looked through the side window to see who could possibly be knocking. To her surprise, it was one of the yard hands with a message. Shelby rolled down her window.

"Sorry to scare you, Shelby, but there is a man in the office looking for you. We weren't sure who he was, so Jayne sent me to get you instead of allowing him to come out here."

Shelby was a little surprised that anyone would show up at her work looking for her. "Did you get a name?"

"I can't remember, but it was Black something."

"Black something… How odd. Well, I'll be there in a minute. Did he happen to mention what he wanted?"

"Nope, just looking for 'Barbie.'"

"Well, that's really strange. He doesn't even know my real name. Give me a few more minutes to finish my log and I'll be there."

Curiosity gnawed at Shelby as she tried to concentrate on her log. But it was difficult to concentrate and she kept making mistakes. "Dammit." She closed the logbook and threw it on the dash. Then she pushed in on the air brakes and moved her truck toward the office building at the front of the property. *Who'd be looking for me here at work but not know my real name?* She wondered. Shelby pulled close to the front of the building and parked. Once inside the office, her curiosity was suddenly replaced with utter surprise and shock.

He stood in the lobby of the office building, holding his black felt cowboy hat in his hands. "Black Jack?" Shelby asked in disbelief.

Black Jack smiled. "Don't worry—I'm not stalking you, Barbie. I just want to speak with you. I've been hoping you would call, but you hadn't and

I was at the truck stop last night where someone just happened to mention you. Through the conversation I was able to find out that you're employed here. I hope you aren't upset, but I really need to talk to you."

Shelby believed Black Jack. A stalker wouldn't be so nervous. Shelby motioned for Black Jack to follow her. "Sure, come on. We can talk out here."

Shelby sat on her truck step and asked, "So what's this all about?"

Black Jack began to explain he was a recruiter for Pig's shipping business. Since meeting Shelby, he felt she would be a terrific asset to the organization.

Shelby liked Black Jack's pitch, but she wasn't sure she liked the way that drivers were recruited. She had a hundred questions, and she never once let on that she had actually been contemplating a change in her current situation. "Wow, I like what you're telling me, Black Jack, but I'm not one to just up and run. Do you have a website or an office that I can visit? Even if I consider your offer, I'll have to discuss it with my husband and he'll want to see things for himself. Not only in writing but physically. He's very protective of me."

Black Jack took another card out of his pocket and a folded piece of paper from his back pocket. He handed both to Shelby. "I totally understand his concerns, and if you were my wife I would feel the same way. Here's another card and this is one of our company fliers. You are welcome to visit our home office in Shreveport anytime. In fact, if you and your husband decide to look at our company, we will gladly fly you down for a visit."

"Really? Wow, that's nice." Shelby looked over the material. "I don't know, Black Jack. My husband and I have been talking about putting me in my own truck. Do you have a leasing program?"

"Yes, we have several trucks leased on with us, and if that's what you want we even have a lease to own program."

Shelby was becoming excited. Black Jack was saying all the right things now. He was even offering her an opportunity to own her own truck, but she didn't want to appear too anxious. "I have to talk to my husband about this before I can even think about giving you an answer."

Black Jack was happy with her response. He knew if he could talk to Shelby's husband he would be able to convince him to let his wife join his team. "I'm going to be in town for a couple days and I would be honored with the opportunity to talk with your husband," he said. "Perhaps you can talk to him first and then I can take you guys to dinner tonight."

Shelby wasn't sure what the hurry was all about but she figured Jack would agree to a meeting with the man. Even if he didn't like the offer he would still understand that she was serious about owning her own truck.

"Okay," she said with a smile. "I'll give him a call and see if he's available for a dinner meeting tonight. I have to make this local, but I think that's all they have for me today so I should be open."

As he shook Shelby's hand, Black Jack was almost relieved that he was close to making the quota that Pig had forced on him. "Great. Just give me a call this afternoon and we will meet somewhere. I'm not familiar with any of the local restaurants so I hope you and your husband can recommend a nice one."

"Sure. There are a few good ones in town that we enjoy. I'll give you a call later today and let you know if Jack is available."

Black Jack took his hat off slightly in a gesture of respect toward Shelby. "Sounds great. I look forward to your call."

Shelby got into her truck, got a pen and paper and stuck her head out the window. "Hold on, Black Jack."

Black Jack waited as she wrote on the little slip of paper. "Here, this is my real name and my cell number."

Black Jack took the slip of paper and read out loud, "Shelby Mathews. Thanks, Shelby. Talk to you soon."

◊◊◊

After dinner, Angelica and Rex took a walk through the city streets near the café. Angelica put her arm through Rex's and they strolled through the night like a cozy married couple, relaxing together in the evening breeze. From time to time he placed his hand on hers, letting his true feelings for her show. Angelica, in turn, patted his hand with her other one, letting Rex know that she understood and felt the same.

"You know, the closer I get to the inside of this operation, the more difficult it's going to be to make contact with you. They've been putting pressure on me to have that chip implant done."

"Yeah, but you know you can't do that."

"You can count on the fact that won't happen. Not just because it will jeopardize my security in this case but frankly, I can't have something like that placed in my body…what an invasion."

"That Pig is some piece of work, isn't he?" said Rex.

"You have no idea," Angelica answered. "He's completely paranoid. Why has he been off our radar for so long? He's been in operation for years and we're just now investigating his connections to the underworld. Has he been that good at staying undetected, or has he had protection from inside?"

"You are correct on both accounts, kiddo. He has been extremely careful and clever. But he's also made some very powerful friends who have been covering for him. We haven't found any of his friends connected to our agency yet, but it wouldn't surprise me. The reason he's just now being investigated is because his name kept coming up in relationship to a rival gang out of LA. We've been investigating Bullets' gang for years now. Apparently Bullets has his eyes set on Pig's organization and he's been doing some really rash things to infiltrate it. Pig is still protected by his loyal clients, but you know when we break this thing wide open they'll go down with him. No one is above the law."

Rex stopped near a little bench along the sidewalk they had been following. He put out his hand for her to sit and then sat next to her. He was worried about Angelica because she was so young and somewhat naive. He knew she was a strong woman, but this operation was dangerous and different from her Marine assignments. "Look, Angelica, I know you can handle yourself and you have proven yourself time and time again in this job, but I'm worried about this case. Pig is vicious and won't hesitate to eliminate anyone or anything that threatens his operations. We know that he has millions of dollars hidden somewhere on his estate and the ability to get rid of any obstacle in his path."

Angelica sat up straight. She was proud that her undercover work was becoming useful. "Yeah, and I think I know where that is too. I took a bunch of pictures of this one specific area of his estate, which is completely forbidden to anyone except him. It's overly fortified too." She leaned back into Rex's arms.

"That's great. I'll download your photos when I get back to the office. Just don't put yourself out there for discovery. Stay low."

"I am, Rex. I know how important it is to remain undetectable. But there is something going on with the leader of Pig's rival gang and if I could get closer to some of the insiders, maybe I could get more information."

"No, Angelica. Just drive the truck and gather what you can for now. We have some other operatives working on the inside of Bullets' gang. Pig and Bullets are gearing up for a showdown unless Pig takes action first. I don't want you getting hurt."

Angelica wanted to go deeper into the operation, but could tell from his tone that she'd better just do what he wanted. "Okay, but don't you find it strange that Pig hasn't already eliminated Bullets? He's got the means."

"Yes, but he hasn't taken Bullets down yet because his connections on the inside have let him know he's being monitored by the government."

"He's got some major players watching his back if he's getting that kind of information."

"Yeah, and you can be assured when he gets the all clear he'll take that entire gang down without blinking, and probably without anyone knowing about it. He's extremely dangerous so stay clear of him and just do what you have been placed in there to do. Collect information and let us know where you are being sent for pickups and deliveries. The more intelligence we get on the man and how he moves his stuff the better. There isn't any need for you to move in any closer for now. Just drive and give me locations."

Angelica relented. "He doesn't know we're on the inside does he?"

"No, not that we can tell. But even if he might be suspicious of someone on the inside, he's protected himself with layers of security. No one has ever gotten that close to him. We don't even know his weak point yet."

"Weak point?"

"Everyone has a weak point. Pig is human, so he has one."

"You want me to see if I can find out?"

"Not right now, but keep your ears open to talk. Someone might say something that could be useful."

Angelica turned to face Rex on the bench. She planted an unexpected but welcomed kiss on his lips. They stayed locked in the kiss for several seconds before Angelica broke away. "What's your weakness, Mr. Rex? I found mine, but I'm not sure what to do with it."

Rex knew he needed to be careful about getting too emotionally attached to his rookie, but Angelica's kiss just proved she was more than willing to give in to temptation. Rex pulled Angelica close and returned the first soft sweet kiss of hers with a passionate kiss of his own. "You."

CHAPTER THREE

Hank was busy in the command center when Pig requested an audience with him on the patio. Pig was never one to relay cartel information over phones or computers. He had paid out millions of dollars for protection from the government, but it was clear his money wasn't enough anymore. His powerful friends had informed him last month that he was being watched closely by the DEA. They didn't know if he had been infiltrated, but they knew he was on their radar. So to keep his clients protected and happy he chose to relay detailed information on the transportation of their product by mouth.

Hank ran to the patio and was almost out of breath when he arrived.

Pig was sipping on a glass of tea, petting one of his several Golden Retrievers.

"I'm here, boss."

"I assume you have already dispatched twenty of my trucks for Mexicali?" Pig said.

"Yes, boss. I did that yesterday. Those that were already loaded are completing their deliveries and all are heading in that direction. Ten will arrive for pickup on Friday night and ten will pick up on Saturday night. The ten on Friday night will deliver in New York Tuesday night and those loading on Saturday will deliver in Texas on Tuesday night."

Pig never smiled or gave compliments. "I have secured their passage through all weigh stations and checkpoints. The deliveries will be met not only by our men, but also the cartel's. This is one of my more important clients and I have assured them that nothing will happen to their shipments. You make sure the drivers deliver on time and without question. Hook and go is all they need to be worried with, and I mean it. Terminate any driver who gets too curious, even if it means making the delivery yourself, understand?"

"Totally."

"If everything goes well and without incident, I'll reward you and my soldiers nicely in your paychecks next week."

"You can count on us, sir."

"We shall see."

Hank loved it when his boss handed out bonuses. They were always big and although he made really good money working for Pig without the extra bonuses, he always enjoyed getting more. Hank petted one of Pig's retrievers and then started back to the command center.

Before he could get through the door, however, Pig spoke up again. "I saw that Black Jack was in Odessa, Texas. Has he reached his quota yet?"

"I believe he's closing the deal tonight on number nine and just has to go to Houston for the final paper closure on number ten."

"Do you have names of the potential drivers? How about backgrounds?"

"All eight of the new drivers have cleared background checks and the man from Houston is under investigation now. Shelby Mathews is the female driver from Odessa, but she hasn't made a commitment yet. Some background has been made and she looks clean so far, but until we get more vital information we can't clear her completely."

Pig was happy with the progress but didn't show his pleasure. "We need more women drivers."

Hank closed the door and returned to the command center.

◊◊◊

Shelby called Jack at work and informed him of her visitor and his intriguing proposition. Jack wasn't sure he liked the fact that a strange man had tracked his wife to her workplace, but he was interested in what the man had to say once Shelby explained what he wanted. "Okay, baby, I think having dinner with him is a good idea. We can meet him at the 42nd Street Steak House around seven."

Shelby took Black Jack's card down from the visor, dialed the number, and gave him the details when he answered. Feeling excited for the first time in weeks, Shelby gave Black Jack directions to the restaurant.

◊◊◊

Angelica left Atlanta with a heavy feeling in her heart. She and Rex had never given into their feelings for each other because they both knew they had baggage. All she could think about was the kiss that Rex had left on her lips. She felt empty as she left the truck stop and headed out for her next load in Mexicali, Mexico. She didn't know if she could ever fall in love again or even if she wanted to, but Rex was on her mind.

Details of the load had not been given out yet, but she knew they would arrive shortly after she crossed the California state line. Her truck was under constant watch, so they knew exactly where she was at all times. The voice and camera monitoring devices in the cab also let the command center know what she was doing inside the truck.

Angelica had been told that the only privacy she had in her truck would be behind her curtain. There were no cameras there, but the voice monitor would record any conversations inside the entire cab. That was why Angelica never turned her private phone on or used it in the cab. She never had conversations with anyone but other drivers in or near the cab area either. She suspected that there was probably a camera in the sleeper, although they assured her there wasn't. Still, she never dressed in the truck. She hated the lack of privacy she had, but it did give her more opportunities to make personal contact with Rex and she liked that part.

◊◊◊

Bullets called an emergency meeting with his gang members after receiving information from some of his connections on the border that the cartel was moving a major shipment into the United States and that Pig had landed the job. Bullets couldn't remember the last time he'd felt so pissed. He planned to either take the job from Pig or mess it up for him so badly that the cartel would never use him again. "Get them all here now, Time Bomb. I mean it! We got a job to do!" Bullets yelled into his cell phone before slamming it down on the table. Several of his enforcers who were in the room moved away from their boss.

Lethal took a deep breath before approaching his boss. "Boss, what's going on?"

Bullets looked at his lieutenant with fire in his eyes. "That Pig has taken the job Tito said I could have. We've got to make sure the bastard doesn't take another one." He slammed his fist down so hard on the desk the papers on it scattered.

The office they used for their meetings was Bullets' brother's legitimate truck body shop. Bullets' brother had kept his nose clean since his release from prison a few years earlier. Bullets had tried hard to get him back into business, but Clark wasn't interested in doing any more time. He had married a gal from down south and they had a little girl. He allowed Bullets' gang to use his shop for their meetings, but merchandise was filtered through other businesses in the community. He wanted no part of that kind of life any more.

Clark was becoming irritated with his brother, especially with all the attention the cops had been paying to his business lately because of Bullets. Clark was really going to lose it when he came in tomorrow and found that Bullets had messed up his secretary's desk. But the gang members feared Bullets more than they feared Clark. Several of the members decided to keep themselves busy by picking up paper. Bullets paced and fumed as he waited for more of the leaders to show up for the meeting.

Bullets was the leader of one of the largest gangs in LA. The membership was well in the thousands, and most were either truckers or bikers. They controlled most of the drug traffic, literally, coming in and out of LA. They didn't distribute it; they simply moved the product from one point to another. They also ran guns, but not on a big scale. However, they didn't have the money or storage availability that Pig had, so the cartel only used them from time to time for emergency load transfers and local deliveries that could be handled by some of the smaller dealers in the area.

Bullets' limitations made him angry. He wanted things on a bigger scale with his cartel friends but they liked doing business with Pig. Pig was very discrete about his business and he had secure storage facilities for their products. His drivers were well trained, very punctual, and never asked questions. Bullets, on the other hand, was a loose canon, boastful about what he did and never reliable. Bullets wanted Pig's business, but even if he could get it he never would be able to handle it. He was not a businessman; he was an accident waiting to happen.

When all the leaders arrived, Bullets began, "Look, I'm not sure why Tito went back on his word to me, but we are riding down to Mexicali tonight and we are going to find out. We are taking trucks and bikes and one way or another, we are leaving there with that shipment. Pig can kiss my ass. I'll take out every one of his drivers if need be."

None of the leaders questioned Bullets, though many wondered what was going to happen when they arrived on cartel turf without being asked. Some of the lieutenants simply loaded their bikes and trucks with guns and ammo, knowing that things were going to get nasty once they got to Mexicali.

Two of Bullets' top lieutenants, Lizard and Rough Rider, talked quietly outside the body shop. "This is suicide, brother."

"I know, but what are we going to do?"

"I hate to do this to the boss, but I'm putting in a call to Bandito to let him know what's coming their way. Maybe he can talk to Tito and put the screws to this thing before it gets started. Bullets is losing it with his obsession over Pig's turf."

"Yeah, he's going after the wrong people. He needs to go after Pig's people, but not on cartel turf."

"You're right."

"Don't rat me out."

"Hell no, man, I don't want my guys getting their asses hung either. If you can stop this thing before it gets out of control, then do it. I'm with you."

Bullets came close to where the two lieutenants were talking. Both men were waiting on their bikes while the others were loading up. "You guys with me?"

"Yeah, man, we're just waiting for everyone to get their shit together. I have to call a couple more drivers. I'll have them meet us on the five."

Bullets mounted his bike. "Good. We are going to need all the trucks we can get." He rode his bike to the front of the pack.

Lizard put his phone to his ear and called Bandito. Then he dismounted his bike and moved away from the ears of the other leaders. Rough Rider covered for Lizard with the other drivers when some wondered why Lizard was being so secretive. "He's trying to get in touch with a couple more drivers. I guess he can't hear with the noise of the bikes."

Lizard made contact with Bandito. Lizard had been friends with Bandito since they were kids. Lizard had actually made the cartel contacts for Bullets through his friend Quatro. Bandito was now very high on the food chain with the cartel, working for them exclusively. Lizard had learned over time, though, that friendship with the cartel had limits and that the cartel wouldn't hesitate to kill even their friends. Money was money and business was business when it came to dealing with the cartel. Friendship didn't count for squat.

"Bandito, I'm not sure how to handle the situation, but maybe you can handle it for me."

Bandito was always happy to help his friend. "What's up, my brother?"

"Bullets is heading us in your direction. He's pissed because Tito gave some loads to Pig instead of us."

"Oh yeah, it was just better to transport that much through Pig since we needed his storage."

"I know that, and you guys know that, but Bullets is losing it because of his obsession with taking Pig out. I think he's really going to make some kind of a major show of authority or try and take over the loads down there."

"That would be a big mistake on Bullets' part. Tito will kill him just for the sport of it."

"I know. I'm trying to prevent that. Can you help me without letting anyone know I told you?"

"Let me see what I can do, Lizard. I'll call you back."

Lizard hung up his cell phone and mounted his bike. The bikes were pulling out to make the trip south. He just hoped Bandito could come up with something before they reached Mexicali or there was going to be a bloodbath tonight.

◊◊◊

Shelby decided while looking through her closet that she wanted to wear a dress, although her profession as a truck driver never called for such attire. Shelby thought a change from the norm was in order and might even impress the man who was so intent on hiring her.

As she put on the short, black, spaghetti strap dress, she wondered if she was overdressing. But as she looked at herself in the mirror, she decided she didn't care. She hadn't had an occasion to wear the dress she had picked out in a while and tonight seemed the perfect opportunity. For whatever reason, Shelby didn't have the normal nervous bubbles in her tummy that she always felt when she was going for a job interview. *Perhaps the nervous feelings aren't there because the pressure of finding a job just isn't a factor*, she considered. *I have a great job, and other than wanting my own truck, I'm under no pressure to do anything.*

When Shelby finally made it to the restaurant, Jack was already there with Black Jack. As she approached the table both men stood out of respect. Jack gave Shelby a welcoming peck on the cheek and Black Jack pulled out her chair.

"Well, I can definitely say this is a first for me," admitted Black Jack. "I've been in the trucking industry all my life and you are not like any driver I've ever come across. What in the world is a pretty little thing like you doing in a truck?" The three laughed, although Shelby had heard similar comments since the first time she stepped into a truck.

◊◊◊

Bullets and his gang had driven down I-5 to San Diego and were now on I-8 heading toward El Centro. Bullets had decided that everyone would meet up at the truck stop in El Centro for a meeting. Lizard figured that Bullets had decided what he wanted to do about Pig while he was riding. Bullets went off the handle often and rarely planned anything out before doing it. Bandito had not gotten back with Lizard but he predicted that if Bandito could come up with something to prevent a scene, he would call soon. If he couldn't, then he knew from experience that Bullets and his gang would be eliminated before they even got within range of the cartel's turf.

Just as the gang pulled into the truck stop, Lizard felt his phone vibrate in his pocket. Without a moment's hesitation, he pulled his bike into a fuel island. He wasn't quick enough to answer the phone, but once he stopped, he started to put fuel in his bike and called Bandito back. Rough Rider was next to him getting fuel and several others had followed suit, but Lizard knew he had to talk to Bandito. Bandito answered his phone and Lizard did his best to keep the conversation from sounding suspicious. "Yeah, I was just wondering where you were at with my truck, Charley."

Bandito knew from the weird conversation that his friend wasn't able to speak openly. Bandito was brief. "Where is your gang?"

Still maintaining his cover Lizard replied, "Yeah, you're supposed to bring the truck to the truck stop in El Centro and you need to hurry because we are going in to get the merchandise tonight."

Bandito had all the information that he needed. "Okay, brother. I'll be there in a few hours with several of my *compadres*. We will make it seem like we accidentally ran into you guys there, and I'll make Bullets understand that whatever he has in mind would not be in his best interest."

"Sounds good, brother."

"Hang tight and make sure Bullets doesn't leave until we make contact. Otherwise, he's a dead man."

"Yeah, I know what you mean. Okay, hurry up."

"Got you covered, my friend."

Lizard hung up and then made an obviously loud conversation with Rough Rider so that some of the other drivers could hear. "Yeah, Charley will be here late as usual."

Rough Rider, in turn, kept the cover going to protect his friend, but wanted more information. "So is he going to make it in time to help us out?"

"Yep, that's what he says."

"Good. We're going to need his truck."

"I'm thinking maybe I need to put another driver in that truck. Charley's a good driver, but he's lazy."

"I know what you're saying." Both men knew Lizard was referring to Bullets and that perhaps it was time to put someone else in his place before he got them all killed.

◊◊◊

Dinner had been wonderful, and the conversation about Pig's organization sounded great. Jack seemed even more excited about the prospect of Shelby going to work for Black Jack than Shelby seemed to be. He laid out two options for her to have her own truck—either she could lease to own or purchase her own truck somewhere else and put it on as just a lease truck. There was also the option of being a company driver for a while and then moving into the owner-op program later. Shelby was leaning more toward the lease-to-own option while Jack thought trying out the company for a while might be wiser.

With still no commitment from Shelby, Black Jack decided that if he was going to get Shelby to sign on he was going to have to bring her to Louisiana. "Well, I can see you are going to be a hard sell, Ms. Shelby. So I think you and Jack need to come to Louisiana and let me show you our operations firsthand."

"I don't know if I can take off that much time from work, Black Jack," Shelby said, glancing hopefully at Jack. "What do you think, baby?"

Jack sipped at his tea. "I think we need to go and check it out."

"Think about it and let me know tomorrow. I'll arrange for plane tickets, a private car, and you can stay on the estate. Our boss has several extra suites and it will be my pleasure to show you personally what our company is all about."

Shelby glanced at Jack again, hoping he would give him the answer she wanted.

"It's your career, baby," he said. "I'm just here to support you. It can't hurt to at least look things over."

Shelby shifted her attention from her husband to Black Jack. "Okay, I'll call you in the morning and let you know what I have decided."

Black Jack could tell from her tone that he had her in his pocket. "I look forward to the call. I have to leave for Houston in the morning, but I'll be back in Louisiana by Sunday. You're going to enjoy PIGT." The waitress brought the three desert and they chatted for a little while longer before parting ways.

At the house, Shelby undressed and got ready for bed. After washing her face and brushing her teeth, she climbed into bed with Jack. He was flipping through the channels on the television when she snuggled in close to her husband. Jack turned off the television and wrapped his arms around his wife. The job opportunity was weighing heavy on her thoughts as she lay in his arms. "What do you think, Jack? Should I check this out or just blow it off?"

"I think you need to decide," he said carefully. "I don't think it will hurt anything to check things out, but the ultimate decision is going to have to be yours, baby. I'll support you either way."

Shelby knew Jack was right. This was her thing, not his, and if she made the wrong decision it would all be on her.

◊◊◊

Angelica had crossed into California where, as predicted, she was given her load information. She was rolling down I-8 and although she would be closer to her destination by cutting across the 98, dispatch had been specific about arrival time. She was not authorized, for any reason, to arrive for her pickup before midnight. She decided to go to the truck stop in El Centro and stay there until closer to her pickup time. She hated the late night pickup and drop off assignments, but it was obvious why it was necessary since most of the shipments were illegal.

Angelica had found a place to park close to the truck stop store. She decided that she would take a little nap since it was going to be a few hours before she could head down to pick up her load. She would need about an hour for travel time and getting to the loading warehouse. Just as she was about to turn out her light and rest, she noticed the swarm of bikers arriving with several eighteen-wheel trucks following close behind. She studied the subjects for a few moments and then almost had a heart attack when she got a glimpse of the club name plastered across the back of a rider's vest. It was Bullets' gang, and they looked like they were on a mission.

She quickly put her shoes back on and her light jacket. Angelica was going to pretend to look for something to eat or use the restroom or whatever she could think of in order to get close enough to hear the gang talk to each other. She knew she couldn't do anything about whatever they were possibly up to, but she was going to find out why they were there. If Bullets' gang was this far away from LA and near Mexico, especially on this particular day, then she knew it had something to do with the cartel loads PIGT was handling. Angelica knew something bad was about to go down.

She got out of her truck and walked toward the store. Several of the bikers were getting fuel and food from inside the store. When she got to the door of the truck stop one of the bikers whistled at her and another opened the door for her. "Don't pay any attention to that, lady. He's just a jackass."

Angelica laughed and probed the biker for information. "Wow, I haven't ever seen so many bikes. Do you guys ride together or something?"

The biker puffed out his chest, obviously proud of his gang affiliation. "Yeah, we run together. We're the 'LA Bad Boys.'"

"Wow, that must be so exciting. I love motorcycles, but I haven't been on one in a long time."

"I'll be happy to give you a ride if we stick around here for a while."

"Oh, that would be terrific. I'm in that big rig over there, and I'm going into Mexicali later tonight. So maybe if you're still here, and before I leave, you can give me a ride around the parking lot." Angelica pointed to her truck from the inside of the store. The man looked out the window toward her truck. "You drive a big truck? All by yourself? You don't look like any driver I've ever seen."

Angelica was flattered but still wanted more information if she could get it. "Yeah, all by myself. It's a good job, but it does take me away from home a lot. So what are you guys doing here, just biking around the country?"

The man was quiet for a little while. "Well, kind of…" he said at last. "But we have some business in Mexicali with a rival gang. They took some of our work and we are going in to get it back tonight."

Angelica knew then that something big was going to go down. She needed to contact Rex, but she didn't want to let her unsuspecting informant know he was being pumped for information. "Wow, that sounds dangerous," she said. "Do you guys have that kind of trouble a lot?"

"No, not really. Just with one outfit."

Angelica walked toward the restroom and said over her shoulder, "Well, I hope you guys get your work back."

The man picked up a couple items from the shelves and stuck them in his pocket. Angelica ignored the shoplifting but decided now was the time to go to the restroom. "I'll be back in a few minutes, I need to use the ladies' room."

The man nodded. "Sure. I gotta get outside anyway. We're fixin' to have a meeting. I'll catch you later for that ride."

Angelica hoped not, but she smiled as she went into the restroom. "Me too."

Inside the restroom stall, Angelica pulled her personal cell phone from her pocket and dialed Rex.

He answered right away. "Hey, beautiful, what's happening?"

"Rex, I'm in El Centro," she whispered. "Bullets and his gang are here at the truck stop. I got one of the bikers to tell me a little bit about what they are doing here, but I didn't get specifics. They are apparently going after these loads we're picking up for Pig."

"Is the cartel involved?" Rex asked in a worried tone.

"I don't know, but he said something about how the work was supposed to be theirs and they were going to get it back. You know as well as I do that most of this stuff we are hauling out of Mexico is the cartel's drugs."

"Yeah, I know," said Rex. "When are you supposed to pick up your load and where?"

"Near Mexicali, Mexico at midnight."

"Just hang out for an hour and I'll see what I can find out. Call me back in exactly one hour."

"Okay."

Angelica hung up the phone and decided to see if she could hear anything more by hanging out in the store. She was disappointed when she saw that there were only a couple of truck drivers left inside. She looked out the window and saw that the gang of bikers and trucks were clustered together in the parking lot. She wanted to get close to where the gang was having their meeting, but knew she would be spotted since they were having it out in the open. She figured her best course of action was to wait and see if any of them came back into the store. Plus, she knew she would catch hell from Rex if she didn't call him back in exactly an hour.

In the store, Angelica looked through books and movies trying to find anything to make her appear to be shopping. She couldn't hear what was going on with Bullets and his gang, but it seemed like the longer they sat there, more members arrived. Angelica was beginning to think maybe she'd better not try and pick up her load, but she didn't know how else she would be able to get out of it without revealing she knew something was going to happen.

While she flipped through the pages of a magazine, Angelica looked at her watch. Fifteen more minutes and she was going to have to call Rex. Just as she was about to put the magazine back, she noticed that a couple of cars and one pickup pulled up to the fuel island. Angelica could tell that the men in the vehicles were from Mexico. Each man in the drivers' seats got out of his vehicle and started to pump fuel.

Then a man from the passenger side of the car that was in the middle got out. He looked toward the crowd of bikers and truck drivers that were gathered together. He shouted toward the group. Angelica couldn't hear what he shouted, but as soon as the sound of his voice reached the group, it parted like the Marines did during a flag salute formation. A man dressed in leathers walked out of the middle of the gathering, through the path of his men, and toward the man who had just shouted.

The minute the man started to walk toward the shouter, the rest of the men in the vehicles near the fuel islands exited and stood nearby. Each man had a firearm, and although they had not put their weapons in position to fire them, each had his hand on a weapon ready to put it into position if need be. Angelica could see that once the gang members saw the defensive stance of the other men in the vehicles, they too exposed whatever weapons they had strapped on; most carried handguns under their leathers.

Angelica looked at her watch. Rex was expecting her call in just a few minutes, but she didn't want to take her eyes off the showdown that was happening in the parking lot. Drivers who had been in the store took their leave and went to their trucks, realizing that something terrible was about to go down.

The ladies in the store got nervous. Only one had sense enough to calm the other two, scolding one of the cashiers who thought they'd better call the police "Leave it alone," she advised. "The cartel will do what they need to and leave. Then we can call the police. But never call the police on the cartel. They'll come after you."

The woman put the phone down and went back to her own business. Angelica breathed a sigh of relief and looked back toward a man walking toward the fuel island. Angelica could tell from the man's face that he was Bullets. She had seen photos of him while studying the case. She couldn't tell for sure who the darker skinned man was, but she figured it was probably Bandito, an enforcer for the cartel. She had memorized the faces of the major players in the cartel.

Bullets put his hand out to greet Bandito. Bandito shook his hand and the tension between the two groups of men dissipated a bit. Bullets was surprised that Bandito was coincidentally in the same place as he was, but knew better than to question the movements of his for-the-moment ally. "My friend, what brings you here?" Bullets asked.

Bandito was a strong-armed enforcer and needed no explanation for his movements since this was his turf. "I was thinking the same of you, Bullets. What are you doing so far from your turf?"

Watching carefully how he answered his "closer than an enemy" friend, Bullets thought about his response. "We're checking out the competition, Bandito. What are you doing here?"

"You aren't here to interfere with my business, are you?"

Bullets was suspicious now. He wanted to know who had tipped off the cartel. He also knew he had to diffuse Bandito's suspicions before there was a gun battle in the parking lot. He was ready for a fight, but not with the bloody cartel. "No, Bandito, never that. We're just here to see about some other business."

Bandito knew Bullets was there to interfere with PIGT trucks. He decided to stay calm and negotiate Bullets out of his plan. He wasn't in the mood to put his men into a blood bath, although he knew his automatic machine weapons would easily eliminate the LA Bad Boys. "Look, Bullets, I'm not sure why you're really here, but I believe it would be in your best interest if you turn your bikes and trucks around and head back to your own turf. We know you have beef with PIGT and that you want all the work we can give you, but you don't have the load transport we need for this shipment. Now save us both a lot of time and blood and lead your men and trucks out of here. We will let you know when we have product for you to move."

Bullets knew Bandito wasn't playing. He also knew if he didn't comply with the request of his Hispanic compadres, he would lose the cartel business he did have and probably his life. His pride and reputation were on the line here, and that was making it difficult to ignore. "Fine, Bandito. I'll turn my men around, but we need to have a meeting, and you need to tell me how many more trucks I need to have in order to capture all your business."

Bandito had no reason to appease this low-life biker but he entertained the man with a response. "You will get the loads we choose for you to run."

Bullets was furious with Bandito's statement. He held his tongue as he backed away from Bandito toward his biker brothers. He held his hand up slightly as he backed away, causing both sides of the dispute to raise their weapons and prepare for battle. Bullets simply pointed and said, "Adiós, my brother." With that, Bullets turned his back to the cartel enforcer and disappeared into the crowd of his gang.

Bandito wasn't sure if he had made his point clear to Bullets. So he stood in the middle of the parking lot, waiting for whatever was going to come next. Bandito was fearless and felt safe, although he was totally exposed to being gunned down at that moment. If Bullets had been stupid enough to gun him down right there in the parking lot, he and all his men would be dead within moments.

Not until Bullets mounted his bike and Bandito saw that the other bikers were also mounting their rides did he back up toward his own car. Banditos' men entered their respective vehicles and moved to the other side of the parking lot, waiting for all of Bullets' bikes and trucks to leave. He wasn't leaving until he was sure that Bullets wasn't going to double back and continue with his ridiculous plan. *He is a hothead after all, with less common sense than a fly heading straight for a fly strip.*

CHAPTER FOUR

Angelica had watched the showdown from the window in the truck stop. She knew Rex was going to be furious with her for not calling in right away, but she had to see what was going to happen between the two gangs. When she saw Bullets and his gang were leaving, she went to the bathroom to call Rex.

In the restroom, Angelica checked to make sure no one was around before she used her phone. Unfortunately, she had to wait until one of the cashiers from the front finished. Angelica pretended to be checking for something in her purse at the counter when the woman came to the sink to wash her hands. She decided to interact a little with the woman so as not to seem suspicious.

Taking out her comb, she started to part her hair. "Kind of exciting around here, isn't it?"

The woman washed her hands silently. Then, as she wiped her hands, she muttered, "Dangerous, not exciting. It would be in your best interest to do what you need to do here and go. I'm not sure who you are or what you're here for, but if you are really just a truck driver then do your trucking and stop hanging out in this truck stop. This is no place for anyone, let alone a woman driving a truck. The cartel owns everything you see for miles around. This is their turf and they will eliminate anyone who gets in their way." The woman left the restroom without waiting for a response from Angelica.

Angelica was taken back. *Was it really so obvious that I've been loitering around the store?* As Angelica dialed Rex's phone she couldn't help but worry that maybe she wasn't as subtle in her undercover role as she had hoped. She decided she was going to have to work on not being so conspicuous.

Rex answered the phone before the first ring even finished. "Where the hell have you been? I've been scared shitless worrying about you."

"I'm fine Rex, but there was some heavy shit going down in the parking lot. Did you find out what it might be about?"

"All I could find out was that the loads you guys are moving for the cartel are going to some warehouses that Pig has on his estate. I also found out that Bullets is furious about not landing the work, but that's all I could get for the moment. So what happened in the parking lot?"

Nervous that someone might come into the restroom, Angelica peered out the door to make sure no one was standing by the door. "I guess Bullets had decided he was going to get those loads anyway because he and a bunch of his gang were just here. They have all pulled out, but not before being confronted by some enforcer from the cartel."

"Are you sure it was the cartel? Are you sure it was Bullets?"

"Positive."

"This is good stuff, Angelica, but you have got to be really careful out there. These guys play for keeps; they don't give a damn who you are. They will kill you just for looking at them funny."

"I know, Rex, and I know I need to be more careful about exposing myself. One of the clerks in this store already finds me suspicious."

"Then you need to get out of that store and go back to your truck."

"I'm going to, but I had to call you."

"I know. Hey, did the cartel leave or are they still hanging around?"

"They moved to the other side of the building when I came into the restroom, but I'm sure they are gone by now."

"Okay, well you be careful. Your job is to observe not to confront."

"I know, Rex. I know." Angelica rolled her eyes.

"Okay, well you be careful and call me later on after you get loaded so I know you're all right and on your way to Louisiana."

"Okay, I will. Miss you."

"Miss you, too."

She tucked her phone into her purse and gathered her things to leave the restroom. Angelica thought as she opened the restroom door and walked into the store that she liked the fact that Rex worried about her. It was nice having someone who cared. She noticed as she walked through the store that there were several Hispanic men looking through items on the shelves. She decided that she had pressed her luck enough in the store and headed toward the exit. But just as she was about to open the door, one of the Hispanic males grabbed the door and politely but intentionally opened it for her. Angelica looked at the man in the face and politely smiled. "Thank you."

The man spoke in broken English. "You welcome."

Angelica nodded and went through the door the man was holding open for her. She continued walking toward her truck but before she could get far, the man was walking next to her. She looked at him and recognized he was one of the men who had arrived with the cartel. Angelica remembered him from his shirt because it was solid white with a black target and a red spot in the middle of the back. She thought wearing a shirt like that would have been stupid, being a man in the cartel.

Again the man spoke to Angelica in broken English. He pointed toward the parking lot and moved his hands like he was turning a steering wheel. "You drive a truck?"

Angelica again nodded but kept walking. "Yes."

The man seemed to think he was making a connection with Angelica and continued to walk with her toward her truck. Angelica was a little nervous not knowing what to expect from the admirer.

"I drive truck, too. But it small." The man laughed, clearly thinking that Angelica would like his rather odd sense of humor. Angelica didn't get the humor but laughed a little to make the man think he had made her laugh.

They reached her truck but she wasn't about to open her door until the man was gone. Angelica knew she was going to have to be careful and not offend the man so she relaxed and decided that a little small talk outside her truck would be okay. She sat on her step and the man hung close, but Angelica could tell he wasn't much of a ladies' man and probably was just trying to impress his friends who were now looking through the windows of the store in their direction.

The man pointed to the PIGT logo on the door of Angelica's truck. "Oh, you drive for Pig?"

Angelica didn't see any harm in confirming the obvious. "Yes."

The man looked even more excited now. "You deliver for us."

Angelica knew exactly who she was delivering for but knew that playing dumb was the safest way through this conversation. "You?"

"Yes." The man pointed toward the men in the window. The men in the window tried to look away as if they weren't really watching their friend put the moves on Angelica.

"Oh, no. I am picking up in Mexicali in a few hours."

The man seemed confused at the language but understood Mexicali. "Oh, yes Mexicali. We go there." The man pointed at Angelica and then to himself and his friends. Angelica was a little afraid of what the man wanted, but she quickly sidestepped the issue and went to another topic.

"You're from Mexico?"

"Yes, Mexico. We go to Mexicali." Again the man pointed to Angelica and himself and the gang at the store. Angelica could tell now that the man had something on his mind. He wanted her to do something, but she wasn't really sure what it was at the moment. She didn't want to speak to him in Spanish because then they would know she spoke their language and she would lose a viable tool for information gathering.

The man reached for Angelica's hand. Angelica wasn't sure whether to go with the man or resist but she decided that she would see what the man wanted. The man guided her toward the other men in the store. Before they reached the store, the men all came out of the store with their leader in front. Angelica gasped to herself when she recognized the face of Bandito. Bandito by reputation and recorded criminal record was a ruthless killer. He needed no reason except his own to take a life.

In Spanish, Bandito questioned and scolded the Hispanic man who had tried to pick up Angelica. The Hispanic man responded with some humiliation, but with determination in Spanish toward Bandito. Angelica knew Bandito had just scolded the man for bringing a stranger into their company and wanted to know why. The man had quickly pointed toward Angelica's truck and informed Bandito that the woman was driving one of the PIGT trucks that were picking up their shipment tonight. Bandito quickly scolded the man again but realized that he was interested in Angelica and trying to impress the others.

Feeling some sense of understanding toward the lowest man on his team and not wanting to make him look foolish in front of the woman he had found attractive, Bandito spoke in fast Spanish while he threw his arms in the air. Angelica knew Bandito had just given his approval for Angelica to be escorted into Mexicali by the gang. The men looked at the one that had picked up Angelica. They hooped and hollered and patted him on the back as if he had just won a prize. Angelica's new friend had just impressed his friends and his boss, but she wasn't sure yet what he wanted with her. She hoped nothing, but figured she was going to have to be careful not to get caught alone or off guard around him.

Bandito looked at Angelica and spoke in perfect English. "You're here to pick up one of my loads headed for Texas?"

Angelica nodded her head and stuck out her hand to the man. "Yes, sir. I'm supposed to be there for pickup around midnight." Angelica hoped stating the time of pickup would encourage the man to let her stay in the parking lot of the truck stop until it was time to pick up the load up. That, however, wasn't going to happen. Bandito turned toward his vehicles with his men close in tow. Angelica stood almost waiting for instructions from this totally take-charge person. "No need to wait here. Follow us on into Mexicali and join us for dinner."

Angelica wasn't sure this dinner invitation was such a good idea, but knowing that a refusal to Bandito could only lead to further problems, she accepted. "Sure." She knew this wasn't proper procedure, but she didn't want to blow her cover. Angelica turned toward her truck and started walking across the parking lot. The man who had taken a liking to Angelica broke ranks and walked with Angelica to her truck. She expected him to simply walk her to her truck, but that didn't happen either.

Politely, but forcefully, the man put his hand out toward Angelica. He motioned to the hand holding her keys, which left no question that he wanted her keys to her truck. She reluctantly handed them to him and panicked slightly when the man walked to the other side of the truck and opened the passenger side door. She did not know what he was up to, but Angelica walked to the other side to see what he was doing. She was shocked and panicked again when he stood there holding the door for her.

Angelica shook her head and pointed to the driver's side. "No, I have to drive," she said with intensity.

The man shook his head in rejection at Angelica's insistence on driving her own truck and pointed to the passenger's seat. "No. Bandito say I drive you." Angelica didn't like the situation that she had just found herself in, but she was powerless to change it.

◊◊◊

Bullets was hot as he left the parking lot. Not only had Bandito made him look like a fool in front of his men, someone in his gang was a snitch. He knew he was out-gunned for the moment, but he was still determined to take out the PIGT trucks. He was just going to have to do it from another location down the road. The more he thought about it, the more he liked the idea he'd come up with and waved for his men to follow him. He planned to lead his men out of El Centro up Highway 86 to Imperial. After they met up, he'd send a couple of men back to keep an eye out for the loaded PIGT trucks out of Mexicali.

Once the scouts were headed back, he and the rest of the gang would go to Brawley and then across Highway 78 to Blythe. They would hold up there until the scouts sent word that the PIGT trucks were rolling out onto I-8. As the scouts kept close watch on the PIGT trucks, he and the rest of the gang would roll down I-10 to Highway 95 south. The plan was to have several members come in behind their scouts and the PIGT trucks on I-8 at Yuma. A few others would go on down I-10 to Phoenix and go in behind the PIGT trucks closer to Tucson on I-10.

Bullets decided he'd only let his top lieutenants know of his plan. Sharing with only a few guys would lower the odds of the snitch knowing his strategy.

◊◊◊

Bandito contacted his boss to let him know only some of what he'd encountered in El Centro. "I took care of the issue in El Centro and made sure Bullets got the message to stay clear of the PIGT trucks, but the guy is unreliable and may go rogue at any time. "Look, Tito," he continued, "I got this guy covered, but it's Quatro who brought him into the organization. I was never given a say about it, but I'm the one dealing with his ass—not Quatro. I'll tell you right now, if this bitch gets in my way again, I'll gun him and his men down like dogs." His men knew that Bandito never said anything he didn't mean.

◊◊◊

Shelby woke up early the next morning and enjoyed the solitude and security she felt in Jack's arms while he slept. She felt her troubles were behind her, including the strain her trucking career had put on their relationship. Jack had become more supportive of her decision. She wondered if taking on a new position with PIGT would cause them problems again since the job required that she take much longer and more frequent trips.

At least she would be close to the house once a week and was assured she could spend her full break time at home. She hoped that at least two nights a week with Jack at home would be enough for him, the hall he caught though. Maybe he would even ride with her from time to time.

Shelby moved out from under the covers. She took off her t-shirt and panties and turned on the shower. *Today is going to be a great start to another adventure on the highways,* she mused.

Jack woke to find his wife already out of the shower and leaving their room in a towel. "Hey, where're you going all sexy in that towel?"

Shelby dropped the towel to the floor, and then laughed as she gathered it up off the floor and headed to the kitchen. "To get some coffee."

Jack saw the towel drop to the floor and scrambled to get out of bed. In the hall, he caught Shelby with the towel halfway around her body. He nailed his wife to the wall by her hands and let the towel fall to the floor again. Shelby giggled as Jack kissed her neck and tickled her for playing with him so early in the morning. "Hold on, little lady. You think you can just drop that towel in front of me and take off without even a kiss?"

Shelby giggled as Jack tickled her. "It just fell down."

"Yeah right."

"Come on, we better stop or we are both going to be late today."

Jack kissed his wife and then let go of her hands. "I have nothing pressing to do today. I think we need to take this back to the bedroom."

Shelby kissed her husband and then bent down to get her towel from the floor. She wriggled away from Jack, leaving him holding one hand on the wall. She wrapped the towel around her body again and went toward the kitchen. "I want to, baby, but we may be catching a plane this afternoon for Louisiana."

Jack turned and leaned up against the empty wall. "Great way to tease me and not please me, Shelby Mathews."

"I think you got a good amount of pleasing last night, and if you're a good boy, I'll give you some more tonight."

Jack laughed in response as Shelby walked back past him in the hall handing him a cup of coffee and returning to their bedroom. Shelby once again dropped her towel at the door as she entered the bedroom.

"You are such a tease. If you do that one more time, you won't be able to use any excuse to keep me from putting you back on this bed and doing what I want."

Shelby laughed as she exited the walk-in closet completely naked and entered the bathroom. Jack laughed as Shelby shut the door to the bathroom in a hurry, knowing that Jack would do what he said if he could catch her.

Laughing, Jack sipped at his coffee. "Tease!"

Shelby put on her bra and panties and started working on her makeup when Jack came into the bathroom for his shower. "So, have you decided about the job?"

Shelby was putting on eyeliner when she stopped to answer Jack's question. "Yes. I think I want to go to Louisiana and check things out. I'm going to call Black Jack here in a few minutes and set things up. You're going to come with me, right?"

Jack looked around the edge of the shower curtain. "Of course. I know the decision is yours, but I would like to see this operation for myself if that's okay?"

"Yes. I definitely want you with me."

"Good. Let's go to Louisiana and eat some mudbugs."

"Oh yuck. You can eat those things, I'll stick with chicken."

Jack laughed from the shower. "What? You don't like watching the eyes stare at you as you suck the head out of those mudbugs?"

"Oh gross! You are a sick man."

"No alligator either?"

"That's as bad as you guys cooking snakes out on the rig sites."

"Oh, now, that's some good eating there, babes. Tastes like chicken."

◊◊◊

Bullets made connection with his men in Imperial and sent two of his best riders back to El Centro with strict instructions not to be seen by any of the cartel. They were simply to watch for the PIGT trucks and call him as soon as the trucks started pulling out of El Centro onto I-8. Bullets signaled his six top lieutenants. "Look, I want this kept between you and me, I don't want any of the others to know that I am still planning on taking out PIGT." None of the lieutenants dared to question their leader's decision in front of him.

"Sure, boss."

"Yeah, we're in."

"Okay, I'll be notified when each truck is heading east. I'm sending Lizard and Rough Rider with your soldiers down I-8. I want you and your men to come in behind the drivers near Tucson. Each truck will be taken over by two of your men and all monitoring devices deactivated. I want the loads hijacked and brought back to LA. You can either bring them back with the PIGT tractors or use our tractor drivers. Once we have the loads in LA, I'll negotiate with Tito on the return of the trucks. I'll ask him to give us all of his transportation work. That's all I want from him, and I'm sure he'll agree."

Lizard and Rough Rider knew Bullets had lost his mind thinking that Tito would ever agree to such a ridiculous manipulation. Tito would agree to the trade, but only to get his merchandise back. Then he would kill everyone involved in trying to exploit his business.

Lizard also knew if he questioned Bullets' plan he would be targeted as a possible snitch. Lizard wasn't sure how he was going to keep Bullets from getting him and his men killed, but he needed to figure out something quick.

What if I avoid the cartel and notify PIGT directly? he thought. *Maybe I can make contact with one of their drivers to let them know what was going to go down.*

He figured if the information came from a driver on the PIGT side then the suspicion would be taken off the gang members. Some of the hijacking would probably need to take place, but maybe some of it could be prevented before the cartel would even know what was going on. Pig would naturally want to keep it under wraps in order to save face with Tito.

Lizard figured he might be able to save his men again from another death sentence because of Bullets' unrealistic obsession with Pig's company. How he was going to do it he just hadn't figured out yet. *I have a few hours to come up with a plan,* he thought as he got on his bike.

◊◊◊

Angelica rode quietly next to her new chauffeur as he drove her south into Mexicali. The man was nice enough and spoke to her occasionally in Spanish and some broken English. She understood every word of his Spanish, but pretended she didn't so that she could possibly get some information. The ride was short and she was relieved when they finally arrived at the loading facility. The man backed Angelica's truck into a dock after two of the drivers from Bandito's security units had exited their vehicles and opened the doors to her trailer.

Once the truck was in place, the man took Angelica's keys and exited her truck. He went to the passenger side of the truck and helped her out before placing the keys into her hand. She was glad when the keys were once again in her possession, but a little nervous when the man led her to a waiting SUV with blacked out windows. He opened the back door for her. Inside the vehicle, Angelica found two men sitting in the front seats and one sitting behind the driver in the back seat. Angelica got into the back seat and with the man's insistence, was forced to slide in next to the other guy. This placed her in the middle of the man who drove her truck and a man she had never met.

She was now at the mercy of these strangers and was helpless if they chose to do anything to her. Angelica fidgeted in her seat. The man who had been driving her truck noticed her uneasiness and grabbed her hand. He spoke in Spanish as the driver left the loading yard and headed into the city lights. "No need to be afraid, mama, we are good men. We will take you for dinner and some drinks and you will feel much better."

The carload of men laughed at the man's words toward his new girl-friend. Angelica tried to appear less uncomfortable, though she knew she was probably failing miserably.

◊◊◊

Black Jack met Jack and Shelby when they arrived at the airport in Shreveport. "Glad you guys decided to check out our operation," he said as he shook hands with both of them. "Let's get your luggage. I have a car waiting out front," he said as he led them to baggage claim.

In the car on the way to the estate, Black Jack explained a little about the security there and gave some highlights of Shelby's potential future boss. He was careful not to expose too much for fear of scaring off his new pros-pect, but he also needed to give them a heads up on what they were about to witness at the estate. "Now don't be alarmed by all the security. Our boss han-dles some really expensive freight for some really important people around the world. He houses much of that freight in warehouses here to keep it safe. Don't be too shocked at the size of the boss either. He is a rather large man, but he's a good boss and works hard to make sure we are paid well for our loyalty and service to him."

Shelby knew he was being vague, but was not going to form any opin-ions until they scoped out the company headquarters and met the proprietor. She became wary as they approached the gates, and saw the guns. "This place needs to be protected with guns?"

Black Jack nodded. "As I said, some of our freight is valuable—thus the need to be prudent."

"How do you protect the drivers when they are transporting such valuable merchandise?" Shelby sat back next to Jack, feeling a little unsure about what she was getting herself into.

"Every truck we own and every truck that leases with us is heavily monitored," Black Jack answered. "When the freight is of extreme value, the driver and the load are protected by armed guards. No need to worry. Those loads are few and far between and handled only by our lead drivers. You will probably never be asked to carry one, and if you ever are, you'll be totally protected with our high-tech security system."

Shelby relaxed, but as they drove down the drive, she kept wondering, *How can a man who only owns a trucking company afford such a lavish estate?*

Black Jack sensed her suspicions. *This gal is sharp, I need to alleviate her concerns,* he thought, then said, "The boss has been independently wealthy all his life. His father left him quite an inheritance and he has managed to invest it well over the years."

Shelby accepted the explanation.

◊◊◊

Pig was working in his office and monitoring the conversation between Black Jack and the Mathewses. Although he hadn't gotten a close visual of Shelby, he found her mannerisms and intellect intriguing. He decided to freshen up before the meeting and called Harry for assistance. Black Jack had already informed Pig that Shelby was a little skeptical about joining the PIGT team but felt that a visit to the estate and a one-on-one with the boss might bring her around to signing on. The brief conversation he'd heard made Shelby a must-have for him.

◊◊◊

Hank met the Mathewses at the front door while a couple of security officers gathered the couple's luggage. Black Jack made introductions. "Hank, here is our communication center supervisor. Hank, this is Jack and Shelby Mathews."

"Nice to meet you. I'm actually second in command here under Mr. Pig. I'm Black Jack's boss, and if you come on board I'll be someone you will answer to as well. Follow me please."

Pig? Shelby thought, *they actually call him Mr. Pig?*

Now that Shelby was at the estate and Hank's responsibility, Black Jack figured he had completed his task. He went to his quarters, miffed by Hank's air of superiority, leaving the Mathewses to deal with Hank by themselves.

Hank snapped his fingers at the security officers handling the bags. "To the west wing, please. I'll be showing them the communication center before they go to their room." The officers obeyed, stiffly.

Hank snapped his fingers at the Mathewses and walked in front of them with a quick step. "Follow me please and don't touch anything." Shelby thought it was rude to snap fingers and bark out orders, but she complied. Shelby was stunned by the breathtaking appearance of the entrance to Pig's massive mansion. "Wow," she sighed.

"It's a foyer," Hank snapped.

"Maybe so, but it's huge. I guess you're just used to its splendor." Shelby's voice was laced with sarcasm.

I'll have to let Pig know this girl has an attitude, Hank thought, but he continued without a beat, "This way, please."

Jack thought Shelby was being a bit too arrogant and gave her a skeptical look, but Shelby ignored him.

Hank opened the door to the command center and allowed the couple to enter in front of him. "In and up the stairs to the left, please."

"This seems like a massive operation for just a trucking company," Shelby observed. "Everything is so high-tech. You guys know exactly where every truck you have is at every moment don't you?"

"Yes we do and we have complete video and audio surveillance on everything that Mr. Pig owns as well." Hank pushed a couple of buttons on the control panel, and the image of the three of them was displayed on every screen in the center. Then hit a button near a microphone. "Ladies and gentleman, meet Jack and Shelby Mathews."

Each operator waved and then turned back to their monitors. With a single button stroke, Hank returned the screens to their previous surveillance. "I have total control from this one panel," he emphasized. I can check on any specific truck, load, warehouse, or room in this mansion. Every inch of Pig's estate is monitored. Pig makes sure he is equipped with the most recent and highly designed high-tech equipment available."

I get that some of Pig's loads are important, but why does everything he own need to be under such scrutiny? Shelby wondered. She had questions, especially about intrusion of privacy, but decided to wait until she met the man. "I'd like to go to my room now until Mr. Pig is ready to meet us. Did you just say every inch of this mansion is monitored… including our room and bathroom?"

"Yes, but it is against policy for anyone to intrude upon another person's private quarters without permission from Mr. Pig himself. There must be a good reason."

Shelby doubted that policy was enforced. She didn't trust Hank and wished they were staying in a hotel instead of on the estate. "Jack, we need to talk…IN PRIVATE," she stressed.

"Wait, Mrs. Mathews, please don't be afraid of the security. I assure you it takes an act of congress to get Pig to allow monitoring of an employee without cause."

Shelby scowled.

"I'm sure he's telling the truth, Shelby," Jack interjected. "They would have to get a person's permission before intruding on their privacy."

She raised an eyebrow.

"Don't worry, baby, they aren't going to see you in your underwear."

"Shut up, Jack."

Shelby moved to the door of the control room, still suspicious of the privacy issue. "Fine, but I want to talk with Mr. Pig about this. And I want it in writing before I sign on with this company that my personal privacy will never be infringed upon without my knowledge."

"You can discuss it with him during your interview," he said, knowing Pig would never give up any aspect of his surveillance. He had one of the security officers take the Mathewses to their room.

CHAPTER FIVE

As Angelica sat in the dark, smoke-filled cantina with her new "friends," she realized she was in a no-win situation. If the men she was with found out why she was there, or if Rex tried to contact her because she hadn't called, she could be killed. She decided just to bide her time and be friendly.

Angelica scanned the large room full of men, women, and even some children. The people were joyful as they smoked and talked, enjoying their food and drinks. It was a family oriented place where parents made conversation with other parents and the children ran around playing games of tag. Some men were gathered in groups in the corners of the room or sat on barstools at the wooden bar at the front of the room.

Food and drinks were delivered by women and when the swinging doors behind the bar moved, Angelica could see other women huddled back in the kitchen preparing the food.

Angelica could tell the men at her table were respected and most likely feared by the community based on the service they received. After a round of cold beer, a young girl brought plates of steaming food.

Angelica sipped slowly at the bottle of beer that had been placed in front of her. She tried to refuse the drink, but her "date" insisted with, "Drink, mama!" He tapped her bottle with his and chugged his beer down as if it were water. Angelica knew she would need to stay sober not only to drive her truck but to keep her wits about her, so she created the illusion she was drinking more than she was actually consuming.

Her minder took a tortilla and with his less than sanitary fingers placed some of the meat on a tortilla. He dipped the end of it into the beans and handed it to her. "Eat, mama, eat." Angelica graciously took the offering and the man smiled with pleasure when Angelica took a bite of his gift.

The other men approved of his attentions towards the lady and raised their beers and cheered him on with "Sí!"

The other men sat at the other tables around their friend and his new companion. "Sí!!!" Angelica knew, for the moment anyway, that she had nothing to fear from these men. She ate and sipped at her beer listening to their conversations in Spanish. She occasionally smiled a flirtatious smile toward her admirer just to keep him happy.

Angelica was proud at how she had made her way into the inner circle of this lower rung of cartel soldiers. And although aware her job was surveillance, she actually found herself enjoying the company of these family men. Although she was aware that outside of these walls these men were ruthless drug dealers and killers, within these walls they were just normal people with families. Or so she thought, until she saw a forty-five pushed into the back of one of her escorts, she realized that no matter where they were or with whom, these men were skilled killers, protecting illegal products being transported into the United States from Mexico. Her job was to find out as much as she could about their activities without blowing her cover.

◊◊◊

Lizard was glad that Bullets had sent him ahead of the others. As he headed into Yuma, Lizard hoped he'd find a PIGT truck and pass along the information about the trap they were headed into before all hell broke loose. It was going to be difficult to get one of the drivers to stop for him let alone listen to him.

He spotted a truck on the opposite side of the highway heading toward Mexicali. "Hot damn. What luck!" Lizard checked to see if any other of his gang members were in the area as he crossed the median before making his move to contact the PIGT truck on the other side. He didn't need anyone telling Bullets that he was a traitor.

With everything his bike could give him, Lizard ran down the truck on the westbound side. He quickly positioned himself behind the truck and trailer. He wasn't going to be able to stop the truck on the highway unless he came up with a reason for the truck to stop. He needed to make up a reason, and the cold handle of the nine-millimeter in his back was the answer. Lizard took the gun out as he moved toward the middle of the trailer, positioning himself so the driver couldn't see him.

"BOOM!" As soon as the bullet left Lizard's gun, it hit the rear inside tire of the passenger's side of the PIGT truck. Lizard quickly put the hot gun into the back of his pants. The heat from the barrel burned his skin but he was too busy avoiding the pieces of rubber that were flying from the now destroyed tire. "SHIT! Maybe that wasn't smart."

The driver heard the boom and saw smoke coming from the rear passenger side of his truck. He quickly hit his brakes and started to move over to the edge of the road. Lizard fought with the scraps of debris and the driver's instinct to slow his truck down. "Dammit. This definitely wasn't a great idea." Lizard moved out from behind the back of the truck and into the hammer lane of the highway. The driver spotted him and hoping that his blown tire hadn't hit the biker, moved over quickly to the shoulder.

Lizard moved around the slowing truck and made sure that the driver saw his turn signal. The two slowing vehicles arrived almost simultaneously at the edge of the roadway.

Lizard parked his bike and walked back to the driver running in his direction.

"Are you okay, man? I'm sorry I didn't even know you were behind me. I'm sorry that tire blew on you. I just don't understand how that happened. Those are brand new tires. I just had them put on last week. Man, if you're hurt my boss will take care of everything," the driver spoke in a hurried panic.

"I'm good, brother. No need to freak. I just stopped to see if you're okay."

The man was a little surprised but accepted the biker's hand of friendship. "Yeah, I'm good, thank you. Are you sure you're alright?"

Lizard chuckled. "Yeah, I'm good."

The two chatted a few more minutes and then the driver wanted to check out his truck.

Lizard took the opportunity to get his information across to the driver without suspicion. "I'll walk with you. Don't know that I can be of any help with the tire, but I can show you which one blew." The men laughed as they walked to the back of the trailer on the PIGT truck. Just as the men passed the logo on the side of the trailer, Lizard pointed at it. "I travel these roads all the time and I see your trucks out here a lot. You guys must have a bunch of these trucks."

The man seemed impressed that someone noticed the company he worked for and was happy to boast a little. "Well, I'm a new driver, only been with this company a couple of months so I'm not really sure what the fleet size is right now, but I've been told it's growing by the day."

"Well, that's great that you got yourself hooked up with an expanding company," Lizard said. "I bet there's room for advancement with them. I use to be a driver and still have a CDL, but I just never found me anything to really stick with. I'm kind of a gypsy."

The man looked under the rear of the truck at what was left of the damaged tire. "I hear you, brother. I've been one myself, but I got kids and a wife now so I can't listen to the wishes of my heart anymore. I've got to be a responsible father and husband. I still got my bike, but I only get to ride when I get home about every other month or so."

Lizard looked at the damaged tire. "Wow! That must be hard not getting to ride more than you do. I'm not sure I could go more than a couple of days without riding."

The men inspected the tire for a few minutes. "Boy, I just really don't understand it. I just had these tires replaced two weeks ago. Pig isn't going to be happy about this."

"Pig, who's Pig?" Lizard feigned.

The man got out from under the truck and dusted off his knees and hands. "Pig is my boss. Well, he's the owner anyway. He's really particular about his trucks and spares no expense when it comes to the upkeep of his equipment. This is great for us drivers, except we tend to get our asses in trouble when shit like this happens."

Lizard knew what the driver was talking about. Pig's reputation was well known by anyone in the trucking business. "Damn, that's not good. Surely he'll understand you had nothing to do with this, right?"

"Maybe, but probably not."

"I remember a friend of mine worked for this company a few years back. He mentioned something about that boss of yours just last week. In fact, I think he was saying something about another company was going to try and hijack some loads from you guys this weekend in Mexicali. You aren't headed there are you?"

The man jerked his attention from the tire. "Hijack loads? Yeah, I'm headed there now to pick up a load at midnight. This isn't good. What exactly did your friend say?"

"Well…all I really remember…," he said cautiously, "…is that he said something about having worked for PIGT Then he laughed and said that Pig was going to be in trouble with the cartel if they were to find out about their loads being hijacked. He may have said something about it going down along Highways 8 and 10 by some gang members. I don't really remember much. What I do recall is that he thought it was funny. Seems kind of stupid to me that anyone would try and take something away from the cartel. That guy must've been talking out his ass. You guys don't run stuff for them anyway… do you?"

I'd better contact central dispatch right away, the driver thought. He knew a lot of the loads he'd been carrying were from the cartel. He didn't care as long as he could make a living for his family without getting killed. And he knew if his load got hijacked by the cartel he would be the first to get nailed.

"No, I don't think we run for the cartel," he told Lizard, "but I need to let dispatch know about this just in case we've gotten hit or we might get hit."

Lizard went with the driver to his truck, hoping to find out what Pig had to say about the hijacking. He stood outside the open driver's side door. "It might be a feather in your cap if you give them some vital information like that, right?" Lizard asked.

"Yeah, I guess, but more than that I just want to stay alive out here."

He picked up his cell phone and made the call. "Yes, this is truck number 5684. I need to report that a stranger just informed me that he overheard that our trucks headed to Mexicali are possible targets for a hijacking."

The man listened to the dispatcher's question. "No, I don't know the informant's name or any details. He wasn't very well informed either." He waited again. "Well, I just thought you might want to know what I was told, but if you don't think it's important then I'll just continue on to get my load after I get my tire fixed." The man listened to the angry dispatcher and replied, "Yes, a tire on my truck blew out…yes, sir."

The man hung up his cell phone and put it in the carriage. He then put his finger to his mouth indicating to Lizard to be quiet while he dismounted his truck. Lizard didn't know the reason for the silence but he complied. The man motioned for Lizard to follow him to the back of the truck again.

Once the men were at the rear of the truck, Lizard watched as the man pointed to a surveillance device attached to the rear of the trailer. The man then leaned down to appear to be checking out the tire again. "We are under constant surveillance," the man whispered. "I have been told to get my truck fixed and continue on to retrieve my load. There haven't been any reports or notifications from any of the other drivers about any hijacking. I want to thank you for the information, but it looks like it was just someone blowing smoke."

Lizard knew it wasn't smoke but he also knew he couldn't force PIGT to believe him without proof. He'd done all he could do until the first truck was jacked. "Yeah, you're probably right."

Lizard got up and replaced his sunglasses over his eyes. He put his hand out for the man to shake. "Well, I need to get going. Wish I could have been more help with the tire."

The driver stood and shook Lizard's hand. "Oh, it won't take long for PIGT's mobile unit to get here. Thanks for your help and take care of yourself. I'm glad you weren't hurt from any trash coming off that tire."

Lizard shook his hand. "Me too and you be careful out there."

◊◊◊

Rex knew he wasn't going to be able to talk with Angelica until she was loaded and on her way to her destination. It made him a nervous wreck. He knew he should not let his personal feelings for her interfere with his job because feelings could cloud his judgment and possibly get her killed. Rex took several deep breaths and tried to relax as he sat back in his chair in front of his computer. At least he'd be able to track her again once she was mobile. Now all he could do was wait.

He knew from the tracker that she was at the loading dock in Mexico, but he wasn't sure why she had gone there early. He was nervous that she had altered their original plan. He also knew she wouldn't change their plan unless she had no choice. His heart began to race. He couldn't continue being her handler if he was falling in love with her.

◊◊◊

Harry escorted Shelby and Jack to their room. "Dinner is at seven in the dining room. Feel free to make yourselves comfortable and explore the estate. You will be redirected by security if you find yourself exploring something that is forbidden. Mr. Pig will be joining you for dinner and I believe the cook is preparing roast beef, one of Mr. Pig's favorite meals. I'm Harry. If you need anything, just pick up any of the phones around the estate and ask for me."

As Shelby unzipped her suitcase, Jack walked Harry to the door. "Thank you, Harry, this room is fantastic," he said and shook the old man's hand.

"My pleasure, Mr. Mathews. Let me know if you or Mrs. Mathews need anything." Jack backed into the room and shut the door.

Jack looked around the room, put his hands on his hips, and then fell back on the king-size bed. "Wow, can you believe this place?"

Shelby took out several of her outfits and hung them in the walk-in closet. Her small wardrobe looked dwarfed in the huge closet. "A little over the top if you ask me. This closet is bigger than our whole bedroom."

Shelby came back into the room and found her husband with the TV remote in his hand. "I see you've found your favorite pastime."

Jack ran through a few channels. "Come over here, baby. Let's check out this sixty-inch flat screen."

Shelby walked toward her husband. She stopped, picked up one of the pillows, and threw it at him. Jack grabbed the pillow and tried to throw it back at her. Shelby ran toward the door laughing. "I can watch TV. at home. I want to go check things out."

Jack tried to grab at Shelby but missed as she ran toward the door. He gave up and fell back onto the bed. "Fine, you go check out this big ass place and let me know what you find. I'm going to stay right here and watch this nice big television until dinner."

"Fine, Mr. Lazy. I'm going to check things out and if I feel charitable when I get back, I might let you know what I found." As Shelby stepped out of the bedroom she felt like she was in a hotel. The hallway was long and wide with closed doorways on either side. She walked to the end of the hall, made a left turn, and after a few more feet came to an open landing that exposed the horseshoe-shaped staircase. The huge lobby was easily visible from the top of the landing.

Shelby stopped and looked over the banister, admiring the exquisite décor chosen to highlight the open spaces of this huge area. She marveled at the size of the chandelier that hung with tremendous grace over the entire area. She wondered what her possible new boss was going to be like if he had such excellent taste.

Shelby slowly descended the staircase as if she was a princess headed to the ball. "So this is what a queen feels like when she enters a room," she murmured. "Well, there has got to be more to this Pig than meets the eye." Her musings were interrupted when the door to the communication center opened.

She noticed there was a tremendous amount of activity and could tell from the traffic in and out of the room that something was going on. She decided to walk over to the door and take a peek inside just to appease her curiosity. But before she reached the doorway she was stopped abruptly by a security officer. "Sorry, Mrs. Mathews, you'll need to either find your way back to your room or check out the pool area. This area is restricted for the moment."

Shelby was surprised that everyone knew who she was but willingly obliged "Okay. I guess maybe I'll go check out the pool. Can you point me in the right direction?"

Several men hurried into the communication center. Shelby pointed at the door. "Is everything okay in there?"

The security officer pointed to the right. "Yes, everything is fine, and the pool is that way."

Shelby tried to follow the guard's directions but as she made her way toward the back of the house, she found herself lost in the library amidst a labyrinth of books. The octagon-shaped room was centered in the middle of the mansion and was accessible from the rooms that surrounded it. The walls were lined with books of all kinds from the hardwood floors up to the sky-lights, which allowed natural light to pour into the room. The furniture was mahogany, complete with an oversized matching desk and chair.

Shelby loved books. As she browsed through some of the titles, she realized that many were rare and possibly very valuable collector's editions, many of them so rare that few people had ever heard of, let alone read them. She was in awe as she took one book she had always wanted to read off the shelf and found her way to a soft chair. *This new boss of mine can't be all that bad if he's got brains enough to read books like these,* she thought.

Before she had a chance to get comfortable, Shelby realized she wasn't alone in the room. From the darkened doorway of one of the entrances to the library a large figure of a man waddled through with a cane. "Good evening, Ms. Shelby. I see you are enjoying one of my rare books."

Shelby knew immediately that the oversized man was Pig. Black Jack had not exaggerated, but the man she'd pictured in her mind was dwarfed by the actual person before her. Shelby composed herself so as not to appear shocked at the man's size. She turned her back on the book in her lap. "You must be Mr…ah… Pig? Harry told us it was okay to check out your home. I hope I haven't offended you by looking around. I am deeply impressed with your collection."

Pig smiled. "Not at all, Ms. Shelby. You may look at anything you like in my home. I don't find it odd that you're in here. Since you were once an educator I would only expect that you would be drawn to this room."

Shelby figured he had learned of her former occupation from her application. "Yes, I love books," she told him. "You have quite a collection here."

Pig found his way to the desk and sat in the oversized chair. "This library was my father's pride and joy. He was very interested in the thoughts and minds of others. He believed the more he read from other people, the more information he could pack into his brain. He was a brilliant but eccentric man."

"Oh, so this isn't your collection?"

Pig knew some women were more impressed with a man's intelligence as opposed to their wealth, but he wasn't sure where Shelby stood on those things just yet. "Well, they belong to me now, but my father was the one who collected them. He used to read a lot of them to me when I was a child. I brought them here and put them in this library when he died."

This large man isn't who he appears to be, she thought, *he's mysterious.* Shelby loved a mystery and she wondered how long it was going to take to figure out this one. "It's wonderful of you to honor your father with such a special place for his memories."

"So you want to drive one of my trucks, do you?" Pig asked, intrigued.

Shelby gave a small smile. "Still haven't made a decision on that yet, but I like what I've seen so far."

Pig's cell phone rang. He picked it up as he slowly moved to get up out of his chair. Using his cane, Pig stepped slowly past Shelby toward the door that she had used to enter the library. "Yes. I'll be there in a moment." He finished his phone call and turned to address Shelby before leaving the room.

Shelby could tell from the brief phone conversation that Pig was probably headed to the chaos in the communication center. However, his abrupt departure without any details let her know that he wasn't going to share the specifics with her. "Everything okay?"

Pig nodded. "Yes, but I must attend to some business. Please feel free to enjoy the books here in the library for as long as you like."

Shelby was impressed with Pig's professional behavior, but her intuition told her there was something more when it came to Pig. "Thank you," she said, trying not to let her suspicion show. "That's very kind."

◊◊◊

It was getting close to midnight at the cantina. One of the men at the leader's table tapped Angelica's "date" on the shoulder. The man stood up and held out his hand to Angelica. The leader of the group and his bodyguards were already on their way out the door when Angelica accepted the man's hand. He escorted her politely to the door and opened it for her. He walked her to the waiting SUV and again she was placed in the back seat between her date and another man.

It took only minutes to arrive at the loading facility. Once they arrived, Angelica heard the leader say in Spanish that she was to stay in the SUV. Still feigning ignorance of the language she tried to follow the men out when they began to exit the vehicle. She was stopped by her date with a gentle but firm hand. "No, mama, you sit." Unsure as to why, Angelica sat back in the SUV without objection.

Once the men disappeared into the warehouse, Angelica quickly looked around to see what she could see. It was dark, and the only light on the property was on the loading dock. She could tell several other PIGT trucks had arrived and were backed into the dock. Several men were busy connecting trailers to tractors and sealing trailers with wire security straps. Angelica couldn't see her truck because of the other trucks that had parked next to hers, but she knew it was where she'd left it. Her observations were interrupted by her escort, who offered his hand to Angelica, saying, "Come, mama."

Angelica climbed out of the vehicle and he led her to her truck then politely took her keys and unlocked the door. He helped her into her truck, handed her the keys, and kissed her cheek. "You go now, mama." The man pointed toward the open gate.

Angelica nodded and started her truck. The man climbed out of Angelica's truck and shut the door. He waved goodbye to her and disappeared into the warehouse.

Angelica felt relieved the man was gone and that she was on her way out of the facility and out of danger. Angelica knew the cartel harbored dangerous men, but it was hard to understand how normal family men could also be killers. She tried hard not to worry herself with things that just didn't make any sense as she drove her truck out of the gate. Several other trucks followed her out of the facility. Angelica knew Rex was going to be upset, but there was no opportunity to stop and call him with an update.

◊◊◊

Lizard was close to the meeting place he had planned with his soldiers. He believed that his attempt to make Pig aware of what was going to go down with his trucks had failed. Lizard didn't know how he was going to get his men out of the predicament Bullets had put them in. He decided the best path was to just get through it and hope for the best. Bullets was an idiot and if Lizard had listened to his gut when he first joined up with the man he might be enjoying a cold beer with his girl right now instead of figuring out how to keep from getting killed by the cartel.

◊◊◊

Shelby had put the book back on the shelf and decided to continue checking out the mansion. She went out the library door Pig had exited through and found herself in a glass-walled hallway. The outside glass wall exposed a glamorous and well-manicured pool area. An automatic door slid open when she walked toward the glass. Shelby left the hallway and made her way to the edge of the bluest pool she had ever seen. She leaned down and placed her fingers in the water, it was warm. Without thinking, she took off her shoes, rolled up her jeans and sat down on the edge of the pool. She put her feet into the pool and let the warm calm water massage them.

As Shelby stared into the crystal clear water, her thoughts were interrupted by Harry. "Ms. Shelby, I see you have found your way to the pool. I just wanted to remind you that dinner will be served shortly." Shelby looked at her watch and couldn't believe it was already ten minutes to seven. "Oh Harry, I'm so sorry about this, I just lost track of time in the library." Shelby gathered her shoes and stood up.

"No problem, Ms. Shelby. Mr. Pig is busy in the communication center; he is going to be late."

"Okay, well I'll hurry." Shelby ran into the glass hallway and stopped. "Harry!"

Harry entered the hallway. He pointed down the hall, knowing without even being asked. "Straight down the hall and turn left. There is an elevator that will take you to the second floor. Go straight and your room is on the left."

Shelby felt like an idiot, but smiled at Harry. "You're the best, Harry. Thank you."

Harry smiled back. "So I'm told. You're quite welcome, Ms. Shelby."

◊◊◊

The command center was wild with activity. Pig had been summoned to the center because of a report of a possible hijacking scheme. The driver was told the report was unlikely and to continue with his orders. However, Hank was not one to put his job on the line for not following up on any kind of report made by a driver. True or false. Hank immediately notified Pig of the report and put everyone in the communication center on alert. No other drivers had reported anything out of the ordinary, but Hank was going to let Pig make the call on whether to continue the alert or stand down.

"Okay, Hank, what is so important that you couldn't tell me about it over the phone?" Pig asked when he entered the control center. Pig saw that all of his operators were on alert and that all of his trucks were lit up on the map on the wall. "Why are we on alert?"

"Boss, one of the operators received information from one of our drivers claiming he was told of a hijacking scheme planned for our trucks headed to Mexicali."

"Who's the driver and where and who gave him the information?

"That's all we have right now. We're getting the driver on the phone so you can speak to him personally."

Pig talked with the driver and questioned him about where he got the information. The driver explained to Pig about the blowout and the motorcycle rider who was behind him. "I don't know how he kept from being hit by the tire debris."

"You said you got this information from a biker?"

"Yes, sir." The driver was nervous speaking with Pig. "He was behind me on the highway when my truck blew a tire. When I got out to examine what happened, we began to talk and he mentioned that he'd just had a conversation with a friend of his who used to work for PIGT. According to this guy's friend, there was talk about some cartel guys hijacking some PIGT trucks when they went to pick up some loads near Mexicali."

Pig didn't want his lower level drivers to have any inkling he was dealing with the cartel. What the driver just told him was too accurate to be coincidental. Pig also found it very suspicious that the information was coming from a biker.

"Well, I do appreciate your loyalty and your willingness to give me a heads up on a potential risk to our business. You will find a nice bonus on your next check. I do want to assure you, however, that the loads my drivers pick up in Mexico are coming from legitimate business associates and not the cartel."

"I'm relieved to hear that from you, Mr. Pig sir. Thank you for the bonus and I'll be sure and keep you informed...."

"Goodbye," Pig said before the driver could finish his sentence.

Pig turned to Hank, "Keep everyone on alert and let me know at once if any of our drivers report trouble. I wouldn't put it past Bullets to try and steal Tito's loads. That idiot is just looking for a bullet in his head. He picked the perfect nickname."

Pig headed out of the control room. "I'm late for dinner with the Mathewses. I think I like our new blonde driver."

Hank wanted to tell Pig what Shelby had said and that he wasn't impressed with her attitude, but he knew not to cross his boss when his mind was made up. Apparently Pig liked her and not liking something Pig liked wasn't a good career move. Hank sat back in his chair. He was beginning to hate his job.

CHAPTER SIX

Bullets' plan to take over twenty PIGT trucks was set in motion. He had his soldiers ready and in place to hijack the trucks as soon as they exposed themselves. What Bullets didn't know was that only ten PIGT trucks would be on the road because Pig had made arrangements with Tito to have ten trucks loaded on Friday night and ten loaded on Saturday night.

Lizard and Rough Rider were waiting in their assigned locations. Lizard called Rough Rider. Both gang members knew what they were about to do was suicide. "Lizard, we have to get our guys out of this. Tito is going to kill us all if we take his loads."

"I know, Rough Rider, but there isn't anything else we can do but wait for the trucks. If we back off, Bullets will know we aren't with him and he'll have our own men kill us. If we take these loads, Tito is going to kill us. We are just dead men. I tried hard to get the info to PIGT but they blew it off as a rumor."

Rough Rider felt hopeless as he listened. He still held hope that they would find a way out of the situation. "Well, I guess we do this then."

"Yep, we do this. I'll see you on the other side, my friend."

"Yes, my brother." Lizard hung up and wondered, *Why did I join a gang anyway?*

◊◊◊

Pig walked slowly down the hall toward the dining room, thinking hard about the information he had received. He knew Bullets was behind whatever was going to happen, if it happened. He also realized that someone in Bullets' gang was not a loyal gang member. It would be nice to know who the traitor was and if the biker might want to work for his organization. Pig was convinced this information was legitimate. *Someone in Bullets' gang knows that taking the cartel's merchandise is deadly and he doesn't want to die.*

Pig stopped by his office to make a few phone calls. First he opened his laptop to see where his ten trucks moving out of Mexico were located and where the ten trucks were parked that were scheduled to pick up the remaining loads on Saturday night. Most of the first ten loaded trucks were already traveling and were between California and Arizona. A couple were stationary and Pig knew they were probably at truck stops.

The trucks that were due to pick up their loads Saturday were mostly stationary along Arizona's highways. A couple were moving toward that area, but none of the trucks due Saturday were in the vicinity of the loaded trucks. Pig was glad the trucks were positioned where they were and he planned to make sure Bullets would only have a small window of opportunity on the loaded trucks. He couldn't prevent the attempts to hijack his trucks, but he could prevent the hijacks. He picked up his phone and made several calls to some of his known associates in the areas of his loaded trucks.

"Look, Yanks, I want your men to protect my trucks and take out anyone who attempts to hijack Tito's prize. Tito is never to know that his loads were ever in any danger. Do you understand? Once the first ten trucks have made it through, I want you guys to protect the next ten due to load tomorrow night. I don't think Bullets knows the trucks have been scheduled to load at different times. I don't think he's prepared to run another shot at them tomorrow. He's a blooming fool to think he can do this, so if you get a chance to take him out, do it. I'll reward you handsomely if you get rid of that pain in my side."

Pig made calls to other protection units and let each of his contacts know where his trucks were and how he wanted things handled. Once he felt he had things taken care of he called Hank. "I've taken care of the rumor, but keep the operators on high alert. Do not interrupt my dinner unless it is an emergency."

Hank attempted to respond, but as usual, Pig hung up on him. "Yes sir, Mr. Pig, I'll take care of..."

Hank hung up his phone. "It would be nice to know what you have done and how many bodies to expect, but that's okay. I'll figure it out when you ask me to cover your ass again," he whispered defiantly.

◊◊◊

Shelby had returned to her and Jack's room. Jack had taken a shower and was dressed for dinner. He was lying across the bed, flipping through the channels on the television when Shelby burst through the doors. "I was wondering if you were going to change for dinner," he said.

Shelby was breathing hard as she threw her shoes on the floor and started undressing. "Yeah, I found the library and the pool and kind of got distracted."

Shelby left a trail of clothing all the way to the closet. When she appeared again in the bedroom, she had on a white, short spaghetti strap dress. A pair of white open-toed heels were in her hands, which she was attempting to put on her feet while running into the bathroom. "Harry told me not to hurry, that Mr. Pig was still dealing with some business. I still don't want to be too late getting to the dining room."

Within a few minutes, Shelby appeared from the bathroom with her hair brushed, her makeup touched up, and a pair of earrings dangling from her ears that matched the shoes and dress. "Well, does this look okay?"

Jack sat up on the bed. "You're a knockout. Maybe we should just stay here and make an excuse that we don't feel well."

Shelby laughed and let Jack grab her around the waist. "You know we can't do that."

Jack kissed his wife and then they left the room together.

◊◊◊

It was almost twelve-thirty when Angelica reached the first truck stop. She quickly turned into the fuel island and took her purse to the restroom. She knew Rex was going to be waiting on her call. She checked the stalls before dialing him on her secured phone. Rex answered immediately after the first ring. "Finally! I'm glad you called. I've been waiting for your call for hours."

"I called you as soon as I could, Rex."

"Are you okay? I saw where you went into Mexico before we had planned."

"Yes. It's a long story and I'll write you a report on the entire thing, but I don't have time to tell you everything right now. I am fine, so you don't need to worry."

"That's all I needed to hear."

Rex and Angelica continued their conversation for several minutes and talked about the next time they could make contact. Angelica liked her job, but she didn't like feeling she was in danger. It was part of the job, and she knew she was going to be in danger from time to time. But now that she might be falling for Rex, she was beginning to question whether she wanted to continue being an undercover operative.

After talking with Rex, she hesitated a few moments before turning the phone off and placing it in her bag. Even long after she hung up, she could still hear his deep, soft voice in her head. Thinking about how warm and special she felt when she talked with him, she looked into the mirror in the bathroom. She took her finger and rubbed her lips and spread out the lipstick that remained. She then took her lipstick out of her purse and put on a fresh coat. With a deep breath, she opened the door to the bathroom and walked into the store. Several hundred miles were waiting for her and it was getting later by the minute.

◊◊◊

Rough Rider and his men spotted their first truck. It wasn't going to take much to take the truck over since it was dark and the truck wasn't traveling at the maximum highway speed. "We only want the load; do not hurt the driver," he reminded his men. "Jameson will ride with Tracks, and when we have the truck, you will drive it back to LA." Rough Rider pointed to an empty parking space near the convenience store where they had gathered. "Put your bike over there; we'll get it later."

A little further down I-10, Turn Coat and his men had spotted a PIGT truck. "Okay boys, there's our target. Do whatever it takes to get that truck to pull over. Archie is waiting with his truck to take the load. We will unhook the PIGT truck from the trailer and Archie will hook up and then take it back to LA." The bikers and trucker went after the prize.

Lizard hoped they wouldn't spot a truck, but it wasn't long before one of his men spotted a PIGT truck running east on I-10. "Lizard, I see one and I think there is another one in front of it."

Lizard ordered his men to stop the trucks. "Okay, half of you and the bobtail go after the truck at the rear and the rest of you follow me. We'll take them down at the same time. Stop the trucks and get the loads. This is about money, not murder, and I'm not doing time for Bullets if this thing goes down wrong."

Lizard's men agreed.

"Ricardo, you bring your truck in from behind so when we get the trucks stopped you can hook and go."

Time Bomb, Lethal, Dirty Player, Turn Coat, and Bullets all had trucks in their sights. Some of the leaders had trucks to help take the loads only. Other leaders were simply going to take the tractor and the trailer. The trucks were spread out so Bullets wasn't aware of how many trucks his men were taking down at the same time. He had ordered his men to take as many trucks down as they could, as quickly as they could, hoping to get all twenty loads before Pig knew what hit him.

◊◊◊

Shelby and Jack had eaten their salads and were snacking on bread as they waited for Pig to join them. Harry had let them know that he had been detained but would join them as soon as he could. Just as Harry was about to have the main course of the meal served, Pig entered the dining room. "I apologize for being late." He took his place at the head of the huge table. Harry poured Pig a glass of wine and placed a salad in front of him.

"No problem, Mr. Pig. I'm also in charge of things in my business so I understand how it is when you are the only one who can fix things," Jack offered.

"Well, we haven't been here long ourselves, sir. I lost track of time in that marvelous library of yours, which made us late," Shelby said.

Pig wasn't much for words during a meal. "I see."

The three adults dined together mostly in silence except for thanking Harry and commenting about the delicious food. Pig finally broke the silence at the end of dessert. He used his cane to help himself out of his chair. "Harry, that meal was divine. I'll take my brandy and cigar at the pool. Shelby, Jack, I would appreciate it if you would join me."

As Harry cleared away dessert plates, Shelby said, "Yes, Harry, that meal was splendid. Mr. Pig, we would be happy to join you." Shelby took her wine glass and strolled toward the door that Pig was walking through.

Pig was amazed at how graceful and stunning Shelby was in her dress. He tried hard not to stare, but he was absolutely smitten with her. *Is this woman really a truck driver? She's too smart and too beautiful to be driving a truck.*

Pig escorted his guests to the pool. He found his usual spot and called for his dogs. Jack joined Pig at his table. Shelby had taken off her shoes and sat down at the edge of the pool. The water felt so inviting that if Shelby hadn't been there for a professional meeting, she would have gone for a swim.

Harry brought Pig and Jack each a glass of brandy and a cigar. Pig's dogs soon arrived at his side. They were very well trained and didn't jump on or bother Shelby or Jack. Pig petted each dog and talked with them for a few moments.

Shelby was impressed with their discipline. "I have never been around a dog that did exactly what he was told."

Pig continued to pet his animals. "Dogs are amazing creatures. They have natural instincts for survival, but if you treat them right and train them correctly, they will be totally loyal and obedient. Sometimes I wish people could be trained like that."

Shelby got up and joined the men at the table to discuss her possible employment with PIGT. She shared her likes and dislikes about what she had already seen at the estate. Pig shared what he was willing to tell her about his company. She asked questions and Pig answered them within his own contrived way. Pig had given Shelby much more of his time and patience than he would have given to any other possible employee. He tolerated her questions and even her criticisms of his business and security, not because he was impressed with her ability to drive a truck, but because of her. Pig had never been so taken with anyone, let alone a woman.

The poolside conversation went on for hours. Pig and Jack drank brandy and smoked cigars while Shelby enjoyed the wine, water, and dogs. Pig had never let anyone other than Harry near his dogs. Shelby was different for some reason and his dogs seemed to instinctively know it, too. They took to her immediately. Pig actually enjoyed watching his dogs play ball and tug of war with Shelby on the lawn.

◊◊◊

Lizard and his boys split up and surrounded three sides of each of the two trucks. Lizard managed to move his bike up next to the driver's side door. He motioned to the driver to move his truck over to the side of the road. "Move over!"

The driver looked at Lizard as if he was out of his mind. He shook his head. "No?" Lizard was glad the man was not complying. Lizard hoped that the other half of his group was having just as much trouble. The longer it took to get the trucks to comply, the longer the drivers had to notify Pig they were in trouble.

It wasn't long, however, before Lizard realized that he and his men were the ones in trouble. Out of nowhere, they were surrounded by a group of men in pickups and jeeps. The men in the vehicles were heavily armed and began using their firepower against Lizard and his men.

Before Lizard knew what was happening, two of his men had been gunned down. Lizard quickly rode his bike to the head of his pack and motioned for his men to back off the hijacking and follow him. He didn't recognize any of the men and they didn't appear to be cartel, but that didn't mean they didn't work for them or for Pig. The protection force didn't follow Lizard but continued to shoot at them as they retreated. Once Lizard and his men were out of the way, the force surrounded the two trucks that had been under attack and escorted them to safety.

Lizard couldn't believe how quickly things happened. It was his intention to protect his men from getting killed, not help them get killed. He led the biker and truck driver who was with them to a picnic area on the other side of the highway. The men were up in arms as they rolled into the park.

"We have to go get Ralph and Stoner."

"They took them out, Lizard!"

"We got to get back in there and get even."

"Lizard, we have to go check on Ralph and Stoner."

Lizard knew he needed to check on his men, but he had to calm his other soldiers down and make sure the force that was brought to fight them off was gone. He didn't want any more of his men to get hit. Once he knew the gunmen were gone and his remaining men were not hurt, he turned his bike around and faced his men. "Calm down and stay here. Ronny, Lenny you two come with me. Archie, you get on your CB radio and see if you can get in touch with any of our other members. Follow us over to the other side of the highway so we can get Ralph and Stoner. We may need to get them to the hospital if they are still alive. The rest of you get on your phones and let the others know what's going on and to watch out. We might not be the only ones getting hit and they need to be prepared."

Lizard pulled out his handgun and ordered his men to follow him back to the area where they had been attacked. Rico followed in his truck, trying to contact any of the other drivers on his CB. It was useless, none of the other trucks were in radio range.

He used his phone to call Archie. Before he could get Archie on the phone, Lizard motioned for him to pull over. Lizard had located the two men and their bikes that had been gunned down in a ditch.

Lizard pulled his bike over and ran to the side of the two men. Ralph was holding his leg and bleeding from his arm. Stoner was face down in the ditch not moving. Lenny and Ronny were just steps behind. Ronny went to help Ralph while Lizard and Lenny went for Stoner. They turned Stoner over on his back. Stoner was bleeding from his head and not breathing. Lizard knew it was too late for the biker as he held him in his arms. "Bastard! I'm done with Bullets and with his stupid plans. He's going to get all of us killed.

You guys can do what you want, but I'm not doing any more of these bullshit suicide missions. Look, what that son-of-a-bitch did to our brother!"

Lenny knew Lizard was right. "I'm with you, brother, and I'll make sure everyone in the gang is with us. Bullets is out of control."

Lizard looked at Stoner then motioned for the others to come help carry his body to Rico's truck. Rico, Lenny, Lizard, and Ronny carried their fellow biker to the truck. Ralph waited in the ditch until the group came and helped him to the truck as well.

The four bikers gathered what was left of the two motorcycles and strapped them to the deck of Rico's truck. "Let's get the hell out of here and get Ralph some help." Lizard's men knew from his voice that Lizard was pissed and that something pretty bad was going to go down when Lizard met up with Bullets again.

◊◊◊

It was close to two in the morning when the party by the pool was interrupted. Hank had put off interrupting Pig as long as possible, but Pig had to know what was going down. Hank had received several calls from drivers reporting motorcycle riders trying to get them to pull their trucks over. Pig's security forces were on site with most of the trucks that were being attacked. Hank had been in contact with the protection units and they were doing all they could to take out as many of the bikers and truck drivers as possible.

Pig's cell phone went off and he reluctantly took his eyes off Shelby to answer it. He spoke with impatience and anger. "What?" He listened to an apologetic Hank. "Okay, so have the protection units taken care of the problem." Pig listened as he started to get out of his chair with his cane in hand. "I'll be there in a few moments." He hung up and called for Harry. Harry came at once. He gathered the dogs and put them in their restricted fenced area a few yards from poolside.

Pig excused himself. "I apologize. Jack and Shelby, please excuse me. I need to take care of some things again in the command center. Please feel free to enjoy the pool. I'll meet with you tomorrow, Shelby, and continue this interview. I believe we have covered just about everything, however. It is up to you now, whether you want to join my team or not. I'll see you tomorrow. Please enjoy your night."

Shelby walked to a chair near Jack. "Thank you, Mr. Pig. I hope everything is okay. I'll give you my decision in the morning."

◊◊◊

Bullets felt a bullet whiz by his ear. "What the fuck?" He turned to see several vehicles coming up behind them as they were attempting to hijack a PIGT truck. The two four-wheel-drive pickups were loaded with armed men in the bed and a gunman in the front passenger side seat. Not knowing exactly what was going on, he pulled out his gun and started firing toward the pickups. "Where the hell did these fucks come from?"

Several of his men had been shot and were in the ditches along the highway. Most of the other men under his command had backed off and were doing everything they could to keep from getting shot. The pickup that Bullets was shooting at sped up and tried to take him out. Bullets decided he was out-gunned and took off as fast as he could. He left his men to fend for themselves against the gunmen.

Time Bomb, Rough Rider, Turn Coat, and Dirty Player were also fighting off the protection squads that Pig had sent to take care of his trucks. The only leader who had not been subjected to an attack was Lethal. He and his men had been watching a PIGT truck that was parked at a truck stop outside of Mexicali. They had been watching it since the female driver had left it in the fuel island and went into the store.

Lethal had been interrupted by several phone calls from other gang members, informing him about the protection forces that had attacked them. Lethal hung up his phone and checked the parking lot. Sure enough, there were two trucks with about ten men parked outside the store, watching the same truck he was watching. Lethal informed his men of the force and the fact that they would take them out before taking the truck.

Bullets had managed to get away from the hit men who were after him. He found a place to pull over and phoned his lieutenants. Most of his lieutenants were busy trying not to get killed. "Lethal, are you guys under attack too?"

Lethal assured his leader he and his men were fine.

Bullets didn't care whether the members of his gang were alive or dead—he wanted the loads. "So go get the load, you idiot, where…"

"Wait, what luck! Another PIGT truck just pulled into the fuel island."

Bullets was furious. "I can't believe you haven't taken down the first truck yet. Where are you at?"

"Truck stop east of Mexicali."

Bullets was breathing hard when he started his bike and headed it in the direction of the truck stop. "Don't let those trucks leave until I get there. Send your men in and have them take out those fucking men. I want to know how and who gave Pig or the cartel or whoever the information about my plan. I'll be there…."

Lethal hung up on him.

Bullets was pissed. He threw his phone to the side of the road and rode like hell to Lethal's location.

Lethal was a killer and knew exactly what he was going to do. He didn't really care about the loads on the truck, but he wanted to kill the men responsible for killing and injuring part of his gang. With a hand motion, Lethal let his men know that they were going to take down the ten men in the pickups. He wanted it done as quickly and quietly as possible.

Several of the men that had been recruited to protect the PIGT had let down their guard. They were talking and sipping sodas they'd bought in the store. Lethal found his opening and took it. Within a few minutes, Lethal and his men had either broken the necks or cut the throats of every man in that protection unit. Lethal and his men quickly moved to take the two PIGT trucks. The driver of the first truck had not come out of the store yet. The other driver was easily overtaken by Lethal and his men. His body was dragged to the pickup trucks and placed with the other bodies in the bed of each truck.

Lethal and his men unhooked both tractors from their trailers and moved in their own tractors to carry the trailers back to LA. Just as they were about to hook Angelica's trailer to their tractor, Angelica appeared from the store. "What the hell are you doing with my truck?"

Lethal caught Angelica from behind and put his hand over her mouth and a gun in her back. "Don't scream. Be a good girl or I'll kill you right now."

Angelica stopped struggling and did as the man asked.

Killing men was something Lethal did without thinking about it, but taking out a woman was not something he particularly liked. He was frustrated with the idea that he had a loose end and it was a damn woman. "Dammit, bitch. What in the hell am I gonna do with you?" Lethal pushed Angelica toward the back of the trailer and out of sight of anyone in the store.

Angelica was afraid, but she recognized some of the men around her from the other truck stop earlier. These guys were part of Bullets' gang, which meant she was definitely in trouble. "Look, I won't say anything," she said quickly. "I'll just walk away and tell them I didn't see anything."

Lethal knew he had a problem and that Angelica was giving him a way out of it. He just wasn't sure letting her go was the best idea. Instead, he handed Angelica over to two men who were standing next to her trailer. "Take her and tie her up inside her tractor and put it on the back line. By the time they find her, we will be long gone and Bullets will have his fucking load." Lethal looked at Angelica. "You tell anyone about me and I'll hunt you down."

Angelica shook her head. "I won't."

The two men took Angelica and put her inside her tractor. Then they drove her and the tractor to the back line of the truck parking lot. The men tied Angelica's hands and legs together and put her on the bed in her sleeper. They put a piece of tape across her mouth and then zipped her curtain shut. They left her in her truck. Angelica didn't like the position she was in, but she was glad she wasn't dead.

Bullets arrived just as Lethal and his men had finished hooking up the trailers to their trucks. Bullets immediately took over the whole operation. Lethal and his men mounted their bikes and none of them mentioned the dead bodies or the woman they tied up in the truck. "Okay, boys, let's get these loads to LA."

A couple of bikers were concerned with their comrades. "What about the others, Bullets?"

Bullets knew there had been a lot of bloodshed tonight, but he didn't care. His plan went almost completely wrong and these two trailers were all he had for a reward. "We can't worry about them right now. I'm sure they can take care of themselves. We have to get these trailers back to LA before Pig lets the cartel know that he lost some of his product." A smile spread across Bullets' face. "I'm sure that's going to be a conversation Pig wants to have with Tito. Boy, would I like to be a fly on that wall."

Bullets' attitude pissed Lethal off and he and others were beginning to think that perhaps they needed a new leader. Lethal decided that he would ride with the group for a while, then head east and find the others. Lethal's little brother, Stoner, hadn't checked in with him and he was concerned. He knew the other leaders were going to need help cleaning up the mess Bullets had made.

◊◊◊

Pig entered a command center in chaos. All the loaded drivers, except for two, had called in to report they were under attack.

Hank handed Pig a printout of the status of the loaded trucks. "Mr. Pig, every truck has been secured except for two. We have their location and they were under protection by one of our teams, but weren't able to make contact with the protection team or the drivers. The tractors are still in the parking lot but it is unclear if the trailers and loads are there. The tracking devices have been disabled. I have another protection force headed their way; they are thirty minutes out."

Pig was not interested in the trucks. For the moment he was more concerned with Tito's product. He could not and would not let Tito know that two of his loads had been hijacked. "I know that Bullets is behind this and he has those two trailers. He's taking them to LA. Send that protection team to LA. and have them intercept those two trailers before they hit I-5."

Hank jumped on the phone. "Okay, Mr. Pig. He got your message."

"Tell them to be clean and precise."

"They are on the way and will keep us informed."

Pig was furious.

CHAPTER SEVEN

Inside her truck, Angelica realized that she was alone in the dark. The video surveillance and voice monitor inside the cab didn't work when the truck was off. She knew the tracking device attached to the outside of the truck was on continually. She knew Pig would eventually send someone for the truck, but just when depended on the priority and importance of her load. A recovery team would arrive immediately if the load was important. If the load wasn't, then she knew she might be stuck there for days.

She decided to focus on getting out of the ropes that held her hands tied behind her back. Her captor had been kind enough to let her live, although she was a hostage. She had heard them zip the zipper on her privacy curtain. She was going to have to get out of the ropes or no one would know she was in there.

She thought about the emergency door, but while one of Bullets' men was putting on the blindfold and ropes, she saw the other one block the door with some wood. Pushing open the emergency doors was not an option. She lay on her back and tried to wiggle her hands out of the ropes.

◊◊◊

Hank had contacted the protection unit that was on its way to the truck stop and relayed Pig's new orders. It didn't take the unit long to find the trucks heading west toward LA. They had their orders and they took no time in following through with them. The vehicles moved in quickly behind the bikers and trucks. There were several bikers behind the trucks and several in front of them. The gunmen in the front vehicle took out the rear drivers in the convoy.

When the bikers realized they were under fire, many of them decided to take the ditch instead of the bullets. Once the protection unit had a clear shot at the truck to the rear, they quickly moved in on either side of the truck. Within seconds, the driver of the pickup was next to the truck driver's door. The passenger in the pickup leaned out the window and pointed his shotgun at the driver. He yelled at the driver, "PULL IT OVER, BITCH!"

The driver realized he had no choice, and after waiting for the truck on his left-hand side to speed forward, he moved his truck to the side of the road.

The second truck wasn't going to be quite so easy to stop. Bullets had seen what was going on behind him from the front of the pack. He motioned for his members on their bikes to move in front of him. He then motioned for the truck driver to follow him close. He got in front of the truck and stayed on the front bumper even when bullets from the second pickup started flying at him.

The trucker put the pedal to the metal and kept up with his leader. The driver became more nervous with every gunshot. The pickup full of gunmen was getting frustrated with the lack of cooperation from the trucker and the idiot biker who was trying to outrun them. "That's it, boys, give it to them. Blow the hell out of that cab and take that bastard out front to the ground." With those words, a blast of ammo flew through the air.

Several flying bullets struck the truck driver. None of them were life threatening, but they left him bleeding and in extreme pain. He put on the brakes and quickly moved his truck to the edge of the highway. Bullets saw that the driver had let up on his speed, which left him an open target. Deciding that he didn't want to die, Bullets leaned forward on the tank of his bike and raced away from the armed protection unit.

The protection unit let Bullets and the other bikers go down the highway. The unit pulled the drivers out of their trucks and confiscated the trucks and trailers, leaving the drivers on the side of the road. "We're taking your trucks back to where you took the trailers. You can pick them up there if you want the tractors back. Next time you decide to hijack some trucks, make sure they don't belong to Pig. Tell Bullets that he will pay us for this mess."

The unit contacted Hank. "Hank we have the trailers in custody and are headed to the truck stop to return them to the drivers."

Hank motioned for the operators in charge of the two trucks to check their screens. They shook their heads. "That's great, Yanks, but we haven't heard from those drivers yet. The tractors are there, but there hasn't been any noise or pictures from the cabs for hours. When you get there, let us know right away if you locate the drivers. We may need to have the trucks driven by other drivers if they aren't located."

"What if we find your drivers dead? Do you want law enforcement informed?"

"No, just let me know if you find them and I'll make a decision then. Make sure they have no PIGT information on them regardless of what I decide to do. Pig won't want any law enforcement involvement or connection to the bodies."

"Got it, Hank. We'll let you know what we find when we get there. Tell Pig we took care of some of the bikers, but his man Bullets got away—for now. We left him a clear message so he knows we're coming for him."

"I'll let Mr. Pig now." Hank was relieved that he could report to his boss that his instructions had been followed, his two trucks were secure, and Tito's loads would be delivered on time.

Pig was settling into bed when Hank called him. "Let's make sure this doesn't happen again," Pig replied to Hank's update. Then he said, "When Ms. Shelby wakes up in the morning, I want you to do whatever it takes to bring her on board. Money, truck, I don't care what it takes. Get her to sign on, and I mean it."

Hank didn't argue, although he had reservations about the woman. "Yes, Mr. Pig. I'll take care of it."

◊◊◊

When Yanks and his boys arrived at the truck stop they found more than they bargained for. "Boss, look, there's Shanks' truck." The security unit moved in close to the pickup. The big rigs parked in the fuel island. One of the men in the back of the pickup suddenly jumped to the pavement, stunned. "What the hell?"

The others got out of their vehicles and looked down into the bed of the first pickup. "Oh my God."

A few guys check out the other pickup. "Yeah, over here too. Boss, they took out our men and left them like garbage. We have to avenge this, boss. They can't kill our members and get away with it."

Yanks checked out the morbid sight. "You're right. Bullets just sealed his coffin."

"Yanks, I think we found one of the missing truck drivers too."

Yanks went to the other pickup to identify the unknown man. "I think you're right. Men, we have to finish this job and then we'll make sure Bullets and his men pay for what they have done to our guys. Fan out and see if you can locate the PIGT trucks. They're probably in the parking lot here somewhere. I'm going to make some calls and get things ready to bring our boys home."

"Yes, sir."

Yanks made a call to his headquarters. "We'll take care of things once we finish this job and get our guys buried. Get some of the wives together and prepare for the bodies. I don't want the cops involved. We will bury them ourselves. I also have one of Pig's drivers. I'll send a couple of the members to you with our bodies while we deal with the rest of this mess."

He waited for a response. "No, I'm not sure yet what Pig will want done with his driver. I'll check with him and let you know." Yanks hung up and dialed Hank. "I got one of your drivers and Bullets has taken out several of ours. What do you want me to do with your man's body?" He waited for a response. "No, there wasn't a woman, just a man." He waited again. "Yes, we are tracking the trucks now." A slight pause. "Okay, we'll take your body too. I'll let you know when we locate the trucks and the female driver."

Yanks hung up and looked toward the parking lot where his men were hunting for the two PIGT trucks. Yanks hated losing any of his men. The protection units were a tight knit family. *Bullets is a dead man.* His thoughts were interrupted.

"Yanks, we located both bobtails at the back of the parking lot. The guys are bringing them around now. There's a driver in one, a female."

Yanks looked at his man. "Is she alive?"

"Don't know, boss." The two men waited for the trucks to be brought to them.

Angelica had been working for hours to try and get loose from the ropes, but as hard as she tried, she couldn't get them to come loose. She had allowed herself to fall asleep from the exhaustion when she was suddenly awakened by someone trying to get into her truck. She kept quiet. She hoped it was someone from PIGT coming to release her, but she wasn't sure and didn't want to expose herself until she knew.

One of Yanks' men unzipped the curtain to Angelica's sleeper. He was sure he was going to find a body, but was surprised when he found a female tied up on her bed. "Hey Jim, look what I found."

"Don't hurt me," Angelica whispered.

"Don't worry, miss. We're here to help you, not hurt you."

"Are you the police? Do you work for PIGT?"

The man sat Angelica up gently and took off her blindfold. "No miss, we are not the police and we aren't PIGT But we do work for them."

Once the blindfold was off, Angelica felt better. "Thank you." One of the men untied her arms and legs while Jim was busy starting and airing up the truck. "You're welcome but we need to get you out of here and find out what Pig wants done next."

"Okay." The men had Angelica stay seated in the sleeper while they occupied the driver's seat and the passenger's seat. They took the bobtail over to where the other unit members had gathered in the parking lot.

Angelica could see through the windshield that whoever these men were, they were heavily armed. The two men who had just rescued her got out of her truck. "We will be back in a minute when we find out what the boss wants you to do. Stay here."

Angelica nodded. She wanted to be more involved, but didn't dare argue.

Angelica looked around the cab of her truck and her sleeper bed. She needed her purse. She hoped that the kidnappers had not taken it with them. She was relieved when she found the purse stuffed behind the passenger seat. It was exactly where she had dropped it when the kidnappers had shoved her into the sleeper. They apparently hadn't noticed or hadn't cared. She reached into the purse to make sure her secured phone was still in her possession.

After feeling around in the bottom of her purse, she breathed a sigh of relief. The phone was still there as was everything else.

She looked at the phone but since the truck was running the cab's voice and camera monitoring devices most likely were activated. She wanted to call Rex and be pulled out of her current assignment, but knew blowing her cover would mean blowing the case. *Two close calls in twenty-four hours is enough,* she thought.

Yanks notified Hank as soon as his men had Angelica. "Hank, tell Pig we have his female driver and she's alive. I guess these bastards aren't into killing women. Mighty big of them with all the other blood they have shed here. What do you want us to do with the loads and with her?" He got a quick response. "Okay, but don't take too long. I got bodies and we need to get them out of here before the cops get wind of what's going on. You've got ten minutes."

Yanks had his men cover the bodies in the back of the pickups with tarps. He then began assigning tasks to his men. "You four men load up in the pickups and get those men back to their wives. The rest of you get those trucks off those loads and the PIGT trucks back on them. Park the other trucks over there and when I find out from Pig what he wants done with the trucks, I'll let you know."

"Yes, sir."

Yanks didn't like waiting for Hank to confirm things with Pig. He wanted to get finished with this mess and start making plans to get Bullets. He moved toward Angelica's truck.

Angelica was in the passenger seat of her truck, watching the activity when she noticed two men walking toward the truck. She waited for the men to open the driver's side door. "Ma'am, we are going to hook you back up to your trailer and once we hear from PIGT we will let you follow their instructions."

Angelica was still a little shaken from what had happened and was happy to let Yanks and his men continue with their job. "No problem. I'm exhausted anyway. I hope they don't expect this load to be delivered on time."

The man who had come with Yanks to the truck moved passed his boss and got into the driver's seat. Yanks climbed down off the truck. "We'll let you know what your boss has in mind for you as soon as they get back to me. Yogi, take her truck over there and hook her up, maybe by that time Pig will have gotten back to me."

"Got it, boss."

Just as Yanks got back to his men, Hank called. "Pig wants to hire a couple of your men to transport both loads to their destination. Do you have any men that have CDLs?"

"Yes, but I need my men. We have bodies to bury and Bullets to find. I'm not sure any of them would be willing to break away. Plus, your female driver is able to drive—she's just a little shaken. Give her some time to rest and I'm sure she'll be fine."

Hank needed the loads on the road immediately. "Okay, what if I…"

Pig grabbed the phone from Hank. "Look, Yanks, I'll make it well worth your while and I'll finance your hunt for Bullets. He's a pain in my ass and I was planning on taking him down myself. But I'll let you have the pleasure and pay for it if you will do me this favor."

Yanks thought for a moment and then decided maybe it would be worth it, especially if Pig was going to put his money where his mouth was. "Okay, I'll send Yogi with your female driver and have Slater drive your other truck. The security team we already agreed on will pick them up in Arizona and follow them and the rest of the trucks to the end of the security zone like we agreed. You need to have a driver ready to take over the trucks once they reach that point. My men are not making the drop for you. I don't deal with your clients out of Mexico. I don't want any involvement with them."

Pig didn't like being manipulated, but he needed Yanks. "Okay, Yanks. I'll have a driver there. I'll contact my female driver and let her know what I want."

"Don't forget, Pig, this is going to cost you."

Pig was annoyed. He shoved the phone back to Hank, "Finish this and give Yanks whatever he wants. I need those loads on time so send two drivers to the security point in Texas in order to cover those trucks for the drop.

Have the female driver ride with Yanks' driver and then have her picked up by one of my personal cars. Bring her back here to the estate. Do you think you can handle this?"

"Yes, Mr. Pig, I got this."

◊◊◊

Shelby and Jack had noticed when they left the pool area the previous evening that things were still busy in the mansion. Shelby had shown Jack the library on their way back to the room and he was amazed by how many books the man owned. She also didn't get lost this time and felt she was finally getting the lay of the land. Pig said they could take a walk on the property the next day.

Shelby and Jack slept in, a rare luxury. Harry checked on them and brought coffee and a full breakfast to their room. As she dressed, she told Jack how excited she was to see Pig's horses. She also wanted to see what he had outside the grassy yard that surrounded the mansion. Pig had warned that there were several buildings that were under heavy security and to avoid them but otherwise, they could make themselves at home.

Their conversation with Mr. Pig over dinner and his assurance that her privacy would never be invaded all but sealed the deal for Shelby. Jack had been impressed almost from the time they'd arrived. Shelby's dream of owning her own truck could have been realized, as Mr. Pig assured her she could lease one with him. However, after their talk, she opted to start off as a company driver. Pig assured her that whenever she wanted to be an owner/operator that he would personally help her get her own truck. Shelby and Jack seemed pleased with the options.

◊◊◊

Hank was exhausted when he met Jack and Shelby in the hallway. "Ms. Shelby, Jack, how are you?" Hank shook hands with the couple. "Have you decided whether you will be joining our team?"

"No, not yet, but I am still considering it. I will have an answer for Mr. Pig this afternoon."

Hank was a little relieved. "I'm on my way to my room, but don't hesitate to let me know if there is anything I can do for you."

She looked at Jack as they turned to walk down the hallway. "What?" Jack asked with a raised eyebrow. "Why didn't you just tell him?"

Shelby shrugged. "I don't know. That guy just rubs me the wrong way. I just didn't want to tell him yet."

Jack laughed. He knew Shelby was an intuitive person and probably had a good reason. "Okay, baby."

◊◊◊

Angelica had received Hank's orders. She was relieved that someone else would be driving her truck since she was so tired. She was told that once they reached a special security checkpoint that another driver would be taking over the load. She would be taken by a private vehicle to the airport and then driven to the estate. Pig wanted to have her checked out by his personal physician. She also figured she would be debriefed.

The driver was a nice person. He didn't talk much and let her rest quietly in her sleeper while he drove. She wished she could've had time to call Rex. She knew she was not going to be able to make the next appointed check in time, which would worry him, but her lack of privacy was going to make it difficult to stay in touch. *Maybe I'll get a call in the next time we stop while I use the restroom.*

◊◊◊

Bullets had made it back to the shop they used for their club meetings. He was in a rage when he rode his bike into the shop area. Several bikers from the job that had just failed had made it back before their leader. None of his lieutenants had made it back and that seemed to enrage Bullets even more. "Where the fuck are my soldiers?" He threw whatever he could get his hands on as he stormed through the building. Finally, he made his way to the stash of cocaine hidden in a hole behind a loose brick in the wall.

The men who had made it back decided they would simply stay out of his way until the other club members returned. Many of the men already had phone conversations with other members and knew exactly what had gone down with the other hijack teams. They knew several of their friends had been killed or hurt. They also knew there was a lot of unrest among the members and several had talked about replacing their leader. But none of them wanted to fuel the fire any further with Bullets. If there was going to be a mutiny, they wanted to make sure they were on the side of the majority. Something that wouldn't be known until the remaining club members returned.

◊◊◊

Lizard and his men had met up with Rough Rider. Several others had joined them as they rode back toward LA with their wounded and dead. Lethal had also met them and after seeing his brother, Stoner, dead he was ready to personally make a change in leadership. They would have to use a more tactical method. "Look, Lethal, I know how you feel. After all, Stoner was one of my men. Bullets has been over the edge for a long time but we have to get the rest of the members behind us before we try and take him out or we will just be killing each other."

"I don't think we are the only ones who will be gunning for Bullets. Bullets has managed to piss Pig off in a major way with this little stunt and I'm sure he is going to be out to get all of us before long. We are going to need to rally the men together and keep our wits about us." Lizard continued. "We can't be divided right now. Together we stand, divided we fall. Hell, Pig might take out Bullets for us if we're lucky. We need to keep our men out of it if we can. We have lost enough already. Let's see what we can do to fix this thing without getting any more of them put in body bags."

"Lizard, I need you to know what we did at the truck stop because Pig isn't the only one who's going to be gunning for Bullets and our club. That bunch of hit men who Pig hired to take us out lost two pickups—and the men in them. I know this because we killed all of them and one of Pig's drivers in a truck stop parking lot."

"Well, I know I shot at a couple of their men and I'm sure I hit several others during the fight today. This changes the dynamics of things some. The groups I'm worried about right now are Time Bomb's and Turn Coat's. Those men and maybe even Dirty Player's group are still with Bullets. I need to figure out the best way to make him take the heat for all of this mess."

"We'll figure something out." Lethal consoled. "Let's go get these men to their wives and girlfriends. We have some soldiers to bury too. Plus, I need a few beers so I can forget all of this."

Lizard's phone rang. "Speaking of our leader." Lizard hit the button on his cell phone.

"Where the hell are you guys?" Bullets yelled. "You men need to get back here so we can figure out our next mission!"

"Bullets, I lost a man today and I have some wounded. I'm taking my men to their families. We will come to the clubhouse after we get done burying Stoner."

Bullets was strung out on coke. "No, you sons of bitches will get here now! We need to go over some ideas I have for another attack."

"Look, Bullets, I'll come to the clubhouse, but my men need to take care of their wounds and I'm sure there are other lieutenants who are doing the same."

"You tell those pussy ass soldiers to get their mother-fucking asses to this club house."

Lizard knew he wasn't going to comply, but he had to figure out how to keep things from falling to shit if he defied this psycho's orders. "If I bring my guys in now that group of militia men that came after us out there on that highway might be watching us. They might be trying to find out where we meet and I would be leading them to the clubhouse. If I send them home and avoid the clubhouse, I might be able to keep them from finding out where you're located. They might want to pull a surprise attack or something."

Bullets paced the floor of the clubhouse. Paranoid, he moved toward a dirty window to the front of the old building. He wiped off a corner of the window and looked out. "Well, shit maybe you're right, Lizard, but I don't see anyone poking around outside."

"Yeah, but they might follow us. I think we'd better be careful for a few days. What do you think?"

"I've decided that my soldiers need to stay away for a couple of days until I make sure things are safe around here. You let the other lieutenants know I've made the order. Or have them contact me and I'll tell them."

"Yes, sir, I'll pass it along."

Lizard let Lethal know about his conversation with Bullets.

"You need to go and take care of your brother and your men. I have my own men to take care of. Bullets is pacified for the moment. I'll meet you for a beer later and we will talk about how we can take Bullets out."

"All right, my brother, I'll meet you later."

The club members parted with a fist bump, a manly shoulder hug, and pat on the back. "Brothers forever."

◊◊◊

Shelby and Jack had spent a few hours walking the estate and checking out the thoroughbreds that Pig had acquired for show. Shelby was sure that Pig had never been on a horse and if he had it wouldn't have been one of the fine specimens he had in his barn. The horses that he kept were well taken care of by the grounds keeper, but without asking, she knew they had not been ridden by anyone in a long time.

A horse came up to the fence and Shelby pet it on the nose. She loved horses and wished she had one, but knew she didn't have the time. Jack liked them but did not have a deep interest in them.

"Wow, to have all these beautiful animals and not ride them. I don't understand people with lots of money. They have everything you can possibly want but it's all for show." She continued to pet the horse as it nudged at her for attention. "Look, Jack, she likes me. If I had this kind of money, I wouldn't just buy things so people would know I had money. I would enjoy the things I'd bought."

Jack looked around at the grounds and thought how wonderful it would be to own such a beautiful place, *but what a lot of work*. He knew Shelby would fit in nicely in such a place since she grew up in the country. He turned his attention back to his wife. She seemed happier now, especially now that he was supporting her career choice in earnest. He watched her play with and pet the horse that had attached itself to her. Her long blonde hair blew across her round cheeks and soft pink lips in the breeze. *How could I have ever been so stupid to have hurt her? She's the best thing in my life.*

"Hey, baby, where you at? You look like you're a million miles away."

Jack laughed. "Right here, sweetie. Just thinking." Jack walked over to where she stood and pet the friendly horse with her.

"What are you thinking about?"

Jack smirked. "You."

Shelby got down off the fence and put her arms around her husband's neck. Jack grabbed her hips and kissed her lips.

"Silly man," she said. The couple walked hand in hand back toward the mansion.

"You think I'm doing the right thing, Jack? I mean deep down inside?"

"I don't know, baby. I think time is really the only way we will know for sure. I mean, the money is good, though Mr. Pig seems a little odd."

Jack was always brilliant when it came to giving advice without really giving it. He had never wanted to be responsible for any decisions that Shelby made when it came to her career, because he didn't want her to blame him if things went south.

"Well, I do think I'm making a good decision. With what I'm going to get paid, I should be able to put plenty away to buy my own truck in about a year. That's what I really want to do, Jack. I want my own truck."

"I know, baby, and that's cool with me. But one thing I truly want to know—we aren't getting any younger. How long are you planning on driving trucks?"

"I don't know, but maybe we could drive *our* truck after you retire. We could travel and work at the same time."

"I'll give that some thought," he said.

The couple reached the backyard near the mansion when they observed several white vans pass the mansion and head in the direction that they had just come from. The vans went straight for the warehouses that were positioned directly west of the horse barn. That area had been cordoned off so Shelby and Jack had not explored it. Shelby couldn't help wondering why there was so much mystery and secret activity going on in this place. With all the armed guards and security people that roamed around constantly, not to mention the surveillance, Shelby felt like they were at Fort Knox. "Wow, I guess Mr. Pig must really have some important clients. He sure goes out of his way to protect their stuff."

"Yeah, we need to keep an eye on this stuff when you go to work here. I don't want you involved in anything illegal."

"You don't really think he's into anything like that do you?"

"Well maybe not, but there's a lot of strange things going on around here. He's been in business for a long time, so if he was into illegal stuff, I'm sure the cops would be watching him. I'm sure he's just protecting his client's things."

"I hope so."

Jack changed the subject a bit as they made their way to the back patio. They took seats next to each other looking out over the pool. "I don't want to sound snobby or rude, and maybe I shouldn't mention this, but last night when we were out here talking with Mr. Pig, did you notice the bad odor coming from him?"

"No, I didn't last night, but I did notice it the other day when I was talking with him in the library."

The couple laughed as Jack waved his hand in front of his nose. "Wow, if it wasn't for the cigar last night."

Shelby giggled. "Jack, that's not polite."

"How does a man with this much money stink like that?"

Shelby and Jack laughed softly together until they were interrupted by Harry. "I've had the cook prepare a late lunch if you are hungry."

Shelby and Jack stopped laughing and hoped no one had heard what they had been laughing about. Shelby responded politely. "Oh thank you, Harry, but breakfast was huge and I'm still full."

"Me too, Harry. Besides, we were thinking of taking in an early dinner at a casino tonight. We planned to leave early in the morning and I wanted to take Shelby out on the town."

Harry bowed as he normally did. "Very well. I'll inform Mr. Pig of your plans."

"I hope we aren't offending Mr. Pig by doing this. If you would also let him know that I need to speak with him. I have made my decision and would like to tell him personally."

"Very well. I shall let Mr. Pig know."

◊◊◊

Pig had been busy all day handling loads his trucks had brought in from the East Coast. The items were weapons from one country that were promised to another. The ships had docked three weeks ago and Pig's men had unloaded the freight onto trucks. The trucks then transported the merchandise to one of Pig's warehouses in North Carolina. The weapons had been kept in storage in North Carolina for several days until Pig was able to clear the way for the loads to be transported to the estate in Louisiana.

Pig was then going to store the weapons in his security warehouse on the estate until his client could inspect the merchandise. Arrangements would then be made for the items to be transported into the buyer's hands. Pig personally handled much of his business with his foreign clients in this manner.

Harry contacted Pig on his cell phone. "Mr. Pig, the Mathewses will not be joining you for lunch today and they will be leaving us this evening for an outing in the city. Also, Ms. Shelby would like to speak with you in reference to her decision to join PIGT."

"Why aren't they staying here at the estate?"

"I guess they made plans to enjoy the evening at one of the casinos."

"Well, tell Ms. Shelby I'll meet her in the library in an hour."

"Yes, Mr. Pig."

Pig had been keeping track of Shelby's activity on the estate all morning. He wanted to make sure she didn't leave the mansion that evening without joining his company.

CHAPTER EIGHT

Harry had made arrangements with Shelby for her to meet Pig in the library. Jack agreed to stay the room to pack their things. Pig, however, was not in the library when Shelby arrived so she decided to take the free time to look through his book collection again. She hoped that through her employment with him she would be able to read as many as possible.

Pig had been monitoring Shelby on the screen of his laptop. He was watching her every move in the library. He liked how she touched the binding on the books and how she moved to read the titles. She was graceful, beautiful, and intelligent—exactly what he had been looking for all his life. How he was going to make her his was yet to be worked out.

He suddenly closed his computer and got off his bed. He knew he was losing perspective of his business and his life thinking about this woman. He needed to be patient and vigilant. He left his room after spraying on some cologne. With his computer under his arm, he locked his bedroom door and walked slowly toward the library. Pig wasn't certain if Shelby was going to go to work for him yet, but he was determined to make it impossible for her to leave without saying yes.

Shelby had once again found herself deep in the first few pages of a novel she had always wanted to read, so didn't notice Mr. Pig enter the room. However, it didn't take long for her nose to realize he was there. She quickly lifted her head and shut the book. "Mr. Pig, I'm sorry, I didn't hear you come in. I found another novel, and of course, I'm lost in the words."

Pig found his usual seat at his desk. "No problem, Shelby. Feel free to enjoy them. In fact, you're welcome to borrow any of them whenever you like. Harry had mentioned that you needed to speak with me?"

Shelby got up and placed the book back on the shelf. The books were way too valuable to borrow and she didn't want to be responsible for any of them in case something happened to them. "Thank you, Mr. Pig, I appreciate it. Yes, I wanted to let you know personally that if you still want me as a driver, I would like to come to work for you. I didn't feel comfortable telling Hank that this morning. I wanted to tell you myself."

Pig was impressed that she wanted to tell him herself. He hoped there was more to that personal attention from Shelby, but wouldn't let himself get excited about such things just yet. "Shelby, I am thrilled you want to work for me, and I believe you will make a wonderful employee. I am sorry you aren't comfortable with Hank. Perhaps I should look into that issue. I don't want any of my employees uncomfortable with my administration."

Shelby didn't want to start any trouble and she didn't know enough about Hank to cause him any problems, at least not yet. She sure didn't want to start off with any issues with anyone at PIGT. "Oh no, Mr. Pig. It's not that exactly. He's okay, I guess. Maybe I just need to get to know him and learn how things are run around here before I voice my opinion about someone."

Pig could tell Shelby was trying hard not to cause problems. He made it easy for her. "Okay, well you let me know if you ever have any problems with any of my employees. I'm glad you're on board. You will need to come back here in about a week so I can get you in a truck. I'll get with Hank on that and he'll be in touch on Monday. I understand you and your husband are leaving us this evening?"

"Yes, but not because we haven't liked it here or appreciated all the hospitality. Jack and I just thought it would be nice to check out the nightlife in Louisiana before we headed home. Once I get back on the road, our time together becomes limited."

"I understand totally. But please allow me to take care of your evening out. It would be my pleasure, and I have many connections in town who will cater to your every whim."

"Oh that's nice, Mr. Pig, but we already made reservations, and..."

"Nonsense, Harry will arrange everything." With those words Pig got up from his desk. He shook Shelby's hand and walked out of the room. Shelby was a little stunned at Pig's forceful behavior, but could only get out a short reply before the man disappeared.

"Okay, well thank you, Mr. Pig."

Pig contacted Harry on his cell phone as he walked back to his office. "Harry, I have insisted on taking care of the Mathewses evening out. Make the limo available to them. I want you to spare no expense. Ms. Shelby will be joining our team next week and I want her to feel welcome."

Harry could tell that Mr. Pig was happy about the new employee and Mr. Pig was never happy about anything. "Yes, Mr. Pig. I'll take care of it immediately."

"Also, let that idiot Hank know that Ms. Shelby will be joining us and to get the paperwork going on her," Pig continued. "I want him to get with me later. I'll explain how I want her handled personally."

"Yes, Mr. Pig, I'll inform him at once."

"Okay. I have another call." Pig answered his cell phone. It was Hank. "What?"

"Mr. Pig, Bullets' men were able to confiscate two of our trailers that were loaded Saturday. They managed to disable the main tracking device on them, but the secondary tracker is still functioning and I have located them."

"Where are they?"

"Somewhere near El Centro, sir. They are still in Bullets' custody as far as we can tell."

"What happened to the security force that was supposed to be escorting them?"

"The security force was unable to prevent the capture of the trailers. They lost one whole team during the original fight with Bullets. They were just spread too thin with having to escort the Friday trucks and then cover the Saturday trucks. I thought I had it contained and covered, but the gang managed to get them somehow."

Pig fumed as he listened to the excuses coming from his top man. Now he was going to have to negotiate with Bullets. The biggest idiot in the world had two of his trailers and he needed them back. He had to figure out a way to keep his friends in Mexico from finding out the two of their loads had been heisted. "Shut up, idiot. I don't need to hear your excuses. I'll pull the trailers up on my computer. I'll figure out what I need to do to get the product back. Get in touch with the warehouse in Florida. I want two trailer loads of the Cuban product I have stored there. I'll replace the Mexican product with the Cuban product until I can fix this problem. Hopefully, neither of my clients will know that the products have been changed out."

"Yes, boss."

"I'll deal with Bullets in the morning. I'm sure he thinks he has the trailers hidden without the trackers. He should know I always have a back-up plan."

"I'll get on it right away, boss. Who do you want me to send to Florida to pick up the trailers?"

"I don't care, moron. The closest drivers, don't you think? I need that product replaced and ready for the customer to inspect on Tuesday morning. I want it to arrive with the other trucks and hopefully no one will be the wiser. Got it, Hank? Can you handle it?"

"Yes, Mr. Pig. I'll take care of it."

Hank knew his boss was not happy with him, but he didn't have any control over the situation. Bullets' gang had always been a pain in the ass and now he was going to have to fix as much of this mess as he could. Hank turned back to his computer and picked out two trucks that were in the area of Pig's warehouse near Jacksonville, Florida. He contacted the drivers and let the warehouse manager know he was sending two trucks to pick up two trailer loads of product for a destination near Philly.

Pig had already found the two stationary trailers near El Centro. He was still fuming about the situation as he worked to fix it. *Bullets. That pain in the ass. It's time to do something permanent about the bastard.* He decided he knew exactly how he was going to do it, too. Bullets wanted his turf, so he was going to give it to him. Just long enough for him to hang himself. He would have control of Bullets' gang and every piece of turf he ran before he was finished.

◊◊◊

Angelica was frustrated and exhausted when she finally arrived at Pig's estate. Over the last few days she had not only been in the forced personal company of some of the most dangerous cartel men in Mexico, but she had been kidnapped and tied up by some LA gangsters. Then she had to ride in her own big truck for hundreds of miles for a day and a half with a stranger. She had been taken from her truck in Texas to an airport where she was put aboard a small plane for two hours. She was finally placed in the back seat of an SUV in Louisiana and driven to her boss' home.

She hadn't slept except for a few hours during the rough ride in her truck from California to Texas. She hadn't eaten anything except for a couple bites of a sandwich she had been given on the plane. She was dirty and wanted a shower. Plus, she was still in a daze from her ordeals in California. The one thing that was bothering her most was that she hadn't been able to talk to Rex. So when Harry and the security officers met her at the front door of the mansion, Angelica was in no mood to be pushed around, questioned, or interrogated.

Harry had quickly moved to gather her things from the back of the vehicle as Angelica walked up the steps toward the waiting security men. "Ms. Angelica, Mr. Pig would like to speak with you immediately,"

Angelica couldn't believe the words that came out of her mouth but she was rather glad she spoke them. "Look, you steroid-injected baboons, I've just been through hell and back and I'm going to my room for a shower and some rest. I realize Mr. Pig wants to speak with me, but it is going to have to wait until the morning. If Mr. Pig doesn't like it, he can fire me and I'll gladly leave in the morning after I have rested."

Angelica rebelliously walked passed the security men toward her room. The officers were amazed that a small-framed woman like Angelica would have the balls to speak to them in such a way, let alone refuse a meeting with Mr. Pig.

Harry, who was carrying Angelica's luggage, simply passed the security officers in a fast pace right behind the determined woman. The smile on his face let the men know he liked the way Angelica had just eroded their macho behavior. Harry was beginning to like the new breed of women Pig was unintentionally surrounding himself with at the mansion.

Angelica walked straight toward the room Harry had given her. She knew the security in the mansion was the same as in her truck, maybe even more strict. She would do her best to find a moment to call Rex somewhere. She had tried a few times on the way to Texas when Slater had stopped for her to use the restroom. There always seemed to be someone in the bathrooms or Slater was within hearing distance. She had managed to get a small text off to Rex, knowing that he would be worried. She hadn't found a secure place yet to check to see if he had responded to her text.

It was dangerous using text messages, especially if anyone got a hold of the phone. She had to use a code word to let him know her status and then delete it. He would always respond with another code word. She would find a way to get off the estate tomorrow and call him. Once she could find a moment, she would discretely try and check the phone when she got to her room. Being detected by security was always a problem when she was at the mansion. They tried to make you believe they never spied on you without a reason, but Angelica knew they always found a reason. Pig had earned his name not only because of his personal appearance and hygiene, but also because he was a pervert. The odd thing was he seemed proud of the moniker.

◊◊◊

Bullets answered his cell phone; he was paranoid by the ideas Lizard had put in his brain. "What? Who is this?"

Time Bomb didn't like the way his leader answered his phone but figured the information he was about to lay on him would change Bullets' tone quick. "Bullets this is Time Bomb."

"Where the hell are you and Dirty Player? We got stuff to figure out and missions to complete, you idiots. But be careful not to let anyone follow you back here to the…"

Time Bomb tried to interrupt his psychotic leader. "Bullets…wait a minute…"

"We don't want anyone knowing how to find…."

"Bullets, listen for a minute…"

"You know they want me dead now… Pig especially…."

"Bullets!"

Bullets stopped rambling for a moment.

"Dirty Player and I got two of Pig's trucks. We are in El Centro and have the trailers on two of our trucks. We accidentally ran across them on our way back to LA. We lost a bunch of our guys, but we have the trailers. We are laying low in an old truck graveyard. We disconnected the trackers, and I think we have the trailers hidden pretty well."

Bullets tried hard to absorb the information from his gang member with what he had left of his brain cells. "Okay, that's great.... Stay where you guys are for now. We don't want anyone to know where you or the trailers are. This is great, just great."

Bullets was stumbling around the hideout, knocking over everything he came near. He was stoned and drunk well beyond function by now. Bullets fell into one of the oversized chairs and dropped his phone to the floor. He tried to scramble to pick it up but he was too wasted to perform the act.

Turn Coat, the only leader who had made it back to the clubhouse, picked up the phone and took over the conversation for his nonfunctioning leader. "Bullets is out of it, Time Bomb. Just stay wherever you are for now. I'm sure that Bullets will be better in the morning."

"Okay, Turn Coat. What the hell is up with Bullets?"

"Bullets has had a little too much of the white stuff up his nose, mixed with a few too many chugs on the bottle of JD."

"Okay, let him know when he comes back to earth that we scored for him."

"Got it brother."

◊◊◊

Angelica was exhausted when she finally got to her room. Harry had put her bags in her room and left her to rest. She knew she needed to call Rex but she was too tired, so she went into the restroom and closed the door. She turned the water on in the sink and the shower. Discretely, she put her purse on the counter and pretended to rummage through it for something. Once she had the phone in her hand she checked it for a response from

Rex. She spotted his reply—he was upset but was glad she was safe. He wanted her to call as soon as she was able to. She splashed her face with water and then undressed for a shower. She didn't like the fact that Pig could be watching her as she undressed, but at this point, her fatigue and tired body was stronger than her modesty. She didn't care if that fat bastard was watching or not.

◊◊◊

Pig decided it was time to deal with Bullets. It didn't take him long to locate Bullets' personal cell number.

Bullets remained loaded on cocaine into the next couple of days. His paranoid and anxious behavior continued as well. So when Pig phoned him, he nearly jumped out of his skin at the sound of his cell phone going off. He had surrounded himself with the men who had shown up at the clubhouse, but he was still nervously keeping watch for the militants that Lizard implied might show up to kill him. The number that came in was blocked, but he answered anyway. "WHAT?" Bullets answered the phone while looking for the hundredth time out the dirty window.

Pig had dealt with Bullets often over the years and knew he was hooked on cocaine. He knew Bullets was an unstable egomaniac. He cared for nothing and no one but himself. It was actually fun for Pig to inflict more ideas into Bullets' mind, causing him to become even more paranoid. Bullets had changed his cell number on a regular basis because of Pig's constant ability to get his number.

This time, however, Pig had to make a deal with Bullets. He hated the man and making a deal with him was a hard thing to do, but if he was going to get his trailers back, he was going to have to bend a little to this rat. The conversation would be short, but he would make a deal that even Bullets wouldn't be able to refuse. "I'm going to tell you this one time and one time only: I want my trailers and loads back. I'll let you have the West Coast and the cartel. But I want my trailers back by the end of the week with loads intact. I'm done playing your stupid games. You're a dead man if you don't give me back my property."

Bullets was still stoned and having trouble with comprehension and speech, but he liked what Pig was saying. "You'll just back away from all of the West Coast stuff and cartel business if I give you back the two loads? Well, Mr. Pig, it sounds to me like there must be something really valuable in those loads for you to be so generous. I think maybe I should take a few days to think about this deal and check out what's in those trailers personally. I know you, Pig. You never give anything away without a reason. What's in it for you Pig? What are you up to?"

"Nothing, Bullets. But if you don't give me back my loads by the end of the week, you're a dead man." Pig hung up his cell phone, leaving Bullets to mull over the short conversation.

Bullets, meanwhile, stormed the clubhouse like an angry animal. "FAT FUCKING BASTARD! WHERE DOES HE GET OFF THREATENING ME? I'LL GIVE HIM BACK HIS TRAILERS AND LOADS WHEN I DECIDE. MAYBE NEVER!" He began throwing things around the room. His men quickly found their way out of the building. Bullets saw them leave, but couldn't do anything about it. "WHERE ARE YOU GOING? GET BACK IN HERE. I'M THE FUCKING LEADER AROUND HERE AND WE HAVE ANOTHER MISSION TO COMPLETE!"

Bullets' men knew Bullets was losing control. Many of the men stood outside listening to their leader storm and rage inside their clubhouse. Several had gotten on their cell phones to let other members know that Bullets was going crazy. It wasn't uncommon for their leader to fly off the handle, but this fit seemed to be even worse than normal.

The men stood outside the clubhouse smoking and drinking beer while supposing what was wrong with Bullets. "Maybe it's the coke?"

"Maybe he's just tripping bad?"

"I don't know, but I think that conversation he just had on the phone was with Pig."

"I think so, too. Plus, he's freaking out about those militant men that hit us during the mission."

"Bullets is out of control and is going to get us all killed."

"You might be right, but he's our leader. We have to defend him."

"He's bringing this club down."

"Where are the rest of our guys anyway?"

"Not here."

"Yeah, and some of them ain't coming back. We lost several of our best guys during that fiasco on the freeway."

"He's so concerned about himself that he hasn't even called to find out who was lost during his 'mission.' We need to do something."

"Let's just hold on until some of the other lieutenants get here."

"That might not be for days. I think I'm going home."

"Yeah, me too."

Several members shook their heads in agreement, but no one was ready to derail things with an open statement putting their leader down completely.

Bullets came to the doorway, staggering, completely strung out on cocaine with a bottle of beer in his hand. He had exhausted himself and realized that he was getting none of the much-craved attention he needed on a regular basis. He needed to pull himself together. "Come on, men. We need to talk about how we're going to get even with these bastards for hitting us. We need to hit back and hit back hard. Pig is caving and wants me to make a deal with him. Those loads Time Bomb and Dirty Player captured must be really important for him to give up his entire West Coast and cartel business. We got him by the balls, boys, and now is the time to squeeze them."

Bullets' words didn't mean much to his men, but they didn't want to let on to their leader that they were questioning his authority over them. Several of the men who had been on their phones hung up without completing their calls, not wanting Bullets to know they were talking with other members about his behavior.

Bullets walked back toward the door. "Come on, we have a lot to work out. I've come up with an idea to get even with Pig and those militant guys."

The men weren't sure they wanted to know the brilliant idea their leader had just come up with while throwing his tantrum but they were willing to listen. The men started filing back into the clubhouse. Bullets was thrilled that he was gaining control of his men again.

Inside the clubhouse, Bullets snorted another line of cocaine from the table in the middle of the room. He leaned back and sniffed each nostril taking the drug in deep. He shook his head and sipped at his beer. "YEAH!"

Stuttering through his words Bullets addressed his men. "Mr. Pig wants his trailers back. He's willing to give me my turf in exchange for them. His demands make me laugh. Mr. Pig will not be getting those loads back and I'm going to have my turf. He must think I'm a blooming idiot to try and bargain with what is already mine."

He continued to stumble and stutter through his plan. Most of the members stood or sat and listened to Bullets while still questioning if he was capable in his current condition of coming up with any kind of idea at all. "Okay, men, this is what I have in mind..."

◊◊◊

Angelica had slept hard during the night. She only woke up when she overheard some talking in the hallway near her door. She couldn't make out what the conversation was about, but she could tell that it was Hank and one of the security guards. Hank's raised voice told her that something big was going on.

Forcing her legs to the edge of the bed, Angelica pulled herself into an upright position. "Oh, God. I don't want to get up." Angelica ran her hands through her hair and pulled out her scrunchie. She then used both hands to pull her long brown hair back into a ponytail. Standing to her feet, she twisted her body around in a couple of circles, and then bent forward to stretch her back out. She stood straight again and leaned back slightly to stretch her back in the opposite direction.

After her morning stretches, Angelica went toward the restroom to brush her teeth. As she moved passed the door to her room that opened to the hallway Angelica could still hear Hank. His voice indicated that he was angry about something, which wasn't uncommon, but Angelica wished she could put her ear to the door and listen closer. She knew it wasn't the best idea, especially if someone was monitoring her room. She decided that she would simply open the door and find out what was happening.

When she opened the door, Angelica saw Hank with his finger in the face of the security officer. Hank was red-faced and angry. The security guard was taking the abuse from his superior, but Angelica could tell that he was close to decking Hank. The security guard was the one who had met Angelica at the front door of the estate the night before.

When Hank and the guard heard Angelica's door open and observed her sticking her head out of the door they quickly stifled their heated conversation.

"Is everything okay?"

Hank quickly gave Angelica and the security guard a stern look. He looked one more time toward the guard. The guard knew without question that his boss meant what he had just said. "Get it done, Masher."

"Yes, sir."

Hank turned and left the hallway without speaking to Angelica.

Angelica looked at the guard and could tell that he didn't want to talk about it. "Mr. Pig wants you in his office in five minutes." He turned on his heels and walked toward the elevator.

Angelica had no intention of going to Pig's office in five minutes. She wanted to take another shower and eat some breakfast before going anywhere. She shut the door and leaned her back against it. She really wanted to talk to Rex.

Angelica contemplated whether it would be smart to try and call Rex inside the mansion. She thought for a few moments and then grabbed her purse from off the floor near her bed and headed to the bathroom. She figured it was unlikely that Pig would be monitoring her from his office this time of the day, so she took the chance. With all the commotion, she figured Pig and Hank must have their hands full with something big. It wouldn't have surprised her in the least that the confrontation in the hallway had something to do with whatever screw up Pig's men had made with the load she was carrying.

Angelica once again shut her bathroom door and turned on the shower. She took off her clothes and wrapped a towel around her body. She had put her purse on the sink. With as much discretion as she could manage, she took out her extra phone, slipping it between her hand and her towel. Then she pulled the shower door open, took off her towel and threw it over the glass door as she closed the door. She left her hand on her phone and used the towel to keep it hidden. She moved behind the towel on the door and shielded the phone from the water with her body.

The shower was big enough that Angelica didn't have too much trouble keeping the phone dry. She quickly called Rex. He answered on the first ring. "It's been hell waiting for you to call. Are you okay?"

Angelica whispered, "I can't talk long, but yes, I'm okay."

"Where are you?"

"In the mansion in my bathroom."

Rex didn't like that Angelica was phoning him from inside. "Angelica, that's not procedure, you are putting yourself and the operation in jeopardy."

"I know, Rex. I have to be debriefed by Pig soon and this might be the only chance I have for a while. I think I secured things well enough that no one will be the wiser."

Rex still didn't like it, but he was glad to hear from Angelica. "Okay, let me know what you can."

Angelica quickly but methodically retraced everything that had happened to her since their last contact. Rex couldn't believe everything that Angelica had endured in the last few days. "I'm not sure what is going on around here right now. This place is buzzing and I just saw Hank get into the face of the head security officer. I'll do my best to find out what's happening when I go in to see Pig."

"Damn, Angelica. Sounds like I should pull you out before you get hurt."

"Rex, I'm fine. My cover hasn't been blown and so far, I've only had a few close calls. I'll let you pull me out when we bust Pig."

"I know, but I'm worried."

"Stop worrying, it isn't good for you or me."

"You're right, but my feelings for you make it more difficult when I know you're in the line of fire."

Angelica hesitated for a few moments before responding. She knew she had feelings for Rex and that he liked her, but until this moment, she had never heard him speak of his feelings for her. She decided to make it humorous just in case he didn't mean what he said. "Feelings huh? Well, I'm a little lonely in this shower."

Rex knew he had slipped slightly but didn't care. "Shower? I'm not sure that's exactly the kind of undercover work our superiors have in mind."

Rex and Angelica joked and laughed for a few seconds. They now knew they both had feelings for each other, but they wouldn't be able to act on those feeling until this assignment ended.

"I better go before someone get suspicious or pulls me up on a monitor."

"All right. I want you to do what you can to get east so we can have a sit down."

"Oh just a sit down, huh?"

Rex laughed. "Well, got keep it business as long as you're under."

Angelica let him off the hook. "I know, Rex, no need to get nervous. I'll see what I can do and call you as soon as I can. I have no idea what this fat man is going to want me to do next."

"Okay, you be careful."

"I will, I promise. Talk to you soon."

Angelica turned off her phone and then took the towel down from the glass as she opened the door to the shower. She stepped out onto the bathroom rug, dripping wet. She did what she could to keep the phone hidden. Her purse was still on the counter where she had left it. She moved to the bag and dropped the phone into the purse while grabbing a bar of soap from the soap dish. She dropped the towel to the floor and got back into the shower.

CHAPTER NINE

Shelby was enjoying a hot cup of coffee on the patio of their home when Jack came out and kissed her cheek. "Gotta go, baby. Are you going out on a job today?"

"I don't know. I have to let Jayne know I'm leaving. I'm not sure if she's going to want me to finish out with a two-week notice or just let me go. I'll call you and let you know."

"Okay, baby, have a great day. I love you."

"Love you too."

After Jack left, Shelby sipped her coffee and thought about how much she was looking forward to her new job with PIGT. Jack reaffirmed that he thought she was making the right decision. She remembered the evening they had spent at the Louisiana casino, dining and dancing. Pig had covered everything, including their gambling. Shelby had a lucky streak and came home with an extra five hundred dollars while Jack lost a good chunk of change. It had been a wonderful evening. If her time at the estate and in Louisiana were any indication of what her employment was going to be like, she had landed a sweet job.

Shelby sipped the last of her coffee and went into the house. She called her office and asked to talk to Jayne. She spent several minutes explaining that she was going to be taking another position with another company. Jayne wasn't happy to lose Shelby, but she was happy that she had found a good position. Jayne told Shelby that she didn't need to give notice and that she could find another driver for her truck. Shelby decided she would spend the afternoon cleaning out her truck and the rest of the week getting ready to go back to Louisiana.

After the conversation, Shelby went to take a shower. Although she was looking forward to the new adventure, she felt kind of sad to be leaving Jayne's company. After all, Jayne was the one who got her started in the trucking business. She took her time in the shower and enjoyed the water as it sprayed her body. Her mind was suddenly brought back to earth when she heard a noise coming from the living room. She listened, but the noise didn't return. Shelby was a little unnerved. *I'm just making something out of nothing. Some leftover paranoia from the Betty saga, perhaps.*

Shelby finished her shower and put her hair in a towel and wrapped her body in another towel. She decided that she would check out the living room before getting dressed just to make sure it was nothing. *It was probably one of the dogs or maybe one of the boys came by for something.*

Steven had moved out of the house months ago and the private solitude that she and Jack now shared was wonderful, most of the time. But Shelby had to admit that she felt lonely in their big house without the noise children always seemed to make even now that they were grown. Although he wasn't living at home any more, he always seemed to come home when he needed things. *It was probably Steven.*

After checking the kitchen, Shelby was baffled that nothing seemed out of place and that no one, including the dogs were around. "Huh." She went back to her room to get dressed. "Shelby, girl, you are losing your mind."

Suddenly the noise came to her ears again. This time she grabbed her robe and went to the living room. She wasn't scared because the noise didn't sound like it was in the house. It was like a banging door noise. Shelby looked toward the front door and realized that the screen door was unlocked and flapping in the soft morning breeze. Shelby unlocked the wooden front door and pulled the outer door shut. "Jack knows better," she grumbled at his oversight.

She turned to close the front door when she noticed a note taped to the wooden door. She pulled it off and realized that someone had attempted an early morning flower delivery. "Jack, you're so sweet."

She took the note to her room with her and dialed the phone number on the card. She let the flower shop know that she was home and they told her that their delivery driver would make another attempt in about an hour. "That will be great. I have some things I need to do this afternoon."

◊◊◊

Pig was dealing with several issues simultaneously, but he had taken a few minutes to call his florist. He wanted to make sure Shelby wouldn't change her mind. *What woman doesn't like getting flowers and knowing that she's appreciated*, he thought. Hank had updates regarding several customers who were waiting for confirmation on deliveries and pickups, a new security man was bringing plans for an upgraded security system, and he had a debriefing with Angelica.

"Hank, I'm flying to LA next week for customer meetings and I have plans to deal with Bullets while I'm out there. Did you take care of the loads I wanted changed out?"

"Yes, sir. I still have the two trailers under surveillance. I haven't been able to confirm the product is still in them but they're still in El Centro."

"Okay, I'll use Parker and my West Coast warehouse guys to help me with the plan I have in mind for Bullet."

"I had Angelica sent to your office for debriefing. Has she arrived yet?"

"No, I've been busy. Harry will have her wait until I get to her. I want her to stick around the estate for a while. I want her available to roll with Shelby Mathews when she gets here next week. Speaking of Shelby, did you take care of her truck and everything?"

"Yes, I tried to call her this morning, but just got her voice mail. I'm sure she'll call me back soon and I'll let her know what you want her to do."

"I want you to be extra nice to this one, Hank. I like her and I want her to stick around."

"Yes, boss."

Hank hated the idea of having to show any kind of kindness or friendliness toward an employee, especially when that employee was a woman. But he knew that if he didn't do as his boss requested, he'd be on the chopping block—literally. Shelby Mathews was going to be a real problem, and Hank had enough problems.

◊◊◊

Shelby had finished dressing and was putting on her makeup when the doorbell rang. She went to the door and was totally blown away at the sight of the enormous bouquet hiding the delivery man's face and body. "Wow! That's some bouquet."

"Yes, ma'am, and that's not all. If I can put this down somewhere I have two more for you."

Shelby had the man come in and place the flowers on her granite top coffee table.

The man went back to his van and brought in two smaller bouquets that went on either side of the larger bouquet. The arrangement covered the entire coffee table. She was surprised that Jack would buy such an extravagant amount of flowers. He knew she loved flowers, but he also knew something like this wasn't necessary to show her that he loved her.

"There you go, Mrs. Mathews, looks like someone really likes you." The man took a clipboard out from under his arm and pulled a pen from his pocket. He handed it to Shelby and pointed to a line at the bottom of the paper. "If you don't mind signing for me right there."

Shelby signed the paper and escorted the deliveryman to the door. "Thank you."

"You're welcome. Enjoy the flowers."

Shelby looked at the flowers and took the small message card and envelope from off its post. She opened the envelope and took out the card. "What were you thinking, Jack?" Her bottom lip almost hit the floor when she read the words on the card. "Welcome to PIGT."

"Oh wow!" *What kind of a boss sends a new employee a table full of flowers for just going to work for him?* she wondered.

After looking over the flowers for a few minutes, she went to her bedroom and found her cell phone. She noticed that she had missed a call from Hank, but she decided that she wanted to talk to Jack first.

"This is Jack."

"Hey baby, it's me."

"What's up, sweetie? You going out on a job?"

"No, actually Jayne doesn't need notice from me and just told me I could clean my truck out this afternoon. But that's not why I called."

"Okay, what's going on?"

"Well, I just got a table full of flowers from PIGT."

"That's terrific. I guess you made an impression on Mr. Pig."

"You don't find this just a little weird?"

"Not at all. I mean usually a company gives you a hat or a t-shirt for coming on board. But I guess Mr. Pig likes flowers. It means he's glad you're coming to work for him."

"I guess so. I've just never received anything like this before. It's unnerving."

"No need for that, Shelby. Mr. Pig is just trying to show you that you're important to him and going to be a real asset to his business. Which we both know is true."

Jack always knew what to say to put her at ease. "Jack, you're nuts. What if I turn out to be one of the worst drivers he's ever had?"

"Shelby, I think you're the crazy one. Just enjoy it, baby."

"Okay, Jack. I guess you're right. They are really beautiful. In fact, they are the most beautiful flowers I've ever gotten."

"Most beautiful, huh…?"

Shelby laughed. "You know I'm kidding, baby."

Jack laughed too. "Oh, you got one coming..."

◊◊◊

Lizard had spent several days getting his men back in shape and attending Stoner's funeral. Most of the club had attended, but Bullets only showed up at Stoner's house with two members acting as his body guards after everything was over. Lizard confronted him in the yard before Bullets and his entourage could make a scene in front of Stoner's wife. "Hey Bullets, didn't know you were coming. Are you sure it's safe for you to be out in the open?"

Bullets motioned for his men to move in closer to him. Lizard was having a hard time holding back his laughter. He knew Bullets was paranoid with all the drugs he consumed, but seeing it firsthand with his own eyes was hilarious. Bullets was crazy and there was nothing to do now but take him down.

Lizard really didn't want Bullets going into the house knowing how Lethal felt about him now and what Stoner's family might be thinking as well. "Hey Bullets, I was just about to leave and go to the cemetery. You want to go with me? It might be safer paying your respects there. You know Yanks might have his men keeping tabs on some of us."

Bullets looked around, using his makeshift bodyguards as shields. "You really think they are here somewhere?"

One of the members looked at Lizard suspiciously. "Lizard, stop making him more nervous."

Lizard broke in between the two guards and put an arm around Bullets' neck like an old buddy. "Come on, Bullets. Let's mount up and go out to the cemetery."

"I better go in and see Stoner's old lady. You know, tell her I'm sorry he's gone or something."

Lizard again turned Bullets around toward the street. "Stoner's wife isn't doing real good right now, Bullets. I think they gave her some downers so she could sleep. Let's just get out of here before Yanks and his boys show up."

By this time the other two members had finally caught on to what Lizard was trying to do. The threat wasn't Yanks and his boys it was Bullets' own men. "Yeah, maybe Lizard is right, Bullets. Let's just go to the cemetery."

Bullets and his two men mounted their bikes.

Lizard moved toward his bike. He really didn't want to go back to Stoner's grave, but if it was going to get Bullets out of here it was worth it.

Lethal appeared on the porch just as the bikes were pulling out. He ran to the street and caught Lizard before he left. "Where you going? What's that asshole doing here?"

Lizard didn't want a scene. "I'll be back. Trust me."

◊◊◊

Angelica took a chair in the small sitting room outside Pig's office. She figured if she sat there long enough someone would notice her on the monitor and let her into his office. She didn't want Pig to know that she had taken her time getting to his office. The man gave her the creeps and she had always made it a point to try and never be alone with him. Pig liked to be in control of everything, and women were no exception.

Hank entered and saw Angelica sitting outside Pig's office. "It's about time you got down here. I thought I told you five minutes. It took you an hour and five minutes."

Angelica didn't like Hank and she didn't like being talked down to. "I was taking a shower," she fired back. "If my response time isn't good enough for you, I'll give you the keys to my truck right now. Besides, how is it that you just happened to know exactly how long it took me to get here? Surely you aren't monitoring my movements in the mansion without my knowledge? I mean that is the policy, right? No invasion of privacy in the mansion without notification."

Hank simply ignored Angelica and walked into Pig's office. He had tried to contact his boss by spy cam and cell phone, but Pig had not responded and he needed an immediate response.

Angelica didn't like being ignored. She followed Hank to Pig's office, but he attempted to shut the door on her. "Don't shut this door on me. I asked you a question and I want an answer."

Pig was busy on his computer with the cell phone in his ear. Hank attempted to make Pig face her by going behind his boss and putting some paperwork where he could see it.

Pig looked up from his computer and cut his phone conversation short. He was shocked by the conflict brought into his office. Hank quickly tried to defuse the situation so that Pig would not think that he didn't have control over the employees. He pointed to the door and said firmly, "Angelica, please step outside and I'll continue this conversation with you in a moment."

"I will not!" she spit back.

"Hank, shut up and get out. Angelica, have a seat. I'll be with you in a minute."

"Yes, sir, but I need the okay on the Pennsylvania job."

Pig glared but responded, "Do it and send me the emails."

"Yes, sir." Hank left without making eye contact again with Angelica.

Pig sat back in his chair, using his hand to direct Angelica to the chair in front of his desk. "Have a seat, Angelica. I apologize for Hank. He doesn't have good manners when it comes to dealing with my drivers. I've had a few complaints about him lately. I guess I better check things out and see what his problem seems to be. Anyway, I need you to discuss some things with you."

Angelica knew what one of those things was—the kidnapping. "Okay."

Pig leaned toward his computer and pushed a button. "I want to hear everything you can remember about the hijacking. But before we get into that, I want to discuss an assignment I need you to take on if you will. I have just employed another female driver for our team and I would appreciate it if you would let her run with you at first. I need you to show her the ropes and keep an eye on her for a while. She is a professional driver with a good record and lots of experience—primarily in the South, West, and Midwest. She doesn't have much experience in the Eastern states, so you will need to keep an eye on her there. Walk her through New York, New Jersey, and the port areas especially. Are you game?"

Angelica wanted to at least appear to be contemplating the idea, but knew she would not be allowed to say no. "Well…sure…but are you sure that I'm the right person for that job? I mean…I'm just a rookie myself, really."

Pig grunted at Angelica's reluctance. "Nonsense, I have complete confidence in you."

"Okay, I guess if you think I can handle it. Who is she and when do I start running with her?"

"Good. Her name is Shelby Mathews. She should be here by next Monday. I have Hank working on her truck and paperwork now." Pig turned his attention to his laptop. "If you'd like I'll give you the next few days off. You can stay here at the estate, or you can go home, it's up to you. You will be paid for the time, but if you don't want to take the time off I'll have Hank schedule you for something local. You'll be paid for your time either way."

Angelica liked the idea of having some time off. It wasn't really enough time to go back East but she really needed some rest and she wanted to do some shopping in town. The downtime would give her the opportunity to look around the estate a little closer and see if she could figure out what Pig might currently be up to. "I think I would like the time off and if it's okay, I'll just stay right here. I'd like to use the pool and spa if that's okay?"

Pig liked when his drivers stayed at the estate. "Excellent! I'll inform Harry that you will be staying with us. If you don't mind, I'm also going to tell Hank that I want you to help him pick out Shelby's new truck. I want her to have one of the brand new, fully loaded trucks I have parked on the line behind the shop. I'm putting you in charge of making sure it is perfect for her when she gets here. Hank doesn't understand what my drivers need, especially the women."

"Yes, sir." *He's going to a lot of trouble for this woman*, she thought. *I wonder why?* Pig had treated her exceptionally well when she came on board, but had not shown any personal interest in her or to the truck assigned to her. "Her name is Shelby?"

Pig did not look up from his computer as he spoke with Angelica, but as soon as she mentioned Shelby's name, he looked up with a smirk. "Yes. She's from someplace in West Texas, I believe."

He quickly turned back to his computer. "Let's talk about your abduction. Tell me about what happened in El Centro? I need to know everything you can remember especially about the abductors. By the way, there is a substantial amount of money added to your paycheck this week for the trauma and inconvenience you suffered. I know money cannot make up for what you had to endure, but I'm hoping it will help some. I also want you to know that I'll gladly pay for any injuries or mental health issues that may come from the incident."

Angelica knew Pig was a ruthless modern-day "Godfather" but he was generous and took good care of his employees. She thought about how conflicting it was working undercover as she took several minutes to go over what she had just experienced. She took a deep breath before going into as much detail as she could remember about what had happened in El Centro.

She had been trained, first in the Marines and then by the DEA, to remember as much information about incidents as possible. But she would not tell him everything.

The conference with Pig lasted a good hour. When Angelica finished Pig didn't look up from his computer. He was intense in some business on his laptop but he noticed when she got up. "Thanks, Angelica. I have recorded everything you have told me about what happened and I appreciate the detailed identifications you were able to give me about the men who abducted you. Let me know if Hank gives you any trouble when you pick out that truck for our new trainee. Just call me on my cell phone. I'll be in LA for a few days."

Angelica left Pig's office and walked down the corridor toward the main part of the mansion. She was going to enjoy her time off this week, especially now that she had some extra cash and Pig was going to be out of town. The first thing she was going to do was go shopping and make time to call Rex. Angelica's plans were quickly diverted when Hank caught her in the hallway near the communication center. "Mr. Pig has informed me that you need to accompany me to the truck line and help me pick out the perfect truck for our new female driver. I have no idea why he is being so particular with this driver, but I guess it's obvious he wants more than her driving experience. Follow me. We'll pick it out right now so that I can have the detailers and mechanics get it ready."

"But I was...."

Hank moved down the hallway to the outer door, he held the door open. "This way, please."

Angelica huffed as she passed through the door. "Fine, but after I finish helping you find a truck, I've got the week off."

"Fine with me."

The two walked in silence toward the truck line. Angelica didn't understand why her opinion on a truck was so important to Pig but she would do what the fat man wanted if it would help her get in closer to him and his secrets. However, like Hank, she believed Pig had an ulterior motive.

"Wonder if Pig knows what you think about Shelby?" she muttered

"That opinion would be best kept silent."

Angelica laughed, she wasn't the least bit threatened by the weasel that was currently her boss. "Hit a nerve, did I, Hanky?"

Hank ignored her and pointed to several of the new trucks on the line that had just come in from the factory. "They are all Peterbilt 379s, thirteen speeds, with 600 HP and except for the two silver ones on the end, they are all fully loaded." He pointed to a pearl blue one in the middle. "That one there has a 70-inch sleeper with a built in flat screen television and sound system. They all have satellite radio and television. Each truck has a built in refrigerator and a microwave and lots of storage. They're pretty much the same except for sleeper size, color, and either wood or carpeted. I'm not sure why Pig wanted your opinion on this decision."

"Maybe he just wanted a woman's opinion. I'll check out the blue one." Hank followed in behind Angelica.

"I doubt that's the reason, but nevertheless, I must comply. Here's the keys."

Angelica took the keys, unlocked and opened the door and hoisted herself into the driver's seat. The cab was chromed to the max with built in CB, GPS, stereo and a small computer, which was mounted for both driver and passenger access. She moved from the front of the cab into the sleeper. "Wow, this truck is really nice. I wish I had one like this."

Hank didn't respond.

Angelica looked through the closets and cabinets. "Man, the storage space in here is great." She opened the refrigerator and the microwave. "Nice."

Hank still didn't comment. He was outside the truck on his phone.

Angelica looked out the driver's door and realized that Hank wasn't the least bit interested in selecting a truck. She decided that she didn't really want to look at any other trucks anyway. The truck was top notch and would be terrific for any new employee. She got out and said, "This is the one I'd pick if it were for me, Hank."

She handed Hank the keys to Hank while he continued on the phone. She didn't wait for a response as she walked back toward the mansion.

Hank took the keys and quickly ended his phone call when he saw Angelica walking toward the mansion instead of another truck. "Wait, Angelica, don't you want to look at some other trucks?"

"I told you that blue one is the one I wanted. You were too busy on your phone to listen so lock it up. I'm on vacation. Don't call or expect me to answer for the next seven days."

He watched in disbelief as she walked into the mansion. "Bitch. No wonder I can't stand women drivers. They have no respect for authority and they use their bodies to manipulate their way into what should be a man's job. Women's rights, the biggest mistake America ever made. Women need to be kept locked away in their little houses with their little brats." Hank took out his phone and continued with the phone call that had been interrupted.

◊◊◊

Bullets had gathered the head lieutenants and several of the members together for another meeting. "Lethal, since you and Rat Hole have CDLs and can drive anything, I want you to get haircuts and get jobs at PIGT."

"WHAT? Have you lost your mind? I'm not going to work for that fat fuck!" Lethal stomped toward the door.

Lizard caught him by the arm and whispered in Lethal's ear, "Come on brother, hear him out. I think he's crazy too, but this could be our chance to take him down."

Lethal turned around, crossing his arms. "Fine. What's your brilliant idea? You already got my brother and a bunch of our members killed."

Everyone looked at Lethal in amazement. Bullets stayed silent.

"WHAT? All of you know I'm right, but none of you have had the balls to say anything. He's so coked up and drunk all the time I doubt he even knows what he's asking us to do right now."

Lizard took the floor to calm the tensions in the room. "Look, let's hear Bullets out."

"Look, Lethal, I know you hold me responsible for your brother's death but that's the price of war."

"YOU MOTHER FUCKER. YOU KILLED MY BROTHER WITH YOUR STUPID MISSION!"

Lizard stepped in and kept Lethal from pounding the crap out of Bullets. "Just listen, brother. Listen."

Lethal pushed back from Lizard and walked toward a corner. He leaned up against the wall and crossed his arms.

Bullets continued with his spiel. "Look, there is nothing we can do about what has happened, but we can get even. Plus, we have two loads of Pig's clients' product and I know he is sweating about that because he's been trying to make a deal with me to get them back. I had the product removed from the trailers and stored in our warehouse. We will use it as leverage and sell what we can for funds."

The members liked the idea that they had the product and that there was the potential for money.

"I have decided that the best way to get even with that fat fucker is to get inside and blow up his communications network. Pig's computers and tracking devices on his trucks, property, and his people are the only protection he has. We take out his network and he won't know where anything is anymore, making him vulnerable."

He now had the members' interest.

"That's why I chose Lethal and Rat Hole. They not only know how to handle a truck, they are ruthless. Once they are in the operation, they can help us get a few more in and then we will let Pig have it. No more Pig trucks!"

"Yeah, Bullets, sounds like a plan."

"Let's get that fat bastard."

Bullets looked toward Lethal and nodded at him. "You in, brother?"

Lethal wasn't willing to admit he liked the idea, but he did like the thought of getting even with Bullets. If this plan was going to get him closer to getting rid of Bullets and destroying Pig at the same time maybe it was going to be worth it. "Yeah, I'll do it, but I'm taking my orders from Lizard."

Bullets nodded and then lifted his beer in the air. "Done. Let's get PIGT!"

After the toast, Bullets motioned for Dirty Player and Time Bomb to meet with him privately. Lizard watched the three men, wanting to know what Bullets had up his sleeve. Before long, the meeting dispersed. Time Bomb and Dirty Player motioned for several of their men to follow them out of the building. Lizard watched as the members filed out of the clubhouse. *What the hell is Bullets up to now?*

◊◊◊

Angelica had taken one of the company vehicles so that she could get some shopping in before she had dinner at one of her favorite seafood restaurants near the estate. Louisiana was famous for its crawfish, which Angelica loved. She was anxious to enjoy a generous portion of the mudbugs.

Before long she was at the mall where she could call Rex. She only wished he was closer and could spend some time with her.

CHAPTER TEN

Pig arrived on a private jet at LAX and his waiting limo took him directly to his hotel. "Good to see you, boss. I hope your trip was pleasant." The limo driver opened the door for Pig. The limo bounced as the heavy man placed his body in the back seat.

Parker was in the limo and ready to give Pig a more detailed explanation of the report he had already sent him via computer. "Hello, sir. Hope your trip was comfortable."

"It was long. Now tell me more about what is going on with my loads."

Parker shifted slightly in his seat so Pig could view his computer. "Mr. Pig, it's like I explained in my report. The trailers are there." Parker pointed to a specific place on the computer screen. "The product has been removed. The information that I've managed to obtain is that Bullets has the merchandise in his warehouse. The exact location of the warehouse where the product is being kept is right here."

"So you've scoped out the warehouse? You are sure my product is in that specific unit?"

"Yes, sir."

"Have you checked the trailers out personally?"

"Yes, I checked them out, but I haven't had them picked up yet. I thought since you were going to be in town, you might want to take a helicopter out to see them for yourself. They did a pretty good job on the trailers, but nothing we can't fix. As for the warehouse, I've had it under twenty-four-hour surveillance since we tracked the product to that location."

"Can we get into the warehouse area and retrieve my merchandise?"

"Yes, Mr. Pig. As you can tell from the attachments that I sent to you, I have prepared an airtight plan of attack. I am limited in manpower, but still, I think I should be able to pull it off."

"Is it going to attract a lot of attention? Do you want me to bring in Head Hunter and some of his men to keep the collateral damage to a minimum?"

"Not right now. I'll take you by the warehouse and get your opinion, but I really think we can take it down without too much trouble."

"Okay, but if we decide to bring in Head Hunter and his men I need to get them on a plane."

"I understand."

"Go to the warehouse. Do not stop, just drive by."

The driver nodded

"And the cartel, what do they know?"

"I've been in contact with Bandito and it doesn't look like they know anything. He said Tito is completely happy with the delivery of the product and that we made it there on time. In fact, he wants to speak with you while you're in LA."

"Yeah, I know, I talked with Tito today and set up the meeting for tomorrow. We will go check out the trailers and then meet with our Mexican friends for dinner."

"Yes, sir."

◊◊◊

Lethal and Rat Hole had taken a plane out of LAX to Shreveport. They met up with one of Bullets' contacts at the airport. The men shook hands after finding each other among the cluster of people. "You must be Lethal and Rat Hole?"

"Yes, and you must be Trigger?"

The men gathered their bags and followed Trigger out of the airport.

Trigger had made a motel reservation for the two men and gotten them an appointment with PIGT for the next morning through Black Jack. The men were exhausted when they reached the hotel. Trigger handed the men their room cards. "Are you sure you don't want to go and get something to eat, Lethal?"

Lethal grabbed his bag from the back of the truck. "I don't really want to be here. Besides, I'm beat. Thanks for the offer, but I'm going to bed, Rat Hole, you can go if you want."

Lethal walked to the door of his motel room, used the card to open the lock then disappeared. Rat Hole decided he was interested in getting some food before going to his room. He climbed into the front seat. "Let's go I'm starved."

"How about some mudbugs?"

"Sounds great."

Lethal looked around his hotel. "Wonderful, stuck in this shit hole." Lethal knew if it wasn't for his extreme hatred for Bullets and the fact that Bullets was going to go down soon, he wouldn't be wasting his time here. "Lizard, you'd better make good on your word to get rid of that psycho. It's the only reason I'm here."

◊◊◊

Parker had picked up Pig from his hotel in a blacked out SUV instead of the limo. A chartered helicopter would be waiting for them at a small private airport outside of LA. "We will fly to El Centro and then I have another SUV waiting for us so you can check out the trailers. I also talked with Bandito and he is waiting for you to confirm where you would like to have your meeting with Tito."

Pig shifted his weight in the back seat. Pig already knew this information but didn't say anything to Parker.

Parker had two other security guards in the vehicle with them. Another SUV with two other guards was waiting to follow the team to the airport. The men in Pig's SUV would be joining him for the trip on the helicopter. The other men would return to their headquarters in LA after Pig was safely delivered to the airport. Pig informed Parker of his plans. "Once we have arrived in El Centro I'll contact Tito and make arrangements with him personally. I don't want to give away too much information too soon."

"Yes, sir."

"Tell me more about your plan for getting my product back, Parker."

"My only concern is the unexpected appearance of any of Bullets' men that may come in on my flank. If they are able to get a phone call out to Bullets before I can infiltrate the compound, I can probably expect back-up in the form of more members. I'm not sure I have enough manpower to handle that kind of attack without making a whole lot of noise."

Pig didn't like noise. "Well, then we need to figure out how we can contain that problem before we go in. I do not want a scene. I am having enough issues with law enforcement right now. Check with Yanks and see if he can help you with that problem. I want my product back as soon as possible. I don't want Bullets to have a chance to sell any of it."

"Yes, sir."

Once the men boarded the waiting helicopter, Pig informed his security officers about his plan to eliminate Bullets. "Once we have my product back I want to take out Bullets and as many of his members as possible. I want it done quietly and methodically. You can take them out one at a time if that's how it has to be, but I want that pain in my ass gone."

"I'll get in touch with Yanks right away. It shouldn't be too hard to come up with something."

"Good."

The helicopter landed. Pig's security men exited and secured the area before Pig left his seat. Pig was then escorted to a waiting SUV.

Parker felt nervous as they approached the parking lot. He stepped out of the vehicle, and panned the area before using his two-way radio to let his men already on location know they were in position.

His men came back on the radio. "All clear, Parker."

Parker scanned the area again. "Come on in closer boys," he called. "I don't think Bullets is going to show his ugly face today."

Parker got back into the SUV and pointed the driver in the direction of the trailers, not knowing that the decision would soon prove to be a mistake.

The SUV's pulled in next to the trailers, which were parked to the rear of the parking lot. The wind had increased and was blowing dust, trash, and sand under the trailers and onto the vehicles, making visibility difficult.

Parker and his men again exited their units, fighting the dust and debris while trying to scan the area near the trailers before opening Pig's door.

Pig exited the vehicle, holding his hat tightly as the wind attempted to blow it off. Parker stayed close to him as they walked toward the trailers.

The appearance of his trailers made Pig livid. He fought the wind as he walked with his cane around the damaged property. One of the security officers opened the rear doors of the trailers so that Pig could see inside. Pig looked and then turned toward Parker. He leaned on his cane and then removed his hat. "I want that bastard dead. If you can't handle it, I'll find someone who can or I'll do it myself. Have these trailers transported back to the mansion."

"I'll take care of it, boss."

Pig put his hat back on and lit a cigar before walking back toward the SUVs.

Before Pig could take several puffs on his cigar, shots rang out across the parking lot. One of Pig's security officers fell to the ground in pain next to him. "OH SHIT! MY LEG!" Bullets flew through the air. Parker pulled out his gun and fired in the direction of the incoming gunfire, doing what he could to shield Pig while pushing him quickly toward the cover of the SUV. The other security officers near the vehicle surrounded Pig, also firing their guns in the same direction. "Stay down, Mr. Pig!"

Pig had been forced to move faster than he cared to. He had to drop his freshly lit cigar and was not one to take orders from anyone, especially someone he employed. "Stop pushing me, Parker. I can use my guns if you will let me get to them."

Parker quickly backed off. "Sorry, boss."

Pig pulled out his guns as if he was going to use them on Parker. He used the door of the SUV as a shield. "Shut up and get those bastards."

Parker's injured man was attempting to pull himself toward the protection of the landing gear on one of Pig's trailers. Parker yelled at the other five security officers. "COVER ME!" As the bullets flew in every direction, Parker ran from the SUV into the parking lot to retrieve his injured man.

He reached the guard, who moaned, "Fuck, Parker! It hurts like hell!"

Parker slid to the ground beside the injured man. "Hang in there, Stretch. Can you move?"

"I think so. I just need a little help getting to my feet."

Parker put his arm around the guard. "Okay, when I tell you, together we are going to get you off the ground. You need to keep your head down and your gun up."

The man nodded his head through his pain.

"Ready?" Parker pulled the man as hard as he could to his feet and with the cover from Pig and the other guards, the two men ran toward the SUVs. Parker helped the injured security officer into an open door on the closest SUV before taking up a position next to Pig.

After letting go with several rounds and dodging the returned fire from the hidden culprits, Pig turned to Parker and asked, "What happened here, Parker? I thought your men secured this area before we got here."

"They did, Mr. Pig. I guess Bullets' men were watching. I didn't put in a perimeter patrol…they must have set up this ambush. I made a mistake, sir, it won't happen again."

"You bet your ass it won't."

The gun battle continued for several more minutes until the sounds of sirens could be heard in the distance. Bullets' gunmen quickly stopped firing and disappeared.

Pig stood up from behind the door. "PUT THE WEAPONS AWAY, MEN!"

They put their revolvers in their shoulder holsters and then placed all their other weapons in the trunk of the SUVs. Pig sat backward into the seat of the SUV, texted a message on his phone and barked out more orders. "Make it look as if we were simply hiding behind our vehicles to protect ourselves from the gunfire." The guards quickly positioned themselves near their injured co-worker.

The police and ambulance pulled into the parking lot. Pig lit another cigar, moving his cane into position to be used as leverage if he needed to stand. "Let me do the talking. If they ask you anything, you lawyer up. Do not speak unless I tell you to."

"Yes, sir."

"What happened here?" a policeman asked.

"My men and I were simply here checking out the damage to two of my trailers," Pig said, pointing out the trailers. "I wanted to see if they still had enough value to have them shipped back to our home terminal. When we finished our estimation of the trailers and were walking back to the SUVs, someone started shooting at us. The gunfire was coming from behind that building and those trees."

Pig pointed in the opposite direction of the actual line of fire, hoping the cops would not find signs of return fire. If they did, they'd have a reason to question Pig further.

"In that direction?" The officer in charge pointed his pen in the direction Pig had indicated.

He turned to look at the position of the vehicles and the men in the parking lot. He shook his head in disbelief and wrote something down in his notebook. The cop knew the gunfire had to have come from another place, since the vehicles and the men would have been shielded by the trailers from that direction.

"Are you sure?"

Pig nodded to confirm.

The officer motioned for his men to check out the area. "Did you return fire?"

Pig's phone rang before he could answer. He put his phone to his ear. "One moment, please."

The officer backed away slightly and motioned for his officers to fan out over the area for evidence.

Pig had texted Tito to let him know what had occurred and that their meeting would be delayed. Tito was concerned with the situation and wanted to speak with Pig personally. Pig didn't want the cops to know he was talking with his cartel connection, and pretended to be speaking with his corporate offices. "Yes, most of us are okay, but I do have one injured man. I want you to make sure he is taken care of. I'll get you that information as soon as I am finished speaking with the police."

Tito understood the underlined meaning. "Very well, Mr. Pig, call me as soon as you can speak freely. Can you give me your location?"

Pig let Tito know where they were before ending his conversation.

As Stretch was being loaded into an ambulance and his security officers were checking out the damage to the vehicles, the lead officer approached Pig.

"Sorry, had to let the home office know about what happened," Pig lied.

"Who do you think may have been shooting at you?"

"I have no idea."

It wasn't long before a group of three vehicles loaded with Mexican men rolled up to the scene. The middle vehicle carried Bandito and several of his men. The vehicle pulled up next to the lead investigator who was standing in the parking lot near Pig. The officer leaned into the window that Bandito had rolled down. Bandito spoke a few words to the cop. Then Bandito and his men slowly moved out of the parking lot after nodding toward Pig. Bandito left the cop bewildered.

Pig's phone rang as he turned away from the officer. "Excuse me."

Parker and his men were leaning up against the back of the SUVs when Pig motioned for them to load up. The officer who had just talked to Bandito radioed his patrolmen off their search. "Let's go, men." In the middle of the parking lot, the lead officer informed his men that they would be closing the investigation. They closed their notebooks, took off their protective gear and threw it in their vehicles with some frustration and left in their police units.

Parker couldn't believe what was happening. Pig returned to where Parker was holding the door for him on the SUV. Pig hung up his phone. Parker looked at Pig with disbelief. "May I ask, sir, with all due respect, what the hell just happened here?"

Pig ignored his questions, found his cane propped up against the door and wedged his fat body in the back seat of the SUV. "Parker, get in the vehicle. We have a meeting to make in Mexico with Tito."

"Yes, sir." He shut the door behind his boss and got in the front seat next to the driver.

◊◊◊

Dirty Player made a call to Bullets when the deed was done. "We did what you wanted but the police decided to show up and we had to split. I'm pretty sure we got one of his men."

"Good. I hope that fat bastard got my message. Did you see any of Tito's men around?"

"No, not while we were there, but we had to leave in a hurry so I can't say for sure."

"It's cool. I'm taking Bandito out eventually and when I do, Tito will be working directly with me."

Dirty Player knew his leader was crazy but he wondered how long he was going to be alive talking about the cartel the way he did.

◊◊◊

Lethal and Rat Hole had been brought from their hotel to the estate in a limo. Lethal looked out the window of the limo as they entered PIGT property. He had heard about Pig's empire but had never seen it. Lethal was amazed and began to question whether he was on the right side of the rivalry.

Once the men reached the mansion, they were treated just like every new employee. They were given their own rooms and treated like guests. Hank set the men up for orientation, driving tests, physicals, drug tests, and a tour of the mansion after they filled out paperwork. Lethal couldn't believe how well he was being treated by the enemy. It was hard for him to remember what he was there to do. He was brought back to reality when he walked into the command center during their tour. "Wow. This is like something out of a spy movie."

Hank assured Lethal and Rat Hole that the center was not from a movie. "Be assured, gentlemen, this center tracks everything and everyone in this company. Every piece of equipment, building, and every person is monitored twenty-four seven. Some of the loyal and permanent employees have implants that contain all their personal information for quick refer-ence." Hank modeled the top of his hand, pointing to the small mole-like spot. "Only those of us who have proven our devout loyalty to PIGT have these, but it's something you might want to work toward."

Lethal and Rat Hole took a closer look at the brown spot and then at each other, intrigued by the tiny device. Rat Hole attempted to touch Hank's hand but Hank pulled it back before he could.

"You have some kind of chip in your body? Is that safe?"

Hank promenaded toward another panel. "Of course it's safe, and the information contained on that chip can be updated daily from my computer. My health and dental records, driving record, financial records, and my personal information; it's all on the chip. I can put anything I want on it, including pictures of my family. It's the most advanced technology on the market today. If I'm ever in an accident or get stopped by a cop, all they have to do is put their phone up to my chip and it will text them all my information."

Rat Hole was amazed. "Impressive."

Hank pushed a button on the panel. "Employees are required to be under constant surveillance. It actually makes the driver safer. The most dedicated employees agree to implant the chip. It's just an option. Mr. Pig is as concerned about his employees as he is about his customers and their merchandise."

Lethal knew there were holes in any system. Proof of that was evident in the fact that two of Pig's loads were now in Bullets' hands. Lethal looked over the center and saw an interesting group of pictures flashing across one of the monitors. He didn't want to appear too interested, so he scanned the walls again before turning his attention back to the screen he'd noticed. They were pictures of the warehouse in LA where Bullets had stored the stolen product.

Lethal could hardly contain himself as he realized that Pig knew exactly where his merchandise was and that he had a complete layout of the whole property. Lethal knew if he gave that information to Lizard, they would be able to move the product somewhere else before Pig had a chance to get to it. But because he wasn't sure he wanted to help Bullets out anymore, he decided to hold the information for the moment.

Lethal looked at the monitors, amazed. There were monitors on and inside buildings, as well as monitors on trucks and trailers and the products they were carrying. Monitors were on the people driving the trucks and security officers guarding the buildings. Lethal was entranced by a huddle of workers monitoring what appeared to be a gunfight somewhere. There were security officers and now police on the monitor. Then familiar faces appeared on the screen. Bandito and his men, in vehicles, near the security guards. He also spotted several glimpses of some of his own members in the background.

Lethal forced himself to turn away and join the tour group. He knew now why Bullets wanted this command center taken down. He also realized why it had been so hard for their gang to take over the territory. Pig was taking from them—and not just small swaths, but all of it. Lethal understood now. *Bullets has no hope of competing against that amount of technology or money. Even if we do take out this command center, Pig is still going to get any-thing he wants. Maybe working for PIGT for real is the way to go.*

He was still curious to find out Pig's weaknesses. Would his employees be so loyal without all the surveillance? Knowing where Pig was vulnerable would give him leverage. Lethal felt emboldened. He was going to take over this organization from the inside out and get rid of his two nemeses—Pig and Bullets. Lethal was going to do what he had to do avenge his brother's death and become the gang's leader.

◊◊◊

Shelby had said her goodbyes to Jack and went through the security check line at the airport. As she waited to board her flight, she wondered what kind of a truck they would assign to her. As Shelby boarded her plane, she felt nervous, but excited about getting on the highways again.

When she arrived a limo driver, holding a sign with her name met her at baggage claim and took her directly to the estate.

Harry was shocked at the warm hug he received from Shelby when she arrived. "Harry, how are you? It is so good to see you again."

"Doing very well, Ms. Shelby. It's nice to see you too."

"It's good to be back. I'm so excited to get started in my new position." Shelby held Harry's arm as they walked into the mansion together like old friends. Shelby broke her clutch on Harry's arm and headed straight to the back doors. "I want to see the dogs before I unpack."

Harry put down her bag and followed her. "Very well, Ms. Shelby, but I must let the dogs familiarize themselves with you before you can handle them. They may not remember you."

Shelby backed away from the fence where the dogs were barking and jumping at her. None of them were growling at her. They appeared to be glad to see her. Harry opened the gate, but before he could get his hands on their collars, they were out the gate and headed straight for Shelby. The dogs jumped on and licked Shelby until she fell to the ground laughing with them. "Good boys."

Harry stood in complete disbelief. The purebred dogs that Pig had spent thousands of dollars to procure and train were now—like their owner—totally infatuated with the blonde lady from West Texas.

Harry walked to where Shelby was playing with the dogs. Harry petted one of the dogs that came to him for some attention while the others were hoarding Shelby's affections. "Yes, you're a good dog."

◊◊◊

Lethal and Rat Hole finished with their tour of the estate and were allowed to finish out the day relaxing on the grounds. Lethal wanted to check out what he could of the property's outside perimeter. "I'm going to go for a walk and check things out, Rat. I'll be back later."

"I'm going to see if there are any women in this place by the pool and get something to eat in that monster kitchen. This place is awesome. Almost makes you want to change sides," Rat Hole responded.

Lethal laughed slightly. "Yeah."

Once outside, Lethal walked down the blacktopped road toward the horse corrals and warehouses. He sincerely liked horses and would be able to convince anyone who might be suspicious of his choice to head there first. His main goal though was to check out the warehouses to see if he could figure out a way to infiltrate them.

On his way to the barn, Lethal was pleasantly distracted when he noticed Harry and a pretty little blonde playing with the dogs. The woman was rolling in the grass like a child with one of the dogs while the other one nipped at her feet. Harry was standing close by, smiling at the playful activity.

Lethal continued to walk toward the horses. The only women he had seen thus far worked in the operations room and business office. He was pleased to know that perhaps there were some women who lived on the property. *I'll find out who the blonde is later.*

◊◊◊

Pig and his men crossed the border into Mexicali. They were met by Tito's men and escorted to a secret meeting place where the Federales and other cartel gangs wouldn't interfere with their business. Tito had most of the government officials and police on his payroll, so they let him be. Some of the other cartel gangs had their own arrangements with the Federales, which could be a problem from time to time. There was always a chance of infiltration by the competition, but Tito didn't want to risk any kind of a gun battle or an unexpected visit from his rivals while Pig was there.

Tito had the largest distribution network throughout Mexico, South America, Canada, Europe, Asia, and the United States of drugs, guns, and other black market items. He lived in Mexico City and Pig had become his primary transportation partner. Pig's trucks not only picked up product on the Mexican-American border, but also transported it throughout North America. While Tito occasionally used alternative delivery methods for smaller scale product, Pig handled all his major loads and proved effective at getting the product to their destinations without interference from law enforcement.

They primarily conducted business via computers or cell phone. However, the Federales and other gangs were confiscating some of Tito's local distribution. He assumed he had a snitch in his organizations or was being bugged. He decided to make deals in person until he found out how he was being infiltrated; it was dangerous but necessary.

When Pig arrived at the secret meeting place Tito came out of the beautiful adobe and Spanish-tiled house with his usual warm greeting. Despite Pig's odor, Tito hugged Pig and shook his hand when Pig got out of the SUV. "My friend, Pig, welcome! Come in, Come in!"

Gunmen surrounded the house, and although Pig was not frisked by the security detail, all of his guards were checked for unnecessary weapons. Pig's detail officers were allowed to keep their handguns, but automatic firepower was placed in the SUVs. Parker joined Pig. Pig was not in any danger with Tito, but Parker knew not to let down his guard, even among friends.

Tito offered Pig a drink and when Pig refused the offer he poured a small portion of Patron into the bottom of a crystal rocks glass. Tito had Pig make himself comfortable on the couch and Tito explained the new assignment. "I've got some important product coming in from South America by way of Key West. My connection in the Keys will take possession of the product when it arrives and will transport it in small trucks to Miami. I want you to pick it up in Miami and get it to my warehouses in North Carolina. Then my people will arrange distribution to my customers along the Eastern Seaboard. We may need your assistance for some of those deliveries. I need your utmost discretion until I find out how the mole is operating and can take him out."

"I understand. I have my own problems with one of my competitors."

"Really? Who is giving my friend Pig trouble? I'll cut him like a snake if you want me too."

Pig knew Tito would do anything to help him but wanted to keep the conflict under wraps until he got his product back. Pig had plans for Bullets and in time he would bring Tito into the situation to help destroy the gang. "Thank you, Tito, but I believe I have it contained. But if I find that I need your assistance, I'll be sure and let you know."

"You know I have your back."

"I think I'll have that drink now," Pig said.

Tito's latest job meant millions of dollars for Pig in the next few months. In order to ensure everything went smoothly, he'd have to do something about Bullets and fast.

◊◊◊

After her romp with the dogs, Harry walked Shelby to her lavish room and put her bags on her bed. "The pool has just been refreshed, Ms. Shelby, if you would like a swim before dinner."

Shelby sat on her bed. As Harry turned to leave, she said, "Thank you, Harry. I think I want to rest for a little bit and then call my husband. I might take a dip after supper."

"Very well, Ms. Shelby." He left her room with a nod.

She looked toward the sun shining through the windows. A large bouquet of flowers sat on a beautiful dark cherry wood table. Shelby went over and took a deep breath of their fragrance. Next to the flowers was a small gold box with a gold bow. A note was attached read: "Enjoy your stay. If you need anything do not hesitate to call. Feel free to use the library. Sincerely, Mr. Pig." Shelby opened the box and found four small pieces of French chocolate. She took a piece before putting the box down. She didn't know why, but she felt weird about the gifts. She decided to call Jack.

◊◊◊

Pig and Parker were on his helicopter after his meeting with Tito. "Parker, I'm not sure what the hell you let happen today but it won't happen again."

"No, sir, it won't happen again you have my word." Pig went into how he planned to take Bullets down.

Once Pig reached his hotel room, he attempted to make contact with Bullets. Bullets refused to take his call. Pig called Parker, "I tried to get him out of his rat trap but he's not playing. Go ahead and take him and his men down just as I asked. Start with the warehouse. I want my product back first."

◊◊◊

Bandito sipped at his beer. "I defused the problem in El Centro, Tito, but I'm not sure Pig can really handle Bullets."

Tito swirled the rest of his drink in the bottom of his glass. "It doesn't surprise me that Bullets is targeting Pig. What I want you and the men to do is eliminate Bullets quietly. Bring him and some of his men into Mexico and help them disappear."

"Yes, sir. I'll try and get him to come, but he's so paranoid that he rarely leaves his clubhouse."

"Do it, Bandito! I have millions on the line with this new product coming in from South America."

"Yes, Tito, I'll get it done."

◊◊◊

Lethal and Rat Hole had eaten their dinner and were enjoying a beer near the pool. They knew the entire place was monitored and decided that they wouldn't talk shop until they could find a place without ears. Rat Hole took a drink. "Man this place is terrific. I just wish it had more women around."

Lethal laughed. "Well, I saw a beautiful blonde earlier today out there by the dog pen. She was playing with the dogs like she knew them, I assume she lives here."

"You got to be kidding me? Why didn't you tell me? I've been dying to meet a sweet blonde honey."

"Yeah, I'll be sure and run right to you the next time I run into a hot blonde. Maybe I might want to hit on her, you fucker. You're on your own bud."

Rat Hole and Lethal laughed. "Well, I didn't see her in the kitchen and she didn't come out her to the pool so maybe she was just visiting."

"Maybe."

◊◊◊

Bullets and his men were celebrating when Dirty Player and Time Bomb returned along with their men. "We are going to take Pig down, men! We have two men on the inside of his operation. Here's to THE LA BAD BOYS!"

Lizard stood back and watched as the men in his gang drank and partied over their victories. He wondered if he and Lethal would ever be able to get rid of Bullets.

CHAPTER ELEVEN

Angelica had spent the majority of her free time in town, talking on the phone with Rex as much as possible. Rex enjoyed every moment of the frequent calls. She had taken him with her to shop, eat meals, and even do some gambling. It was the next best thing to being there with her.

Now it was time to go back to work and her first assignment was to train the new female driver. She was a little nervous since she was an operative and not a real trucker. She hoped she had learned enough to actually train someone who was already a licensed commercial driver.

◊◊◊

Shelby had fallen asleep after she had talked to Jack. She had been more tired than she knew because she woke up still fully clothed. She turned over on her back and stretched, then got up. She was excited about the day. She was going to meet her trainer and get her truck. She had to go through her orientation, driving test, physical, and drug test this week, but figured if everything went well, she'd be on the highways by the end of the week.

As soon as she stepped out of the shower, Harry called to invite her to breakfast with Hank and Angelica, the driver who would be training her. She assured him she'd be there soon.

Hank wasn't happy that he had to wait on Shelby. "I have to get to the operations room. Angelica, when Ms. Mathews decides to come bring her to my office."

A few minutes later, Shelby entered the dining room. "Sorry, I'm late. I fell asleep last night and didn't have my alarm set." She looked around the room. "Where's Hank?"

"He had some things to attend to, Ms. Shelby," Harry said. What can I get for you for breakfast?"

"Damn, that's all I need, to make him mad at me." She looked at Harry. "Just a couple over medium eggs and toast, please."

Angelica saw her opening to introduce herself. "God knows there is hell to pay when you make Hank mad." She stood up and offered her hand to Shelby over the table. "Hi, I'm Angelica. Don't worry about Hank. He's an ass to everyone."

Shelby salted her eggs and took a bite out of a piece of toast. "Harry tells me you'll be training me."

"I'm not much of a trainer. I'm sure I'll be learning more from you, since you have more experience driving a truck then I do. But Pig wants me to show you the ropes around here."

"That's exactly what I need. I don't want to look like an idiot."

Angelica liked Shelby. *Maybe this training thing isn't going to turn out so bad after all.*

Angelica assumed that Shelby was unaware of what was going on at PIGT. It was probably a safe assumption, although with Pig's unconventional hiring practices, anything was possible. Shelby, however, didn't seem to be the type to be involved in drug and gun running.

◊◊◊

Pig was on his private jet, returning to Louisiana. He'd left Parker in charge of getting back his merchandise and taking out Bullets. As soon as they maintained altitude, he made a call to Hank.

Lethal and Rat Hole entered the office just as Hank picked up the call from Pig. He pointed for them to wait in the chairs outside his office and returned to the call. "Yes, sir, I received your email and I have several new drivers ready to head out and dispatch is making the necessary arrangements. He listened to Pig's next question, "Yes, sir, she's here and will be going through orientation today. I should have her on the road by the end of the week…" Pig interrupted him. "Yes, I can have her ready to roll by Thursday with Angelica. I'll put them on those first loads out of Miami…Yes, her room was as requested…Alright, I'll make the staff aware of your arrival time…see you soon, sir."

Hank hung up the phone. "That man is going to kill me." He got up, opened the door, and motioned for the waiting men to come into his office to complete their orientation. "This session is to explain the specifics of what we expect here at PIGT. The Pig rules."

◊◊◊

Angelica took note of the two men leaving Hank's office when she and Shelby arrived. She stared at them as they walked down the hall. The expression on her face made Shelby curious. "What's up, lady driver? You know them old boys?"

Angelica wracked her brain. She only got a glimpse of one man. She wasn't sure if she had seen him before or if the man just looked like someone she had seen. Angelica had a knack for recognizing people. She found it hard to forget a face once she had seen it, which was one of the reasons the DEA had hired her. "No, I don't think so. He just looked familiar. Probably just looks like someone I know."

"Well, come on let's go talk to butthead so we can ride the roads."

Hank was working on his computer when Angelica and Shelby walked in. "Come in, ladies. Have a seat. We have a lot to do. Mr. Pig wants me to get you through this paperwork and have you on the road ASAP."

Shelby sat down. "That's what I'm talking about. Let's get on with this."

Hank looked up from his computer. "Well, we just landed a rather large account from South America and we will be transporting the new client's merchandise from Florida to North Carolina and then up the East Coast to New York City."

Shelby shifted in her seat. "Wow, that sounds fantastic. What are we hauling?"

The room went silent. Hank shifted some papers on his desk and gave Angelica a stern look. "What? I just met her this morning and haven't had any time to explain things yet."

Hank put the papers down rather forcefully. "Find the time."

"What did I say? Find the time for what?"

Angelica patted Shelby's arm. "I'll explain later. Let's get this paperwork finished. I have to show you your truck. Pig had me help choose a good one for you."

Hank put a package of paperwork in front of Shelby. "Please fill these out and when you have finished, I have arranged for one of the security officers to take you for your physical and drug test. Once you finish those you can go with Angelica to get set up in your truck. Tomorrow, after you have been cleared on your medical exam and drug test, I'll put you through a crash course orientation. You'll take your driving test with our truck manager on Wednesday. Mr. Pig has requested that you and Angelica be ready to roll by Thursday morning. The two of you will be picking up in Florida and going to North Carolina. You will run your loads out of the same warehouses."

Shelby took the package of paperwork and looked through it. "Alright, let's get started. I'm ready to roll."

Hank pointed to the door. "There's a table in the other room that you can use to fill out that paperwork. Angelica, I need to talk with you privately for a moment."

"Yes, sir."

Shelby left the room and shut the door, leaving Angelica and Hank to talk. As she walked away, she wondered why knowing what the loads contained was so hush-hush. *What if it's hazardous material or illegal stuff? What if I get stopped by DOT and am not placarded, or carrying stuff that could get me in trouble?* She wasn't sure she liked that idea.

I'm just being paranoid; it's like the security camera thing. Maybe I just needed to chill out. Mr. Pig seems like a real straight shooter. Besides, if Jack had noticed anything odd he wouldn't have given me his blessing. Shelby calmed her thoughts, she knew she was pretty good at reading people, and other than his smell, she hadn't found too much wrong with Mr. Pig.

◊◊◊

Lethal and Rat Hole got their new trucks and were waiting in the yard for a call from dispatch. Lethal said, "I told you I saw a cute blonde around here and now we know there's a beautiful brunette, too."

Rat Hole took a long drag from his cigarette. "Yeah, I saw those babes going into the boss man's office. Maybe we'll get a chance to run some loads with those hotties before we blow this place to pieces."

Rat Hole looked around at the estate while he smoked. "You know, it's really a shame to have to blow up such a nice place. Too bad it's owned by a fat asshole."

Lethal had to agree, wondering if he should let Rat Hole in on the idea that he had about not blowing it up but taking it over. He decided to keep it to himself for a while. "Yeah, it sure is, but we got a job to do. Did you contact Bullets? I told Lizard what was going on and that we had made it into the company."

"Yeah, I told him."

"Did you see the set up in that command center? I mean, Pig has really spent the money to insure his stuff, hasn't he?"

Lethal picked up a small rock in the driveway and tossed it back and forth in his hands. "Yeah, but I think we need to check things out a little more. I'm just not sure Pig is stupid enough to confine all his security to one area. I'm thinking he has a secondary mobile unit or something that he can access his security and tracking devices on. I'm thinking that it's tapped into that laptop he carries around."

Rat Hole didn't spend time thinking through much of anything. "I think you're thinking too much. I'm sure when we blow this place to hell Pig and his computers will go up with it."

"Maybe." His phone suddenly rang and so did Rat Hole's. Both men answered their respective phones and spent a few minutes with their dispatchers before hanging up. "Well, it's go time. Where you headed?"

"New York City."

"Me too."

"Then let's load up and roll, brother. We're headed to the Big Apple."

◊◊◊

Parker had contacted Yanks and the two men were meeting at Pig's warehouse office in Long Beach. "Come on in, Yanks. Can I get you a beer?"

"Not for me, but my two men will want one."

"I'll get them while you guys have a look at the pictures on the computer. Those are from the surveillance my men and I have been conducting on Bullets' properties."

Yanks looked at the pictures of several warehouses and the guards protecting them with automatic weapons. There were photos of the men in a control room near the front of the warehouse. The control room apparently was for monitoring the security cameras scattered around the property. Parker had not been able to locate all of the cameras, however.

Parker had located Bullets' clubhouse, which was inside an old body shop in the Carson Township. He had several photos of Bullets and his men coming and going from the clubhouse. His surveillance had also produced photos of meetings of the gang and several photos of groups leaving and coming for what Yanks thought were probably jobs.

There were photos of funerals and houses of several of the gang members. There were photos of vehicles, motorcycles, and trucks that the gang members used. Parker had also acquired times for the warehouse guards' work schedules. Times for members being at the clubhouse varied, but it was clear from their observations that the clubhouse was occupied by someone twenty-four hours a day. Parker and his men had not been able to enter the clubhouse.

Yanks was impressed. "Wow, you sure did your homework didn't you?"

"Pig wants his shit back and I want to keep my job. I've found that the only way to beat an unpredictable son-of-a-bitch like Bullets is to be one step ahead of him."

Parker went through each picture and explained how he wanted to take down the warehouse. "Pig wants his product back before Bullets can sell it, so we need to get in there soon. Pig also wants it done without a lot of noise. We'll start with the guards in the security house and disable all the surveillance."

"I suggest just breaking their necks or using knives instead of guns to eliminate the noise." Yanks interrupted.

"I agree. Once we have control of the surveillance room, I'll send you and your men in to take out the other guards. There are ten men at all times watching the warehouse." Parker showed Yanks some of the possible openings for getting to the guards. "There are five inside the compound and five outside. They roam around the property but stay pretty much in their designated areas. I assume the security house checks in with Bullets at an arranged time. I'm not sure what that is, which could be a problem if they don't make one of those appointed calls."

"So how close are Bullets and his men to the warehouse? How much time will we have before they figure out what's happening?"

"I found his clubhouse by following one of the guards. I also followed several of the guards to their homes. Since we have no idea just when those calls go into Bullets, I calculated the distance from the clubhouse and some of the guard's houses. The closest guard is ten minutes away and the clubhouse is thirty-five. I figure we'll have at least ten minutes…at most, thirty."

"Where is it in that place? It looks pretty big. We aren't going to have time to search for anything. Besides, how are we getting that shit out of there? I mean even if I bring my entire army of men that's two semi-truck loads of product."

Parker pulled up more pictures. Satellite photos of the warehouse came up and pictures of two semi-trucks with box trailers. "The merchandise is located here." Parker pointed to the area on the satellite picture. "Once you and your men have secured the facility, and my guys have taken out the security house, we will meet at the building where the product is located."

"How do you know that's where the stuff is stashed?"

"Several reasons, first, I've been studying the way they bring things in and out using my computer's surveillance program. They never move anything around in that area and it's under heavy security twenty-four hours a day. Plus, I have a friend who knows one of the guards and they have had a couple of conversations about the stash. He has assured me that what we are looking for is in those buildings."

"So when do we do this thing? What about Bullets? I want to take him out soon."

"The best time to hit them would be in the middle of the night. This Friday preferably, that way Bullets and the majority of his men will either be drunk or on their way to being drunk. As far as Bullets goes, Pig wants him dead, but unless he shows up here and accidentally gets himself shot, I want to let him feel the pain of losing that stolen merchandise before I take him out."

"Sounds good to me on both points. I want to be in on the kill for sure."

Parker knew Yanks had a score to settle with Bullets because of the men he lost at the truck stop. Yanks was a loose cannon and did what he did for the fun of it. He just hoped he could keep the man in check until the job was complete.

◊◊◊

Lethal and Rat Hole were hauling ass to New York City. They had decided that they would follow Highway 20 until it hit Highway 95 in South Carolina. Rat Hole got on the CB. "Lethal, I miss my bike, but this sure is fun."

"I think so too, Rat Hole. It's nice getting out on the open road in a truck again. I haven't driven a truck in years."

"When we get to where we are picking up our loads I'll tell you what I've been thinking about. I can't tell you what I want to do over the radio, but I have an idea that might make our friends happy."

Lethal figured it probably had something to do with either women or lifting something. "Okay, but we're twenty-two hours from our destination. I don't know about you, but I know how I'm going to spend the night in about seven hundred miles…catching some Zs."

"Pussy! I knew you were too old to hang."

"Shut up, Rat Hole. I know you ain't gonna make the full fifteen hundred miles without shutting it down somewhere."

"Watch me."

"Yeah, this I gotta see." The men continued to dig at each other but soon agreed that they'd stop about halfway to their pickup point and Rat Hole would let Lethal know what he had in mind.

◊◊◊

Angelica took Shelby to the truck line. "Pig bought all these new trucks just a few weeks ago and this blue one here is the one I thought you might like best."

"Wow! This truck is beautiful."

Angelica unlocked the door. "Come on, take a look inside first and then we'll check out the engine, lights, and trailer."

Shelby climbed into the driver's seat. "Oh my God this is awesome. The dash is so shiny with all the chrome." Shelby turned to check out the sleeper. "Oh wow, I've never had a sleeper this big. It's already furnished with linens." Shelby looked inside the closets where she found towels and toiletries. She checked out the microwave and flat screen TV, and when she opened the refrigerator there was five hundred dollars and a note from Pig. Shelby read the note. "Welcome aboard, here is a little cash for food and anything else you might need for your first run."

Angelica couldn't believe the special treatment Shelby was receiving. She knew now that Pig had more interest in Shelby than she had at first suspected. Angelica knew she'd have to keep an eye on Shelby to make sure she wasn't as naïve as she appeared. Shelby was obviously unaware that this kind of treatment for a new employee wasn't customary. Angelica would watch and see what else Pig had in mind before she rained on Shelby's parade.

Shelby moved back into the passenger's side seat. "Wow, this is terrific. I can't believe that Mr. Pig treats his new employees so well. Did you get all these nice things when you started?"

Angelica chose her words carefully. "No, I think these are new incentives Mr. Pig has just put into practice to help lure new drivers."

"I'm surprised people aren't lining up around the block to get on here."

Angelica couldn't help but mutter, "Yeah, lining up around the block."

◊◊◊

Hank informed Pig that Parker sent an email confirming that he and Yanks were a go for Friday night. He also said that they would be using two of Pig's trucks that he had parked at the warehouse in Long Beach.

"Yeah, he sent me the same email. As soon as they have my shit back I want it transported back to that locker in Florida before my friends down south find out I borrowed it."

"I'll make sure it gets taken care of at once."

◊◊◊

Back at the mansion, Angelica asked Shelby, "I'm going to go change and go swimming. Would you like to join me?"

"Okay. But I want to go to the library first and get a book to read while we're out there."

"Okay, I'll see you in a little while."

"Okay."

Shelby walked to the library, determined to read as many of Pig's antique books as she could. Once there, Shelby lost herself again in the titles. She was having a hard time deciding which book to choose. She took three down that she thought might be interesting, sat down in an armchair, and read a few words from each one.

Pig walked into the library as she was perusing the books. Pig shut the door and moved toward his desk. Shelby turned and gasped when she saw him.

Pig pretended to be shocked. "Oh, I'm sorry, Ms. Shelby. I didn't mean to disturb you. I had no idea you were in here reading."

"No, Mr. Pig, I'm sorry. I was just checking out the books again. I wanted to take one with me poolside to read. I hope that will be okay. I'll take good care of it."

"Absolutely. I told you to feel free to read any and all of them."

"Thank you, Mr. Pig. I have decided on this one. I also wanted to thank you for all the wonderful gifts you have showered me with since coming to work for you. I've never been treated so special."

Mr. Pig found his chair and sat down. He had been watching Shelby since she arrived back to the mansion and knew he'd find her in the library. He intended on showering Shelby with more gifts in the future. "You are most welcome, Ms. Shelby. We are very glad to have you on our team."

The conversation went on for a few more minutes until Angelica stuck her head into the library. "Hey Shelby, I thought you were... Oh, I'm sorry. I didn't know you were in here, Mr. Pig. I hope I didn't interrupt anything."

Shelby rose to her feet and hurried toward Angelica. "No, I think I intruded on Mr. Pig. I got a book and I'm ready to go get my suit on. Thank you again, Mr. Pig."

Pig pretended he was doing something on his computer. "No problem, Ms. Shelby. Enjoy the pool. I'll be out there after a while to exercise the dogs."

Angelica knew she probably better tell Shelby what Pig was up to, but she needed to wait a little longer, she needed to make sure she had enough evidence for the DEA to bust both Pig and his clients. They would be leaving for Florida in a couple of days, which would give her the opportunity to tell Shelby some things, as long as she didn't blow her cover.

The trip she and Shelby would be taking to Florida was going to help put another nail in Pig's coffin. She was finally going to get a look at some of the men working for the South American drug and gun runners.

◊◊◊

Lethal and Rat Hole had gotten to Columbia, South Carolina when they both decided it was time to shut down for the night. "What? I thought you wanted to make it a straight through run, Rat Hole?"

"Well, I figured I could stop for the old man part of this team, let him get some rest."

"Yeah, you son-of-a-bitch, you can't hang like you use to either."

As they sat down to eat, Lethal asked, "What you got planned, asshole?"

"Well, this is what I was thinking, I'm not sure I can, but when we get to the loading facility, I want to take a look at what kind of security they have and what kind of security they are putting on our loads. If we can get away with two of Pig's loads, I think we can get away with a whole lot more, just in smaller portions. You know, take a little off the top."

"What? Are you trying to get us killed? That's a stupid idea, Rat Hole, and you know it. Bullets put us in here to blow up the communication center and get as much information as we can on his operations. It would be suicide for just the two of us to try and take from Pig. Let's just do what we came here for and see where it leads."

"Maybe, but I'm still going to check it out and see if it's at least possible."

"Just be careful. Don't get me killed!"

CHAPTER TWELVE

Except for a few streetlights and security spots placed around the building, the absence of the moon made the darkness around the warehouse nearly impossible to navigate. Parker and Yanks had their men ready to infiltrate their target. The two trucks they had brought were waiting on side streets close to the buildings, but out of sight of any gang members who might show up unexpectedly. Both trucks had been loaded with hydraulic lifts and forklifts. Parker wasn't taking any chances on not being able to get the product out once they got into the warehouse.

Yanks and his men separated from Parker and his boys. Everyone had been briefed on their missions. After a brief moment of watch-checking and last minute instructions, everyone seemed ready and pumped for what was about to go down. They were going to hit them fast and hard and hopefully Bullets wouldn't have a clue what had happened to him until morning.

When Parker's watch hit twelve-thirty, he and his men went toward the security room. They didn't want to alarm the whole facility, so one unarmed man went to the door and knocked. One of the men in the security room came to the door but didn't open it. He simply shouted through the small thick glass window in the middle of the upper half of the door. "What do you want? This is a secured area and you aren't supposed to be here."

Parker's man acted as if he couldn't hear and made his voice sound as if he was in a panic. "What? I'm sorry. I can't hear you. I need help. There is someone chasing me. Please help me!"

"I said you can't be here. You have to leave."

Parker's man knocked with more intensity. "Please, I need to call the police. I'm in trouble."

The security guard armed himself and opened the door slightly. "Look, I said you have to...." Before the guard could finish his sentence, Parker's man had pushed the door wide open and the guard landed on his back. The guard quickly tried to remove his handgun from his side holster. Parker's man immediately grabbed the man by the shirt and punched him in the face. The guard collapsed.

Within seconds, several other men stormed the door. The guards sitting at the computers attempted to set off the alarms to alert Bullets, but Parker's men stabbed one and broke the neck of the other guard. With all three guards in the security room subdued, Parker texted Yanks, letting him know that his men were successful.

Now Yanks and his men were clear to continue with their part of the attack. Yanks motioned to his men fanned around the outside perimeter of the warehouse to move in. Within seconds, the front gate was opened. Parker and the rest of his men went through the gate with Yanks and his men. One by one, Yanks' men took out their assigned targets. Parker and his men continued through the warehouse yard to the buildings that housed Pig's stolen merchandise.

Parker took bolt cutters and removed the chain and locks that were holding the large overhead door down. Once the locks and chains were removed, Parker was held back slightly from making an entrance because the overhead door was locked from the inside. Parker quickly located a locked electric power box on the side of the building. He didn't know if destroying the wiring in the box would release the door locks, but time was running out.

Just as Parker opened the box, the two eighteen-wheel trucks they had brought backed in near the doors he was trying to open. He pulled at the wiring in the box until sparks started to fly. When he had removed most of the wiring going to the electrical fuses, he checked to see if the door locks were released. With a profound domino-like clatter the locks on most of the warehouse doors unhinged, including the doors that Parker was trying to access.

Several of Yanks' men had arrived to help load up the product at the same time Parker's men were opening the doors and backing in the big rigs.

As soon as the trucks were in position, two men climbed into the back of the trucks and started the forklift. Others attached the ramps to the backed in trucks.

While their men were setting up the trucks, Yanks and Parker checked out the warehouse. They found the product that they had come for stuck in the back of two rooms covered with tarps. "There it is. Let's get it out of here."

"Come on, boys, we've located the prize. Parker wants it out fast." Both Yanks' men and Parker's men moved to load the merchandise as fast as possible.

Parker watched the time and waited for the men in the security house to radio him if any phone calls or anyone came into or near the warehouse. Parker checked the warehouse to see how much product the men still had to load. Parker checked his watch again. Yanks looked at Parker. "Nervous, brother? We almost got it."

Parker looked in the back of the trucks and watched as another two loads were loaded. "Yeah, I just want to get everyone out of here before Bullets gets wind of what's going down and we have to wake up the neighbors."

"Only a couple loads left. It's all good."

Just as Parker's watch hit thirty minutes, one of the men from the security room notified him on the radio. "Boss, we got a phone call coming in. What do you want me to do? Answer it or let it ring?"

Parker looked at the men with the last two loads. "Let it ring. We're shutting up the trucks now. We will be up front in a minute, you men be ready to roll."

As soon as the last latches on the trucks were secured and the eighteen-wheelers were rolling out of the warehouse yard, Parker and his men parted ways with Yanks and his men. "Thanks for the help, brothers. Pig will be sending you your well-deserved fee."

Yanks and his men hung back. "Alright, Parker, tell Pig I'll be expecting it soon."

Parker was concerned that Yanks was going to make noise, but he would take it up with Pig when he had the trucks in the clear and on their way to Louisiana.

Yanks had his men meet him a block away from the warehouse where they had left their trucks. When the men reached the spot, Yanks picked out four of his men to complete a mission he'd planned before they arrived at the warehouse. He hadn't shared his plans with Parker. He was pretty sure Parker would have told Pig and Pig wouldn't have wanted him to complete his mission.

"I want you four men to watch and take pictures of what goes on here after Bullets finds out that he just lost five million dollars' worth of flake. Then after he and his men get done cleaning up the mess, I want Bullets followed and I want to know where he lives. I'm taking that bastard down for killing our men and dumping their bodies in the back of trucks like dogs."

"We want Bullets dead too, Yanks."

Parker contacted Pig as soon as he and his men were on I-10 heading out of the LA area toward Riverside. "The mission was a success without noise. Your merchandise is on its way to you."

"Excellent."

"My partner and his men stayed behind, but I'm not sure why, sir. I didn't have time to ask, but I made it clear you didn't want any unnecessary disturbances before we went into the warehouses."

"Let it go, Parker, Yanks won't piss me off. He wants to get paid. Just make sure that product gets to me as soon as possible."

"Yes, sir."

◊◊◊

Bullets was stoned and drunk but when Time Bomb informed him that the guards in the security room at the warehouse didn't respond to several calls, he suddenly sobered up. "What? Call them again!"

"I did, Bullets. No one is answering. We need to send someone over there to check things out. I don't like this."

Bullets threw his beer bottle across the room. "Me either! Rough Rider, you and your men go to the warehouse and check things out. Let me know why the hell those jackasses aren't answering the damn phone."

Rough Rider took his men and headed toward the warehouse. When they arrived, Rough Rider went into the security house. He soon emerged with his cell phone at his ear. He yelled at the men, "They've hit us! Check out the rest of the place and let me know what you find. Check to see if Bullets' prize is still in its place."

Rough Rider's men split up and went into the warehouse yard.

Bullets was livid when Rough Rider called to let him know what he had found. "WHAT THE FUCK! IS MY SHIT STILL THERE? FIND OUT WHO DID THIS. I WANT THEM DEAD! DO YOU UNDERSTAND ME? DEAD!"

Rough Rider understood, but the place was a mess and he was going to have to get help cleaning it up. He was pretty sure Pig was behind the hit, which would be confirmed once he knew if the loads were missing. One of his men met him halfway into the yard and gave him information that he really didn't want to hear. "They hit us bad, Rough Rider, and they got Bullets' prize. It's all gone. All the guards are either dead or hurt badly. This wasn't done by amateurs. It was Pig's men."

"Yeah, I figured that was who was behind this. I better let Bullets know so he can get down here and check things out."

Rough Rider's man looked around the yard. "What are we going to do with the dead ones? They're all over the place."

"We'll have to wait 'til Bullets gets here." Rough Rider got on his cell phone to let the Bullets know the bad news.

◊◊◊

By Wednesday, Shelby had finished her orientation and passed everything with flying colors. She and Angelica received their dispatch orders to Miami. She couldn't wait to get out on a long haul again.

Angelica and Shelby would have an eighteen-hour ride to Miami. They decided that they would leave early Thursday morning. The first day of their roll would take them to Tallahassee. They would spend the night there. Then roll down I-20 to Jacksonville before taking I-95 to Miami on Friday. They were to pick up their loads after midnight from one of Pig's warehouses and take them to North Carolina to another warehouse.

Shelby and Angelica had spent a lot of time together in the last few days and were becoming close. Shelby had had several friends back home, especially when she was teaching, but since she became a truck driver the majority of her friends hadn't kept in touch. Her co-worker friends had been men. Shelby hadn't had a close female friend in a long time and Angelica was terrific fun.

Angelica was rather reserved when it came to her personal life, even to Shelby. She did open up a little about herself a couple of times while they were sunbathing by the pool and Shelby chose to respect her new friend's privacy.

Angelica liked Shelby and having female companionship. Shelby was not only funny, she was brave and had faced a lot of adversity and danger since becoming a trucker, although she hadn't shared much detail about that. Angelica regretted having to hide her true identity from Shelby, but did not want to put either one of them in danger by revealing too much.

◊◊◊

Rat Hole and Lethal arrived in New York and were headed to pick up their loads from a Brooklyn warehouse. They had found a truck stop off I-95 that they could hole up in until it was time to pick up their loads. Rat Hole had enjoyed the company of a local lot lizard while Lethal slept. They weren't allowed to pick their loads up until two o'clock that morning. Lethal figured that was going to be a better time to enter the city anyway. Although New York never slept, the traffic would be somewhat lighter and easier to handle in the early morning hours.

It took the men some time to locate the warehouse, but once they arrived, it took the dockworkers less than twenty minutes to load the product on both trucks. Rat Hole had gotten out of his truck to check things out, but was forced by gunpoint back into it. Soon, several guards with guns arrived at Lethal and Rat Hole's trucks. Lethal and Rat Hole were not allowed out of their trucks or anywhere on the docks while they were at the warehouse. Rat Hole was pissed that he couldn't get a better view of what he was hauling, but he let it go since he was going to open the trailer later anyway.

Rat Hole got on the CB. "Well, I guess these guys are pretty serious about keeping us in the truck."

"You think? You're crazy, Rat Hole. They told you in orientation not to get out of your truck when loading and unloading unless you're asked to."

"I know. Don't you find that a little weird?"

Lethal tried to get Rat Hole to shut up since he knew the trucks were being monitored. "Yeah, but rules are rules. We get paid to drive, remember?"

Rat Hole got the message. "Yeah."

Lethal knew Rat Hole was going to be a problem and he was going to end up giving away their cover. He was going to talk with Lizard and see if another member could come in and take Rat Hole's place. He needed someone who would stay on track with the mission. Rat Hole was known for his over the edge behavior and his taste for nose candy. Lethal also knew Bullets had put Rat Hole with him for that very reason. Bullets wanted Rat Hole to cause problems and do crazy things that would drive Pig insane. Realizing this, Lethal knew his life was on the line too.

When the two drivers had their loads, they were escorted out of the warehouse by the armed guards. Before Rat Hole left, one of the guards gave him a warning, "You have been paid to drive the truck; stick to that for your own good."

Rat Hole saluted in military style and laughed, "Yes, sir."

The guard let Rat Hole go, but quickly picked up his phone and contacted Pig, letting him know his suspicions.

◊◊◊

Shelby and Angelica had driven to Midway, Florida where they decided to shut down for the night at Exit 192. "It's been a while since I've done this, so after we eat I'm going to take a shower and go to bed," Shelby said.

Angelica laughed. "I've been doing this for a while now and I'm still tired after eleven hours of driving. I'm with you on the sleep."

The women went into the truck stop and found a table in the restaurant. After they ordered from the waitress Shelby sat back in the booth, glad to be out from under the truck's monitoring. "Angelica, I know you told me that I'm not supposed to ask questions about what we are hauling and that are we to stay in our trucks when we load and unload…but I can't help but wonder. Is there anything you can tell me?"

Angelica thought about how she was going to answer the question. She needed to keep her identity concealed, but she had become friends with Shelby and it was hard to lie to her. "All I can tell you, Shelby, is that if you want to stay working for Mr. Pig, you can't ask questions. If it's really a problem for you, maybe you shouldn't roll for him. He likes things kept quiet."

"What are we hauling that's so secret? Is it illegal?"

Angelica had to remain discrete. "I'm pretty sure if we were doing something illegal, the law would already have shut Pig down. Think about it, Shelby. He's been in business for years. I just think it's because of the clients he hauls for. They don't want the drivers stealing from them."

"Yeah, that's what Jack and Black Jack both told me." Shelby stretched out again in her booth. "I guess you guys are right. Sometimes I'm too paranoid for my own good. But I still say it's weird."

Their food arrived and they ended the conversation.

◊◊◊

Bullets had arrived at the warehouse and was not only loaded but pissed. He walked into the security house. When he saw the dead guards and his computer system in shambles he started throwing stuff around the room. "SON-OF-A-BITCH! THAT FUCKING PIG WAS BEHIND THIS! I WANT THAT FAT BASTARD!"

Rough Rider reluctantly interrupted. "Look, Bullets, I know you're pissed but we have to either call the cops or do something with all these bodies."

Bullets didn't want the police in his warehouse, and he wasn't sure how he was going to explain all the bodies. "Let me look over the area and you guys lock down everything except for the buildings where the merchandise was held. Then call the cops and we will get out of here before they get here. I'll have Lizard come over and deal with the cops since he's got a cop on the force. Hopefully, they will just report it as a robbery and not dig too deep. That way I can take care of Pig myself."

Rough Rider and his men did exactly what Bullets had asked him while Bullets checked out the rest of the warehouse. Pig's men had managed to do a nice job of making a real mess out of the place. Because Parker had taken out the electrical fuse box, Bullets' men had to manually secure each door in the warehouse. Bullets and the rest of the men left just as Lizard was arriving to take over.

Yanks' men had taken hundreds of pictures and watched the place until Bullets and his men were leaving. "Come on, we need to get going so we can follow that son-of-a-bitch." Yanks' four men got to their pickup and fell in behind Bullets' gang on I-5. Once the gang reached their clubhouse, Yanks' men began their stakeout. Yanks wanted to know where Bullets lived, so they were going to have to wait until Bullets left the clubhouse again to get that information.

◊◊◊

Angelica and Shelby had made it to Miami, but they were going to have to wait until midnight to pick up their loads up. They found a place to park near the warehouse and went in search of something to eat.

"Let's just get a taxi and go to a local restaurant area," Angelica suggested.

"Sounds great," Shelby agreed. "I'm hungry and I want to get out of the truck and walk around for a while."

They arrived by taxi in Coconut Grove. "Oh my, this place is beautiful." Shelby looked at all the stores and lights. She and Angelica checked out some of the quaint little boutiques before finally deciding to get something to eat.

"I love Italian food and wine," said Angelica, truly enjoying herself for the first time in days.

Shelby sipped at her wine. "Me too."

◊◊◊

Lethal and Rat Hole left New York with their loads. Rat Hole was still angry about having a gun pointed at him at the warehouse. Once they stopped in Pennsylvania for food and coffee, Rat Hole finally told Lethal what he was going to do. "After we finish eating, I'm going to go out to that trailer, open it up, and see what's inside. Of course, I already know what's in there, but I'm going to help myself to some of it before we take it to that other warehouse. I'm pretty sure a few pounds won't be noticed."

"You can do what you want, Rat Hole, but they put security cameras on those trailer doors. Pig tracks everything we do. I'm pretty sure he even has cameras inside the trailers that tell him who enters. Hell, he might even have surveillance with alarms letting him know when the security tape is removed. You're crazy, Rat Hole, you're gonna get caught."

Rat Hole jumped up and walked toward his trailer. "I don't give a damn. I plan to hit Pig where it hurts—in the pocket."

Lethal wanted to take Pig down too, but he wanted to take him out, not just injure him. Lethal felt what Rat Hole was attempting wasn't going to do anything but get him thrown out of PIGT.

Rat Hole went to the front of his truck and then returned to the back of the trailer with a pair of bolt cutters. Lethal saw Rat Hole cut the padlocks and the security strip off of his trailer. He shook his head as Rat Hole held up each piece after cutting it off. Rat Hole opened the trailer doors and hopped into the trailer. He was inside the trailer for several minutes but when he appeared at the rear of the trailer again, Lethal couldn't believe that he actually had two bags of cocaine in his hands. He held them up and then put them on the floor of the trailer.

Lethal moved a bit closer to Rat Hole. "You're an idiot!"

Rat Hole laughed. "Yeah, but I'm going to be a rich idiot. Hell, I'm thinking of taking the whole load. There's enough flake in here to make me a very wealthy man."

"Two questions for you, Rat Hole. How are you going to get this shit out of here? And how long do you think it will be before Pig's customer finds you, literally peels the skin off your body, and then roasts you like a pig on a spit?"

Rat Hole thought for a few moments, but then took his two bags of cocaine and closed the trailer doors. He then put the security tape in his pocket. "I'll just tell them someone in a truck stop must have broken into the trailer while I was sleeping. They can't prove I did anything."

"Unless they got a camera on you."

"I doubt it. No one can have that much security."

◊◊◊

Pig received an alarm on his computer that he had only heard one time before. He quickly checked out the information. The security tapes had been removed from one of his trucks coming from New York. Pig quickly contacted Hank and had him contact the driver. Dispatch was attempting to get in touch with Rat Hole at the same time he was lifting flake from the trailer. When they were unable to contact Rat Hole, they called Lethal.

Lethal answered his phone. "Hello?"

"Where is Rat Hole?" Hank demanded.

Lethal couldn't snitch on his friend. "I'm not sure. We stopped to get coffee and I think he was feeling sick. He might be in his sleeper. I'm in the store right now, but I can check on him and have him call you. Is something wrong?"

Hank wasn't sure he believed Lethal, but he was going to give the new driver a little rope. If he found out they were stealing, he would use that rope to hang them. "Yes, have him call me at once. There is definitely a problem."

"Alright. I'll check on him."

Lethal found Rat Hole packing his truck and putting his stuff outside on the ground. Lethal stood at the bottom of the steps and waited for Rat Hole to come out of the truck again. "What the hell are you doing, man? Pig's people have been trying to call you."

Rat Hole continued to unload his truck. "I'm done, Lethal. I want to take some of the coke from the back and disappear. All I need you to do is buy me a little time."

"We had a mission to complete, and now you're bailing on me?"

Rat Hole finished recovering his stuff from inside the truck before he went back to the trailer. He opened it one more time and took several more bags of coke from the stock. Rat Hole shut the trailer doors and then returned to his things. He stuck the cocaine in his bags and zipped them closed.

"You son-of-a-bitch. You're going to leave me here to clean up your mess?"

Rat Hole grabbed his bags and started walking toward a car that was waiting for him in the parking lot. Lethal couldn't believe Rat Hole was taking off and that he had apparently been planning to leave all along.

"Sorry, Lethal, but I just needed a reason to get out of California and back to Ohio. I also need something to help me get started and this is it."

"You suck, man!"

Rat Hole threw his bags in the back seat and got in the front with a female who was driving. "Yeah, I know, but Bullets is going down soon and I just want out."

Lethal watched as Rat Hole left. He honestly wasn't that upset that Rat Hole was taking off. He was just wondering how he was going to get Pig and Hank to believe he had nothing to do with any of the missing product. After Rat Hole was gone, Lethal called Hank. "Hank, this is Lethal. I checked Rat Hole's truck out, and he's gone."

"GONE! What the hell do you mean GONE?"

"Well, his truck is unlocked and everything in it is gone. I think he's taken off."

"SHIT!"

"Lethal, check the security strip and locks on the trailer and let me know if it's still in place."

Lethal pretended he didn't know anything and followed Hank's instructions. "Okay just stay on the phone with me and I'll go and check."

"Fine, just hurry up." Lethal left his truck and went to the rear of Rat Hole's truck. He looked at the trailer. "Hank, sir, there is no security tape and it looks like the locks have been cut off. The trailer is even slightly open."

"DAMN IT! Okay, secure the truck and go inside and purchase some new locks. I need to let Mr. Pig know and send another driver to get the truck. I need you to stay with the truck until the other driver arrives. Don't enter the trailer."

"Yes, sir."

Hank was about to hang up when he said, "I thought this guy was a friend of yours. You came in together, didn't you? Are you sure you are telling me everything?"

Lethal knew he was going to have to make Hank believe he had nothing to do with what Rat Hole had done or he was going to be blamed for the missing cocaine too. "Yes, Hank, I have told you everything I know and no, Rat Hole and I were not friends before we came to work for PIGT. I met him when we were both picked up by Black Jack."

Hank wasn't convinced and Lethal could hear the doubt in his voice. "Well, I have to tell Mr. Pig. You stay with the truck until I get back to you."

"Okay, I'll be here." Lethal wasn't sure if he should run or wait it out and see what happened. He secured the trailer and then went into the truck stop to purchase the padlocks. He hoped the worst scenario was that he'd get fired and sent back to California.

◊◊◊

Yanks' men were getting tired. "Come on, this guy isn't going to leave that building any time tonight. I suggest three of us get some rest in the truck and one keep watch. Then every two hours we change out." The other men agreed.

Just as they were about to decide who would pull the first shift, Bullets left the clubhouse. "Wait! Look, the ass is leaving finally." The four men went to their vehicle and followed Bullets for several miles until he got to what they figured was his house.

Tomahawk called Yanks. "Yanks, we located what looks like that asshole's house. What do you want us to do?"

"Go home. I'll take care of that bastard myself."

"You got it, boss."

◊◊◊

Lethal looked at his phone, knowing that he was going to have to contact Lizard and let him know that Rat Hole had bailed. He wasn't sure if he should give Lizard the complete story. Rat Hole running out on the gang was a crime against the club and Rat Hole could lose his life over it. Lethal decided he would just tell him Rat Hole had gotten arrested for some old warrants and the judge wouldn't give him bail.

CHAPTER THIRTEEN

Pig was furious when he entered the command center. "Hank, I know we have a security breach on truck 6716. I've been tracking the movements."

"I've had Lethal secure the truck and wait there with it until another driver arrives. I talked to Lethal and he says he doesn't know Rat Hole very well and doesn't know if he's taken anything from the load, but since the security of the trailer has been breached it's logical that someone has been in that trailer."

"Where is Black Jack?" Pig asked.

Hank pulled Black Jack up on the computer. "He's in Illinois recruiting."

Pig thought again as he puffed on his cigar. "Put him on a plane and have him meet Lethal and the replacement driver at that truck stop. I want him to check out the load and give me an in-person evaluation of Lethal. I want to know if that man is being truthful or if he's holding something back. Then, I want you to find Rat Hole. If he's stolen from me, I want his balls cut off."

"I'm on it, sir. I'll send you a report as soon as everything is set."

Pig didn't respond and went back to monitoring his computer. *This is why I want everyone chipped. If it were a requirement for employment I could avoid these inconvenient, pain in the ass problems.* He was currently monitoring Shelby's truck. She and Angelica had reached their destination and had been sitting near the pickup point for a few hours. Pig had turned on the in-cab camera but Shelby's curtain was closed so he figured she was probably resting. He turned off the camera. *I'll check on her later.*

◊◊◊

Angelica and Shelby planned to drive to a truck stop and spend the night once they had their loads. Shelby watched as two pickups and an SUV rolled into parking spots near the dark warehouse. Within a few minutes, two men with guns opened a small warehouse door and disappeared inside. Several minutes later, a set of outside lights came on near two overhead doors and floodlights lit up the dock in front of the large doors. Shelby watched as the two men with the guns motioned for the others in the vehicles to join them.

One driver opened the back passenger door of the SUV for a man seated there. Shelby couldn't see the person, but felt he must have been someone respected and important by the treatment he was receiving from the others. They gathered together inside one of the dock doors. Several minutes later, that man disappeared with the two men with the guns further into the darkness of the warehouse. When they returned, the VIP man was escorted back to his SUV and driven away.

Shelby watched with great interest at the activities playing out in front of her. She began to feel anxious about her new job. *This is not normal behavior for warehouse personnel, being strapped with weapons and loading trucks late at night. Who does that? What the hell am I delivering?* She wanted to know more. *I'm not going to lose my CDL or go to jail for anyone.* But she also knew she had to be careful.

Her thoughts were interrupted by a sudden knock on her driver's side door, which caused her to jump. She looked through her window at a man on the ground near her door.

"Back your truck into the dock door closest to the trees. Turn off your lights and get into your sleeper with the curtain closed. We will wake you when we have loaded you."

"Can I...?"

The man had already turned around and was headed back to the dock before the words left Shelby's lips. "Wow. What the hell?"

While Shelby was turning her truck around, she saw Angelica was doing the same thing into the other dock. *Does Angelica ever question the strange activities? Am I just being paranoid and overly suspicious? No one else seems to be bothered with these strange procedures.* Even when she made eye contact with Angelica after reaching her dock position, Angelica seemed to be more interested in getting into her sleeper than what was going on with her load. *Something's not right. I don't know what, but I'm going to find out.*

Shelby followed Angelica's lead and moved into her sleeper, but sleeping wasn't an option for her. She couldn't shake the feeling that she was being watched.

◊◊◊

Lethal had stayed with the trucks at the truck stop for several days and was relieved when Black Jack finally arrived to take possession of the load. Black Jack knew Lethal and Rat Hole hung together on the estate and that they were friendly, but had no idea that they were friends or part of Bullets' gang. Lethal hated that Rat Hole had abandoned their mission, but he had a job to do and he wanted to take on Pig. He had to make it clear to Pig and Black Jack that he had nothing to do with the heist. He had called Lizard to let him know that Rat Hole had been arrested and that he was still working on getting close to the inside of the company, but that was it.

Black Jack opened the trailer up and took inventory of the contents. He was on his cell phone and securing the contents with locks when Lethal approached him at the rear of the trailer. "Yes, Hank. I sent the pictures to Pig and placed the new locks on the load. I'll be following Lethal and his truck back to the estate." Black Jack pointed at Lethal to let him know he would be with him shortly.

Lethal nodded and backed away, but not so far that he couldn't hear the conversation. "Yes, Hank. He's here and he's being very cooperative. I doubt seriously that he has had anything to do with any of this. Think about it, you idiot. What sane person do you know that would wait around to be interrogated or if he's going to get knocked off if he's involved? Don't be stupid. Tell the boss I'm bringing the trucks and Lethal back to the estate and we will be there tomorrow night."

Black Jack hung up his cell. "Idiot." He put the phone in his shirt pocket and adjusted his belted jeans around his waist. He moved toward

Lethal. "Well, I truly hope you are not involved with any of this 'cause Pig is out for blood on this one and Rat Hole is a dead man."

"No, sir, Mr. Black Jack. I assure you I had nothing to do with this. I was totally taken aback when I discovered Rat Hole had taken off and found the locks cut off the trailer. I just shut the doors and called in just like they trained me to do. Mr. Black Jack, I need this job and I don't want to do anything to get fired. Believe me when I say, I truly had nothing to do with any of this."

"I believe you, Lethal. Let's get a cup of coffee and head back to Louisiana with these trucks. I'm sure if you tell Pig exactly what you have just told me he'll believe you as well."

"I hope so, Mr. Black Jack. I hope so."

◊◊◊

Getting rid of Bullets was not going to be as easy as Yanks had thought. Once he called to let Pig know that they were ready to take Bullets out, Pig had a change of plans. As Yanks listened on his phone, his face reddened. "That's just bullshit, Pig. My men and I have lost friends and family. We have risked being arrested, or worse, getting shot, and now you tell me we have to wait? What the fuck does the cartel have to do with it? The cartel pricks dictate everything for you, don't they? Maybe I need to take a few of them out too?" Yanks became more incensed. "Fuck you, Pig! I'll give you twenty-four hours and then I'm taking that bastard and his gang down." Pig hung up on him.

Yanks threw his phone across the room. "Fucker! I'll do whatever the hell I want, when I want." Yanks' men gathered around him and listened to the details of the heated conversation. Yanks was now even more determined to get rid of Bullets, regardless of Pig's wishes.

◊◊◊

Lethal had no idea what kind of interrogation he was going to have to endure from Pig's organization once he and Black Jack returned to the estate. He was ready for anything they threw at him.

At the estate, Lethal was removed from the driver's seat of the truck at the gate and placed in one of Pig's black SUVs. Black Jack and one of the gate guards drove the two trucks full of product toward the back of the estate to a secured warehouse. Lethal watched as much of the transfer process as he could from inside the SUV before he was quickly rushed toward the main house. He knew he would soon be face-to-face with Pig and Hank. He wasn't nervous about the interrogation; he just wished he had some backup.

Just as Lethal was stepping out of the SUV he was surprised to see that the two guards assigned to removing him from the SUV were familiar faces. The two guards remained unemotional as they took him from the vehicle, one on either side of his body. Two more members of his LA gang were now guards for Pig. He tried to suppress the surprised expression on his face in order to conceal the fact that he knew the two men. *Things are going to go a lot better now that I have some reinforcement.*

Pig was relaxed when Black Jack and the guards brought Lethal into his office. Hank arrived a few seconds behind the group. The new guards had just been hired and once Hank entered the room he quickly excused them. "You two can wait outside the doors. I'll let you know if we need you for anything."

Lethal sat quietly in the chair that had been pointed out for him to occupy. Black Jack had taken off his black cowboy hat and was fiddling with it while standing near the wall by one of the windows.

Hank immediately went behind Pig's desk where he was looking over some information on his computer. He whispered into his boss' ear, "Parker says that Yanks may be up to something because he noticed that he had one of his guys spying on Bullets. He doesn't know for sure what Yanks is thinking, but Parker knows that Bullets and his members are going to be heading to San Diego tomorrow. The members are picking up a small amount of product and carrying it to New Mexico."

"Damn, I bet Yanks is going to try and take Bullets out against my orders. Tell Parker to get word to Bullets somehow without him knowing the information is coming from me. I want Bullets gone, but in my time. If Yanks is stupid enough to go against me then I guess he's stupid enough to die."

"Okay, sir, I'll let Parker get on that at once." Hank waited for Pig's next order.

Lethal knew exactly who Hank and Pig were talking about, but he did his best to pretend he knew nothing about what they were whispering about to each other.

Pig moved his computer lid down and stared at Lethal with a blank expression. "Thank you, Lethal, for staying with my shipment until I could get another driver there to bring it in safely. My customers are going to be very happy that only a small portion of their freight was taken. Do you know what was in the trailer?"

"I'm really not sure, Mr. Pig. I didn't go into the trailer. I followed the procedures according to what I was trained to do in orientation."

"You weren't even curious why your partner took off with some of my shipment?"

"I really didn't know the man well enough to know why he did any of what he did. We had only met when we got hired on together. I guess I kind of know what might have been in the shipment, but I would only be guessing. I really don't care anyway. I just need this job, sir. I have a lot of child support to pay and this job pays real good."

Black Jack and Hank looked at each other. They knew their boss and he was not very forgiving when it came to people who knew more or thought they knew more than they should know. Pig tapped on his desk with a pen. "So you didn't get into the trailer? You had no knowledge of what Rat Hole was up to?"

"No, sir."

Pig decided to let it go with a warning. "I believe you, but if I find out in the future that you had any knowledge or you helped Rat Hole in any way, you're a dead man. Do you understand?"

"Yes, sir, I understand."

Black Jack put on his hat and moved to the side of the chair where Lethal sat. Hank looked somewhat upset that Pig had not been harder on the driver. He crossed his arms and backed away from Pig's chair while glaring at Lethal.

Lethal stood and attempted to shake Pig's hand in gratitude. "Thank you, Mr. Pig."

Pig didn't offer his hand for the handshake so Lethal put his hand down and turned to leave.

"Lethal may return to driving," Pig told Hank, "but I want him running with Angelica and Shelby. They will be picking up a load out of New York and bringing it back here. Lethal, you can meet them on their way out of North Carolina. Give him the information, Hank."

"Yes, sir," Hank said.

"Thank you again, Mr. Pig," Lethal said.

Black Jack walked Lethal out while Hank stayed back with Pig. "Keep a close eye on him," Pig instructed. "I want his monitoring on your daily report to me. Now leave me alone. I have some work to do."

Hank left quickly. "Yes, Mr. Pig. I'll keep him on close watch." Hank shut the door and left Pig in privacy.

Pig opened his computer and pulled up Shelby's truck. He checked to see if he could see her on the onboard camera, but she was in her sleeper. He activated the camera in her sleeper that he had secretly installed. Shelby was resting quietly. Pig liked the way Shelby slept with her blonde hair laying gently across her pillow. He activated the sound control inside the truck so he could hear her breathe. He sat back in his chair and just stared at her calm sleeping body. The more Pig watched Shelby, the more he wanted her.

Pig decided he was going to treat his future bride to a lavish weekend in Las Vegas. He would treat her like a queen. She would see what being with him could provide. Beautiful clothing and jewelry, not to mention fine dining and dancing. Las Vegas shows and unlimited gambling would make it hard for her to resist his gracious doting. Pig figured Shelby would have to be blind and stupid to resist the promising future he had in mind.

He closed his computer and planned to have Harry make all the arrangements for the Vegas weekend at Caesars Palace in the morning. He would make sure that the other drivers going to Las Vegas would also be accommodated so that Shelby wouldn't feel singled out, although he did want Shelby and Angelica to have suites on the same floor as his. He just wanted to make sure that he would have ample time alone with her. *She'll willingly give up her current marriage and marry me in time. I am going to do everything possible to make sure of it.*

Pig's phone rang, taking him out of his reverie for Shelby. Caller identification was unknown so he knew it was either cartel business or one of his high-end customers. As much as he liked occupying his mind with thoughts of Shelby, business always came first.

◊◊◊

Lethal rested in his truck while it was parked at the yard. He wanted to make contact with his fellow club members, but knew if he did it might seem suspicious. He was going to leave in the morning for I-95 to meet up with the two drivers who he had been assigned to roll with in Harrisburg, Pennsylvania. The dispatchers gave him the route he was to take. Once he met up with his team they would then continue together to a small town called Johnson City, New York where they would pick up their loads for Las Vegas.

Lethal knew it would take him about two days to make the trip. He wasn't thrilled with having to go to Vegas, but he was glad he still had his head. It was going to take the two new club members time to obtain the trust and confidence of the staff at Pig's estate. He hoped that by the time he finished with his load to Las Vegas they would send him to LA for a load back to the estate. He hoped they would not send him toward Mexico because the cartel would recognize him. If they sent him there, he would have to figure out some way to either get out of the load or hide his identity. His main goal was to get in touch with Lizard to formulate a plan to take out Bullets—and hopefully Pig too. Patience and precision were going to make their vows of revenge on their two enemies become reality.

CHAPTER FOURTEEN

Shelby heard a knock on her driver door. Before she could roll down her window, the man motioned with his hands that she could leave. Shelby looked toward Angelica's truck. Angelica was in her driver's seat putting on her seat belt. She looked toward Shelby and smiled, motioning for Shelby to follow her out of the warehouse area. Shelby fastened her seat belt and pressed in on her air brakes, still wondering about Angelica's blasé attitude.

Once the two lady drivers were on I-95, Angelica spoke to Shelby over the CB radio. "How about you, Barbie?"

"Go ahead, you got Barbie. Hey, what's your handle anyway?"

"Well, I don't have one yet, Barbie. Maybe you can help me figure one out."

"Okay, I'll start thinking of one."

"Since it's so late, once we get up here a few miles north of Fort Lauderdale, we might want to go to a truck stop and rest 'til tomorrow. What do you think?" Angelica said.

"Sounds good to me, you have one in mind?"

"Actually, I do."

The truck stop was small, but it did have a store and it was open. Shelby needed to use the restroom so she pulled in behind Angelica and the women backed their trucks into two empty slots. Shelby motioned to Angelica through her window after they were parked that she was going to the store. Angelica nodded back her understanding. She also let her know that she wouldn't be too far behind. It was kind of a code among women drivers never to give away their locations or movements once they were parked. That's how they kept themselves safe from weirdos.

Shelby found the restroom. After washing her face and brushing her teeth, she went back toward the register where she found Angelica buying some water.

Angelica took her change and walked toward the restroom. "I'll be out in a few minutes, just gonna get ready for bed. We can have breakfast in the morning at the café across the road. I'll give you a holler on channel eight."

Shelby walked toward the sliding doors. "Okay, see you in the morning. Sleep well."

"You too."

Shelby walked toward her truck. She was tired and she couldn't wait to go to sleep. She hated the fact that her truck had surveillance cameras and voice recording equipment inside of it, but she was tired and could ignore it. She climbed into her truck, turned on her dome light, and pulled the curtains around her windows. Still feeling uncertain of her privacy, she only took her shoes, socks, jewelry, and belt off. Shelby closed her bed curtain and got into her bed. It didn't take her long to fall asleep.

Angelica took her time in the restroom. After she felt that Shelby had enough time to get to her truck, she took her private phone out of her pocket. Dialing Rex's number gave her a silly girlish feeling in her stomach. When his voice finally came over the phone, her heart seemed to leap in her chest. "Hey, it's me," she said quietly.

Rex tried hard to remain professional, even though he wanted to be more personal. "Glad to hear from you. Everything okay?"

"Yes, everything is fine. I've picked up a load out of Miami with that new female driver I told you about earlier. I think from the glimpse I got of the ringleader, it's Chavez, one of the Cuban cartel leaders. It was a small transfer of goods, only two loads going to Pig's warehouse in North Carolina. We're delivering it there in the next couple of days."

The information was good. The more she found out, the easier it would be to shut down Pig's operation. "That's great, Angelica. How are you doing?"

"I'm hanging in there. This new driver Shelby is keeping me company and I really like her."

Rex was cautious. "Is she on the inside track?"

"No. She's not familiar with anything that's going on and she really doesn't like the secrecy of everything. It's been hard just keeping her mind on the job. She's really smart and I'm pretty sure she realizes that things aren't right. I'm thinking maybe I need to let her in, but I don't want to alarm her. She might quit and that would raise suspicions, I think."

"I would just keep putting out the fires for now and just see how it goes. Don't bring her into anything yet. Your instincts are good, Angelica. You'll know when it's the right time."

Angelica wanted so much to tell Rex she wished she were in his arms instead of sleeping in a cold truck bed alone, but their relationship had to remain professional for both their sakes. "Okay, I'll do my best. I just hope I can keep her from quitting. Pig has a thing for Shelby and it would be a great asset to have someone who can get really close to him. Although I'm pretty sure she's like every other woman who comes into contact with Pig—rather repulsed by his stench."

Rex and Angelica had to laugh together on that comment. The agents talked for a while longer. "Well, I'd better get back to my truck, Rex. I wouldn't want Shelby or Pig, if he's watching, to get suspicious about anything."

"I know. You be careful and let me know where you unload. You are giving us great intelligence on Mr. Pig. When we bust him it will all be because of your hard work, little lady."

Angelica felt her cheeks blush. "Thank you, Rex. I'll continue to do my best." She left the store, got into her truck, secured herself in her sleeper, and slept until her alarm woke her the next morning.

"Hey Barbie, time to get up."

Shelby was already awake but she had been lying in her sleeper trying to decide if she wanted to get up. She went to the CB. "I'm up."

"Good. I'm going to walk across the street for breakfast. See you over there in a little while."

Shelby got out of her sleeper and grabbed her shower bag and some clean clothes. "Okay. I'll be there in a few minutes. I want coffee."

"I'll get some for you." Angelica got out of her truck and headed to the restaurant.

Shelby grabbed her things and headed into the truck stop store for a quick shower. She took her phone so she could call Jack while she had privacy.

◊◊◊

Yanks knew Pig was never going to let him take Bullets out on his own. He had decided that he and his men were going to take care of Bullets and most of his gang regardless of what Pig wanted. Yanks had learned that Tito's cartel gang was going to have Bullets' gang deliver a small load of product into New Mexico.

Yanks called his boys together to share his plan. His men listened as he laid out the details.

Yanks' men never questioned his missions but one of his men spoke up, "You know, Yanks, I'm down with anything you want to do, especially when it comes to eliminating Bullets, but are you sure you want to go against Pig? And are you sure you want to do anything that will interfere or get us involved in cartel stuff?"

Yanks respected his men enough to let them question his missions. "I'm not concerned with Pig, but you are right in being concerned with what the cartel will do if we mess with their business. I'm hoping that we can take them out right after they finish their job for the cartel, that way we won't interfere with their shipments at all."

His men nodded their heads in agreement. They would go with Yanks' plan against Bullets.

◊◊◊

Shelby had finished her shower and was on the phone with Jack while she walked toward the restaurant. "I miss you too, baby." Shelby waited on Jack's response. "Yes, I like the job, but there are some really weird things going on. I'm not so sure this company is on the up and up. For one thing, we only pick up or deliver at night, and usually at warehouses located outside of warehouse districts. You know the kind of warehouses that look abandoned in old slummy neighborhoods? Plus, there are always a lot of guards with guns. They never let me inspect my loads either. I have no idea what the hell I'm carrying."

"Tell me what you're thinking."

"I know we were assured that the weapons were security for the valuable property that Pig handled for his clients, but I'm beginning to wonder just what kind of property his clients have in those places. Seriously, Jack, if you had valuable paintings or expensive stuff you wanted transported or stored, would you leave it in a run-down warehouse? It seems weird to me."

"I trust your instincts," said Jack. "Why don't you see if you can find out anything else before you make any decisions."

"Okay, I'd better go now. Thanks for listening. I'll talk to you later, baby."

Shelby found Angelica sitting in a corner booth in the café. She slid into the opposite seat across from her, turned over her coffee cup, and poured coffee from a decanter on the table. Angelica was looking through a newspaper and eating her breakfast. "Sorry, I got hungry and went ahead and ordered."

"No biggie. I had to check in with my hubby this morning. He worries about me out here on the road."

Angelica put down her paper and concentrated on her food while the waitress arrived at the table to take Shelby's order. "I'll take two eggs over medium with dry toast and some fresh fruit if you have it," Shelby said.

"Sorry, honey, we don't have any fresh fruit. I can get you some fruit cocktail, but it's from the can."

Shelby put a little sugar in her coffee and then sipped at it. Angelica took a bite of her toast then swallowed. "So, what's a proper lady like you doing out here on these roads driving an eighteen-wheel truck? Especially with a husband at home that worries about you?"

Shelby sipped at her coffee while she thought about how she could explain the last few years of her life without discussing all of the details. "Well, I like driving big trucks."

"Come on, Shelby, no one gets into this business with your obvious level of education and your 'write your own ticket' looks without a reason. Level with me, what the hell are you doing out here? You do not fit the bill at all."

Shelby wanted to tell Angelica, but ever since the Betty Burton debacle, she still had trust issues with people. Besides, she didn't want to get into any dramatic issues this morning. She sipped at her coffee. "Well, I could ask you the same thing. You're a beautiful woman. What are you doing in this business?"

Angelica ate at her breakfast, wanting to tell Shelby what she was really doing, but it just wasn't the right time. She decided she'd try and probe Shelby in another direction to get more information. "Well, thanks for saying that, but I was just curious about you that's all. So did you know Pig before you came to work for him? I didn't. I just got recruited."

Shelby's food arrived and she peppered her eggs and cut them up. "No. I didn't know Pig or even about PIGT until I met Black Jack at a truck stop one night. Actually, I hadn't given him any information about myself except my handle that night. Somehow he found Barbie in West Texas and showed up where I used to work. I'm still not sure exactly how he found me. Anyway, he offered me a job, and it had been a while since I'd been long hauling. I convinced my husband that it was time to get back out on the road. So here I am, but I'm beginning to wonder if I made the right decision."

"So your husband doesn't mind you being out here on the road?"

"Not now. For a while he did, but I guess it was for a reason since I was being stalked by a crazy woman. That woman is dead now so he's more supportive."

"You eluded to something when we were talking at the library on the estate, but I didn't realize who you'd been stalked by or that your tormentor was dead."

Angelica made Shelby feel comfortable and she decided to open up to her. "Yes, a real out-of-her-mind lunatic. She was wanted for murder as well as my attempted murder. To this day I don't understand how I got in her crosshairs. She did a lot of really nasty stuff to me and my family."

Angelica knew if the crazy woman was or had been wanted by the law she would be able to find out about her through Rex. Maybe there was some connection to drugs and guns. "Was it on the news? Maybe I heard about it and just didn't know it? What was her name?"

"Betty Burton."

Angelica had heard about the case. The case had been turned over to the FBI when Betty Burton started crossing state lines on her murderous rampage. What Angelica had not realized until now, is that her current trucking partner was the woman that Betty Burton had been trying to kill. "Holy cow! I did hear about that on the news. That crazy woman was chasing you? That story was all over the radios out here too. Truckers were looking out for her all over the place. She was some weirdo wasn't she?"

"To say the least. She caused havoc in my life for years. I almost lost my life, my marriage, and my children to that insanity."

"Wow! I'm trucking with a real hero. I'd love to hear what really happened. You know how truckers like to exaggerate. I'm sure the stories told out here were inflated to make them more dramatic."

Shelby smiled. "I know they do, but I'm no hero. My family, some of my trucker friends, and some really good cops brought that bitch to her demise."

"You mentioned kids, how many?

"I have three great sons and I have four beautiful grandchildren."

Angelica raised her eyebrows. "Grandkids? You don't look old enough to have grandchildren."

"Well, thank you, but I do. How about you? Are you married? Any kids?"

"Nope. And no kids."

"Boyfriend?"

"Maybe, but it's kind of new, so I wouldn't go so far as to say, 'boyfriend,' just someone I'm seeing."

Angelica needed to tread lightly, but she also thought Shelby could be an asset for her and Rex, especially with Pig's infatuation with the little blonde. "So you think coming out on the road was the wrong thing to do?"

"Not the driving…but this company. There are a lot of really weird things going on." She lowered her voice, "I don't think things are on the up and up for some reason. I even told my husband what I was thinking this morning, but he told me I was just being paranoid. I don't think so."

Angelica focused on her food. "What things do you find weird?"

"Come on, you can't tell me you don't find the way we do things out here weird. I mean, I know we aren't supposed to question the loads or even check on them, but don't you find it odd that we only pick up and unload at night? What about the guns those guys carry? The places we deliver to and pick up from—you know those aren't normal warehouse facilities. I am inclined to believe we are working for some kind of drug dealer or something. I know you told me to keep my mind on my job and not to ask questions. I'm not looking to get in trouble for questioning anything this company does. It just seems odd. I'm not sure I want to stay."

Angelica didn't want to lose a possible inside informant and maybe even a new friend. She chose her words carefully. "Shelby, I know things are not conventional with PIGT, but don't quit. I really like running with you and there aren't a whole lot of us female drivers working for Mr. Pig. Please, just stick it out for a little while. I promise you that staying will pay off. Please put up with the weird activities for a while. Not for Mr. Pig, but for me. I'll tell you what I can when the time is right."

Shelby had still had doubts, but she liked Angelica and her new truck. "Okay, I guess I don't really have anything better to do right now anyway."

Angelica was relieved. She just needed to keep Shelby engaged until she could reveal the truth. "Great. Now, I know it's weird, but we do have to unload tonight after midnight in Dunn, North Carolina."

Shelby rolled her eyes.

"I know, but I really think you are going to like the place we are headed to with the next load we pick up."

"Tell me."

"After we unload in North Carolina, we'll take a break. Then we're going to meet another driver in Harrisburg, Pennsylvania. Once we connect with the other driver in Harrisburg, we'll pick up our next load in a little town called Johnson City, New York."

"At night again?"

"Yes, but guess where we are taking the loads out of Johnson City?"

"Where?"

"Las Vegas!"

"Really? That's awesome! I haven't been to Vegas in a long time. Do we get to take a break and spend some time on the strip?"

"Yes, we do."

I wish Jack could come with me, she thought. "Awesome. Let's get out of here. I need to get fuel before we leave."

Angelica and Shelby slid out of the booths and headed to the register. Angelica grabbed the ticket and Shelby threw a few dollars on the table for a tip. "How much do I owe?"

Angelica handed the cashier a credit card and the ticket. "Don't worry about it, Shelby. I got this one."

"Okay, but I got the next time."

"Deal." Angelica was glad that Shelby, at least for the moment, had leaving off her mind. "Let's get fueled up and roll."

After they were on the road for a while, Shelby had a thought. She keyed up her radio. "Hey Angela," she said, "I've been thinking about a handle for you and I think I have a good one. How about Mystery Lady?"

"That sounds great. How'd you come up with that one?"

"Obviously because you're so mysterious!" Shelby laughed.

◊◊◊

Bullets and the men he had decided to take with him were going to pick up their small packages from Tito's men in San Diego. The product was going to be smuggled back through the tunnels near the border. The tunnels had been built by the cartel over several years and had been used to get drugs, weapons, and illegal goods into the United States without detection. Only those who had been labeled loyal distributors for the cartels had been privy to the location of the tunnels. Bullets' gang had never been considered loyal. The cartel always made drops in the States with them.

Bullets knew about the tunnels from rumors drug runners had inadvertently mentioned. He had tried many times to get Tito to let him pick the product up near or in the tunnels, but Tito always refused. Bullets hated the fact that Tito and the cartel didn't trust him with their secrets. He wanted to be their only distribution line in the States but Pig was in his way. *I have to get rid of Pig and take over his business to get what I want.* That is why he had placed Lethal and others inside Pig's organization. Once Pig was gone, the cartel would have to work with him. He knew he was taking a chance by backing the cartel into a corner, but he didn't care.

◊◊◊

Lethal called Lizard when he got to the truck stop. "Lizard, this is Lethal. I haven't been able to talk to you because they have been watching me like a hawk. I just wanted to check in with you and let you know that I saw the two new guys you got in at Pig's estate. Make sure they keep their heads down and remember that Pig has every inch of that property and equipment under surveillance."

"Good to hear from you, Lethal. We are on our way to San Diego to do a little job for our Mexican friends."

"I don't have much time Lizard, but I need to let you know that Yanks is up to something. I overheard Pig discussing it with Hank yesterday. I know you guys are already on your way to pick up the product. Be careful, because they think that Yanks is planning to take you guys out at some point."

"Wow. I haven't heard anything about Yanks trying to take Bullets out recently. Bullets did say he was going to meet with an older club member somewhere in Arizona. That meeting might be to let him know what's going down."

"Yeah, I'll bet that's what that meeting is about. But you need to be careful and watch your backs. Don't let anyone know that I gave you a heads up. There were only a few of us in the office when Hank told Pig about Yanks. Pig is smart and he'll figure out that one of us in the room leaked the ambush. I'd be on the top of the list since they already suspect me for helping with the theft out of Rat Hole's truck." Lethal had forgotten he'd told Lizard that Rat Hole had been arrested.

"Theft? What theft?"

"Well, Rat Hole really didn't get arrested, Lizard. He took off with a shit load of Pig's merchandise."

"Really? Why did you lie to me? Where is he?"

"I'm not sure, Lizard. He didn't tell me and I didn't ask. He did take off, though, and left me holding the bag."

Lizard was glad that Bullets had enlisted other club members to help with the infiltration of Pig's Company. He wasn't happy that one of the gang's top leaders had jumped ship. "Shit, Bullets will kill Rat Hole for sure if he finds out."

"Yeah, I know. Don't tell him anything until we find Rat Hole. I just hope we can find him before Pig does, 'cause Pig is out for blood. Rat Hole just doesn't think straight."

"That's because he's always got his mind on that nose candy. I think you're right, we will just keep this to ourselves. I'll put out some feelers and see if I can locate him. If the club finds out he flaked on a job they'll want to take him down. Damn it."

"Okay, I got to go before someone sees me on this phone. You guys watch your backs and I'll let you know what I hear on the inside."

Lizard hung up his phone and placed it in his pocket. He sat up straighter on his bike and began to watch his surroundings with more attention. Now that he knew Yanks was hunting the club, he was determined to stay alert. He would deal with the Rat Hole issue later. Right now he had to keep himself and his club members alive. He really didn't care if Yanks took out Bullets, since that was some of the other club members' plan anyway. But Yanks wasn't taking him or his brothers out without a fair fight.

◊◊◊

Bullets had made arrangements to meet one of the elder bike members at a truck stop in Quartzsite, Arizona. He had used the location several times for meetings because it wasn't overly popular with truckers and secluded to some degree. When the bikers arrived, they parked at the rear of the truck stop to avoid detection from the cops. Bullets went into the store and located High Roller who was flirting with the cashier. "Come on, baby, just a quickie in the back room. No one will notice. It's not even busy tonight."

High Roller stopped his conversation with the young cashier when he spotted Bullets. "Bullets!"

Bullets shook the elder club member's hand and patted him on the back. He then looked at the young cashier. "Don't let the age of this old man fool you, he can go all night for sure." The cashier blushed red with embarrassment as the two men laughed and moved to a small table in the corner.

"So what's up, High Roller? You sounded pretty serious over the phone."

High Roller got close to Bullets and whispered the information that he had received from a hooker he had been keeping for a while. "I didn't want to tell you over the phone because I didn't know if you were still under the scope of the cops. You know how those guys tap phones and stuff these days?"

"Yeah, I know."

"Look, this old pro I've been doing for a long time told me that she heard from one of her other Johns, who is apparently one of Yanks' boys… Anyway, I guess Yanks is planning to take you guys out in New Mexico. She didn't really know much but I thought I better let you know what I heard. You guys headed to New Mexico?"

"Yes, we're supposed to make a drop tomorrow. I really didn't want to have to deal with that bullshit right now. I got a lot in the works and Yanks is just a nuisance."

High Roller could see that Bullets wasn't happy about the news. "Look, I can gather up some of the old riders I run with and we can help you out."

"Maybe, High Roller, I need to talk to the club members and figure out how we are going to handle this. I'm glad you gave me a heads up, brother. I can't figure out how Yanks and Pig are tracking my activities. I'm thinking maybe I got a rat."

"Maybe they're spying on you. I can't believe one of our brothers would be a traitor."

"Me either, High Roller, but Pig and Yanks always seem to know what I'm doing." Bullets opened the door for his fellow club member. "Come on, let's go talk with the other riders. I'll be damned if Yanks is gonna take us out. Did that whore say anything else that might help us figure out where they might be waiting for us?"

High Roller quietly sorted through his drug-ravaged brain for information. "Something about dumping the bodies in the trees or forest or something, I think... But honestly, I can't remember everything, Bullets. I was busy doing the bitch and stoned to boot."

Bullets called his high-ranking lieutenants to his bike. High Roller joined the meeting but didn't say anything. Pulling a vial of coke out of his pocket, Bullets put a little of the white powder on the top of his fist, snorting the powder into his nose. After feeling the coke hit his brain, he let his leaders know what High Roller had told him in the store.

"I think he's gonna try and hit us after we deliver the product," Lizard said. "Yanks doesn't want trouble with the cartel; he wants our blood. It would make sense that he'd try and hit us on Highway 60 since it's not busy, especially at night."

Bullets began to fidget, feeling the effects of his nose candy. "I think Lizard is right and I think we need to be prepared. Yanks and his men are probably already set up." Bullets couldn't think straight. "I'll be right back." He went into the store for a beer.

Lizard took over since Bullet was too buzzed. "This is what I think we should do. Let's have High Roller and his friends make the drop for us. I'll head out now and check out what Yanks might have set up."

"Won't Yanks take out High Roller and his guys instead if they don't know it's not us?"

"Yes, but they don't want to mess with the cartel so they won't do anything while the product is being delivered. Let's just send High Roller and his guys out of town on Highway 25. Half of us will hide out on sixty and the other half will split between Yanks' men who will follow High Roller, and the ones who meet Yanks on 60."

Dog Killer had doubts. "How do you know Yanks will set things up like that? How do you know he won't kill High Roller right after the drop?"

Bullets finally returned with his beer. He had no idea what had been said while he was gone, but he didn't care. "Trust Lizard, brothers. He knows what he's talking about. Now, Lizard, tell me what we're doing and let's ride."

"I think we'd better rest a bit before we head that way, Bullets. We don't want to get there before Yanks if our plan is going to work."

High Roller interrupted. "I got a place we can rest for a while."

Bullets liked the idea. "Good. Let's ride."

Once the men arrived at High Roller's whorehouse, Bullets found a couple of women and some more beer and disappeared into a private room.

◊◊◊

Parker had let Pig know that he had gotten the word to Bullets and his men. "They know Mr. Pig. I'm not sure what is going to happen, but the warning has been delivered."

"Good. Now I can be rid of Yanks and I'll take Bullets out soon as well. Thank you, Mr. Parker. Once I have Bullets and his gang eliminated I'll give you top leadership of all my West Coast operations."

"Thank you, Mr. Pig. I won't let you down."

CHAPTER FIFTEEN

As Lizard and his men rolled toward Socorro, Lizard had plenty of time to think over a few things. The drugs the club members had been transporting had been taken to High Roller and his biker friends' bikes. Lizard had given orders to the rest of the club members to leave about an hour after High Roller and his friends. They would be traveling to Socorro on Highway 60.

Lizard had decided that he would leave Bullets to his whores, drugs, and drinking knowing that once Bullets sobered up, he would be pissed that his members had left him behind. Bullets would then get on his bike and race to Socorro to play leader. Lizard had decided that with all the confusion this would be the perfect time to take Bullets out, blaming it all on Yanks and his men.

Lizard was right. As soon as Bullets sobered up, he was pissed. "Where the fuck did they go, you whores?" Bullets stormed around the house, throwing things everywhere. He located his clothes, boots, and his gun. He placed his gun in the backside of his pants while grabbing a few swallows of an open beer left on an end table.

The women in the house were afraid of Bullets, especially when he reached for his gun. "We're sorry, Mr. Bullets. They left about two hours ago. They told us to let you sleep."

Bullets threw the beer bottle at the wall, smashing it before leaving the house. He got on his bike and raced toward Socorro.

◊◊◊

Yanks and his men arrived in Socorro on Highway 60 just as Lizard had suspected they would. Lizard and his boys had already set up in separate places around the drop location. Time Bomb called Lizard, letting him know that they were set up behind Yanks on 60. "We are about a mile from Yanks and his boys with their pickups."

Dog Killer spied things out for Time Bomb. "Looks like there are about four pickups with three to four men in each pickup," he relayed to Lizard.

"What are they packing, can you tell?" Lizard asked.

"Dog Killer says semi-autos."

"Okay, we need to separate all of the trucks. I think two of the trucks will probably follow High Roller to the drop location. I want you guys to take out at least one of the pickups if you can. I'm sure that one will fall back and make contact with the rest of Yanks' men on Highway 60 once High Roller leaves on Highway 95 instead of 60. We will take out the one that goes after High Roller. Dirty Jack will take half of us here in town and follow the one that falls back."

Time Bomb nodded. "Okay, Lizard. We'll take care of it."

Lizard and his men waited patiently for High Roller to roll into town and make contact with the cartel's men. Just as Lizard had suspected, Yanks sent two of his trucks of men in behind High Roller. It wasn't too hard to follow Yanks' men; they did very little to avoid detection. High Roller and his men met the cartel in a little bar. High Roller took his time in the bar, drinking a few beers with the cartel men. Lizard watched Yanks' men as they waited for High Roller to leave the bar.

Dog Killer and the other LA Bad Boys waited until the first two trucks left to follow High Roller. Once they had the first two pickups out of the way, Time Bomb, along with several of the other gang members, spied on the other two pickups. One group was busy talking and examining their weapons, and the other men had been distracted by some pretty young girls. Time Bomb decided the ogling men would be easiest to take out. He instructed his men to ditch their bikes and pretend they were drunks looking for girls. The gang members did as they were instructed while several of the members came in behind the pickup.

Walking unsteadily as if intoxicated, the gang members crossed into the path of the young girls that Yanks' men had been checking out. "Hey baby, want to hook up with a real man?"

Yanks' men were furious with the intruders. "Look, assholes, they don't want your old asses!"

The girls ran off. Before Yanks' men knew what had hit them, Time Bomb and his men slit the throats of the two men nearest the pickup. One shot in the head each was saved for the remaining two men. Time Bomb quickly had the two who'd been shot dragged by their feet into some nearby trees. The two near the pickup were placed in the bed. One of the gang members, Naked Boy, was given the assignment of driving the pickup out of town and abandoning it in the forest.

After hiding the truck, Naked Boy got a ride with Malt to the highway. To everyone's surprise, Bullets suddenly appeared out of nowhere. The bikers stopped along the road to make contact with their leader. Bullets parked his bike. After getting off, he leaned on the seat rubbing at this face and puffing on a cigarette waiting for his members to explain their actions. "So, I see things are going according to Lizard's plan."

"We thought you were going to stay at the brothel."

Bullets threw his half-smoked cigarette to the ground. "So I was told."

Bullets decided to let his men off the hook. "It's cool, men. Go and finish what you have to do. I'll wait here and see what Lizard has to say for himself."

They took off on their motorcycles toward the other members. The closer they got to town, sounds of erratic gunfire alerted them to get ready for battle.

Lizard had decided that he was going to switch places with Dirty Dog. Bullets would probably be rolling into Socorro soon and he wanted to take care of him before he blew the whole operation. He called Dirty Dog on the phone, "I think I'd better take the other truck. Yanks is in that truck and I want to make sure he goes down."

"Okay, Lizard. High Roller and my squad will take care of our truck and then come in behind you to clean up the rest."

Lizard came alive as he watched High Roller and his friends leave the bar and mount their bikes. "Sounds good, brother, 'cause High Roller just left the bar. It's rock and roll time."

As soon as High Roller and his friends headed toward Highway 95 the two pickups split off from each other just as Lizard expected. Lizard and his squad moved in behind the pickup that Yanks was in. Yanks and his men finally realized that they were being followed and quickly tried to lose their tail. Lizard and his men didn't give into the maneuvers of the pickup. Yanks ordered the men in the back of the pickup to start firing at the bikers. With bullets flying, Lizard and his men took evasive action, taking side streets but still maintaining a visual of their prey.

Yanks didn't have the time to make contact with his other drivers. He soon realized that he had made a terrible mistake in setting up his ambush against Bullets. "Damn it!" He ordered his driver to find the other trucks and prepare for a gun battle. He looked over his weapons and prepared for a fight. "Shit, those bastards apparently found out we were coming for them. I'll bet it was Pig. Find James and Alex now. We're gonna have to face them head on."

"We have better weapons, right boss?"

Yanks nodded and watched the side roads for the bikers. "Right."

Before they could stop the pickup, Yanks found himself in the scopes of several of Bullets' gang members. Bullets' men had lined up in the road with their guns aimed straight at the speeding pickup. It took Lizard and the other members only a few seconds to empty their guns into the pickup and men coming at them. Just as the pickup was about to hit the gang members in the street, it swerved to the left, running head-on into a patch of pine trees.

Yanks' driver had taken a bullet in his face and lost control of the pickup. The impact of the crash threw both men who were standing in the back of the pickup over the cab and into the trees. Yanks' body was trapped in the pickup by the impact that had pushed the engine into his chest. The LA Bad Boy members reached the crash site. They found the driver dead with Yanks pinned in and bleeding to death in the passenger seat. One of the men from the back of the pickup was lying dead on the ground. The other man had been thrown into a tree with such force that a branch had gone through his body.

Lizard shot Yanks in the head before leaving the scene. "You guys make sure these assholes are dead. I'm going to go help High Roller and the rest get rid of that truck of men on 95. Finish up here and go help Time Bomb get rid of the pickups that are still on this end of town. Lizard had no plans of backing up Dirty Dog and High Roller. Lizard had to find Bullets before the battle was complete and take him out.

Avoiding contact with the pickup that was parked but now on high alert because of the sounds of gunfire, Lizard found his way to his men. Lizard parked his bike and made contact. "We already took out four of them and got rid of the bodies and pickup," Time Bomb said.

"Looks like they are trying to make contact with Yanks but that won't be happening."

Lizard reloaded his gun while walking back to his bike. "You guys take care of these four. I'm going back over to the other side to make sure Dirty Dog and High Roller don't have any problems with the last four."

Before Lizard could leave, Malt confronted him about Bullets. "Hey Lizard, when Naked Boy and I came out of the forest after getting rid of the pickup Bullets was coming toward town. We pulled over and talked to him and he stayed there. He didn't even know why we left him at the whorehouse. He was pretty mad and said he would discuss it with you when we finish."

"Really? He's here? Why didn't he come help us?"

Malt shrugged. "Don't know."

Lizard finished loading his gun and put it in his belt. "Doesn't matter right now. I have to get back to Dirty Dog and the other members. Where did you leave Bullets?"

Malt described where they had left Bullets along Highway 60.

Lizard started his bike. "I'm sure he'll be okay there until we get done here. I'll talk to him and explain it was for his safety. Don't worry about Bullets; he'll be fine. Help Time Bomb get rid of these jokers."

Malt moved back toward the other members as Lizard spun out on his bike.

Lizard headed in the direction of Dirty Dog, but when he was out of sight of the other members, he doubled back heading toward Bullets. Rolling down Highway 60 Lizard was surprised to find Bullets' bike parked along the highway but Bullets nowhere around. Lizard didn't trust Bullets so he rolled on past the bike.

Down the road about a mile, Lizard found a clearing. He parked his bike and walked into the wooded area on the side that Bullets' bike had been parked. He walked back toward the parked bike under the cover of the trees. There, Lizard found Bullets propped up against a tree in the woods.

Bullets waved his gun loosely at Lizard. "Have a seat, Lizard. I think we need to have a little talk." The sight of some white powdery substance on Bullets' nose let Lizard know that Bullets was stoned.

"What's there to talk about, Bullets?"

"Oh come on, Lizard, we are brothers. We have a lot to talk about. Why did you ride by me and walk back here? Yeah, I saw you go by." Bullets waved his gun again but remained seated.

Lizard decided to indulge Bullets for a few minutes while he figured out how he was going to take Bullets out without a fight. "Well, I didn't see you so I thought I would see if I could find you down the road a ways. When I didn't see you on the highway I figured you might be in the woods."

Bullets laughed. "Very good, Lizard, you passed the leadership lie test."

"Test?"

Bullets tried to get to his feet but he stumbled and fell back to his seated position laughing. "Oh come on, Lizard, time to be honest. Between brothers, you left me in the whorehouse, knowing that I would be pissed and come after you. Well, here I am. What now, brother? What you gonna do with me now? I knew the minute you rode by on your bike you were coming for me. I have known for a while my time as leader of this gang was coming to an end, but I never thought you would be the one to take me out. How are you going to explain my disappearance to the others?"

Lizard took his gun out of his belt and put one shot into Bullets head.

Blood gushed from Bullets' head and his gun fell to his lap from the hand he had been holding it with only moments earlier. He was nothing more than an empty body exposed to the elements of a quiet and silent forest.

Lizard went to Bullets' body and closed his eyes. He took the club medallion that hung around his neck. Then he went to the highway and rolled Bullets' bike into the woods. He hid it as far back into the woods as he could before returning to his own bike. He had no idea what he would say to the men—probably nothing. He rode fast and hard toward the area where his men were fighting against Yank's boys.

Once he reached the area where the gang members had been battling with the militants, Lizard took side roads so it appeared that he was coming from the other end of the battle. Sirens were blaring now and the gang members had picked up their bikes and were hauling ass out of the area. Lizard caught up with the riders and pulled up at the rear of the posse, moving fast down Highway 60. No one questioned Lizard's appearance.

Lizard called Dirty Dog. "Hey Dirty Dog, everything okay with you guys?"

"Yep, we took Yanks' men down. We would have come and helped you guys, but the cops were screaming toward us and we had to get out of there."

"No problem. See you guys in Phoenix."

◊◊◊

In Dunn, North Carolina, Shelby and Angelica waited for the warehouse watchman to open the gate. It took several minutes before the watchman would let the two women drivers into the facility. It was early in the morning and both were exhausted. Shelby keyed her radio. "I'm so tired. I wish they would hurry up."

"Yeah, me too. Shouldn't be too long now. I see the guard coming."

The watchman finally approached Angelica's truck. "I need you ladies to pull right over there by those trailers. Two men will be there waiting for you. They will dolly down your trailers. Once they dolly you down they will have you pick up one of the empty trailers parked there. Listen to them and they will tell you what to do."

Angelica relayed the information from the guard to Shelby.

"Follow me to those stacked trailers to the left. Once we get there, two guys are gonna park us and then dolly our trailers down. Don't get out of your truck, just watch your spotter and do what he tells you. We are getting rid of these trailers and picking up two new ones for our loads in New York. Shouldn't take too long and we will be on our way to the truck stop and some rest."

Inside the yard, two men met the women near the stacked trailers and did exactly what the guard had said they would do. Shelby was surprised this time that none of the workers were strapped with weapons. "Wow, no guns."

Angelica held her tongue. "Yeah, that's good." She'd spotted several stealthy gunmen scattered around the yard. Angelica knew every location she'd been sent to while employed with PIGT was fully equipped with armed men and surveillance equipment. This one was no different except for the two yard workers who apparently had put their guns away in order to make the load transfer easier.

Once the women had their loads dropped and were backing into their new trailers, Shelby felt a little less suspicious about Pig's company. This warehouse seemed fairly normal. She still didn't like not knowing what was in her cargo, but she was too tired to care. *Angelica's right. I just needed to relax and enjoy the job. Still, I want to know more about this company.*

◊◊◊

Lethal had made it to his next stop and was ready to crash. He'd stopped a couple of times and made calls to Lizard, but Lizard had not responded. He hoped they hadn't been ambushed by Yanks. He pulled into the truck stop and then went into the restroom to try Lizard again.

"You got Lizard."

Lethal quickly checked under the stalls. "Hey Lizard. How'd it go in New Mexico?"

Lizard wanted to give Lethal the good news about Bullets, but thought it best to not say anything for a while. "We took care of it, Lethal, nice and clean. Yanks and his men won't be going home tonight. Doubt the cops even got wind of what went down."

"Good. What about Bullets? What'd he fuck up?"

"Nothing. He actually stayed out of the way and let me run the plan."

"Really? That isn't like him. At least you took care of that pain in the ass. Next we need to figure out what to do about Rat Hole. I think I know where he is and I want us to get him before Pig does."

"Where do you think he's at? Do you want me to send some members to take care of him?"

"My guess is he's in Indiana with some family."

"You sure? That's halfway across the fucking country."

"I know…" Two men came into the restroom. "Look, I gotta go. I'll call ya tomorrow."

Lizard hung up, pissed. "Shit, just got rid of one fucking drug head and now I have to get rid of another. When are these guys gonna learn to sell the product, not use it?"

◊◊◊

Although Jazz and Drake got jobs at Pig's estate as security guards and enjoyed the associated perks, they remained loyal to their gang. It had been difficult to get access to the command center, but they had managed to scope out a good portion of the estate in the short time they had been employed and even took pictures with their cell phones. Their objective was to blow up the command center and they needed to devise a plan. They hoped they'd get a chance to talk during their outside guard shift.

Drake said, "They keep that thing locked up tight and guarded 24/7."

"I heard some talk about the company's annual ball, attendance is supposedly mandatory," Jazz said.

"When is that supposed to go down?"

"In about a month."

"Well, somebody's got to be on guard duty. They probably exclude the newest employees; nothing was said about it in orientation."

"I wonder if there is a way to request being assigned to the command center without making them suspicious?"

"Let me check it out," Drake said.

◊◊◊

Lizard and his gang met up in the bar in Apache Junction that High Roller had suggested. The place was packed when they arrived, but as soon as the bikers rolled up, most of the locals took their women and left the bar.

Lizard ordered a beer at the bar and the others gathered around him and followed suit.

Dirty Dog lifted his beer in the air. "We did great today, my brothers. Here's to Yanks and his men, may they rest in hell."

The others cheered in response.

Time Bomb noticed that Lizard had not joined in the toast. "What's up, Lizard? The way you took out Yanks and his boys was mind-blowing. Bullets is gonna be proud of the way you handled things."

"Thanks. It's been quite a day. Guess I'm not as young as I used to be."

Time Bomb patted his friend's back. "I understand, brother." He turned and yelled, "Anyone of you bastards seen our leader? Is he at the whorehouse?"

"Me and Naked Boy saw him outside Socorro when we were headed back from dumping that truck," Shanks said. "Guess he could be back with the whores."

"Well, if that bastard was near Socorro and didn't help us he'd better have a damn good reason," Lizard sneered. "I didn't see him anywhere after we left and rolled down 60. Did any of you guys see him on 95?"

The bar buzzed with comment. No one had seen Bullets on the highways.

Lizard felt the medallion in his pocket. The gang members' responses made it apparent that he could never let on that he'd killed Bullets. "I guess I'll go check the whorehouse and see if Bullets wandered back to his women," Lizard said. "I need to find a bed and get some rest anyway. We got to get back to LA tomorrow."

As Lizard made his way out of the bar, Time Bomb could tell that something was bothering Lizard.

◊◊◊

The morning snuck into Shelby's truck too soon. She threw back the covers and sat up on the edge of her bed. It was pitch black in her sleeper. Shelby pulled at the leather curtains, causing the snaps to give way. She stood up and looked at herself in the mirror before sliding into her driver's seat. It was still dark inside her cab as her side windows and windshield covered with another set of cloth curtains.

She sat in her driver's seat, grabbed her hairbrush, and brushed her blonde hair. She was up two hours before her alarm was to sound, but she couldn't force herself to go back to sleep. She got up, went to her closet, picked out clothes for the day, and then grabbed her shower bag, keys, and some money for breakfast.

Shelby stepped outside and took in several deep breaths of the cool diesel-tainted air. The sky was a light bluish-grey to the east and a darker blue-grey to the west. Shelby surveyed her surroundings. Angelica's truck was humming quietly from the generator next to her own truck. Several more trucks lined the parking lot, all idling in the stillness of the morning. She walked toward the truck stop store.

Shelby hated entering a store with her pajamas on, but she was determined not to change clothes in her truck. She still felt as if someone was watching her constantly. She showed the clerk her fuel ticket from the night before and got a key to the showers.

◊◊◊

Lizard turned over with a shuttering jerk, sat up straight and wiped the back of his hand across his face. He had paid for a room in the whorehouse, but passed on having a girl join him. His mouth felt dry from too many beers. His head pounded with the same thought: *How am I going to explain Bullets' death?* The medallion was heavy in his pocket. He got out of bed and dressed.

When he entered the main room of the brothel, he saw several of his gang sprawled out on chairs, beds, and couches with different women. The madam of the house intercepted Lizard just as he was about to turn the knob on the front door. "Who's paying for the favors, big boy?"

Lizard reached into his pocket and pulled out a roll of bills. Club money Bullets had given him to cover expenses for his assignment. He handed the women several hundred-dollar bills, moved past her, and walked out the door.

She leaned against the door frame with her sheer robe exposing her assets. "Your business is greatly appreciated," she yelled after him.

Lizard stopped and turned. "Wake up those lazy ass bikers and tell them to get out. I need them back in LA by tonight."

◊◊◊

Angelica stretched as she got out of her sleeper. It was time to check in with Rex. She couldn't wait to hear his voice. She gathered her things and stuffed her personal phone in her pocket. Just as she hit the ground Shelby came towards her. "Hey girl, I just finished my shower. Want to get some breakfast?"

"Sure, but I'm gonna take a quick shower and make a phone call or two. I'll meet you over at that diner in about forty-five minutes?" she said, pointing across the street from the parking lot.

"That'll work. I need to finish my makeup and put my stuff away. I'll get us a table and some coffee."

"Order me two eggs and some sausage. Over easy."

"You got it."

Angelica stepped into her assigned shower and phoned Rex.

"Hey sugar, how you doing?" he answered.

Angelica felt a flash of warmth rush over her body. "I'm doing good, Mr. Handler. How are you? Do you miss me?"

"You know I do, but you also know that this is a secured line and every thing we say is being taped and monitored."

"Yeah, I know…professionalism," she relented.

"How are things?"

Angelica put Rex on speaker while she got ready to take a shower. "Okay. We got to Dunn and after breakfast we are headed to Harrisburg to meet up with a new driver. They're using several different types of warehouses to store their goods. Some are heavily secured and others are monitored by security systems. Pig seems to know how much to keep out in the open and how much to keep hidden."

"It's a smart strategy, but if he is leaving something vulnerable we'll figure it out. How's Shelby? Is she still asking questions?"

"She's still curious, but I don't blame her after what she's been through."

"I read her case, but you still need to be careful and know how she is going to react before you tell her anything."

"I'll take it slow. I'll see what happens when we get to Vegas. I'm sure we are going to be sent back toward Mexico to pick up product after that. I'll let you know once we get the details."

"I gotta go, Sweet Pea. I have another agent calling in. Be careful out there."

CHAPTER SIXTEEN

Shelby found an empty table near the door of the dive. She brushed away crumbs left on the seat before sitting down and avoided contact with the wet, sticky table. The musty, stale smells were soon replaced with the aroma of fresh bacon and coffee brewing, which made her stomach growl. A little round waitress with a stained white apron smiled boldly as she placed a menu in front of Shelby. "Hi sweetie, what can I get for you to drink?"

"I'll have coffee and a rag to clean this table."

"Sure, I'll be right back with that. Sorry about the table. I guess it got missed after the early morning rush."

A few seconds later, the waitress returned with a rag and a cup of coffee. She stuffed the wet rag into her apron pocket and took out a pad and pen from the other pocket. "Do you know what you would like or would you like a few minutes?"

"Let me finish this cup of coffee and then I'll order."

"Okay, sweetie, no problem."

Just then, Angelica slid into the booth across from her. "Good morning."

"What can I get you to drink?" the waitress asked.

"Coffee, with milk and sugar."

When the waitress left, Shelby said, "Good morning, sunshine."

The waitress came back with the coffee, a small pitcher of milk and sugar packets. "Are you ready to order?"

They placed their orders and made small talk as they waited for their food.

After their plates arrived and their coffee cups were topped off, the waitress turned her attention to other customers. Angelica took a bite of her food and then asked, "So, you ready to meet one of our new drivers?"

Shelby shrugged. "Yeah, I guess. Aren't we meeting up with him in Pennsylvania somewhere?"

"Yes, Harrisburg. It's gonna be a long ride today. Once we meet up with the driver we're headed for another early morning pickup."

"Look, I know you've told me to just do my job and mind my business, but the way things are done here just aren't normal. It worries me that I may be doing something illegal. I don't want to get into trouble and lose my license."

Angelica chose her words carefully, "You're right. I do find some of the things we do questionable. If I tell you what I know, promise me that you won't cut and run."

"Cut and run? What does that mean? I'm not looking for trouble."

"I'm not telling you anything unless you promise me that you're not going to empty your truck and leave. Doing that would put me in danger. I need someone else inside who I can trust. I'm hoping that person is you because if it's not, I've just opened myself up to getting killed."

Shelby sat there, stunned. She looked around the diner, it was filling up and the waitress was occupied with other diners.

Angelica held her cup close to her lips and spoke quietly across the cup. "Shelby, I'm going to let you in on what I'm really doing here."

"What do you mean by that?"

"First, I need you to promise me you'll stay on the job." she put down the cup and started to eat as Shelby thought about what she'd just been told.

"What if after what you're about to tell me I can't keep the promise?"

"Then I can't tell you anything and I'll just have to take my chances that you won't get me killed."

"This is nuts. This sounds like some spy…wait…"

Angelica raised an eyebrow and drank some more coffee. She put down her cup, put her plate to the side, and folded her hands together under her chin, with both elbows on the table. "First, promise you won't tell anyone or leave."

"Okay, if you promise to tell me the truth."

The women shook hands.

"My name really is Angelica, and I do drive trucks. I'm an undercover DEA agent. We are investigating Pig for narcotics, guns, stolen goods, and human trafficking. My job is not to bust him, but to build an airtight case against him and bring down as many of his co-conspirators as possible with him when he does fall."

Shelby couldn't believe she was involved in more drama—spy drama. "Oh God, I think I'm gonna vomit." Shelby slid out of her seat and went to the restaurant restroom.

Angelica signaled to the waitress for their check. The woman came over and Angelica handed her a twenty-dollar bill, and said, "When my friend finishes in the restroom let her know I'll be at our trucks waiting for her."

As Angelica walked across the parking lot, she hoped her assessment of Shelby was correct. She wished she could talk to Rex for assurance.

Shelby was by her side a few minutes later. "I'll keep your secret and I won't run, but I'm scared. Especially after everything that happened to me with Betty Burton."

"I understand, and I'll let you know more as time goes on. I appreciate you having enough faith in me to stick it out and keep quiet. I won't ask you to do anything that will put you in danger. My job is to collect intelligence. Just letting me know if you hear or see anything will be help enough. I'll protect you, I promise. If I think Pig is becoming suspicious, I'll have the agency pull us out."

"Okay."

"Thanks for trusting me. It's going to be okay."

"My track record isn't that great for staying out of trouble but I'll trust you, Angelica. Jack and my boys will never let me drive another truck if something happens."

"Understood. I'll get with you on the radio in a minute. We need to get to Harrisburg if we're gonna make that meet with the new driver."

"Got it. Let me do a quick pre-trip and we will head out. Oh yeah, thanks for breakfast. I owe you."

◊◊◊

"Guess Bullets hightailed it to LA?" Spider said at breakfast.

"Probably. He's not answering his phone. He's probably mad we did the job without him," Lizard said.

"Still, this isn't like Bullets. I think something might be wrong. You know Malt and Naked Boy did see him near Socorro."

"If they saw him there, how come he didn't come on into town and help us?"

"It's just not like Bullets not to help out," Time Bomb said, "even if he was pissed about being left at the whorehouse. Do ya think maybe something happened to him? Maybe a couple of us should go back that way and check things out."

"Not a good idea, my brothers," Shanks said. "The cops are going to be all over that place. We don't want them looking at us, do we? Some other business must have come up and he's back at the club."

"You're right about laying low, but why isn't he answering his cell phone?" Time Bomb insisted. "Where the hell is he? Malt and Naked Boy said he looked strung out. I hope he didn't get nailed by the cops."

Lizard interrupted the conversation, "Well, I don't know about the rest of you guys, but I'm headed back to LA. I'm sure Bullets is there or he'll make contact with us soon."

"Yeah, Lizard's right. I'm heading back to LA, too," Time Bomb decided. "Bullets will either be waiting in LA pissed as hell or let us know where he's at."

Lizard walked out of the restaurant. Those who were coming could follow him. He wasn't going to say another word about Bullets. Just as Lizard reached his bike his phone rang.

"Hey man, have you sent any of the guys to check out Rat Hole yet?" Lethal asked.

"Not yet, Lethal, we just finished that job in Socorro and Bullets is missing. We are headed back to LA but I'll send two guys out now. Several of them are still in Phoenix so I'll have Spider and Trigger leave from there. I suppose we should bring him back to LA."

"Yeah, but you guys better hurry because Pig's men are hunting him down. I'm also going to have trouble contacting you for a while because they're putting me with two other drivers. I just hope you guys get to him before Pig does."

"We'll try, Lethal." He ended the call and called Spider. "Spider, this is Lizard. Lethal just called me. He hasn't been able to get a hold of Bullets so he needs a couple of us to go to Rat Hole's family house in Indiana and pull him back to LA. Apparently he has fallen off the speed wagon and Pig is looking for him over some drugs he lifted. I'd go, but I'm already on my way back to LA. Do you think you can grab Trigger, go round that tweaker's ass up, and drag him back before he gets himself killed?"

"Oh shit, yes. I'll get Trigger and go find the bastard."

"Thanks. Give me a call when you have him." Lizard put his phone in his pocket and continued his ride toward LA, determined to keep the gang together.

◊◊◊

Shelby and Angelica were on their way to Harrisburg with a sense of camaraderie.

Shelby had an idea and got on the radio. "Hey, I've got an idea about a handle for you. How about we call you Cover Girl?"

There was silence.

Shelby repeated the call. "How about Cover Girl?"

Still no response.

"That's for you Angelica. This is Barbie."

"How'd you come up with that handle?"

"I chose it because you're as pretty as a magazine cover girl."

"Thanks, Barbie. I like it."

"Thanks, partner. I think it fits you real nice. Now we need to get to Harrisburg and check out the new driver."

"Yes we do, and we need to haul so we can make our appointment time in Johnson City, New York. Pig doesn't like us to be late for pickups or deliveries."

"I know, and I sure don't want to miss out on our trip to Vegas."

"I can't wait. If I know Pig, it's going to be over the top."

"I sure hope so."

◊◊◊

Pig had been monitoring Shelby and her truck for a few hours. An unusual slight smile crossed his face when he heard that Shelby was looking forward to her time off in Vegas. He quickly shut his computer and called Hank. "Is everything ready for this weekend in Vegas?"

"Yes, sir. Flowers, champagne, and the best suites in Vegas."

"Good. I'll be leaving today. Have my jet ready."

"Yes, sir. Any specific time?"

"Two hours. Have those two new guards ready to fly with me as well. I think I want to get to know them a little better."

"Very well, sir. I'll have Drake and Jazz waiting for you. Should I notify Harry for you?"

"No, I'll call him myself." Pig hung up before Hank could finish and redialed. "Harry, be ready to leave for Vegas in two hours. I have some shopping to do there. The drivers are supposed to arrive early evening on Friday. I want to make sure everything is just right."

Three hours later, Pig and Harry arrived in Las Vegas along with the two new security guards. Harry unpacked his boss' bags while Pig and his two bodyguards went shopping. Pig's first stop was the Forum in Caesars Palace. He went to the dress shops, shoe stores, and jewelry stores, sending a wide variety of each item to Shelby and Angelica's rooms, keeping his interest in Shelby camouflaged. Pig made reservations for dinner at Rao's. He also made arrangements for the drivers to have a few thousand dollars of spending money for gambling and tickets for any shows they chose to see. Pig contacted a rare book collector and made arrangements to have several interesting books sent to Shelby's room wrapped in fine wrapping paper.

◊◊◊

Lethal had made his destination and found out from dispatch that the other two co-drivers would be arriving within an hour. He was nervous, not knowing who might be watching him. He hadn't met either of the drivers that he was going to be rolling with, but he knew they were female. He had no idea how close they were to Pig so he'd have to be careful. Drake had called him back while he was on his last break. He wasn't able to pass along much information except that he and Jazz would be joining Pig in Vegas. Lethal hoped he would be able to make a connection with them there. He was curious whether Pig had located Rat Hole and wanted to know about their plans for the takeover of PIGT. Lethal had not been able to reach Bullets, which didn't bother him, but he was nervous about being left out of the loop. Lizard had assured him he would keep him posted.

◊◊◊

Angelica and Shelby had made contact with the new driver. They had been driving hard and were about to pull into the Pilot Truck Stop in Harrisburg. "Well, let's see if we can find our co-driver in this mess of trucks. You check out the line while I check out the fuel island."

Shelby spotted the PIGT truck. "I got it here on the line, Cover Girl."

At first, Angelica didn't recognize her handle. After a few seconds, she responded. "Good. Is he in the truck?"

Shelby had already gotten out of her truck and was talking to Lethal.

Lethal noticed the PIGT truck parked in front of him. Shortly after noticing the truck, he heard a knock on his driver's side door.

"Hey, I'm Shelby from PIGT. Are you Lethal, the driver we are supposed to be hooking up with today?"

Lethal was surprised to see such a pretty woman truck driver. "Yes, I'm Lethal."

Shelby got down off his step and waved for him to follow her. "Great, head to the fuel island with me and we'll meet up with Angelica, the other driver going with us to Vegas."

Two beautiful women. What luck! He saw Shelby's wedding ring, but still felt optimistic. *She might still be up for a good time*, he hoped. "Sure, be right behind you, sweet cheeks." Lethal maneuvered his truck in behind Shelby's.

Shelby got on the radio. "Hey Cover Girl, I got our little-lost ram over here. We're headed to the fuel island."

"Great, Barbie. I'm fueling now too. Make sure the ram gets everything he needs before we leave. It's gonna be close making our pickup time."

"10-4, Cover Girl."

After putting fuel hoses in her truck and washing her windshield, Shelby found Angelica fueling her truck. "Hey Cover Girl, you about ready to go?"

Angelica replaced her fuel hoses and took off her gloves. "Yeah, I think I'm about ready. Need to go in and get my fuel ticket, use the restroom, and get a few things. What about the new guy?"

Before Shelby answered, Lethal appeared and interjected, "The new guy is ready whenever you two beautiful ladies are ready." Lethal shook hands with Angelica and Shelby. "They call me Lethal, but little Barbie here seems to have given me a new handle—The Ram. I think I like it."

"Well, let's move these trucks and get our tickets. We just have a few hours before we need to be in Johnson City to pick up our loads."

Shelby walked away with Lethal while Angelica climbed into her truck. "Vegas, here we come. Yee-haw!"

◊◊◊

Shortly after Lizard arrived at the clubhouse, Bullets' wife drove up in her SUV, got out, and demanded to know where her husband was. "Where is Bullets? I've been trying to call him for two days now and he won't answer his phone." She pulled at Lizard's arm. "Nothing happened to him. Right, Lizard? Where's my Bullets?"

"Look, Lori, I don't know where Bullets is. We've been looking for him too. We got separated outside of Phoenix. We've been trying to call him. Most of us figured he just came on back to the clubhouse. But if he's not with you… and he's not here…it's hard to tell. He might have had business with someone and couldn't keep his cell phone turned on, or maybe it died."

"Right, the leader of this huge biker gang just up and disappears and none of you guys know anything about where he is? This is bullshit, Lizard. Bullets told me something was going on with you guys in the club. That some of you wanted him out. I told him he was paranoid. Now I'm beginning to believe he was right. WHERE THE FUCK IS MY HUSBAND, LIZARD?" Lori moved toward him and began beating on his chest. "WHERE IS HE?"

Lizard took Lori by the wrist and gathered her tight in his arms. "We are looking for him, Lori. He's out there, he's okay. We've just got to find him." It took a little while to calm Lori down and convince her to go home. Lizard wondered how the hell he was going to keep how Bullets really got killed to himself. Before too long, either his club members or the cops would find Bullets' body. He decided he needed to go home and take a shower and drink a couple of beers. *This isn't going to be easy, but my survival depends on me being able to lie really well.*

◊◊◊

Shelby, Angelica, and Lethal pulled into Johnson City, New York around 7:30 p.m. and found the warehouse in a rundown part of the city. They agreed to meet at the TA in Binghamton once they were loaded.

The warehouse was completely dark except for the spotlights that suddenly illuminated the area when the trucks pulled up to the gate. A guard came out of the guard shack and took down the truck numbers of each truck before allowing them to pass through into the yard. Once inside the yard, several men approached Angelica's truck and pointed toward the dock area.

As they drove into the yard to collect their loads, Shelby wondered, *What kind of intelligence is Angelica going to get from this place?*

It took a couple of hours for the yardmen to load the three trucks. As usual, the drivers were not permitted to get out of their trucks. Shelby got on the radio, "Angelica, do you have any idea what is taking them so long? I really have to pee."

Angelica laughed. "Have to hold it, girl, they should finish soon."

She knew just couldn't wait any longer and when they got ready to leave she convinced the guard of her predicament and he gladly let her use the bathroom in the guardhouse.

At one in the morning the three finally made their way to Binghamton.

◊◊◊

The phone rang, waking Lizard from a sound sleep. "What the fuck?"

Lizard reached for his cell phone and sat up in bed, causing his live-in girlfriend to complain. "Damn, Lizard, it's three o'clock in the morning. Can't that bastard Bullets wait? You just got home!" She turned over and covered her head with the blankets.

Lizard listened to Time Bomb. "What?... You're kidding... Where?... Damn it…. Yeah, I'll be there in a few minutes. Are the cops still there?... Don't let her say anything to the cops…. No, she can't tell them anything about where Bullets was going. If she does, it will implicate all of us in that shit that went down there. Just tell the bastards to get out of her house…. Yeah, I'm on my way."

Lizard's girl rolled over. "Everything okay, baby?"

Lizard pulled on his clothes and boots. "No, all hell is breaking loose. Sit tight and I'll call you later."

Lizard knew he had to get to Lori and calm her down. The cops had come to her house to let her know that the New Mexico State Police had found her husband, and he had been shot to death. He had no idea what Bullets may have told Lori or let slip about business. It was gang policy to never discuss business with family or girlfriends, but since Bullets was either high or drunk most of the time, it was hard to know what he might have let slip.

Lori had called Time Bomb because he only lived a few blocks from her. She was crazy with grief. When Lizard finally arrived at Bullets' house, Time Bomb was at his limits on what to do with Lori. The cops had left after Time Bomb told them to. Lizard noticed an unmarked cop car with two cops inside down the street from Bullets' house. He quickly dismounted his bike and went straight into the house. Time Bomb was sitting on the couch with Lori.

When Lori saw Lizard, she rushed him screaming and hitting him with her fists. "YOU BASTARD! YOU LIED TO ME! YOU TOLD ME THAT BULLETS WAS OKAY AND THAT YOU WOULD FIND HIM, THAT HE WAS DOING BUSINESS. YOU LIAR!!" Lizard held Lori close and let her cry against his chest. He made eye contact with Time Bomb and tried to pretend he had no idea what was going on. He mouthed the words to Time Bomb. "What happened?" Time Bomb mouthed back. "I'll tell you later."

Several other bikers arrived within the hour. One of the bikers brought some sleeping pills to help Lori relax, and a couple of the bikers' wives had come to help take care of Lori and her kids. Once the other women and the gang members had Lori in her room, the gang was able to discuss what they thought had happened.

Time Bomb opened the conversation. "The cops said someone found Bullets and his bike in the trees outside of Socorro on Highway 60."

Naked Boy popped off. "I told you that we saw him there! One of Yanks' men must've got to Bullets. Man, I told you Bullets was there!"

Dirty Dog said, "I don't know. We had Yanks and his men all tied up in and around Socorro. They found him somewhere closer to that ghost town. Unless there was a straggling group of Yanks' boys coming into Socorro later, but I don't think it was any of Yanks' guys."

Lizard played dumb. "I don't know, guys. What else did the cops say?"

Time Bomb continued with the only specifics that the police had given to them.

Lizard wanted them to think about something else. The less conversation about Bullets, the less chance of anyone really finding out what happened. "I think that for now, we just need to help Lori get through this and get our leader back here. We need to get him buried and then we can concentrate on finding out who did this to Bullets."

Most of the gang members agreed, but Naked Boy couldn't let it go. "I bet it was Pig."

"Maybe, Naked Boy, but let's concentrate on Lori and Bullets until we have some time to really figure things out," Lizard suggested.

◊◊◊

Shelby was in a deep sleep when she heard a knock on her door. She moved her curtain back and spotted Lethal outside her driver's door. She opened the door slowly, still half asleep.

"Hey, good morning, beautiful. I was wondering if you want to have breakfast? Angelica says we need to be on the road soon. I guess Pig wants us in Vegas and unloaded by Friday night."

Shelby stretched and wiped her hands across her face. "Wow, that's cutting it kind of close, isn't it? Pig usually doesn't push things so hard."

"Don't know, but those are the orders from dispatch."

"Okay. I'll be there in a few minutes."

Twenty minutes later, Shelby found her way to the table to join Angelica and Lethal. "Sounds like our boss really wants these loads in Las Vegas in a hurry."

Angelica had just finished her breakfast and was sipping coffee. Lethal was still eating. "Yeah, we've got to make a three and half day haul in three," Angelica said. "I have everything planned out. I think we can do it. Since most of our over hours will be at night, we can doctor our logs a little to help make them legal."

The waitress came to the table. "Can I get you anything?" she asked Shelby.

Shelby pointed at a coffee cup. "Just coffee and dry toast please."

Angelica took out a map and showed Lethal and Shelby the route she had chosen. "We can stop in South Bend, Indiana and then Grand Island, Nebraska for our shut down before we head to Salt Lake. If we think we can make it further, fine, but if we have to shut down, those will be our best places. It's only five hours from Salt Lake City down Highway 15 to Vegas, so we can make that for sure on Friday."

"Let's head to Vegas," Shelby said.

CHAPTER SEVENTEEN

Lizard and the gang members gathered at Lori's house after the funeral. Lori hadn't spoken to Lizard since she learned about the cops finding Bullets' body. Lizard had sat on the patio, drinking a beer away from the other members. It had been hard seeing Bullets in his coffin. His eyes were closed, but Lizard couldn't get Bullets' face out of his mind after he killed him. Bullets' eyes seemed to see right through him.

No one had asked about the medallion until the funeral. It was tradition to let the leader wear the medallion until the body was put in the ground. Lizard had placed the medallion on a shelf in Bullets' house the night he went to see Lori. No one noticed it. Lori finally found it the day of the funeral.

She called Time Bomb about her discovery. "I found Bullets' medallion here at the house. It's real strange, Time Bomb. Bullets never would have left his medallion at home. Especially, not where I found it."

"I know that doesn't sound like Bullets, but how else would it have gotten there?"

"I don't know, but I knew my husband, and he never would have left without his medallion."

"Let it go for now, Lori. The club will work on finding Bullets' killer as soon as things calm down."

"I miss him so much. What is going happen to me and the kids now?"

"Don't cry. You know we take care of our own. Bullets was our leader. The club will always be there for you."

"Okay, Time Bomb. I'll hold you to that."

Lizard stood against the banister on the patio and sipped at his beer, thinking about the things he had already put into motion. Suddenly, the sliding glass doors opened and Lori came out onto the patio. She was dressed in a solid black short skirt and sheer blouse. She sipped at clear liquid from a glass, which was probably vodka. "Well, Lizard you're being extremely anti-social." Lori moved in close to Lizard.

"Look, Liz, I'm sorry about getting mad at you the other day."

She began to cry. "I'm just really scared, I have no idea who I am without Bullets."

Lizard held Lori while she cried and spilled most of her drink all over him.

Malt and a couple other gang members found their way out to the patio. "Sorry to disturb you, Lizard, but some of the guys were thinking we better get to the clubhouse for a meeting. Time Bomb has decided that we need to have a vote tonight."

Lori was outraged. "What the hell! My Bullets isn't even cold in the ground yet and you bastards want to replace him?" Lori stormed back into her house, looking for someone who would at least pretend to care she'd just buried her husband.

Malt spoke out, "Sorry, Lizard. We didn't mean to upset her, but Time Bomb is right. We need to vote in the next leader tonight. A lot of shit's happening and we really can't afford to be without a leader any longer."

Lizard drank the last of his beer. "I know, guys, but don't you think we should wait 'til morning out of respect for Lori?" Lizard moved toward the sliding glass doors and then turned back. "I'll meet you at the clubhouse in the morning. I'm not going to disrespect Lori today. If you think you can, go ahead and name a leader without me. But I'm head lieutenant and you can't change any leadership positions without me, unless of course, you want to kill me."

The gang members knew Lizard was right.

Lizard knew that Time Bomb was the one pushing for a vote because he was just under him. Time Bomb was hoping he could get the other members to vote him into the spot instead of Lizard. Lizard also knew that Lethal was also in position to be the next leader. Lethal wasn't there, but if he was, Lizard would gladly concede to his friend, but he would never concede to Time Bomb.

Shanks decided to follow Lizard into the house. "I don't know about you guys, but we all know who's going to be the next leader. I, for one, am not going to be the first one to piss off the boss. Let's give the rest of this day to Lori and Bullets' memory." Most of the rest of the members out on the patio agreed but opted to stay on the patio.

Lizard found his way into Lori's kitchen and took another beer out of the refrigerator. Time Bomb entered the doorway of the kitchen and leaned against the door frame holding a drink. "So, you decided to make an executive decision."

Lizard took the cap off his beer and threw it in the trashcan. "I didn't make any decisions, Time Bomb. I just told them I wasn't going to the club-house today to vote on anything. Today is Lori's day."

Time Bomb sipped his drink and moved to a chair near the table. "It's Bullets' day, too. Maybe you're glad Bullets is out of the way; maybe you know more about what happened to him than you're, saying Lizard. Lori called me this morning. She found Bullets' medallion right here in the house, on a shelf in the living room."

Lizard leaned against the sink and gulped his beer. "Time Bomb, it seems to me you're the one who's glad Bullets is gone. You're the one wanting to hurry away from his funeral and have a vote."

"Fuck you, Lizard. You know I had nothing to do with Bullets' death. I want the vote over with so we can get on with club business. That still doesn't explain how Bullets' medallion ended up in his house."

"Look, Time Bomb, I have no idea about the medallion. Maybe Bullets just forgot it the last time he left the house. He was drunk and high most of the time lately. It's hard to tell why it was here, but we can be glad it was here and not on him. Someone might have stolen it or the cops might have kept it. Then we wouldn't have it at all."

Time Bomb knew Lizard and Lethal hated Bullets and that they both were working to get him out, but he had no solid proof. He knew Lizard was going to be the next leader, which irked him. He sipped at his drink. "Fine. I guess waiting until tomorrow won't hurt anything. I still think there is more to Bullets' death, and I'm not going to stop 'til I know for sure what happened."

Lizard took another sip and toasted toward Time Bomb. "I plan to do the same, brother. We owe it to Bullets and Lori."

◊◊◊

The trip to Las Vegas was long and hard, but the three drivers made it to the destination warehouse in three days. Angelica pulled up to the security gate and a guard instructed her to lead the trucks to a parking lot on the right. "Park your trucks together over there in that parking lot and wait. There will be someone over there in a few minutes to tell you what to do next."

Angelica got on the radio. "Okay, partners, the man wants us to park over here in the parking lot and wait."

Shelby was surprised that they were going to make a delivery during the day. She was glad they'd made it to Vegas and was sure excited about getting to spend a few days enjoying the sites. "I hope they don't spend all evening deciding what they are going to do with our loads."

Lethal agreed. "I am sure looking forward to a cold beer and some fun."

The three drivers got out of their trucks and congregated in front of Angelica's truck.

"I hope we don't get into trouble by getting out of our trucks," Shelby said.

"I don't think we are breaking policy," Angelica said, hoping Shelby wouldn't comment any further. "The guard didn't tell me that we needed to stay in the trucks."

Shelby didn't pick up on her tone and said, "I wonder if they expect us to drive our trucks to the hotel?"

Just as Shelby spoke those words, an SUV with four men and a large black limo pulled up behind them. Angelica, Lethal, and Shelby looked at the vehicles in front of them, surprised.

"Guess not," Shelby said.

The four men left the SUV and walked toward the three drivers. The limo driver got out of the driver's seat. He walked to the back of the limo and opened the rear door. Then he stood by the door waiting for his passengers. The driver of the SUV approached the drivers and pointed toward the trucks. "These men will take care of your trucks. Pig has sent the limo to take you to the hotel."

Shelby and Angelica both went toward their trucks. "We need to get some personal items from our trucks," Angelica explained.

"Me too," Lethal said.

"No need for any personal items. Mr. Pig has provided everything you could possibly need for your weekend stay in Las Vegas."

Angelica spoke out again. "I'm sure he has, but I need my purse at least."

"Me too," Shelby said.

Lethal just wanted to make sure he had his phones.

"Very well." Reluctantly, he let them get what they needed from their trucks.

Inside the limo, Shelby and Angelica sat in one seat while Lethal sat across from them. The limo bar was well stocked with beverages and snacks. Lethal took no time in helping himself to a beer. "I've been waiting for this all week. You ladies want anything?"

"I'll take a bottle of water," Shelby said.

"Me too," Angelica chimed in.

"You're out of the trucks ladies, you can legally drink now."

Shelby looked around the limo as they moved toward the hotel. "Wow, I haven't been in a limousine since my high school prom. It wasn't even close to this luxury. I sure have received first class service since I've been with PIGT. Is this normal, Angelica?"

Angelica shrugged. "This is a little over the top for Pig, but he always been pretty decent to me since I've been here."

Lethal gulped at his beer. "Over the top or not, I could get used to being treated like this." The drivers laughed and talked all the way to the hotel.

Pig and his two bodyguards waited at the hotel for the drivers to arrive. Pig was anxious to see Shelby again and looked forward to spending as much time with her as she would allow.

One of the guards interrupted Pig's thoughts, "Sir, they are within four minutes of the valet parking."

Pig moved his fat body out of the oversized chair. "Very good, let's go down and meet the ladies."

"Welcome to the Caesars Palace," the valet said as he opened the limo's doors.

The three truck drivers exited, wearing blue jeans and t-shirts and carrying small duffle bags. A bellboy took the small bags from the drivers and loaded them on a large luggage carrier. When the limo driver indicated that was the extent of the luggage, he shrugged and pulled the three small bags on the gold luggage carrier into the lobby.

Pig and his bodyguards, Drake and Jazz, were waiting just inside the lobby. Lethal recognized his two club members but did his best not to let on that he even knew who they were. The guards played dumb as well. Pig spoke out as the three passed through the glass front doors. "Welcome to Las Vegas. I hope your trip was safe and pleasant."

Angelica was the first to approach Pig and shake his hand. "Yes, sir, it was fine and we made really good time, just as you asked."

"That's good, Angelica."

Pig shook Angelica's hand and quickly let go to take Shelby's hand. He gently shook her hand and stared into Shelby's face. "Shelby. I'm so glad you made it safe and sound. Are you ready for a wonderful weekend of fun and freedom?"

Shelby shook Pig's hand but tried hard to avoid his stare. She looked around the lobby of the huge hotel with wide eyes. "Oh yes, Mr. Pig. I am definitely excited about this weekend, thank you." Shelby pulled her hand away from Pig's. She did not want to be rude, but she felt a little creepy with her hand in his.

Pig nodded to Lethal but didn't offer his hand. He motioned for his guards to lead and follow the group to the elevators. "Let's get you to your rooms so that you can freshen up before dinner." The group entered the elevator with the bellboy who pulled the luggage carrier. Shelby and the others were well aware of the stench their boss carried with him but none mentioned it. They simply put up with it until the ride was over.

Once the group reached the reserved floor, the bellhop escorted Pig and his guards to his room first. Pig's guards opened his room for him and Shelby noticed that Harry was waiting. "Dinner will be at seven o'clock. I have placed a few nice things for you in your rooms. Enjoy your afternoon and I'll see you at dinner." Pig disappeared into his room. Drake and Jazz stood outside the door as they had been assigned.

The bellhop escorted each driver to their rooms, leaving them with their bags and key cards. Shelby couldn't believe her room when she walked into it. It was lavishly decorated with a separate bedroom, living space, and huge bathroom. The bedroom had a king size bed and dressers made of dark cherry wood. The room was filled with fragrant fresh flowers.

Several beautifully wrapped packages were neatly stacked on Shelby's bed. Shelby opened the boxes one at a time on the bed and was shocked to find very expensive shoes, under clothing, sleepwear, clutch purses, and three priceless necklace and earring sets. The jewelry was definitely not costume, but fine diamonds and gemstones. Shelby opened the closet, which contained several designer cocktail dresses and outfits. Everything was in her exact size and most were colors that she herself would have picked out if she were doing the shopping. "How in the world did Pig know all this about me?"

Shelby checked out the bathroom. Next to a very large shower hung a beautiful bathrobe and slippers. The garden Jacuzzi tub placed in the center of the bathroom was lavishly decorated with fine towels, bath oils, and aromatherapy candles. A double sink was lined with several imported hair salon products, body lotions, tooth care, and facial cleansing needs. The makeup table was well supplied with hairbrushes, hair jewelry, and styling equipment. There was also makeup that Shelby had heard of but had never tried because of the price. "Wow, I can't believe this is all for me."

In the living room area Shelby was greeted with another room dressed with flowers and a huge basket of fruit, chocolates, and fine wine. The bar was stocked with everything imaginable to drink and snack on. Several nicely wrapped gifts rested on the coffee table in front of the sofa. Shelby opened each package and was shocked to find a variety of newly released bestsellers and a couple of finely preserved older additions of books that she dearly admired.

In the coat closet, Shelby located two very expensive furs that were absolutely gorgeous. Shelby took one of the furs and put it on before she sat down on the couch. She liked everything that Mr. Pig had provided for her for the weekend. *This is all too much. I could never keep any of it. I'm not even sure I should wear any of it. What is Pig doing? Why is he being so nice to me? He's a criminal with lots of money who just buys what he wants.* Shelby's thoughts were interrupted by a knock on her door.

She got up, took off the fur, and hung it back in the closet before answering the door. "Hey Angelica, come on in. I was about ready to call you."

Angelica entered Shelby's room and looked around. She helped herself to some grapes as she sat down on the couch. "I see Pig has lavished you with the finer things in life too." Angelica looked over the books that were neatly placed on the coffee table next to the lavish wrapping paper. "I didn't get any of those, but I'm sure Pig had his reason for giving them to you."

Shelby sat down next to Angelica. "What's going on here, Angelica? What is all this? You can't tell me that Pig does this for all of his drivers."

Angelica reached for one of the chilled bottles of wine and took out the cork, which had already been released from the bottle. She poured herself and Shelby each a glass and sat back on the couch. "No, Shelby, he doesn't do this for any other drivers. I'm not sure exactly what Pig has on his mind, but I suspect it has something to do with you."

Shelby sat back on the couch and sipped at her wine. "Me? What the hell does that man want with me? I'm a truck driver. I'm married and I've never given him any reason to think I had any interest in him."

Angelica got up from the sofa, grabbed more grapes, and turned on the stereo.

"What's with the loud music?" Shelby asked.

Angelica put her finger over her mouth. "We have no idea if he is listening to us in this room. I doubt he's watching, but I'm sure he has some kind of listening device going in each room. Never underestimate Pig. He's a pervert and a devious businessman. You are the first woman that I have ever seen Mr. Pig take any kind of interest in."

"Terrific. I don't need or want anything from that fat man."

Angelica laughed. "I know, Shelby, but I suggest you just play along with his ploys. Enjoy the gifts and take advantage of his attempts to woo you.

He's going down soon and if you play your cards right, you might get to take some of his loot with you."

"Right. Jack won't like me taking these kinds of gifts from Pig. He's going to have a cow when I tell him about all this."

Angelica got off the couch and went toward Shelby's bedroom. Shelby followed, wondering what Cover Girl was up to. Angelica opened her closet and looked through the boxes on the bed. "Wow. I didn't get near what you did. Pig must really have it bad for you." Angelica took out a pair of the panties and danced around the room, laughing. Shelby grabbed them and threw them back on the bed.

The women laughed together and fell onto the bed. "Enjoy it, Shelby. Take what he wants to give you. It's not going to last long."

Shelby sat. "Okay, but what do I do if he tries to make a pass or expects some kind of return on his investment? It grosses me out just thinking about that man putting his hands on me."

"Don't worry, Barbie. I'm here and I won't let anything happen, I promise. We'll just stick together and spend lots of money, drink lots of booze, and eat lots and lots of really good food."

Angelica got off the bed and looked at her watch. She downed the last part of her wine before walking toward the door. "That reminds me, we have three hours before we need to meet our fearless leader for dinner. I'm going to go to my room and take a nap and then get ready. I'll see you at dinner, Barbie."

Shelby walked her friend to the door. Angelica handed her the empty glass and opened the door. "Dress to kill, sweetie, your man is waiting."

"Shut up, Cover Girl. That's just nasty."

Shelby shut the door and turned off the stereo. She grabbed one of the books off the coffee table. In the bedroom, she took the shoes out of their boxes and placed them beneath the dresses in the closet. She placed all the lingerie and underclothes in drawers. The jewelry she left in the leather bound boxes that they came in, placing them in the top drawer of one of the dressers. She then placed all the empty boxes in the top of the closet. She wanted to keep all the boxes so that when the weekend ended, she could return all the items to her boss. No matter what Angelica said, she was not keeping any of the gifts Pig had showered on her. Jack would have a fit if she brought any of it home.

After organizing things, Shelby started a hot bath, lit the candles, and poured some of the Arabian Oil into her bath. Shelby loved the soft but bold musky smell of the oil. She had used it before in her baths or applied it straight on her skin. Her son Mark had brought her some of the same type back from the Middle East when he was deployed in Iraq.

It was weird that Pig would have even known about the oil and how much she liked it. Shelby put it off as just coincidental. She had already taken off her clothes and put on the soft robe while she filled the tub. After the bath was full, Shelby dropped the robe on the floor and lowered her body into the warm water. The book she had taken from the living room rested on a towel near her head. She soaked for a few minutes before drying her hands and opening the book. This moment was perfect and she was going to enjoy it for as long as she could.

Lethal was enjoying his own accommodations. He had been given three suits, a pair of shoes, some socks and underwear. The bathroom had a few toiletries and the bar had been loaded with beer and snacks. Lethal thought he had hit the lottery. "Wow, I think I could get used to this job." He grabbed a couple of beers and walked out into the hallway. He knew he had to play stupid, but he wanted to make contact with his club brothers. "Hey guys, I know you're on duty and all, but I thought I would bring you a beer."

Drake and Jazz remained very professional. "Thank you very much, sir, but unless Mr. Pig gives us permission to drink we have to decline."

Lethal put down the beers and shook his head. "I understand, no problem, just thought I would offer a company member a beer." Lethal took one of the beers and opened it. He took a drink and walked back toward his room. He turned around and indicated to his friends silently that he would find time to make connection with them tonight.

Drake nodded his head confirming that he understood.

While Shelby bathed and Lethal drank beer, Angelica laid on her bed and thought about Rex. She knew Pig had their rooms bugged and she could not take the chance of contacting Rex. *Here I am in Las Vegas with beautiful clothes, a huge hotel room and a whole weekend of fun. The only thing missing is the one man who has managed to melt my heart.* She had built a shell around herself since the death of her fiancé, but Rex had managed to crack it. She hugged her pillow and whispered. "Damn, I wish Rex was here."

Shelby left the makeup table, still trying to put on a necklace when she heard a knock on her door. "Coming." She looked through the peephole and saw Lethal and one of Pig's guards. Shelby opened up the door and held onto the necklace. "Come in. I'll be ready in a minute."

The two men entered Shelby's hotel room.

She looked toward Lethal. "Can you help me with this, please?" she asked, holding out the necklace.

"Sure." Shelby turned so Lethal could help her hook the necklace. Lethal took hold of the necklace while Shelby moved her long blonde hair. Lethal hooked the clasp on the necklace. "There you go." Lethal moved back toward the door after taking a long look at the blonde lady driver as she headed back into her bedroom. Lethal looked at Drake and smiled. "She doesn't look like any truck driver I've ever seen." Drake smiled and nodded.

Shelby came out of the bedroom in a short red and black strapless cocktail dress. She wore black stilettos, held a red clutch purse under her arm, and wore the ruby and black stone necklace and earrings that Pig had purchased for her. She stopped and spun around for the two men who stared in amazement. "How do I look?"

It took Lethal and Drake a few seconds to stop foaming at the mouth before they responded. Lethal answered. "Shelby, you look amazing."

Shelby smiled. "Thanks. Well, I guess we'd better go."

The three walked out into the hallway and went toward Angelica's room. Shelby knocked on the door. When Angelica answered it she was dressed in a short, light blue spaghetti strap cocktail dress. She wore light blue heels and carried a white clutch purse. A pearl necklace with matching long pearl earrings made her deep brunet hair stand out.

Shelby smiled and took her friend's hand. "You look magnificent, Angelica."

Angelica smiled back. "You look pretty magnificent yourself, sweetie." Angelica looked at the two men. "Well, are you two going to just stand there with your mouths open, or are you going to escort two beautiful women to dinner? I think the man who paid for all this merchandise might be waiting on us."

Lethal and Drake backed out into the hallway, allowing the two women to enter the hallway still holding hands. Angelica looked at Shelby. "Shall we go get some dinner and check out Sin City?"

Shelby nodded. "Yes, I think we should."

Just as the four were entering the elevator, Shelby's cell phone rang—it was Jack. "Hi baby, what are you doing?" Shelby listened as Jack explained that he had been working and missing her. "I miss you too, darling. Wish you were here in Las Vegas with me. We're on our way to dinner right now. I tried to call you earlier, but I guess you were busy at work."

Jack was glad she was having a good time and wished he were there too. He wanted to know when she would be able to come home for a few days.

"I'm not sure when I'll get to come home, sweetheart, but it should be soon." Shelby talked with Jack the entire time they rode down on the elevator and all the way to the restaurant. "Sweetheart, we're at the restaurant. I'll call you when I get back to the hotel room. It will probably be late, but I'll call and kiss you goodnight."

Shelby placed the phone in her clutch before entering the restaurant. Lethal had tagged along behind and waited for her to finish her call so he could escort her to the table. When Lethal and Shelby approached the table, Angelica was already seated. Drake and Jazz were standing nearby.

Pig got up from the table as Shelby waited for Lethal to pull out her chair and then sit between Angelica and Shelby across from Pig. Pig found his seat. He was mesmerized by her. "You ladies look absolutely beautiful tonight. I hope the clothes and accessories were to your liking. I want my drivers to feel like they are being well treated."

Angelica put her hand close to Pig's but was cautious about touching him. "Mr. Pig sir, the clothes, accessories, and rooms are absolutely wonderful. Thank you so much for everything. I truly feel like a princess tonight. Thank you again."

"Yes, Mr. Pig, thank you. Everything is beautiful. I've never been treated so well by an employer before," Shelby said with a cautious tone.

"I'm glad you are enjoying everything." He motioned for the waiter to begin serving their meal. "I hope you don't mind, but I went ahead and ordered for us. I know that you will want to check out the city and do some gambling after dinner."

The waiter poured wine for Lethal and Shelby. Then he placed a salad in front of each person. Pig picked up his salad fork. "Shall we eat?"

The other three followed suit.

The meal was decadent and filling. They discussed some work but mostly Pig wanted to know how things were going for the drivers and if they were happy. He told them he wanted to improve their jobs and make things better for them. Most of his comments, however, were directed at Shelby.

The group made small talk over dinner and a dessert of chocolate cheesecake. The dinner ended with a snifter of brandy. Before they got up from the table, Pig reached into his jacket and pulled out several envelopes, and handed one to each driver. "Enclosed are a few hundred dollars for gambling and fun for the evening." Angelica and Lethal looked in their envelopes but Shelby wasn't sure she should take the money. Pig noticed her reluctance. "It's a bonus, Ms. Shelby, for getting the loads here to Las Vegas so quickly and safely. Please, take it and enjoy yourself this evening."

"Very well, Mr. Pig. Thank you," she said, stiffly.

Pig's phone rang and Jazz brought it to the table. Pig looked at the phone screen. He handed it to Jazz before getting up from the table. "Tell them I'll call them from my hotel room."

Jazz took the call and repeated Pig's instructions.

Pig gave a slight bow before placing his hat on his head. "Ladies and gentleman, I apologize, but business is my life. I must leave you to your pleasures. Please enjoy yourselves tonight and I'll see you tomorrow. Breakfast will be brought to your rooms and I have left orders with the limousine company to take you anywhere you wish to go."

Pig and his two guards started to leave the restaurant. Pig looked at his guards. "I'll only need one of you to escort me to my room. Harry will be fine taking care of me tonight. You may have the night off as well. Enjoy yourselves and watch after my drivers, please."

"Yes, sir Mr. Pig, we will keep a close eye on them."

The drivers wished their boss good night. Pig tipped his hat and left the restaurant with Jazz.

Pig was slightly upset that he wasn't going to be able to spend more time with Shelby. He was glad, however, that she was wearing the items that he had purchased for her. He intended to spend a few hours with Shelby tomorrow.

The drivers and Drake finished their wine. Lethal was anxious to get away from the fine dining atmosphere. He wanted beer, gambling, and fun. Lethal also needed time to speak with Drake and Jazz.

Drake's phone rang. It was Jazz. He was waiting at the limo for him and the drivers. Drake motioned for the drivers to follow him. "Jazz is at the limo waiting on us."

Lethal and the others arrived in the limo at a nightclub on the strip. The men eagerly rushed to be the first to help the women out of the limo. Angelica and Shelby thought it was sweet that they were trying so hard to be gentlemen. Lethal's phone rang. He looked at it. "Damn, I have to take this call, guys. Get me a beer and I'll find you in the bar." Jazz and Drake gladly took Angelica and Shelby into the nightclub.

Lethal stood outside the club with his phone. "Hey Lizard, what's up?"

"Look, man, I know you and I don't have any love lost for Bullets, but he's dead. We buried him today and the club is going to vote me in tomorrow as club leader. I just wanted to make sure it's okay with you if I take the leadership. I know you and I are both in line for it, but with you gone, someone needs to be in control."

"Wow, how'd he go down, brother?"

Lizard explained to Lethal what the cops had said but didn't tell him what really happened.

"Damn, Lizard, something sounds really off about the whole thing. I'm not accusing you of anything, but are you sure you don't know more about his death? Not that I give a shit that the bastard is dead, but I really would want to know if you did us that favor. As far as the leader thing goes, you know you're better with the club members than I am."

"Well, my brother, when you get back here after we take over PIGT, we'll catch up over some beer. I'll keep you in the loop on everything and we'll run this club together. By the way, where are you?"

"Hell Lizard, we're in Las Vegas, eating, drinking, gambling, and spending time with two of the hottest lady truck drivers I have ever seen."

"Sounds like maybe I need to ride to Vegas and join your party. Things around here are a downer."

"Come on, Pig is footing the bill. We can party every night and I'm telling you the truth about the women."

"Tempting, brother, very tempting, but I need to keep things going here."

"I know, but you are sure missing out."

"I'd better go. Tell Jazz and Drake about Bullets. Let them know about the vote tomorrow too."

"You got it. I'll let them know. Ride safe and keep me posted."

"You know I will."

Lethal hung up and went into the nightclub to find the others. Angelica and Shelby were seated between Jazz and Drake in a booth close to the stage. Another woman was seated on the outside near Jazz, but Lethal had no idea who she was. "Well, move over and hand me my beer."

Angelica handed Lethal his beer. "Here you go, Lethal. Everything okay? That phone call sounded important."

"Everything is fine. Let's party." Lethal gave Drake and Jazz a pointed look. They all raised their glasses in a toast.

"Here's to us, the best drivers in the country," Lethal said.

Drake added, "And to the best bodyguards ever!" Everyone laughed and drank.

◊◊◊

Pig's phone call was from his friends in Mexico. "Pig, after your drivers pick up their loads in Tijuana, I want two of the trucks to stop in Mexicali for some extra product there," Tito said.

"Got it." After finishing the call, Pig went to his computer and turned on his locator in order to find Shelby. The limo was parked near a bar on the strip not far from the hotel. He wasn't going to go to the bar, but he was going to go down to the hotel's bar and casino for a smoke and some gambling. He would let his guards know that he was there and perhaps they and his drivers would stop and visit before turning in for the night. He wanted to see Shelby before the night was over.

Drake answered his phone after several rings. He had been laughing and enjoying the evening until she heard Pig's voice on the other end of the phone. His face turned sober as he listened to Pig. "Yes, sir. Are you sure you do not need one of us to escort you there, sir? Okay, very well, sir. We will check on you as soon as we arrive back at the hotel. Yes, sir, no problem." Drake ended his phone call.

Taking several drinks of his beer, Drake decided he needed to relieve himself. Lethal and Jazz looked at each other. "Everything okay?" Jazz asked.

Drake stood by the table. "Yes, Pig is just going to the casino in the hotel for some gambling. I really need to go to the restroom."

Lethal and Jazz decided to join him. "Hold on, I need to use the head too."

Shelby and Angelica laughed with the other lady who was sitting with them. "I thought women were the only ones that went to the bathroom together." They continued to laugh as the three men headed to the men's room.

In the restroom, Lethal checked to see how many other men were in the bathroom and waited for them to leave. Lethal then stood near the door. "I need to tell you guys a couple of things before anyone else comes in here. Bullets was murdered and they buried him today. Tomorrow the gang is swearing Lizard in as our new leader." Drake zipped his pants and Jazz finished washing his hands.

"You're joking, right?" Jazz said.

"No. Bullets was killed or murdered during the ambush in Socorro and Lizard is taking over tomorrow to keep things together."

Neither Drake nor Jazz liked Bullets, but it was hard to believe he was dead.

Drake looked in the mirror in front of him, turned off the water, and wiped his hands. "Dead, huh? What about us? We don't get to vote?"

Jazz sat on the counter of the sink, folding his hands and crossing his legs. "What about this job we're doing now? Who are we supposed to report to here? Does Lizard even know what we're doing? Shit, we're just about to take that bastard Pig down. We're the ones out here with our junk swinging in the air."

"Everything is going to stay in motion. Lizard is well aware of what's going on, and yes, you will report to him. Hell, he's the one who set everything in motion. Bullets was out of touch for a long time."

Drake and Jazz stared at each other.

"Okay, we'll report to Lizard," Jazz said. "But if we don't have back up when we blow up that command center and we get killed, Lizard is going to pay, even if we have to come back from the dead and haunt him."

"Don't worry, guys," Lethal said. "Lizard is well aware of what we're into and wants Pig to go down as much as we do. By the way, what are our plans for Pig?"

Drake walked toward Lethal. "You should be the one leading us Lethal, not Lizard."

"Lizard is best for the position right now. Our commitment is to this job until Pig is eliminated."

The men nodded and Drake began to explain the plan. "Pig has a formal ball every year with his employees and several of his top clients. We are going to volunteer for guard duty on the communication center for that night and …." A man came into the restroom so the men knew they would have to finish the conversation later. The three men shook hands and returned to the bar.

They resumed their places next to the ladies and talked and joked.

Shelby sat quietly, listening to the conversations of the others. It was becoming boring and she wanted to go back to the hotel. She scooted toward Lethal and Drake who were blocking her exit from the booth. "Excuse me, ladies and gentlemen, but it's time for me to get some rest."

Drake and Lethal moved out of the booth to allow Shelby out.

Lethal decided it was time for him to return to the hotel as well. "Yeah, I think I'm going to go back to the hotel too. I'm tired." Lethal looked at Shelby. "May I escort you back to the hotel, Ms. Shelby?"

"Yes, that would be nice, Lethal." Lethal said goodbye to the others and followed Shelby to the limo.

Pig had been monitoring the limo movements from his cell phone. He saw that the limo was headed back to the hotel. The cocktail waitress came to Pig's table. Pig lifted his glass. "Another one, please." He decided he would wait to see who showed up at the hotel before returning to his room.

Shelby and Lethal entered the hotel. "Thank you, Lethal, for coming with me. I think I'm going to take a dip in the pool before bed."

As they entered the elevator, Lethal thought that taking a swim was a good idea but didn't want Shelby to think he was stalking her. "Sounds great, Ms. Shelby, but I think I'm going to bed." He held the door open for her when they reached their floor. "See you tomorrow."

Pig remained in his seat after hearing Shelby say she was going to the pool. He planned to go to the pool area after Shelby came back down from her room.

Soon after Shelby and Lethal left, Drake and Jazz put their beers on the table at the same time. "Well, ladies, it's time for Mr. Pig's guards to return to duty." Jazz reached his hand out for the woman that he asked to join them earlier. "I got to say goodnight, babe."

The woman was a little taken aback with the gentleman-like behavior of her new male friend. She had figured Jazz was going to ask her to his room or invite her to another bar. "Okay. Will I see you again?"

Drake helped Angelica into the awaiting limo while Jazz gave a quick wave of his hand to the woman who had joined them for the evening. The woman was left on the sidewalk outside the bar as her three companions entered the limo. Jazz spoke quickly as the limo driver was waiting on him to shut the door. "Perhaps."

CHAPTER EIGHTEEN

The light on the pool's security door flashed green as Shelby slid her hotel card through the card reader. The smell of chlorine from the pool hit Shelby in the face as she opened the door. Spotting the spa, which was completely empty, Shelby walked across the wet tile. She removed her swimsuit cover and flip-flops, placed her property in a lounge chair near the spa, and walked down the spa's steps. She lowered her body into the hot, bubbling water. She found a comfortable spot with jets that massaged her back and leaned back, resting the back of her neck and head on the tiles along the outside frame of the sunken spa. "Oh, how wonderful this feels, I could sleep in here tonight."

Unaware that Pig had entered the pool area, Shelby sat there with her eyes closed and her back to the door, enjoying the soothing pulses of the water coming from the jets of the spa.

Pig was ecstatic that no one but Shelby occupied any part of the pool or spa area. He didn't want to frighten or make Shelby feel uncomfortable, so he raised his voice upon entering the area. "Wow, there is no one in the pool. I think I'll go get my suit and take a dip."

Shelby was shocked by the loud voice. She turned her body around and saw her boss standing next to the pool just inside the door. Pig pretended not to notice Shelby until she turned to check out the voice. Pig then turned toward her with a feigned greeting. "Shelby, how nice to see you, I had no idea you were in here. I hope I haven't startled you. I couldn't sleep, so I thought I would walk. I didn't think anyone was in here."

"It's okay, Mr. Pig. I just wanted to soak for a little while before going to bed."

Pig walked toward where Shelby was resting, still carrying his laptop. "Well good. I am glad to see that you are enjoying yourself."

"Yes, Mr. Pig, I am. Thank you."

As Pig moved closer, he saw that Shelby was wearing the swimsuit he had picked out for her. He found a chair and table near the spa. The chair groaned under his weight, but he ignored it as this spot gave him a clear view of Shelby. "The wardrobe I had sent to your room is pleasing to you?"

Again Shelby didn't move. "Yes, Mr. Pig. I am taking great pains to be very careful with each item so that when I return them to you. They will be in excellent condition."

"No need for that, Ms. Shelby. Those are gifts from PIGT for you to keep and they will not be taken back."

Shelby opened her eyes and turned to see that her boss had positioned himself uncomfortably close. "Oh, I didn't mean to offend you, Mr. Pig. I just didn't figure you would want me to keep such extravagant items. I'm not sure I would feel comfortable accepting such beautiful things without paying for them."

"The gifts are yours to keep and I'll not for any reason take them back. I reward my drivers well with gifts and bonuses. Giving them back would be disrespectful."

"Of course I'll keep the gifts, Mr. Pig. Out of respect for you. I thank you very much for your generosity," she said rigidly.

"You are very welcome. I'll continue to reward you as long as you work for me. Did you get a chance to read or look at the books that I chose for you?"

"Yes, Mr. Pig, I have started reading one already and it was hard to put down before dinner tonight."

"Excellent. Tell me about the book."

Pig enjoyed listening to Shelby explain the details of the book. He let her speak for what he judged was an appropriate amount of time and then said, "Well, Ms. Shelby, it is time for me to retire to my room for the night. Enjoy the rest of your spa time and perhaps we can meet for lunch tomorrow?"

"Lunch sounds good. Just let me know."

"I'll send one of my guards to fetch you around noon."

Shelby moved toward the steps. It was time for her to get out and go to her room as well. "Okay. See you tomorrow."

◊◊◊

Lizard was the first one to arrive at the clubhouse. The area in back of the garage where they held meetings and conducted business was a disaster. Lizard got right to work on cleaning things up and going over what he was going to say. He knew he was going to have some opposition, but he was ready for it. He wanted to be their leader, but was more interested in keeping the club together and finishing what they had started with PIGT.

"Hey Lizard, can I help you clean things up?" Time Bomb stood in the doorway with his hands in his pockets.

"Sure."

Time Bomb began picking up empty beer bottles. "Bullets never was one for keeping things clean. I'm sure if you get voted in today that will change."

The sarcasm was obvious. "Look, Time Bomb, I can handle this alone."

"No, it's cool man, I want to help the new leader all I can. Especially since I'm pretty sure my objecting to his advancement will land me with the same fate as the former leader."

With one swift movement, Lizard was in Time Bomb's face. "Time Bomb, why don't you just leave unless you've got something you want to say to me?"

Ronny, Lenny, and Rick walked through the door. "Wow, did we miss something?"

Backing away, Lizard went back to cleaning up the place.

Time Bomb straightened his shirt. "Nah, we were just having a little close conversation. You guys want a beer?"

Other members came in and took seats. When everyone was there, they got down to business.

Lizard was glad when the vote was over. Spider and Naked Boy shook hands with Lizard after the vote. Most everyone else toasted him with beer bottles and encouraged him to say something. "Well, I have no plans to change much of what our brother Bullets had been doing. I do think we should focus on Pig and the takeover of his company. We also need to continue to look for Rat Hole. We sent out scouts to find him, but he's disappeared. With Yanks and his boys in the ground, things should run better. I'll continue to reach out to Tito for loads to keep the club running."

Somewhat tipsy, Time Bomb, who had voted against Lizard, lifted his beer in the air. "Here's to our new leader and to the old leader. The dark side knows the truth, even when it's not spoken here today."

Rick grabbed Time Bomb and walked him out of the room. "Come on man, let's go take a walk."

◊◊◊

Shelby was returning from lunch with Pig, but before she entered her room, Angelica was on her heels. "Please tell me you see what is going on here, Shelby? That boss of ours is trying his hardest to win you over."

Shelby slid her card in the card reader, allowing her and Angelica in the room. "Yes, I see what he's doing, but what do I do? You don't want me to quit and if I'm mean to him he might fire me. Then where will we be in trying to bust this guy?"

Angelica picked up the remote and turned the stereo on loud to cover their conversation. She sat down on the sofa. Shelby kicked off her shoes and sat cross-legged, holding a pillow to her chest.

"I know it's hard. Maybe you should get a little friendly with Pig," Angelica suggested.

"Seriously? You're kidding, right?"

"Okay, you're right, maybe getting close to him would be too danger-ous. I wish he had a thing for me like he has for you. It sure would be easy to get information out of him. But you're right, that would be too risky for you."

"Maybe I should just be mean to him or ignore him. Maybe he'll send us on some really dangerous runs to get even with me."

"You could be right. Maybe if you ignore his attention, he'll try and get you to notice him in other ways. Are you sure you can handle whatever might come out of this plan? I mean it could get dangerous."

"I don't mind dangerous truck runs, but please don't ask me to stay in the room very long with that stinky man."

"Okay then, that's what we will do. You do your best to avoid him and turn down any offers he makes."

"Okay, and I'll be rude. I won't show up for dinner tonight and I won't return any of this stuff, although I really think I should. I won't even say 'thank you' anymore. You need to be my lookout so I can avoid him."

"That sounds great. I'll be sure and run interference as much as possible, starting tonight."

◊◊◊

Pig waited in the restaurant for Shelby and Angelica to show up for dinner. "Sorry I'm late Mr. Pig, but I was looking in on Shelby. She apologizes, but she has a really bad headache and doesn't feel like eating. She said she was going to go to bed early with one of the books you gave her."

"That's too bad. Perhaps I should send a doctor to her room."

"Oh, I don't think that will be necessary. I think she just needs to rest."

Pig was no fool. He knew very well what "headache" was code for. He grabbed his glass and gulped down the water. "Well, I hope she's feeling better tomorrow. We're going to cut the weekend short. I need loads picked up early in Mexicali. I want her with you on this run. Hank will be in touch with you tomorrow after you are taken back to your trucks. You will deliver the loads to Southern California. Then deliver loads from there to Mexicali. You will then deliver the loads from Mexicali to Florida. I was really hoping to let Ms. Shelby know about this myself."

"I'll let her know."

Angelica grabbed a roll, putting butter on it.

Pig huffed, grabbed his cane and stood up. He looked at Jazz who was standing by. "Have my meal sent to my room. Suddenly I'm not feeling well myself."

"Very good, Mr. Pig."

Angelica ate at her roll. "I'm sorry you feel bad, Mr. Pig. Hope you feel better. Maybe it's something going around?"

When Pig was gone, Angelica ordered food and wine and then reached for her cell phone. She sent Shelby a text: *Pig's not feeling well either. We R leaving early A.M. Poor stinky, you hurt his feelings. LOL.*

Shelby texted back: *Glad to leave. I like Vegas, but not like this.*

Lethal finally showed up and saw Angelica sitting by herself. "So where's your partner?"

"Oh, she's in her room with a headache."

Lethal grabbed a roll and ordered from the waiter. "You hear? We're leaving tomorrow"

"Yeah, I heard."

"After we deliver in Florida, I hear we're bringing back some special cargo to the estate. We'll be there just in time for Pig's annual ball."

"Wow, where has the time gone? I didn't realize it was already time for that shindig."

"I haven't had the pleasure of attending, but everyone I've talked to tells me it's pretty awesome."

"I guess. It's just a bunch of Pig's business partners and their dates rubbing elbows. We're invited so that it looks like Pig has a lot of friends. It's all for show."

"Oh, I thought I was important to Mr. Pig."

"Seriously, Lethal, you haven't figured out yet that we are just pawns in Mr. Pig's big chess game? We don't mean anything to him and neither does anyone else."

"Oh, I wouldn't say that. Mr. Pig has his eye on Ms. Shelby."

"Is it that obvious? We thought we were the only ones that noticed his infatuation with her. That's kind of why she got a headache tonight. She didn't want to deal with him."

Lethal sat back in his chair and sipped at his drink. "Oh, I see. I can understand her feelings, being married and everything. I haven't been with this company long, but there are some things that seem odd. I know we aren't supposed to talk about stuff, but don't you find the way we do stuff far from normal? I've been a trucker for years and I've never delivered loads without knowing the contents."

"Look, Lethal, let's change the subject before someone overhears and we both get canned."

"Okay, but I'm just saying things are strange here."

Angelica liked Lethal but she knew she couldn't risk another person knowing what was going on. "Let's just do our jobs, enjoy the perks, and make lots of money. I have plans to get rich and dump this job, but it's not gonna happen overnight."

"Yeah, I guess you're right. Save me a dance at the ball?"

"Alright."

◊◊◊

Pig was furious that Shelby wasn't able to attend the special night he had planned for her. "Harry, I want you to pack my stuff and be ready to leave first thing in the morning. I need to get back to the estate. I have several loads arriving there and I want to personally inspect the cargo."

Harry bowed. "Very good, Mr. Pig. I'll see to it."

Pig took his computer to his bedroom. He connected with Shelby's room and saw that she was not in the living space. He couldn't see into her bedroom, he had tried to give her some privacy but now he wished he hadn't. "Dammit." He scanned over a few other things before closing his computer. He didn't believe she was ill. He had never allowed anyone to get to him the way Shelby had. He was losing control. *Enough is enough. I can't allow some woman to gain control over my thoughts. Although I should get what I paid for.*

His phone broke his train of thought. "Yes, Hank."

"Mr. Pig, I wanted to let you know that information just came in that Bullets is dead and so is Yanks and his gang. It happened in Socorro, New Mexico. Supposedly Yanks and his men set up an ambush against Bullets' gang, but it was foiled. Bullets' men killed Yanks and his men and somehow Bullets ended up dead outside of town."

"Who's the new leader of the LA Bad Boys now?"

"Lizard. He was just voted into that position today."

"What do we know about him?"

"Not much. He has some issues with some of the gang members. He probably won't be much of a problem."

"I'm glad Bullets is dead, but I told Yanks I would take him out myself. Guess Yanks got what he deserved, too."

"Yes, sir."

"Harry and I will be back at the estate tomorrow."

"Yes, sir. Frank called and they have some new loads coming into the Keys."

"I'll deal with it tomorrow. He sent me an email."

"Yes, sir. We will be ready for you tomorrow."

"How are things going with the ball?"

"Everything is right on schedule."

"Any word on Rat Hole?"

"Yes, my informant told me they have a good lead on him. Hopefully we will have him back at the estate to answer questions soon."

"Good." Pig disconnected from the conversation.

CHAPTER NINETEEN

ngelica clutched her phone in the bathroom stall. "Hey Rex, it sure is good to hear your voice."

"Yours too," he said. "So, did you do anything you need to 'leave in Vegas?'"

"Very funny. If you were here that might have been a possibility, but since you're not it's really been kind of boring."

"So what you got for me, party girl?"

"I told you I thought Pig had a thing for Shelby?"

"Yeah."

"Well, I was right. He's trying to get her, but she's not the least bit interested. In fact, she wants to quit, but since she knows about the operation, she's willing to hold out for a while. I think she's going to be a real asset."

"Okay, but be careful. We don't want any civilians getting hurt."

"I know."

"The reason I called is because Pig apparently got upset when Shelby blew him off last night. He moved our job up and we are leaving for Tijuana today."

"Did he give you any specifics?"

"We are going to Tijuana and meeting with a man named Omar. I haven't been to this unloading location before but it is really close to the tunnels."

"Are they gonna let you out of the trucks?"

"No, but I'll try and see as much as I can. "

"Try and get at least a mental picture of Omar."

"I will."

"I wish you could've come to Vegas."

"I know, me too, but that would have definitely blown your cover."

"Really? Now, how would your being here have blown my cover?"

"Because I wouldn't have let you out from under your covers all weekend. I'm sure Pig would have figured out something was up."

"You're funny. Maybe I would have been the one keeping you under the covers."

"All right, guess I'm coming to Vegas now."

"Sorry, we are pulling out in just a few minutes."

"Damn it, I missed my chance."

"This time."

"Won't be long, Sweet Pea, and you will be off this assignment and safe."

"I know. I gotta go, someone's coming."

◊◊◊

"I sure wish we could have stayed through Sunday. I was just beginning to like being pampered," Lethal blurted out over the radio as the three drivers headed out of Vegas toward San Diego.

"Not me, I'm glad we are on the road again. I get restless sitting around, Barbie said."

"Sitting around? With all there is to do in Vegas? It must be because you're married, Barbie."

"Yeah, it's hard to have too much fun without the hubby."

"Well, I had a good time too, Lethal. How you feeling, Barbie?" Angelica lifted off the mic key.

"My headache is gone. I'm just glad to be on the road again. I don't know what I'm gonna do with all this stuff piled in my truck. Wish Mr. Pig would have let me give it back."

"Those things were a bonus from Mr. Pig. We do our job and he rewards us with our pay and special bonuses like this weekend."

"I know, but I don't feel right taking things like this from him. Besides we have to report these gifts on our tax returns."

"Not to interrupt, but I need ya'll to be aware of what were are going to be dealing with when we get to Tijuana. I'll give you more details when we stop for lunch, but this is the gist of what to expect."

"Go ahead, Cover Girl, we're listening."

"Okay, the three loads that we have now are going to be swapped with three other trailers near the border. A guy named Omar is going to be waiting for us. I've never delivered to this specific location, but they are all pretty dangerous down there so we need to stick together. Don't get out of your trucks unless I give you the okay. They will back us in, and we will unhook with their assistance. Then we will be directed to another location for our loads to Mexicali. Everyone understand?"

"Yes, ma'am."

"Good. Now when we stop for lunch, I'll let you know more."

The three trucks moved swiftly down the highway toward San Diego. Shelby was glad the weekend had ended early, but she was still worried that Pig hadn't gotten the hint.

◊◊◊

"I don't care what it takes. I want that Rat Hole and I want him now."

"Yes, sir, we know the house he's holed up in. Getting to him has presented us with some problems. The house is located in a very heavily populated area."

"Get the men in that house—whatever it takes. I want that thief at the estate so that I can deal with him. He'll be a prime example of what happens when you steal from me."

"Yes, sir. Listen, I hate to bring this up, but we have something going on with the warehouse in Miami. I've tried to contact Jamal but no one is answering. The surveillance cameras are down throughout the warehouse."

"I noticed that earlier this morning while I was leaving the hotel. I called Larry, he's going to check it out and let me know." Pig hung up.

Hank called Casey and Black Jack. "Casey, the boss says to do whatever you need to do to get Rat Hole and bring him back to the estate. I know it's going to be difficult, but try not to make too much noise. Although Pig wants him back here no matter the cost, you and I both know he doesn't want attention."

"I know, Hank, but it's going to be tough. I'll do my best."

"Let me talk to Black Jack."

Black Jack took the phone from Casey. "Yeah, Hank."

"We got trouble in Miami. Do your best to get that cleaned up and get to Miami as soon as possible. Pig has Larry on it, but he's a moron and I'm sure he'll screw it up. The whole security system on the warehouse is out and I suspect it's been raided."

"Yeah, that sounds like what's happened. It's gonna take a while to get Rat Hole to come out of hiding. Maybe I'll fly on down to Miami and see what is going on down there. What about the other warehouses?"

"The others are still coming up on the security system in the central command center."

"Okay, well I'll make sure everything gets done here before I leave for Miami. I'll take care of it, Hank."

"I know Pig will know where you are when he checks his computer, but I think it will be best to have you there."

Black Jack ended the call. "Casey, I'm going to leave for Miami. Do you think you can handle things here for a while?"

"I think so. I mean how hard is to watch this house and wait for that bastard to come out of it? The hard part is going to be pinning him down once we have him in our sights."

"I know, but remember to do it as silently as possible."

"I'll do my best. Pig has to be kidding if he thinks we won't make any noise capturing this guy."

"What about trying to break into a basement window of the house?" Black Jack pointed at the broken cardboard covered window.

"We thought about it, but it's too small for any of our guys."

"Okay, we'll figure something else out. I've got to go. Keep me posted."

◊◊◊

"Lizard, we're on our way back to the estate this morning. Since you're the new club leader I thought I would let you know what we plan to do."

"Sounds good, Jazz. I was the one that came up with the plan to take down Pig, but I understand you guys have come up with a plan to get into the command center."

"We are going to volunteer for security duty during Pig's annual ball. I found some explosives in a locked warehouse the other day when Pig had me doing some security checks on the estate. He thinks he has everything tight and secure with all of his gadgets. I have news for Pig—I'm the best at breaking into secure places."

"I know you are, Jazz. Keep me posted and let me know when you plan to take it down. I'll send you back up."

◊◊◊

"Man, it sure is dark around here, don't they believe in lights?" Angelica scanned the loading area. "I sure hope Omar is wearing white so we can see him."

"Angelica, there's a man coming up to your driver's side door."

Just as Shelby spoke the words Angelica jumped from the knock at her door. "Thanks, Barbie."

In broken English, Omar directed Angelica. "Truck back there."

"Okay." She moved her truck toward the area and got on the radio. "You two hold up until I get turned around and backed into the dock. Without any lights it's going to be hard to see. Turn your bright lights on so I can have a little more light. Once I get in, I'll direct you into your spots."

"Okay you got it, Cover Girl."

Angelica's truck moved slowly as she pivoted it around in the small warehouse parking lot. After finding the target area, Omar waved her back into position. Angelica then waved Omar to her truck. "I need to help my drivers get backed into the dock."

"No, stay put. I'll do it."

"Let me do it. I'll back them in and then get right back in my truck."

"Only you."

"Yes, only me."

Angelica got on the radio, "Okay, guys, Omar is letting me direct you into position. Barbie, you come at me first. Lethal, you watch her then do the same."

"They actually let you out of your truck?"

"It's too damn dark out here to do this without a spotter."

Angelica looked over the area while backing in Shelby and Lethal. It wasn't hard to notice that there were several holes in the dilapidated chain link fencing. Just beyond the fence there were several abandoned buildings. Angelica thought she spotted people going in and out of the buildings. The people seemed to disappear and then reappear on the other side of the fence. She knew this was possibly a connection point to the underground tunnel system that had been spoken of in many of the briefings she had attended.

After the trucks were parked, Omar made Angelica get back in her truck. "You in truck."

To her surprise, just as she sat in her driver's seat, several men appeared from out of nowhere. Within minutes all three trucks were dollied down. Omar asked each driver to pull forward. Once all three tractors were away from the trailers, he approached Angelica's truck again.

Through the already opened window, Omar gave her a piece of paper with a map. "You follow map to pick up load, give map to Poncho."

Angelica waved. "Okay." On the radio, she said, "We have a map to follow. I sure hope we don't get lost."

"I still can't believe they let you out of your truck."

"Yeah, I know. They probably wouldn't have if the other guys had been on time. Looked to me like Omar was the only one there for a while. Let's see if I can figure out this map. We aren't too far according to the miles on these roads, but whether we can find the roads is another subject."

"You can do it, Cover Girl."

"Follow me, drivers; if I'm getting lost so are you."

The roads were bumpy and small as the three drivers made their way through uncharted territory. "This reminds me of some of the roads I've traveled in Arkansas and Oklahoma—small."

"At least we're not in the LA traffic. Talk about messy and tight."

"So, Lethal, you've driven in the Southern California area before?"

Lethal knew he had given out too much information. "Yes, ma'am, been through LA and over the grapevine many times in my life."

"Maybe you should be leading this exploration?"

"No, Cover Girl, you're doing just fine."

◊◊◊

Pig stormed around the communication center. "Dammit, Larry, what the hell is going on down there?"

"Mr. Pig, the cops have everything cordoned off. I can't get within two blocks of that warehouse."

"Hank, where the hell is Black Jack?" Pig bellowed.

"He's on his way to Miami, sir. Remember you had him in Ohio looking for Rat Hole."

Pig's face was scarlet. "I don't care where I had him. I want him in Miami, now!

"Yes, sir, I'll check on his location." Hank tapped on his tablet. "He is in Miami, sir, and it looks like he is only a few blocks from the warehouse."

"Get him on the phone."

"Black Jack, Mr. Pig wants an update on the warehouse."

Pig yanked the phone from Hank's hand. "Black Jack, I want you in there now. My friends aren't going to be happy if their product has been compromised. I'm not sure which one of these idiots missed the alerts on that warehouse, but someone's head is gonna roll."

"I just turned onto the street. Oh shit! It looks like the building caught fire."

"Fire?"

"Yes, sir. I can't get close enough yet to see how much damage it caused."

Just as Black Jack moved closer, a man of Cuban decent touched his arm. "Hold on, Mr. Pig. I have to call you back." Black Jack hung up quickly.

The man who had approached Black Jack motioned for him to follow him. "Come, Santiago is waiting for you over here."

Black Jack knew who Santiago was and followed the man.

Several blocks away, the man led Black Jack into an ordinary looking house. But there was nothing ordinary about the men inside, strapped with firearms. Santiago was seated at the table and saw Black Jack enter.

"Black Jack, it is good to see you. Sorry it's under such horrible circumstances. Please, sit here." He motioned to a chair across from him.

Black Jack complied. "What happened, Santiago? The command center received an alarm on the building early this morning but no one contacted Pig."

"We're very sorry about Pig's property, but the building was compromised by some young people."

"We just transferred the last of the product brought in from Cuba last night. How is the product?"

"The product was not compromised, I assure you, but the fire caused other damage in the building. Since the building was gutted, I removed the security guards. The electronic security was left on, but failed for some reason."

"Failed? That system is almost flawless. The only way anyone could have entered that building was if the system wasn't armed. It also would have alerted Pig if the system had been down for too long. Come on, Santiago, what aren't you telling us? Why haven't you answered your phones?"

"I can't tell you anything more than that, Black Jack."

"So you're telling me the building was destroyed by the fire, the product is safe, and you have no explanation for why some kids were in the building or why you didn't answer your phone?"

"Yes."

Black Jack was suspicious. He stood up and put his hand on his gun near his hip. "Save the lies for Pig, Santiago. Where is the product?"

Santiago shifted again, folding his hands on the table. "It's safe, but I can't disclose the location right now."

"That product isn't yours and the people who do own it will have your head. You're a dead man, Santiago." When Black Jack turned away from the table, the other men near the table pointed their guns at him.

Black Jack strode past them to the door. "You better pack up your men and your families and leave Miami. I'm not sure what you're thinking you're going to gain from all this Santiago, but you're playing with the money of some very dangerous men. They won't just kill you and your men, but your entire families." Black Jack let the screen door slam behind him.

Santiago followed Black Jack into the street. "Black Jack, listen. I am not stealing from Pig or his clients." Santiago motioned with his head to the house.

Black Jack understood they were being watched and nodded his understanding to Santiago. "I'll tell Pig you have betrayed him," he said, feigning anger.

Santiago knew Black Jack understood.

Black Jack left and called his boss from the car. "Mr. Pig, it appears that the warehouse is gone. The product was removed and transported last night so it's apparently safe."

"Where is it?"

"I don't know, but Santiago assured me it's safe."

"You don't know? You believe him? Why hasn't he been answering his phone?"

"He can't. He's being watched and he's possibly been bugged. He's trying to protect you and the product."

"Who is investigating him?"

"I'm not sure."

"Something is going on, Black Jack. This is the third warehouse issue we've had this year. I want you to stay in Miami and get to the bottom of things."

"Perhaps we have a mole?"

"I doubt that. But if there is a leak, I'll find it. I've been thinking that it's time to have everyone who works here chipped."

"It might be time."

CHAPTER TWENTY

The DEA brought several agents in for a briefing. The director stood in front of the briefing room. Rex was in the back of the room. The director began, "Many of you know that we have been investigating a trucking organization involved in drug and gun trafficking. We have several agents on the inside feeding us information about locations and major players involved in this operation. I want the players apprehended by the end of this year, or sooner, if possible." He pushed a button on the remote he held and pictures appeared on a screen behind him. "This man, Samuel Laurence Piggott, aka Pig, is our main suspect. He is in bed with several cartels, from Cuba to Mexico and throughout Central and South America."

Other pictures and names were displayed. "It's not going to be easy to invade this man's operation, and the busts that we have made so far have come up empty. He is very well protected. As we get information from those inside we will feed it to you. Rex back there is the handler for one of our embedded agents. Rex, do you have anything to add?"

"Not at this time, sir. Just be careful and cautious. Mr. Pig and his associates are dangerous killers."

◊◊◊

Angelica and Shelby entered the truck stop store. Lethal had declined their offer to join them. They purchased some bottled water and slid into a booth to talk freely.

"What's up?" Shelby asked.

"Things will not be as strict in Mexicali. For example, they won't make us stay in the trucks. They aren't afraid of anyone knowing what they do there."

"Really?"

"Yep, Rex told me it's because they murder. Anyone caught snitching or turning them in for anything ends up dead, along with their families."

"How come the U.S. Government doesn't just go in and shut them down?"

"Well, the government allows a certain amount of that stuff to go on. They let the little fish operate in hopes that they will lead them to the bigger fish."

"So why do you do this? Aren't you afraid of these people?"

"I like being an agent and doing what I can to eliminate as much of the bad in the U.S. as possible."

"I'm scared to even talk through my truck window with some of these guys."

"Never let them see your fear. I had dinner with the group we are going to see in Mexicali just a few months ago. I thought at first I was a dead woman, but after we got to the cantina in town and started drinking, they seemed just like normal people. Of course, I wouldn't turn my back on any of them, but they were fun."

"You have a strange notion of fun."

"One of the guys seemed to have a crush on me, so that was kind of a safety net. I'm pretty sure he kept the others from hurting me for sport."

"Oh, Lord. I hope nothing like that happens to me. I'm not sure I can handle anything like that going down."

"Don't worry, I've got your back. Just follow my lead. If they invite us to have dinner, we can't say no. That would be an insult and give them a reason to hurt us. I'll protect you, so don't let them spook you. Try and have a good time."

"It's hard to fake having fun."

"They might not ask us. I just wanted you to be prepared, just in case they do."

"I hope they just load us and let us go."

"Me too, sweetie."

◊◊◊

Pig had tried to contact some of his government friends, but none of his known associates were returning his calls. He knew something was going on since several of his warehouses had been searched. In addition, his trucks were being stopped at checkpoints and searched. To his credit, none of the merchandise belonging to him or his customers had been discovered or seized. However, the possibility of that occurring was becoming more probable with each encounter with the law.

"What the hell is going on, Hank? I can't get Senator Obemen or Congresswoman Poleg to return my calls. Not to mention the police chiefs I have taken such good care of over the years with donations to their personal charities. The governors who I have so graciously contributed to also won't answer my calls. Did you invite them to the ball?"

"Yes, sir. All of them have received invitations. They may be busy with their political campaigns. I'm sure all of them will be here for the ball. After all, there will be lots of money thrown around."

"Whatever is going on, I need to put a stop to it and fast. It won't be long before some dimwit rookie cop stumbles across my product and blows everything up. I can control most everything from the inside. It's those unknowns on the outside that worry me."

◊◊◊

"I feel guilty sleeping so late," Shelby told Angelica over coffee.

"We can't pick our loads up until later tonight, besides we needed the rest. I had hoped I'd find a place where I could call Rex, but I couldn't risk it. I sure do miss him."

"Are you getting serious about Rex?"

"No! Well maybe. I wouldn't mind bringing him with me to Pig's ball."

"Lethal mentioned the ball. Would it be safe having him there?"

"I think so. Pig won't know who he is, especially if we use a fictitious name. How about you? Are you bringing Jack?"

"I'm not sure. I want him there, but I'm afraid if he finds out that I'm in danger, he might pull me away before you get a chance to bust Pig."

◊◊◊

While the women had breakfast, Lethal had gotten a key to the showers so he could check in with Lizard. "Hey Lizard, we're on our way to Mexicali and then we're delivering these loads somewhere out East."

"Any more updates about Pig's ball?"

"Nothing more than what Jazz and Drake told me. Have you found Rat Hole?"

"We sent scouts out to find him but that was useless. I hope he stays hidden."

"Pig will kill him for sure if he's discovered, but what can you do? How are things going with the club?"

"Business as usual. Time Bomb hates my guts and is doing his best to turn some of the men against me, but I'm dealing with it."

"Hang in there. Once we take over Pig's operation everything else will fall into place."

"I will, brother."

Lethal went to return the shower key and saw Shelby and Angelica eating breakfast. "I see you ladies finally made it."

"How are you today?" Shelby asked.

Lethal slid in the booth next to Shelby. "After all that sleep and a great shower, I'm ready for some food." He motioned for the waitress and she came and took his order. As he waited for his steak and eggs he asked, "So where are we taking the loads after we finish in Mexicali, boss?"

Before Angelica could respond, her phone vibrated. She took it out and checked the screen. "Damn, Central Command. Excuse me for a minute."

"What's that all about? They gonna change our loads again?" Lethal asked Shelby.

"Probably not, maybe just where we'll unload."

"We still going to make it back to headquarters for the ball?"

"I think so. Isn't attending mandatory? You really want to go to it?"

"Sure, I think it will be fun rubbing elbows with the higher-ups."

"I think it's going be another boring weekend."

"What? You didn't like all the pampering you got in Vegas?"

"Not really. I'm just a Plain Jane kind of girl."

"Well, I like the party life."

Angelica slid back into the booth. "Well, we're going to be unloading at a warehouse in southern Louisiana. Then Pig has a few small loads he wants us to run next week before the ball. It's going to be a low-key week."

"About time," Lethal said.

"What about me going home? Pig told me I could go home for the week before the ball," Shelby said.

Angelica shrugged. "Guess you'll have to ask Mr. Pig about that when we get back."

◊◊◊

Drake pulled Jazz behind a tree in the yard near the dog pen. "Look, we have to try and get as close to the communication center as possible. I need to get in there and look around so I know where to put the explosives."

"I have no idea how we are going to get into that room before the night of the ball," Jazz said. "I'm pretty sure we are just going to have to blow it up sight unseen."

"We need to find other places to put some explosives too. Like in the kitchen and some of the hallways upstairs. This whole place needs to go up in smoke."

"Do you seriously think you and I can do all that on our own? I thought Lizard was sending backup."

"He is, but we need to create distractions so they can get past the gate guards."

"I have a bad feeling that we are going to end up dead."

"No way, we are going to take Pig down. Lizard will get us the backup. Maybe we can get them into the ball as guests."

"Yeah, right. Can you picture Time Bomb blending in?"

"It'll need to be a cop or a judge, someone Lizard has on the take."

"Sounds, good. Now let's see if we can make friends with those dogs. They might come in handy."

◊◊◊

The three drivers arrived in Mexicali on time. Angelica led them right to the loading facility. "This shouldn't take too long."

The Mexican man that had been "her date" on her last visit knocked on her door. "Miss Angel. I drive your truck now." Angelica got out of her truck and hugged the man. He then got into Angelica's truck and maneuvered it into position.

Two other men did the same with the other trucks. Shelby and Lethal gathered with Angelica in the middle of the dirty, dark lot. "Should we be letting them drive our trucks?"

"Just try and stop them."

"So we just stand around here and wait for them to load us?"

"Yes. And they may invite us to their favorite cantina afterward."

"I'm not going anywhere with those guys," Shelby protested.

"Shelby, it will be fine, just be friendly."

"I'm with Shelby. We don't have any way to protect ourselves," Lethal said.

"They're harmless as long as you don't mess with their business."

The Mexican man who was so fond of Angelica walked up to her. "Come." He grabbed her hand and motioned for the others to follow. Shelby hung close to Lethal as they followed Angelica and the man. He led them into an open door in the warehouse next to where their trucks were being loaded.

Angelica took mental notes of everything that she saw as she entered the warehouse.

The Mexican man led the three drivers to a small room with a refrigerator, chairs, and a table. On the table was a plate of tortillas, a bowl of beans, a bowl of shredded meat, and several bottles of beer. "*Hay es comida.*"

"Have a seat, guys, I think he wants us to eat." The Mexican man smiled as he held a chair for Angelica. "*Gracias,*" she said to him.

Shelby and Lethal each took a seat at the table.

Shelby picked at the food. "I'm not really hungry. Do you think it will make him upset if I decline?"

Angelica opened one of the beers. "The way Lethal is scarfing it down, I doubt he'll even realize we didn't partake. You want a beer?"

"I don't really like beer that much."

"That's okay, Shelby, I'll drink yours, too."

"Thanks, Lethal, I wouldn't want them to think I'm being rude."

"I'm just glad they didn't invite us to join them at their cantina further inside Mexico," Angelica said.

"They took you to their cantina in Mexico?" Lethal asked.

"Yeah, why?"

"Well, that's quite unusual for the cartel to invite anyone but their money-makers to their private drinking holes."

"Really? And just how do you know about the cartel, Lethal? Or even that these people are cartel?"

Lethal swallowed hard. "Well…I really don't know that for sure, but everyone knows the cartel is really cautious. If you guys haven't figured out that these people are cartel or cartel associates, you're pretty stupid." He took a swig of his beer.

"It's probably a safe guess that they're cartel," Shelby said. "We'd better be careful so they don't cut our heads off or something."

"Yep, I heard they do a lot of that too," Lethal said.

"These people might try to kill us at any time," Shelby whispered.

"That's not likely," Angelica said, "especially since we're their transportation into the U.S."

"You got that right, Cover Girl."

Angelica decided to change the subject, "So, Shelby, have you decided what you are going to wear to the ball?"

The man returned while the gals talked about fashion. He smiled as he looked at the table, pleased that most of the food and beer had been consumed. "You like?"

Angelica smiled back at him. "Yes, very good."

Shelby and Lethal nodded their approval.

The man looked at Shelby, making a steering wheel motion with his hands. "She drives too?"

Angelica introduced the two, "This is Barbie and Lethal."

The man laughed. "Barbie? Doll?" He reached over and gently touched the end of Shelby's long blonde hair, continuing to laugh. "Doll."

"Yes, Barbie."

The man took Angelica's hand and led her toward the door. "You go now." He waved for the other two to follow. "Come." The three drivers were led out of the building and to their trucks.

The Mexican man escorted Angelica all the way to her truck. He opened the door and helped her up inside the truck. With a wide smile of affection, he kissed her hand. "You come again?"

Angelica smiled. "I'll be back, I'm sure." She waved as he dismounted her truck. She got on the radio, "Okay, guys, let's get these loads to Louisiana."

"Looks like Cover Girl has a boyfriend," Lethal said.

CHAPTER TWENTY-ONE

"I am so glad they let us come back to the estate for the weekend. I'm going to call Rex and see if he can come out for the whole week and go to the ball with me."

"I need to talk to Hank or Mr. Pig about letting me off this next week. Pig said I could go home this weekend, but dispatch has me on duty all week."

"Good luck with that, Shelby. Once they have you scheduled, it's hard to get Hank to change anything."

"Pig said I could go home. Guess I'll just have to remind him of what he promised me."

"Will you bring Jack back with you for the ball?"

"I'm not sure if I'm coming back for the ball."

"You have to come back for the ball. Even with all the snobs it's still fun."

"We'll see. To be honest, I just want to go home and see my husband."

◊◊◊

Jazz scanned the command center. "You've changed things since the first time I was in here, Hank."

"Yeah, we made some upgrades. Pig wants every one of his employees on the chip program by the end of next year."

"Is that where they put information chips under your skin?"

"Yeah, it's not that big of a deal. They insert it with a needle. All your information is available with a simple scan. No more need for printed credentials, and if you're ever lost, the tracking device locates you at once."

"Sounds creepy. What happens if you want to quit or don't want the chip?"

"It's easy to remove, but I promise you, it won't be long until everyone in the world will be using the chip identification system. It eliminates a lot of fraud and theft. Even your banking will be done with the chip. No more identity theft."

"What if we refuse to get the chip?"

"You won't be able to work for PIGT any longer."

"Goodbye to privacy."

"Sure there are drawbacks, but seems to me the positive aspects outweigh the negative. In fact, I haven't felt like my privacy has been infringed upon at all."

"But you're a boss; you have control over who sees what."

"Not really. There are security measures to prevent abuse of the system."

"I'm still skeptical."

"Let's get back to business. Here is what I need you and Drake to do during the ball. No one is to enter the command center unless Mr. Pig or I am with them. You will be the only two operators in the center and will be held responsible for protecting it. You will be posted outside and unless we tell you to enter the center you are to stay and guard it. I have several guards working the outside perimeter, so you won't need to worry with anything other than this area."

"You think the outside guards will be enough to protect us inside the building?"

"We've never had any problems in the past, ten guards should be sufficient. The rest of the security staff will be attending the ball."

"We can handle the assignment. Have a good time and don't worry about the command center."

"Let's hope so, it's not that difficult to stand in front of a steel door and watch out for people who don't belong."

On the way out of the command center, Jazz took note of the door's thickness. "Will we be provided with keys in case of an emergency?"

"Mr. Pig will give one of you a key, but it will be armed with an alarm to alert us if the key is used without notification."

"Just one more question. If something does go wrong, how long will it take you guys to get to us if we need help?"

"It's is about three minutes from the ballroom to here." Hank's cell phone rang. "I have to take this. You should have all the information you need." He turned his back on Jazz.

Jazz went to retrieve his jacket from behind a chair. He took out a small notebook and pretended to make some notes, staying as close as he could without drawing suspicion.

Hank said into the phone, "Yes, I'll be right down. Has Mr. Pig been notified? Alright, I'll contact him and be right there." He finished the call and dialed his boss. "Mr. Pig, they have Rat Hole in the outside warehouse near the dog pen. Okay, I'll let them know you're on your way."

Jazz moved quietly to the door and slipped out of the center.

Hank looked around, thinking he'd heard the door. Seeing no one enter or leave, he dialed his cell phone. "We're on our way."

Jazz hurried down the hallway to his room. He went in the bathroom, turned on the water, and took out his phone and called Drake. "Hey, I just heard they got Rat Hole here. They have him in the warehouse near the dogs. There is no way we can get to him now and if we try and rescue him, we'll be putting the whole operation in jeopardy. Rat Hole should have come back to the club where we could have protected him—now he's a dead man. You need to call Lizard and let him know what's going down."

◊◊◊

Shelby had tired of the book she was reading and wanted some fresh air. She stepped out onto the balcony of her room. She looked over the estate and saw the dogs were restless in their pen. They obviously needed some attention and she needed someone to talk to about her dilemma. She had been contemplating how she was going to approach Hank about her time off.

Shelby left her room and approached the dogs, calling to them through the fence. Without hesitation, both dogs came for affection from their new friend. She reached through the fence and rubbed each dog on the head. "You guys look like you need to get out of that cage and run for a while. I'll ask Mr. Pig about that after awhile, okay?" She sat down next to the fence and continued to talk to them and pet.

Shelby stretched out on the lawn. She continued to talk to the dogs, telling them everything that was on her mind. She looked up through the trees to the starry sky. *What the hell have I gotten myself into—again?*

As she refocused her attention on the dogs, Shelby noticed that Mr. Pig and Hank were riding in a golf cart toward the warehouse behind the dog's pen. *Now what the heck are those men doing out here tonight?* Shelby stood up and hushed the dogs. She tiptoed away and quietly followed Mr. Pig and Hank to the warehouse.

Mr. Pig and Hank entered the warehouse along with two other guards. Rat Hole had blood coming from his nose, eyes, and mouth. His hands were handcuffed behind his back and he was on his knees in the middle of the floor. Casey and two of his men were doing their best to hold his limp, beaten body up.

"What, you couldn't wait for Mr. Pig to arrive before making hamburger out of his face?" Hank growled.

"He kept trying to get away, Hank."

Pig wore his fedora and a cigarette hung out of his mouth. He walked toward Rat Hole, his cane pounding the floor. Casey pulled Rat Hole's hair back so that his face was toward Pig. "Well, well, Mr. Rat Hole, I have been looking all over for you. You took something that belonged to one of my best customers and I had to cover your theft out of my own pocket. I don't like having to do that. Do you know what happens to thieves in this business?"

Rat Hole was almost unconscious and didn't respond.

Pig pulled a handgun out of his vest and in one swift motion, pointed the gun at Rat Hole's forehead and fired. Rat Hole's body slipped to the floor as the men holding him up let go. Pig put his gun back in his vest. He turned toward the door, Hank following. "Casey, clean this up."

Shelby had made her way to the outside wall of the warehouse. Keeping her body against the wall, she crept over to the doorway. She had intended to listen to the conversation between the men inside and had not expected to see an execution. "Oh my God." She knew she had to get away from the warehouse and ran as fast as she could toward the dog pen. She only stopped when she found the spot that she had occupied just minutes earlier. The dogs were barking when she returned.

Compose yourself, Shelby, they can't know that you heard or saw anything. Shelby focused on the dogs. "Calm down, boys. Calm down, it's okay."

Shelby wanted to scream and cry at the same time. "Oh God, oh God, I don't know what to do," she whispered and put her hands in the fence and rubbed the dogs' heads. They were agitated and they sensed something beyond her presence. She tried hard to calm them down.

"Boy, they are sure upset about something," Jazz said, startling Shelby.

"Yeah, some noise came from over there near that warehouse and they just went nuts. I'm not sure what it was, but it was loud."

Jazz had seen Shelby running from the warehouse and knew she had witnessed what had just happened to his friend. "Really? Well maybe we should go check it out?"

"You can if you want, but I'm going to try and calm down the dogs."

"I'll just go and let Mr. Pig know that there was some kind of noise that upset the dogs. And you? Are you okay? You look like something is wrong."

"I'm fine. I'm not sure it was anything; maybe a car or truck backfired. Maybe we shouldn't mention it to Mr. Pig, he's always so busy."

"Are you sure? I can go investigate and make sure it wasn't anything major."

"No, let it go. I think the dogs just need some extra attention."

Just as the two were getting the dogs calmed down, Mr. Pig and Hank got in the golf cart and headed toward the mansion. "Hey, there goes Mr. Pig and Hank now." Jazz started to wave at them.

Shelby pulled his hands down. "I don't think that would be a good idea. What if they did something over there and we aren't supposed to know about it? Don't you think they might be upset with us?"

"Yeah, you might be right. I'll go check things out in a little while. Maybe I'd better walk you back to your room. You don't look so good."

"I am feeling a little dizzy. I must be coming down with something. I do need to go to my room."

Jazz helped Shelby to her feet and escorted her back to her room.

Jazz left Shelby and went back outside to call Drake who was taking care of some business for Mr. Pig at another warehouse away from the estate. "Can you talk?"

"Yes, but only for a couple of minutes."

"They killed Rat Hole. I heard the gunfire and I know that blonde female driver saw everything."

"Shit. How do you know she saw anything?"

"I was almost to the warehouse when I heard the gunfire. I hid behind a tree and she ran right by me toward the dogs. She was white as a sheet and scared. She didn't tell me she saw anything, but her actions said otherwise."

"That's not good. If Pig finds out, he'll kill her just to keep her quiet. You sure it was Rat Hole?"

"I haven't seen his body come out of there yet, but I'm positive."

"I've got to go. You need to watch that girl. If she talks, it might be a problem for us too."

Shelby leaned her head against the door until she was sure Jazz was gone. Then she ran into the bathroom. "Oh my God, what am I going to do?" She threw up in the toilet, got up, and wiped her face with a wet washcloth. She was startled by a knock on her door.

"Hey Shelby, I was thinking maybe we could go out for a drink?"

Shelby went and opened the door. She slowly put her index finger to her lips. "Shh!" Then announced, "Let me put on a little makeup and then we'll go."

Angelica knew from Shelby's face that something was terribly wrong. She followed Shelby to the bathroom, stopping on the way to turn on the stereo.

"What the hell?"

"Shh! Let me put on some clean clothes and some fresh makeup and we'll go to the casino." She got ready as Angelica called for a ride into town.

Neither of them spoke as they rode into town. They arrived at one of Angelica's favorite bars. "We will call you when we need a ride back to the estate," she said.

They went into the bar, found a secluded table in the corner, and ordered drinks from the waitress. After their drinks were served and they were alone, Shelby finally broke down and let some of the tears she had been holding back fall.

"Oh Angelica, it was horrible. Pig just shot that man in the head and they let him fall to the floor like a piece of trash."

"What are you talking about?"

"I don't know why or who he was, all I know is I saw Pig kill him in the warehouse behind the dog pen. I was out playing with the dogs and saw Hank and Pig walk toward that warehouse. I thought it would be a good time to talk to both of them about me going home next week, so I followed them over there. Just as I got to the doorway, I saw Pig put a gun to that man's head and shoot him."

"Oh no. Does Pig know you saw anything?"

"No, I got out of there as fast as I could. I was by the dog pen with Jazz when they came out of the warehouse."

"Did Jazz see anything?"

"I don't think so."

Did you tell him anything?"

"No, and I stopped him from going to talk to Pig and Hank when they left the warehouse."

"Do you think he might say something to Pig?"

"I don't know."

"This isn't good, Shelby. Maybe it would be best if you quit and went home now before Pig gets wind of the fact that you might have seen something. God only knows what he might do."

"I'm going to call Jack tonight and tell Hank I quit tomorrow."

"I need to call Rex and let him know what has gone down. You sure you didn't recognize the man?"

"He was beaten so badly, Angelica, I don't think he had a face anymore."

"He must have done something really horrible for Pig and his men to do that to him. I remember hearing something about one of the new drivers. I think it was the one who was paired with Lethal. You remember that guy?"

"No, I think I had just started rolling with you."

"I can't remember what they called him, I'll have to ask Lethal. But I think that guy took something from his truck and then took off. Not much was ever said about it after it happened. I'm sure if he did take something, Pig was looking for him. Pig never forgets anything, especially when something is stolen from him."

Angelica got up from the table. "Give me just a minute, I need to call Rex. I'll be right back."

Shelby put her arms on the table and rested her head on them. "What am I going to do?" she murmured.

Angelica got Rex on the phone. "Hey, we have a situation. Pig killed one of the drivers tonight and Shelby accidentally witnessed it. I really think she's in danger if she stays on with us."

"How did she witness something like that? Did he do it out in the open?"

"No, he did it in a warehouse on the estate. She was in the doorway when he killed the man."

"Does Pig know she saw anything?"

"Not that we know of, but one of the guards found her by the dog pens in a state of panic. I'm sure he knew she saw something. We just don't know if he's going to say anything."

"Yes, you should advise her to get out now!"

◊◊◊

"Mr. Pig, the men are going to put Rat Hole's body under the foundation of the new warehouse," Hank said.

"Good. Now we can get down to business. I need to make sure this ball is spectacular. I have several people who I need to impress. Business is down this year and I want to make sure next year is much better."

"Yes, sir Mr. Pig."

Jazz entered Pig's office. "Hank, I'm sorry to interrupt but I need to speak with you."

Pig nodded at Hank. "What is it?" Hank asked.

Jazz was nervous. "Well, sir, I thought you might want to know that I just walked Ms. Shelby back to her room. She was over at the dog pens. She appeared to be upset about something. She said she had heard something that sounded like a car backfire coming from the warehouse behind the pens. I was going to check it out, but thought I'd better check with you first. I also think maybe someone should check on Ms. Shelby."

Hank looked at Pig who ignored his glance. "Did she say anything other than hearing the noise?" Hank asked.

"No, but I could tell she was shaken by something. Do you want me to check out the warehouse, sir?"

Hank walked Jazz to the doorway. "No, no, we will handle it. We are already aware of what occurred there. Mr. Pig was storing an old vehicle and it backfired when we tried to start it. But thank you so much for your concern."

After Jazz left Hank and Pig, he called Drake and let him know what had happened.

"You do understand that they are going to kill that woman?"

"I told them she only heard the gunshot. I doubt they will do anything."

"Maybe. We're all involved in a dangerous business."

"Club comes first, my brother."

"Agreed."

When Jazz was gone, Hank looked at Pig. "You want her taken care of, sir?"

"No, not yet, you idiot. I think I want to know whether she saw anything first."

"I'll have her interrogated right away."

"No, I think I'll speak with Shelby myself. I'll be able to tell whether she knows anything or not."

"Very well, sir. I'll send for her."

"No, not tonight. I'll speak with her tomorrow."

"Yes, sir."

◊◊◊

"Look, Angelica, I know you and Rex want me to hang in here and help you, but I can't anymore. I need to go home. This is just too much."

"I understand how you feel, Shelby, and I don't blame you for wanting to leave. I think you're right. If you stay around, you'll be in more danger."

"I'm glad you understand. I'm going to call Jack tonight and let him know that things just haven't worked out here. I'll tell Pig and Hank tomorrow."

"I'll miss you." The women sat and talked for a while longer before calling for the limo.

Clutching her cell phone, Shelby sat in her bathroom, hesitating before dialing Jack's number. "Jack, I'm coming home."

"Really? That's great, baby! When will you be here?"

"I should be there either tomorrow or the next day. Depends on how long it takes them to processes me out."

"Process you out? What's that mean?"

"I'm coming home for good. This situation just isn't for me. The money is good, but I just don't like being away from you so much."

"Okay, sweetheart, you sound strange. Is anything wrong?"

"No, nothing is wrong, I'm just a little tired."

"What did you do, stay up all night?"

"Yeah, I went to bed late. Angelica and I went out for a couple of drinks."

"I hope you didn't drink too much. You know you don't handle liquor too well."

"No, baby, I only had two. We went to one of Angelica's favorite casinos."

"Casino? Are you coming home broke?"

"I didn't do any gambling. I'm coming home with a pocket full of money."

"I love you darling; it will be good to have you home."

"I love you and miss you too, sweetheart. See you soon." Shelby hung up, went into the bedroom and stretched out on the bed.

A knock at the door woke her up. It was 5:00 a.m.

"Ms. Shelby," she heard through the door.

"Yes?"

"Mr. Pig requests an audience with you after breakfast in his office, please."

Why does he want to see me now? I tried to get in to see him and Hank all day yesterday, but they didn't have the time. Did Jazz say something to them? What am I going to say to him? Will he think I want to quit because I saw something? Will he try and kill me? The thoughts running through her mind petrified her. She finally found the resolve. *I'm going to tell him I'm leaving, then I'm getting the hell out of here.*

After breakfast, Shelby knocked softly on Pig's office door.

"Come in."

Shelby entered the room. Hank was there standing behind Pig as usual.

"Have a seat. Hank, give us a minute, please."

Hank left the room, but left the door open a crack.

"How are you, Shelby? Have you been enjoying those books I gave you?"

"Oh yes, Mr. Pig, I have enjoyed them very much."

"How's the job going? Are you liking it here at PIGT?"

Shelby chose her words carefully. "I have enjoyed working here, Mr. Pig…."

"Good," Pig interrupted. "I have a special job I want you to be on next week. It's a very important delivery and it should put you back here just in time for the ball on Saturday night. "

"Well, Mr. Pig that's…."

"No need to thank me, it comes with extra pay too. You can go ahead and have Hank come on in when you leave."

Hank entered the room before Shelby could stand to leave. "But, Mr. Pig, I…" Hank came over and took her by the elbow and escorted Shelby through the door. "Thanks, Shelby, Mr. Pig has an important phone call to take. I'll get with you later."

Shelby couldn't believe what had just happened. Not only hadn't she been unable to quit, but Pig had put her on another job. *What am I going to do?*

Pig turned around in his chair. "She knows, Hank. I don't know how she knows what happened in that warehouse, but she knows. She was ready to quit. I just put her on a run to Mexicali. Let Tito know she's coming. I hate to see her go, but she has to disappear."

"You want me to have them kill her?"

"No, she's too much of a commodity. She'll net a good chunk of change on the human market down there. Maybe someday she'll find her way back to the States."

"I'll take care of everything today and send her out in the morning."

"Make sure you jam her company phone. I'm sure she has a personal phone too. See what you can do about disabling it as well. Don't give her any ideas about what I have planned for her. We don't want her to run."

"I'll take care of it, sir."

Shelby had returned to her room after her brief conversation with Pig. She went into the bathroom and turned on the water. She felt she still needed to be cautious. She took out her phone and called Jack. "Hey honey, Mr. Pig talked me into doing one more delivery for him. I'll be back here on Friday. Do you think you can make it down here on Saturday night for the big ball?"

"I'll definitely try."

"Good, if you're here it will be easier for me to tell him I'm quitting."

CHAPTER TWENTY-TWO

Hank handed Shelby a piece of paper with instructions. "Hank, where is Angelica? I haven't seen her since the day before yesterday. Isn't she going on this haul?"

"I have her on another run. You'll be going with two other drivers. Don't worry about her. Just make sure you make your delivery and pickup on time. See you on Friday."

The other two drivers were pulling out of the yard while Shelby was airing up her truck. She tried to contact them on the radio but neither of them answered. "Well, I guess I'm making this haul alone. Won't be the first time and sure won't be the last." Shelby was actually pleased to be pulling this haul by herself so she could make her own time and not be limited by what others wanted to do.

Angelica had tried to call Shelby all morning on both the company and her personal phones. She had a weird feeling about things and wanted to talk to Rex. She reached a spot where she thought she could pull over and try Shelby again on her personal phone. Unlike the previous attempts, this time she left a message: "Hey Barbie, it's Cover Girl, I heard you got roped into another load. Call me as soon as possible. It's important."

◊◊◊

"Did you take care of everything, Hank?"

"Yes, sir, the two drivers I put with her are unloading and picking up at other locations. She'll be alone when she gets to her delivery spot. Tito said he would be glad to take her off your hands and put her to work."

"Good, he knows not to kill her?"

◊◊◊

Shelby decided to take a break in Weatherford, Texas. As she waited for her food order, she took out her cell phone, turned it on, and waited for it to power up. Once it was powered up she noticed she had several voice mails. Jack had left a message letting her know a client was scheduled to be in town on Saturday, but that he would join her on Sunday to take her home. Shelby was disappointed, but understood. Then she moved on to Angelica's messages. All three said: "Call me it's important."

Shelby called her back, "Angelica, this is Shelby. I'm in Weatherford, taking a break. Call me." Shelby then called Jack.

"Hi, baby."

"Where are you?"

"Taking a break in Weatherford. I was thinking I could stop by the house on my way through tonight."

"That sounds great. I'm sorry about the ball. My guys really screwed up. One of my best customers wants me to personally to fix the mess."

"I understand. I really didn't want to go to that stupid ball anyway. It won't be necessary for you to come Sunday. I'm not even going to tell Pig I'm leaving. I'm just going to pack up my stuff when I get back on Friday and head home."

"Are you okay, sweetheart? Your voice sounds funny."

"I'm okay. There is something wrong, but I don't want to talk about it over the phone. I'll tell you about it when I get home. Things just didn't work out for me here. Maybe I just need to buy my own truck and work for myself. I can't seem to find anyone I really like working for anymore."

"We'll talk when you get home, but I agree, you need your own truck."

Shelby's phone buzzed. "Hey baby, I've got to go, Angelica's calling. I'll see you tonight."

"Okay. I love you."

"Love you, too." She switched calls. "Hi Angelica, what's up?"

"I'm glad I finally got in touch with you. I've been so worried. Where are you?"

"Pig put me on a small delivery to Mexicali. I'm in Weatherford right now."

"I thought you were quitting?"

"I tried, but that fat pig wouldn't give me a chance to talk. I decided to take this one last load. I'm just going to leave when I get back on Friday."

"I've been so worried about you. They sent me out really early the morning after we talked. I didn't have a chance to tell you before I left. When I realized you weren't on the job, I figured you might have quit already. I didn't want you to leave until we had a chance to say goodbye. Hank told me you were going on another haul."

"I'm supposed to be going to Mexicali with two other drivers, but I'm rolling by myself right now. They took off before I could even get my truck aired up."

"Careful, I have a funny feeling about this. Something doesn't seem right."

"I'm okay. I'm going to stop by the house tonight and see Jack."

"Good. Is he coming to get you on Friday?"

"No, he has to work, but I'll be all right. I'm not even going to tell Pig. I'm just going to leave."

"They have me hauling loads to southern Louisiana until Saturday morning. Please keep in touch. I'll probably need to contact you sometime soon about what you saw Pig do. But that won't be until after we take him down for good. That's going to happen really soon from what Rex tells me."

"I promise. I'll call in and check on you."

"I sure am going to miss you, my friend."

"Me too, Cover Girl."

"Take care, Barbie. Call me when you get home so I know you made it safely."

"Will do."

They called out her number for her food and Shelby got up to retrieve it then took it back to the booth. She felt lonely without Angelica, but she also felt relieved that she would soon be gone from PIGT.

"Is this chair taken?" Shelby looked up and recognized her old friend, Buck from her sand hauling years.

She sprang to her feet. "Buck!" She hugged his neck.

"How are you doing, Shelby?"

"I'm doing great, Buck! Please, sit."

Buck sat across from her. "It's been a long time. What have you been doing?"

"Oh, I'm hauling for PIGT. How about you? You still hauling sand?"

"Of course. Not for the same company. I'm driving my own truck. I also have a couple of other trucks that I lease out."

"Sounds like you're doing well. I've been thinking about buying my own truck and leasing on somewhere. How's the sand business these days? Hear from any of the drivers we use to run with down south?"

"Mundo and White Lightning are running the other two trucks for me. The sand business is still strong. I'm doing well financially, too."

"I've been thinking about getting back into sand hauling, but this time, I want to do it in my own truck."

"What about PIGT? I heard they're a pretty good company to work for."

"Oh, the money is okay, but I think there's some shady stuff going on."

"Well, let me know if you decide to get back into sand. I'll hook you up with some good companies."

Before Buck left, they traded phone numbers.

As Shelby moved along the highway she thought about her conversation with Buck. *Running into him was a good omen*, she thought.

She didn't bother to let dispatch know that she would be taking her overnight break at home. *The command center knows where I am at all times. I don't give a shit if they get upset that I'm staying at my own house.*

Jack met Shelby at the door. "Hi baby. I'm so glad you're home."

His hug and kiss made Shelby feel safe. "I'm glad I'm home too. Feels like I haven't been here in forever." Her dogs, Buddy and Pooh-bear jumped up on her lap as she sat down. "Hi guys, it's so good to see you. I've missed both of you." She looked up from the dogs. "I also miss our boys. How are they? Seems like when I'm home I know everything that's going on with them. When I'm gone I feel like I know nothing about their lives."

Jack put his arms around his wife. "Those boys are fine, Shelby Mathews. You raised them to take care of themselves. You did a great job, sweetheart. They're busy with their own lives, just like we were at their ages."

"I just worry about them and hope they're safe."

"That's what mothers are supposed to do. Now, tell me what's really bothering you. Does it have to do with why you're quitting PIGT?"

"Jack, don't freak out, but I accidentally saw Pig shoot someone in the head."

"What! Oh my God, Shelby."

"Please don't go off, I really just need you to listen."

"Okay, Shelby, but you're not going back to that estate."

"I'm not. Just listen…I realized soon after I started working that something was off with the company. We were never allowed to see our loads. Most of the time we loaded in the middle of the night. Sometimes the people we were loading or unloading for would do it for us while we either waited in our trucks or in waiting areas.

"At first…I just let it go…but as time went on…I was afraid I might be hauling things that were not legal. So, I decided to just leave, but then I met Angelica. We became friends and after some time passed she started to trust me with a secret…. She's an undercover DEA agent. They have been investigating Pig for a while. The stuff we are hauling is illegal…. I'm not sure what the loads are, but I believe they are drugs, guns, and other contraband. I stayed with it because Pig has a thing for me and Angelica thought I might be able to get information out of him if he ever decided to confide in me."

"Just how close did that fat pig get to you?"

"Don't be stupid Jack, you know me better than that. I couldn't stand his smell let alone let him get close."

"You should have gotten out of there sooner."

"I promised Angelica I would stay on a little while longer and keep my ears open. Everything was going okay until we got back to the estate this last week. I was out playing with the dogs when Hank and Pig drove by in a golf cart they use to get around the estate. I had been trying all day to talk to them about coming home this week for a break. I walked toward the warehouse they had entered, hoping to talk. I got to the doorway and just as I was about to go inside, I saw Pig with a gun to some man's head. The man had been beaten really badly. I couldn't even tell who it was, his face was so disfigured and blood covered. I ran from the doorway as fast as I could."

"Did anyone see you? You could be in danger if anyone knows what you saw."

"I don't think so. I ran back to the dogs and pretended I was playing with them. Pig and Hank left in the golf cart. I don't even think they saw me with the dogs."

"Why the hell did you agree to take another load out for him?"

"I tried to tell him I was finished, but he didn't let me get a word in when I went to his office. I thought I'd just take this one last load and then leave Friday night after I returned the truck."

"Well, I'll be there Friday."

"You don't need to do that. In fact, it will be easier for me to get my stuff and leave if I don't have to explain why you're there. This load is a simple drop and go. I'll probably be back there on Thursday if I don't mess around in the truck stops too much."

"Okay, but I want you to call me every five hours so that I know you're safe. Did you tell Angelica about what happened?"

"Yes." She gave me her number and Rex's number. Rex is her 'handler.' Once they take Pig down they will need me to testify about what I saw."

"You're sure these people are with the DEA?"

"Yes."

"How do you get yourself into these situations, baby? I can't believe one little woman can attract so many bad things in her life!"

◇◇◇

Pig was scanning his computer when he noticed that Shelby was at her house. He called Hank. "Did you give Shelby permission to spend her break time at home?"

"No, sir. I did see that she was there. I thought that if I said anything to her, it might tip her off about what you have planned for her."

"Fine, let her spend one last night with her husband."

◊◊◊

Shelby left the house early the next morning. She wanted to get to Tucson quickly. A familiar voice from her past came on the radio, "How about you, Barbie?"

"You got Barbie, who is this?"

"You got Grumpy. How you been, Barbie?"

"Hey Grumpy, I've been good. Where are the boys hanging out these days?"

"Rooster is still hauling in South Texas, Shade Tree and Widow-Maker are still running long-hauls in all 48 states. J.R., Slick, Light-Foot, Bean, and Papa Wolf are rolling with me right now. We just dropped loads in Bakersfield. Headed back to the dirt bowl now."

"It's been a long time since I've seen y'all. You guys got time to stop for coffee in Voca? I'm headed to Phoenix for the night and then dropping this load in Mexicali."

The radio buzzed with chatter about Barbie until all the drivers were parked at a restaurant in Voca. Shelby felt like a princess being escorted into the establishment by all her friends.

"Table for about ten, please. There might be more coming, but this is all for now."

"Yes, sir, this way please."

"So, what you hauling, Barbie?"

"Oh, a little of this and a little of that."

"We miss the Sand Queen, you know."

"Well, I've been thinking about getting back on the throne again. I've been spending a lot of hours away from the house."

"Oh, that hubby of yours doesn't want you gone too much? I don't blame him. If you were my wife, I wouldn't let you out of the house."

"Very funny, Slick. Hubby doesn't have anything to say about what I do."

After a great, but short visit with her friends, Shelby headed toward Tucson. Over the years, Shelby had made hundreds of friends on the highways. Good friends who had gotten her out of some really awful situations more than once. She knew those friends would always be there to help her if she ever needed them again.

◊◊◊

Angelica contacted Rex. "Something is going on here and I think you should see if you can send in the team earlier."

"I've already put in for the agents to bust Pig next weekend. I still haven't received confirmation from the director."

"I think Shelby is in danger. They've separated us and sent her to Mexicali with two drivers I don't know."

"I'm doing my best to get you and her extracted out of there next week."

"I just don't know if we have the time. I think Pig is up to something or he knows that Shelby saw him kill that driver. She could be in trouble especially going down to the border by herself."

"Angelica, calm down. Pig isn't that stupid."

"I don't know; he's done some pretty crazy stuff."

"You just keep in touch with Shelby and I'll do my best to get the director to move on this quickly."

"He's never moved fast on anything."

"Just keep tabs on her and I'll let you know what we are going to do."

"Are you still going to be my date to the ball?"

"I'll be the one in the SWAT vest."

"Funny. Even if they don't extract us during the ball, I still want you here."

"I'll try, Angelica, but I can't promise. Keeping you safe and getting you out of there is my priority. If the director decides to hold off with the extraction, the exposure to those involved with Pig could really be beneficial. I'll let you know."

◊◊◊

"Drake, are you sure you guys have everything under control? I don't want to lose any more club members."

"Just make sure those twenty brothers you're sending get here by Friday. Everything is in place to blow Saturday night at midnight."

"They will leave Monday morning and definitely be there on Thursday."

"Good, we are going to need the back up when the shit hits the fan. Are you sure that twenty extra men will be enough?"

"I think so. If most of the guards will be unarmed at the ball."

CHAPTER TWENTY-THREE

The lot was dark when Shelby arrived at her destination. She remembered the warehouse from the only time she had been there with Angelica. However, this time, no one was around. She continued to slowly pull into the warehouse's parking lot. She turned her truck around and backed it into the warehouse dock. "Well, if no one shows up I can drive straight out."

Shelby punched in a text message on her truck's computer to the command center: *Arrived at location. Parked at dock. No one around, no sign of other drivers.* A few seconds later, she received a return message stating: *Stay in your truck. Someone will contact you shortly.* Shelby sat silently. Her personal phone vibrated in her pocket. She knew she couldn't answer it in the cab because of the camera, so she moved to her sleeper.

It wasn't safe in the sleeper either, but she figured she could hide her activity with her pillow. The phone call was from Angelica. She had two other text messages from Jack. She texted Angelica first: *In my sleeper, can't get out of my truck, have to text. Made it to the warehouse, but no one here. I'm spooked, but dispatch told me to just sit in truck and wait.*

Angelica texted back: *Don't know what's going on. Be careful. Don't go anywhere with anyone. If they tell you to get out of your truck. DON'T. Stay in truck and get out of there as soon as possible. I don't like the smell of things. I think you might be in danger.*

Shelby replied: *Okay I'll try. It's hard not doing what these people want with those big guns they carry.*

Angelica responded: *I know. But it's best not to get out of truck. If that man that I introduced you to shows up, he's nice. But they are all part of cartel, so nice is still dangerous. Don't go with him anywhere.*

Shelby heard something: *I'll try. Someone coming. Call Jack, 555-455-7888 tell I'm okay for now. Got 2 go.*

Shelby stuck her phone into the front pocket of her jeans before responding to the knock on her door. She rolled down the window and had a moment of relief. It was the man who Angelica had introduced her to the last time she was here.

"You come."

Shelby's relief suddenly turned to fear. "No, I can't leave the truck."

"You come, I drive for you."

The man attempted to open Shelby's door but she had locked it. The man's face turned from pleasant to angry. "You open, come. I drive."

She shook her head. "No. I can't. The truck is already parked." The man tried again to open her door before climbing the steps. Shelby rolled up the window. She tried to swallow her fright. She sat up straight in her driver's seat and decided that the best course of action was to drive out of the yard.

She released the air brakes and attempted to pull the truck from where she'd parked it against the dock. To her shock, several men came out of nowhere with automatic machine guns, stood right in front of her truck, and pointed them at her through the windshield. Shelby knew she was in trouble. She put the truck back into park and put her hands up.

The man again stepped up onto her truck. "Open."

Shelby complied.

The man waved her over into the passenger seat. "Sit there."

Shelby again complied as the man took over her truck. The men with the guns moved aside. Shelby rode silently in the passenger seat until the man motioned for her to get into the sleeper. "Back there."

Shelby complied.

Once she was in the sleeper, Shelby attempted to use her cell phone to let Angelica or Jack know what had happened. *They have taken me and my truck. Help me, please. I know we are going into Mexico but I don't know where.* Shelby sent the messages but they were returned "undelivered." Then it dawned on her, *I'm in Mexico I don't have phone service in Mexico.* Shelby couldn't hold back the tears anymore. She was in big trouble.

◊◊◊

A couple of hours later, the truck came to a stop. The man put on the air brakes before pulling back the curtains to the sleeper. "You come now."

Shelby was afraid. Angelica had warned her about getting out of the truck. She moved back onto her bed. "No. I want to go home. You leave me alone."

The man pulled a small handgun out of his belt. "You come, I no want to hurt you. Angelica my friend. Me be you friend."

Tears streamed her face. "Please don't hurt me, I want to go home." Shelby grabbed her jacket.

The man grabbed the blanket and pillow off the bed. He handed them to Shelby. "You need." Shelby reached over and opened the driver's side door.

The morning dew stuck to the dust on the ground. It was still dark but the sun was attempting to poke through the streaks of clouds to the east. All she saw were well-worn buildings lined up in rows, separated by dirt roads, one of which her truck was now parked on. The man pushed Shelby to move across the street toward a dilapidated building. "Go."

Shelby walked toward the door that was barely hanging on by some old rusty hinges. He pulled the door open and motioned for Shelby to enter the room. Shelby entered the dirty room and the man shut the door. He placed a brick at the bottom of the door and a two-by-four across the middle. The door was penetrable and Shelby knew she could easily escape, but where would she go?

She looked through cracks in the walls and tried to see out at the area. All she saw were several other old buildings and more dirt roads from the west wall. The rising sun was warming the door side of the building, which told her the building was facing east. She saw a few hills beyond the buildings through the southeast wall. A market area was in the distance through the north wall. She was apparently in the middle of a town somewhere. Few people walked along the roads, no one seemed to pay much attention to the building she occupied. *Where the hell am I?*

Shelby knew she was in Mexico. The time she spent in the truck while the man drove was about two hours. She wasn't sure which direction they moved, but she knew they went south out of the warehouse yard in Mexicali. *Even if I could get a hold of anyone, how could I let them know where I am?* She reached into her pants' pocket and realized she still had her cell phone. "Great, no service." She slipped the phone back into her pocket.

Shelby looked around the room. It was dark except for the morning light that was shining through the large cracks in the walls. In the middle of the room, a metal table and one chair pressed their heavy legs into the dirt floor. A small cot lined the west wall. She went to it and sat down. The dust from the cot filled her nostrils She placed her blanket and pillow over her face and coughed, and then wiped the dust from her face. Tears fell again from her eyes. "Well, you got yourself into something you might not be able to get out of now, Shelby Mathews."

◊◊◊

"Hi Jack, this is Angelica, Shelby's friend."

"Oh, hi Angelica. Shelby told me about you when she came home. What's up? Is Shelby okay?"

"Yes, at least I think she is for now. She was at her drop off location and said she was fine. She wanted me to call you and let you know."

"I appreciate that, Angelica. Was she going to try and call me later?"

"I believe she plans to do that as soon as she can. I'm going to try and call her later just to make sure she's on her way back to Louisiana."

"Please keep in touch with me and let me know that she's okay."

"I will and if she calls you, please remind her to call me so I won't worry."

"Will do."

◊◊◊

A creaking door woke Shelby up and she realized she'd fallen asleep while holding her pillow and blanket to her face. The man who'd brought her to the building entered with a plate of food and a beer. He put his delivery on the table. "You eat, I be your friend. Angelica my friend. No trouble. Okay?"

Shelby got up and walked toward the table. She wasn't hungry but she wanted something to drink, even if it was beer. "Thank you." She reached for the beer and went back to the cot.

"Angelica my friend."

Shelby didn't really understand what that meant but she responded, "Angelica is my friend too. Why am I here? I want to go home."

Shelby saw a flicker of kindness on the man's face. "I be your friend." The man left, securing the door just as he had before.

Shelby sat back against the wall and sipped her beer. The feeling of hopelessness wasn't as strong as it had been when she first arrived. "I've got to get out of here."

◊◊◊

Angelica tried to call Shelby for hours. She tried Jack too, but he had not answered his phone. Finally, she called Rex. "I can't get a hold of Shelby. I'm worried that she's in trouble."

"Well, I hate to tell you this, Angelica, but the high ups won't approve taking Pig down yet. They say we need more of the people he's involved with before we can shut down the operation."

"What about the ball? Will they be able to bust his connections there?"

"I thought so, but they say they don't have enough evidence to prove that Pig is moving their product."

"Seriously? After all the information that I've given them?"

"I know, be patient. We will take him down soon."

"What about Shelby? She might in deep trouble."

"Calm down, Angelica, I'm sure she's fine."

"I don't know, Rex, I've been trying to call her all day."

"She's probably doing her best to get back home. Didn't you say that this was her last job?"

"Yes, but I'm still concerned."

"Be an agent, Angelica. Remember, 'don't get involved.'"

"Too late Rex, I'm already involved. She's become my friend and I'm seriously worried about her."

"Be professional; stay calm. Wait until you haven't heard from her for a week.

"A week? Are you crazy? She could be dead by then! What is wrong with you? You do not sound like yourself at all."

"I've got to go, Angelica."

◊◊◊

"Get your agent under control, Rex, she's not focusing on her objective."

"I'm working with her sir, but she has made friends with this Shelby Mathews. She's not one to be concerned or emotional over something unless she has some basis for it. Angelica is very level-headed and professional, sir."

"Maybe so, but she needs to remember that her job is to help us take out his supply lines and make sure that he can't do business anymore. Her objective is to shut Pig down."

"Yes, sir."

After the director left, Rex attempted to reconnect with Angelica. She would not or could not answer her phone. He left a voice message. "I can't explain everything, but when you get this message call me back. I'm going to be at the ball, but if you can call me first I can give you an update."

◊◊◊

Jazz and Drake had taken the night off to meet several of their gang brothers at a casino. When they walked into the bar they were shocked to see over fifty of the members had arrived to help them take down Pig. With fist pounds, back pats, and high fives, the brothers greeted each other. "LA Bad Boys forever, my brothers."

"Forever."

"We have a chance to expand our territory this weekend!" Drake lifted his beer. The other gang members followed. Jazz took a map that he and Drake had drawn up out of his pocket. "Gather 'round, we'll show you the plan."

The men gathered around a pool table and Jazz laid out the map. "This is the main entrance. It is heavily fortified. But once we take out the command center inside, it will be easy for you to take out the guards at that gate."

"Is this the only entrance?"

"It's the only one we were told about, but I know there are more. Pig only uses those in special circumstances. Everything comes through the front gate."

Drake pointed to specific points on the map. "We need you guys to be ready to storm the estate the minute we take down the center. Most of the guards will be at the ball, and although they won't be packing officially, no doubt their weapons will be nearby. The faster you guys get in, the more control we'll have."

"Pig isn't an idiot; he's not going to leave himself exposed that much."

"I'm sure that not only will his guards be packing, his guests will have heat or be accompanied by their own armed guards."

"Possible, but we are going to blow the shit out of his command center, take out his front guard shack and blow the doors off of several of his warehouses at the same time—we're talking major chaos. It's going to take Pig several minutes to realize just what's hit him. By that time, you guys will be on top of him, taking out anyone who tries to resist."

"I'm ready, it's about time Pig pays for all the shit he has done to us."

"Payday, brothers." The gang members drank to their future success and challenged each other to games of pool for the rest of the night.

◊◊◊

Shelby was startled again when the Mexican man returned with some clothes. "You change to these. We have to go."

The tight fitting leggings and crop top looked like something a whore would wear. "No. I'm just fine in the clothes I have on."

He moved in close. "You put this on, we go."

"No!"

The man turned red and pulled the gun out of his belt. "Put on. Now."

Shelby remained defiant, yelling "No!" and running toward the door.

He caught her by her hair and pulled her to the ground. Before she knew what was happening another man came into the room. They spoke in Spanish while Shelby lay face down in the dirt.

The Mexican man pulled Shelby up off the floor and pushed her toward the cot. The other man grabbed the clothes off the table. "Put this on."

"No. I won't"

"Then we will kill you."

"You speak English? Then you can understand, kiss my ass. I don't care what you do to me but I'm not putting that on. You are not going to make me do anything I don't want to do. Go ahead, kill me, I don't care."

The Mexican men conversed in Spanish.

"You will regret not cooperating with us, guera."

"You will regret taking me, you idiots."

The men left, securing the door behind them.

Shelby gasped for air. "Oh my God. Oh my God. They are going to kill me," she said as she paced. "I've got to get out of here." She tried the door. It gave at the bottom near the rusty hinge. She looked around the room for something that might help her pry the hinge loose, but there was nothing but rats and dirt.

She looked at the chair and had an idea. She took the chair and used the leg like a hammer on the hinge. After about ten blows to the hinge, it broke loose from the rotting wood on the door. Just as she was pulling the hinge loose with her hand she heard footsteps and men talking in Spanish coming toward her door. She quickly put the chair back and sat on the cot. The door opened and three men walked in.

Shelby hid her face from her visitors. "Why won't you put on these nice clothes, mama?" The man said in perfect English.

"I'm not your mama, my name is Shelby. I won't wear those trashy looking clothes. I'm not a whore and you're not going to make me dress like one."

"I am Tito. I apologize for my men and their lack of respect. I don't want you to be uncomfortable. We were only trying to supply you with some clean clothes. We want you to join us for dinner."

Shelby stood up and faced the well-dressed man. "I don't give a damn who you are or what your intentions might be. Why am I here? I demand you take me home now."

Without flinching, Tito backhanded Shelby across her face. She flew back onto the cot, hitting her head on the wall. Shocked, Shelby grabbed her face and curled up on the cot in a fetal position.

"I'm sorry that you forced me to do that. No one talks to me like that. This is my territory and everyone does what I tell them to do, even you."

Shelby found her resolve; she stood up, and lifted her hand to her burning cheek. "Not me. I want to go home—and if you have no plans to let me go home, then go ahead and kill me. I will never cooperate with you."

The man struck Shelby on her other cheek. Shelby remained on her feet.

"In time you will agree to my terms." Tito turned toward the door speaking Spanish to the two men. The two men grabbed the clothes before leaving.

As night fell, the room plunged into darkness. Shelby was relieved the men left without noticing the hinge was missing from the bottom of the door. She waited for a few hours before going to the door in case the men came back again. This time, she finished removing the rotten wood where the hinge had been. The door still would not give enough for her to squeeze through the bottom. Shelby grabbed the chair and used it again to hammer on the middle hinge of the door. She hoped her captors did not hear her escape attempt.

CHAPTER TWENTY-FOUR

"**L**ook, Angelica, I know you're worried about Shelby. But we don't even know if she's in Mexico. If we want the director to send in the agents, then we need to give him what he wants."

Angelica turned and stormed down the hallway of Rex's hotel, her red evening gown rustling with each step. "I don't believe that idiot has any plans to close out this case, or help Shelby," she bristled.

Rex chased Angelica to the elevator. "I know you're angry that the director seems unconcerned with Shelby's safety. He's not going to take a team of agents into Mexico if it compromises our cases against the cartels there. That could cause international problems with Mexico."

Angelica crossed her arms. "Bullshit! That bastard doesn't care if Shelby gets killed. To him she's just a casualty of war. I know something has happened to her. I've tried getting in touch with her for three days. Her husband doesn't even know where she is. She told me she intended to turn her truck in on Friday—that was yesterday. No one at the estate will tell me anything. She's missing and I know that Pig has something to do with it. He probably paid the cartel to take her."

"We have to have proof. We can't cause an international incident over one missing person."

"You want proof? I'll get you proof. If she's not at the ball and Pig denies knowing why she's not there, you'll know I'm right. He's had a thing for Shelby since she started working here. He's made sure he knows exactly where she is every minute. How is it that he suddenly doesn't have a clue where one of his drivers is located? Where is her truck? I'm going to ask him, and his lie will prove I'm right."

"Maybe so, but what can I do?"

"Nothing. I'll find her and get her out of the hands of those animals myself."

"I believe you, but we can't blow this whole case on a hunch."

"It's not a hunch. I know she's down there somewhere just waiting for us to come get her. She was willing to help me when I needed her; now it's my turn to help her."

"Let's try and enjoy the night."

"Right, we will party and booze it up while Shelby is probably fighting for her life."

They rode the elevator in silence. The couple moved through the lobby to the limo waiting for them outside.

◊◊◊

It took Shelby two days to remove the hinge from the door. Neither Tito nor his men came to check on her. *They're probably trying to starve me into cooperation,* she thought. She didn't care about food, she was thirsty, however, and it was time to break out of her prison.

The two-by-four was the only stronghold on the door. Using one of the hinges Shelby pushed up on the two-by-four until the board fell off the door and to the ground. She stepped back into the room and waited to see if anyone would come to see what had fallen. It remained quiet and she stepped out into the dark night. It was cool and she was thirsty, but she didn't care. Shelby was determined to find her way back to the States, whatever it took.

Shelby looked up at the early evening sky to get her bearings. The quarter moon's position indicated east. "I need to go northeast, that will get me to the States if I walk in that direction." Shelby stayed as close to the buildings as she could "Keep your head down, Shelby, just walk."

◊◊◊

Drake and Jazz were at the top of the stairs with security wands, checking each guest as they entered the ball. "Looking good," Drake said when he spotted Angelica.

"Hey Angelica, how you doing?" Jazz asked.

Angelica gave both Jazz and Drake a small hug. "I'm okay. This is my boyfriend, Rex."

Drake and Jazz shook hands with Rex, and then exchanged 'nice to meet you greetings.'

"Sorry," said Drake, "I still need to wand you both."

"Just doing your job, man," Rex said with a smile.

Angelica and Rex scanned the ballroom. The enormous man was hard to miss.

"Look over there, that's Tito with a couple of his men and Oman and Rodriguez. Looks like Pig has representation here from every cartel."

Rex took two glasses of champagne off the server's tray. He handed one to Angelica. "Looks like he has someone from almost every organization we've been tracking from Central and South America to Mexico and Afghanistan."

"See, now, if the director would have done as I suggested he could have taken down a whole room full of suspects," she whispered.

"That's the point; they're suspects. What we need is proof."

"What more proof do you need than them all being here together?"

"Let's dance." Rex placed their glasses on a table and tried to move closer to Pig.

"So, did my little package get delivered to you?" Pig asked Tito.

"Oh yes. She is quite the little spicy one too."

"Yes and beautiful. I sure hated letting her go, but I couldn't take any chances."

"I understand, she'll definitely bring a pretty dollar on the market. I'm having to teach her a lesson in obedience, however. She is not cooperative, but a few days without food and water will cure her."

"I told you to not kill her, Tito. I wanted you to treat her well. She's too beautiful and smart to be broken down like a common whore."

"I know what you want, Pig, but I have her now. I'll do whatever it takes to bring her into submission. Hell, I might even keep her for myself 'til she's broken in."

"Just don't kill her. If it comes to that call me. I may want her for myself when I visit south of the border."

"We'll see." The men sipped champagne and watched the guests dance.

"Look, you moron, I want to talk to Mr. Pig. My name is Jack Mathews, and my wife Shelby Mathews works for this company. I haven't heard from her in over a week. I want to talk to Mr. Pig now."

Drake and Jazz were busy letting the registered guests into the party. "I'm sorry, Mr. Mathews, but this is really a busy night. I can't let you in right now, but if you will wait out by the gate I'll be sure and let Mr. Pig or Hank know you're here."

"I'm not leaving until you either let me in to see Pig or he comes out here."

Drake knew they only had minutes before all hell was going to break loose. "Okay, Mr. Mathews, if you will just stand over there by that pillar. Let me finish letting in the last of these guests, then I'll go find someone for you."

Jack wasn't happy but he walked over by the pillar to wait.

◊◊◊

Shelby was exhausted and felt like she'd been walking for hours.

"You need help?" A little old woman spoke to Shelby as she rested next to an old building.

"You speak English?"

"Un poco."

"Water, please."

"Agua?"

"Sí, agua."

The lady helped Shelby to her feet and took her into her small house. "Sit."

Shelby sat down at a small, but clean table as the woman poured a glass of water. Shelby forced herself to drink slowly so she would not get sick. Then she put her arms up on the table and laid her head on them.

"Come…you rest."

Shelby knew she needed to keep moving, but her body craved sleep. The woman presented her with a clean, soft bed.

"Gracias."

Shelby took off her boots while the woman pulled back the covers. "De nada."

"I'm American, I was kidnapped by some man named Tito."

"Tito? We know Tito. He very bad man."

"I need a phone."

"You rest, I bring my son to you." She covered Shelby with a heavy blanket. Although it was warm outside, Shelby shivered.

Shelby was not sure how long she had been asleep when the woman returned with a bowl of soup. "Come…eat."

Shelby took several sips before handing it back to the woman.

"I really need a phone."

◊◊◊

"Having a good time, Ms. Angelica?"

Angelica turned to see Pig standing next to her. "Yes, sir, thank you. Mr. Pig, this is my boyfriend Rex."

The men exchanged pleasantries.

"I haven't seen Shelby here tonight, Mr. Pig."

"Neither have I, come to think of it. I suppose I should check with Hank and find out why she's not here."

BOOM!

"What the hell was that?"

BOOM!

The ballroom shook and the lights flickered before completely disappearing. Smoke and dust began to fill the room. Women screamed and men scrambled for hidden weapons scattered throughout the room. "Angelica, are you okay?" Rex grabbed Angelica's hand.

"I thought you said the director wasn't sending in a team tonight?"

"He didn't. Something else is going on. Let's get out of here."

BOOM! BOOM! BOOM! The walls started to crack and parts of the ceiling fell to the floor. Pig was quickly covered by his guards. "Get me my computer."

Hank ran toward the command center. Harry did his best to exit through the kitchen entrance. "Harry, where is my computer? Get me my damn computer!"

Tito and his men gathered together with several of the other cartel leaders. All of them had retrieved weapons they'd stashed in the ballroom. With weapons drawn, the men were prepared to take on whatever came through the ballroom doors.

Angelica and Rex decided to exit through the kitchen since everyone else was attempting to leave through the main door.

Harry brushed by them. "I have it, Mr. Pig." Harry was carrying Pig's computer.

BOOM!

The ceiling above Harry fell as he raced to serve Pig.

Angelica saw the ceiling come down. "Oh no! I think Harry went down with that ceiling."

"Angelica, we need to get out of here. We need to call for fire and rescue." Once they reached the patio, Rex dialed 911. Before he could make connection, another explosion went off, taking out the warehouse near the dog pen. "Get down!" Rex covered Angelica with his body and coat.

They found cover under a tree near the patio. "Oh my God, Rex. Someone has declared war on Pig."

"Yep, and we are right in the middle of the firefight. Come on, let's go around to the front this way. I think we need to try and get to the front gate. This looks like an inside job."

"It has to be. No one could have gotten that close to Pig. I bet they got to the command center."

◊◊◊

Shelby had slept for several hours. The little old woman, placed her hand on her forehead, startling her awake. "You better?"

Shelby sat up, pushing the covers off her sweaty body. "I need a phone." She tried to stand, but was dizzy and sat back down. "I really need a phone, please."

The woman went to the next room and came back with a young man. "This my son, Ricardo."

Shelby stretched out her hand. The young boy shook it. "I'm Shelby. Do you speak English?"

"Yes, some."

"Where am I?"

"You east of Pitiquito. Santa Ana is just east of here a few miles."

"Do you have a phone I can use?"

"Mama says you are here because of Tito?"

"Yes, his men kidnapped me from a warehouse in Mexicali. I need to get back to the States. Are we near Mexicali?"

"No, Mexicali is several miles away. If Tito's men took you they probably took you near his home in Hermosillo."

"I'm confused as to where I am then."

"Arizona is east and north of us."

"Okay, well I still need to get to a phone."

"That will be difficult here, Tito owns this town and most of the towns around here. If you are running from Tito you must be very careful. Most people are afraid of him and won't help you for fear he'll kill them."

"My being here puts you and your mother in danger?"

"Sí, but my mamá knows Tito's mamá, he won't hurt her. He might hurt me if he finds out I helped you, but he won't hurt mamá."

"I don't want to put you or your family in harm's way. Just tell me how to get to a phone." Shelby stood up and balanced herself so that she could walk. "I have to get out of here."

"Be careful, guera," the woman said.

Shelby hugged the woman. "Thank you for all your help."

Ricardo helped Shelby walk until she could manage for herself. "I'll take you to a phone at the store, but the store owner is under Tito's control. Just pretend you're a lost visitor and you need to make a call."

"What if he won't let me use the phone?"

"He will unless one of Tito's men is there. I can't go in with you. Tito will kill me if he knows I've helped you. Make sure there isn't anyone with a gun in the store. If there is just leave and head north. If Tito has put out the word on you the man will know. If the words not out yet, just make your call and leave."

"How far am I from the border?"

"About seventy-five miles. I don't know how you'll get across the border, but at least you will be close. Stay away from as many of the border towns as you can. Tito has spies everywhere. You will be lucky if they don't capture you again."

◊◊◊

Angelica and Rex reached the front of the mansion. There were people running out of the building that now looked like a pile of rubble.

"Pig really pissed someone off," Angelica said.

"I'll bet it was the LA Bad Boys. Let's get back over here out of sight." They moved behind hedges near the corner of the mansion. "We can see most of what's going on from here."

"Shouldn't we call 911?"

"Even if we call them, Pig isn't going to let them in here. Who are those guys going into the building with weapons?"

"Those aren't any of Pig's guards."

"LA Bad Boys, for sure. Stay here. I'm going to see just how close we can get up there."

Just as Rex tried to move, gunfire rang out.

"Rex!" Angelica pulled him back behind the shrubs.

"Dammit. Guess we'll just have to stay under cover until things quiet down. I haven't heard any more explosions, so maybe that part of their assault is finished."

"You really think the Bad Boys are smart enough to pull off this kind of attack? Bullets can hardly handle his crew, let along something like this on Pig."

"Sorry, I haven't had time to bring you up to speed on everything. Bullets is dead and so is Yanks."

"When were you going to fill me in?"

"Priority, Angelica, priority."

"Who's in control of the gang now?"

He ignored her question. "Who's that guy over there in the jeans and button up shirt?"

Angelica looked at the man standing behind some bushes near one of the front pillars. "Not sure, haven't seen him before. He's hiding and he's not packing, maybe he's part of the catering team."

"I doubt it, he's yelling something, but I can't hear what he's saying."

"He's not trying to leave either. Maybe he's looking for someone?"

"Maybe I need to get closer. Stay here Angelica." Rex waited for the gunfire to subside slightly. Then he bolted toward the place where the man he and Angelica had spotted was standing. Angelica waited a few moments and then she bolted toward the same place.

"Shelby! Dammit Shelby, where are you?" Angelica heard Shelby's name just as she reached him.

"Shelby? You know Shelby?"

"Yes, she's my wife."

"Jack? What are you doing here?"

"How do you know my name? Do you know where Shelby is?"

"I'm Angelica. I've been talking to you on the phone about her."

Jack turned back to watch the chaos in front of the mansion. "Oh yeah, you're the agent who is supposed to be Shelby's friend. Well, I flew here this morning to try and find her. I haven't heard from her since she left our house on Monday. I can't get her on the phone and no one at this damn company will tell me anything. Now, I'm in the middle of a goddamn gunfight. What kind of business is this?"

Rex approached them and Angelica said, "Rex, this is Jack."

"I'm a DEA agent, too," Rex said. Why don't you move back over here by Angelica and let me have your spot? I need to get some pictures of these people."

"Well, I really need to find my wife."

"Your wife isn't here, Jack. I think Pig is responsible for her disappearance, but I'm not sure yet what he's done. Come back here and let Rex get some pictures until this thing cools down. Then we'll get out of here and go find Shelby."

"Okay, but I don't know how pictures are going to help. Where is the law? Why aren't they here?"

"This place is like a fortress. Pig isn't going to permit the law on his estate, not unless he's dead."

"I don't give a damn about Pig, his estate, or these people. I want to know where Shelby is, and I'm not leaving till that fat Pig tells me."

"Hang in there with me, Jack, I think Pig probably had her taken into Mexico by the cartel out of Mexicali. That's where her load went to and that's the last time any of us have heard from her. I've made some friends in that cartel and I'm sure I can get them to tell me where she may be. Trying to get anything out of Pig is futile. He's now got bigger concerns on his hands and probably won't even see you."

Rex joined them. "She's right, Jack. If he makes it out of this mess alive, he won't be stopping to talk to anyone."

"What's going on around here?" Jack asked.

"Pig's a big-time drug and arms dealer," Angelica said. We've been investigating him for months."

"Be careful what you divulge," Rex warned.

"He's not stupid. He's already in the middle of this crap anyway." She continued her explanation to Jack, "We had planned to take him down tonight along with several of his business partners, but the director wanted more evidence against the partners. We didn't expect this either. We suspect one of Pig's rivals is responsible."

"So Shelby really has been working for a drug lord? She told me something about this over the weekend but I didn't think she was in any danger. This is unbelievable."

"I know. We'll find her. I'll get the State Department to help us locate her."

"They might be able to locate her, Angelica, but you know they won't go get her," Rex said.

"If we have to Jack, we will go in and get her out ourselves."

"She's got a lot of friends on these roads. I know they'll help her. She's been in so much shit since she became a trucker, more than I think anyone has ever been in their whole life. She seems to be attracted to trouble. Now she may get killed."

"We won't let that happen, Jack."

"I've got to get out of here and find her."

"We're not going anywhere until one of these rivals kills the other one. They are fighting for Pig's turf. If we go now, they'll shoot us just for being in the way."

"He's right, Jack. Let's just wait this out for a little while. Once the shooting stops, we'll be able to make a run for the gate."

"I have my rental car, it's over there." Jack pointed at a little grey four-door a few feet from the opening of the circle drive. "Don't know if I can get it out of that mess of people and vehicles, but I'll try."

"It might come in handy, Jack, but I'm not sure it will go through the gate. We have no idea who's in control of the main gate or if we can even get through it. But it will be better than nothing, at least we won't have to walk or run down that damn long drive."

"I'm going to the back, Rex."

"What the hell for, Angelica?"

"It will be easier to get through the gate in my truck."

"That's a pretty good idea, but can you get to it without getting shot?"

"I think so. I think everyone is pretty busy trying to defend the mansion and command center. I don't think they will be concerned with one truck."

Rex kissed Angelica. "Be careful." He turned to Jack, "I'll wait for you to let us know that you have it. Then we'll meet you on the road in the rental car."

CHAPTER TWENTY-FIVE

"What the hell just happened here?" Pig threw his computer across the ballroom. "I want the bastards that just killed my best man." He looked down at Harry who had been so faithful to him for so many years. Some of the guards who were still protecting Pig removed large pieces of ceiling from Harry's lifeless body. "Go and find me the person who is responsible for this. Now!"

All but two men turned and headed toward the command center.

Hank was stuck in the hallway near the entrance to the command center. He had been pinned down by gunfire.

"Hank, can you get into the command center?"

"No, it looks like the door has been blown off. I'm not sure where these people came from, but it looks like they have control of the center. They are coming in the front door. I think I even saw a few come in from the back."

Gunfire exploded as Pig's men moved to eliminate the infestation from their house. Head Hunter shouted for his men to move out along with several guards of the cartel who had joined Pig's team. "That way! Move down the hall. That way! The rest of you follow me. We have to take out the ones at the front door and the command center." The men moved forward, shooting everything that moved.

"How did this happen, Hank?"

Just as Black Jack spoke, Hank spotted Drake with a gun pointed in his direction. Drake was using the steel door of the command center as a shield. "I think I know. Look behind the steel door; it's Drake. I'll bet his partner, Jazz, is in the Center. Those bastards have betrayed us."

Black Jack looked toward the steel door, then with a short aim Drake's head went backwards. Hank watched as Drake's body fell against the wall. It slid down the wall leaving a trail of blood all the way to the floor.

Jazz saw Drake go down. He stuck his head out of the command center. "Drake!" He looked toward Black Jack and Hank. He raised his gun and fired in their direction. "Bastards! You will pay for taking down another LA Bad Boy."

Hank and Black Jack took cover. "So that's who is behind this."

"How the hell did those guys get in here?" Hank asked.

"I don't know, you're in charge of the background checks."

"When they haven't got a background, it's hard to know who they really are."

"No time for finger pointing, Hank. We need to take these guys out."

Hank noticed that Black Jack's shirt was soaked with blood on the left side. "Black Jack, you've been shot!"

Black Jack bent down slightly and touched his wound. He removed his hand and looked at the blood. "Yeah, it's just a flesh wound."

◊◊◊

"Thanks for helping me. I'll always remember you and your mother's kindness."

"Be careful; these men are dangerous," Ricardo said, and slipped away.

Shelby entered the small, cramped store. The counter and walls were filled with food, trinkets, jewelry, and brick-a-brac. There was a large man behind a glass-encased counter, reading a Spanish language newspaper and smoking a cigar. Shelby didn't see anyone else in the store. "Do you have a phone I can use, please?"

The man put down his paper and looked curiously at Shelby.

"Teléfono?" Shelby put her fingers to her ears like the old-time phones.

The man pointed to a pay phone on the wall before picking up his paper again.

Shelby dug into her pockets. She only had two quarters and a penny. She showed it to the man. "No tengo dinero."

The man seemed put out, but he put down his paper. He placed an old rotor dial phone he kept behind the counter out for Shelby to use.

"Thank you." The man said nothing, he just went back to reading his paper.

Shelby quickly dialed zero. She wasn't sure if she would be able to dial Jack's number directly from the phone. When the automated machine answered the phone, she quickly answered each question. She requested to speak directly to an operator who spoke English. It took several minutes before the operator answered. "May I please place a call to 555-455-7888 and reverse the charges?"

"Yes, you can place the charges on that phone, your name?"

"My name is Shelby Mathews."

The operator placed the call.

Jack's didn't recognize the number, but he answered anyway, "Jack here."

"This is Operator 9671. I have a collect call from Shelby Mathews, will you accept the charges?"

"Hell yes, I accept the charges." Jack waved at Rex. "It's Shelby." He went back to the phone. "Shelby, where are you?"

"Jack, I don't have much time. I'm somewhere outside of Santa Ana to the west. I don't know exactly where but…"

The connection was poor and Jack was only able to get a little bit of Shelby's message. "Where? Shelby?" Jack yelled at the phone.

"Jack, I'm west of Santa Anna, but Tito is probably looking for me. I'm going to try and get to the nearest border town north of here. Tito has control…."

"Shelby! Shelby!" The line went dead.

Shelby knew she had made a mistake by mentioning Tito's name. She hung up quickly. "Thank you." The man heard Tito's name and removed his face from the paper. Shelby was already almost out of the store when the man got up and followed her to the door.

"Tito?"

Shelby shook her head. "No."

"Tito."

"No!" Shelby ran from the store in an easterly direction.

The large man tried to follow, but his bulk and wheezing cough kept him from pursuing her.

I have to get to Santa Ana. If I remember correctly, from there I can go northeast to a border town called Douglas. Can I make it? She knew she had to try.

"We've got to get out of here. Shelby is in trouble. Someone named Tito is after her near Santa Anna."

"Tito?" Rex looked at his phone. Angelica had just texted him.

"Okay, Angelica has her truck. She's bringing it around the other side of the mansion. We have to get over there somehow. I don't think we can use your car; that will take too much time. Let's cut around the vehicles over there. We have to stay down, though, we have no idea who's shooting at what in there."

As the men made their way around the mansion, Angelica pulled her truck off the line and headed toward the east side of the building. Gunfire flew from every direction, but she didn't care. She forced her truck through the congestion near the side and front of the mansion and headed straight for the road that led to the entrance gate. "Where are you, Rex?"

Before she knew what was happening, Rex was hanging onto the passenger side door. Angelica stopped the truck long enough for both men to get inside.

"Drive, baby, drive. They just started shooting at us. Someone is pissed off that we just took this truck."

"At least no one is manning the gate." Angelica slowed the truck down enough to make a right turn out of the gate.

Jack looked out the window. "I see why. All those guards are on the ground. Why hasn't the law showed up? I mean with all the explosions you would think someone would notice and call the cops."

"Pig isn't an ordinary citizen. The cops pretty much leave him to himself around here. It's financially more beneficial for the police department to let Pig deal with his own problems," Angelica said.

"Shelby contacted Jack while you were getting the truck. She's somewhere near Santa Ana and Tito's men are after her."

"Tito? But we saw him and some of his men at the ball."

"I know. But Shelby thinks Tito is responsible for kidnapping her."

"So I was right; Shelby has been kidnapped."

"Yes, but it sounds like she escaped and is on the run in Tito's turf."

"That's a big area, Rex."

"She said she was near Santa Ana."

"Wow, that's a long way away from Mexicali. How did she get there?"

"Look, guys, I know you're trying to figure out what to do, but I'm really concerned about my wife."

"We are too. I just need to get us out on the highway so we can head that way."

"How long will take to get there?"

"A couple of days. But we're going to ask the State Department to send in some agents to help us find her."

"Will they?"

"We'll find out soon enough."

◊◊◊

Shelby ran as fast as she could away from the little store. The proprietor took note of her direction before going into the store and phoning one of Tito's men. Shelby knew she had to keep going, even if Tito found out where she was headed. *At least Jack knows I'm near Santa Ana. It'll take him a couple days to get here. I have to make it to Douglas. I'll call him from there once I get to the border.*

◊◊◊

"Get these bastards and get them now." Pig paced the ballroom, waiting for the firefight to end. "I need to know what is going on out there."

"We are doing our best, Mr. Pig. They have the command center under their control."

Tito and several other cartel leaders were gathered in the ballroom. "Pig, do you need us to take down these guys?"

Pig was fuming. "No! My men can get them."

303

Tito's phone rang. "Really?...When?...Where?...Okay, we have run into a situation here at Pig's party. We're leaving now."

Tito pointed toward the back of the ballroom. "Pig, you're gift has escaped from my men. I need to get back and round her up before you have another issue that will need your attention. We are leaving out the back."

"She has escaped? How?"

"Don't worry about it. I'll make sure I get her back before you get this mess in here cleaned up."

Tito and his men left with their guns drawn through the rubble now piled up in the back of the ballroom.

◊◊◊

Shelby did her best to hide as she moved toward Douglas. She was exhausted, but knew that she had to get out of Mexico. *Once I'm in U.S. custody I'll be able to explain everything to Border Patrol. Jack and Angelica will pick me up and I can go home. I just need to find a place to hide and rest for a little while.* She noticed an old warehouse up in front of her. The seeded grass had long since been mowed. Patches of it climbed half way up the side of the building. Broken panes and spiderwebs took the place of the paned glass of several windows. Large holes protruded without explanation on all sides of the building. With caution, Shelby slid her hand along the rough and sometimes sharp metal of the outside walls of the building. She looked in front of her and behind her as she slipped into the wide opening of the entrance.

Shelby found several rooms inside the building. Each separated by broken or missing pieces of plywood, exposing the two-by-four interior walls. Dirty and dust-covered machinery were stacked in piles throughout the unattended building. It appeared that no one had occupied the property for some time.

Shelby found an old cardboard box that had fallen apart from the weight of the heavy metal items that had once been placed in it. Moving what was left of the metal objects from off the cardboard, Shelby pulled at the piece. Dust flew through the air, attaching itself to her already filthy body and hair. Shelby coughed and dragged the box to a corner of the cluttered room. She placed the cardboard on the dirt-laden floor behind the pile of junk. She hoped she'd be shielded from the eyes of anyone who might be looking for her.

◊◊◊

Angelica drove as fast as she could toward Douglas. They were going to need help once they reached the border and Rex had been on the phone with the State Department. "What? But she's been kidnapped and is inside Mexico somewhere. Are you telling me there is nothing that you can do for her?... You aren't going to do anything for one of our citizens?... Fine I'll remember this when it comes to one of our diplomats getting stuck in a foreign country....You can take my badge. Getting rid of me won't change anything. I'll do whatever I have to and you can't stop me."

He hung up and said to Angelica, "I've called in every favor anyone has ever owed me and no one will do anything. They say they have to go through diplomatic channels and that could take months. No one is going to lift a finger to get her out of there, at least not right now."

"That's not happening, guys, even if I have to go in there myself and find her and get her out, I'm not leaving her in there," Jack said.

Angelica had turned the driving over to Jack so she could make some phone calls of her own. "Oh, I don't think you're going to need to do that, Jack. Some of my buddies out here in the trucking world are already headed toward Douglas. I think that's where Shelby is headed. The borders there are penetrable and they have tunnels. We should be able to get into Mexico through that border much easier than one of the ones that are used most often. Shelby is smart, she'll figure that out."

Jack pulled out his phone and handed it to Angelica. "Go to my contacts and pull up a name, Shifty Gears. Call him. He'll get all of Shelby's trucker friends together. They'll gladly help us out. You also need to contact my friend Bones. He's a member of my motorcycle club and will help us out. I figure if we have to go in and get her we can take out a border or two with all her friends and their trucks."

Angelica didn't hesitate to contact Shifty Gears and Bones. Both were willing to dispatch as many truck drivers and bikers as they could find. Angelica tried to contact Lethal but he didn't answer. She wondered if he had been caught up in the battle at the estate. With help on the way, the three headed for the border.

◊◊◊

The firefight was beginning to die out. Lethal had slipped out to the back of the estate. Things had not gone as the gang had wanted. They had managed to destroy a good portion of Pig's estate, but Pig's men were still maintaining control. Lizard had not sent enough men to take over the whole operation. Lethal figured he would have a better chance of survival if he got in his PIGT truck and left the party. Most of his men were either dead or going to be soon. Pig would be in control again, and he wanted to be far enough away from the estate that no one would suspect he was even a part of it. He headed back home to LA.

CHAPTER TWENTY-SIX

"Who was the idiot that let her get loose?" Tito yelled. A gray-headed man stepped forward as the other men took stepped back, aware of what was about to happen.

"I did, sir. I was doing as you had instructed. I left her to herself while you were away. I didn't check on her enough."

Tito recognized the man, it was his father's brother. He had been a loyal man. Tito knew he couldn't kill him but he had to do something to show his authority to the others or they wouldn't trust in his viciousness. "Uncle, you have left me in very hard position. You must be punished for letting her get away." Tito stepped up to his Uncle. He pulled out the pistol that was lodged in his belt. He hugged his uncle's neck and then shot him in the foot.

"Ohhh!! Tito! I'm sorry."

Tito let him fall to the floor screaming in pain. Blood seeped from the hole in the man's shoe, quickly drowning the leather with the thick red liquid.

The man grabbed his wounded foot and begged for help. "Tito. Please don't let me die here. I am your father's brother."

Tito pointed at several of his men. "Take this man to his family. The rest of you spread out and find that woman. The shopkeeper in Pitiquito saw her yesterday. Search there first. She'll be trying to reach the border. Find her and stop her or the next bullets will be in your heads."

◊◊◊

Pig looked over the damage with Hank at his side and waded through the rubble of blown up sheet rock, wood, metal, glass—and bodies. "We have to get these bodies out of here before they start stinking."

Hank handed the phone to Pig. "It's the police. They're out front and want you to come outside."

Pig pushed the phone away. "Tell them I'll be out there shortly. I want to check out the command center first." Pig stepped over the bodies of several LA Bad Boy members who blocked the command center's entrance. Black Jack was propped up against the wall holding his side with the bullet wound. "They're all dead, sir. I cleared out the command center, but it's in shambles."

"Hank, get Black Jack to a doctor." Pig glared at Black Jack and then pointed at two lifeless bodies in the doorway. "If you hadn't hired those two lowlifes right there, we wouldn't be cleaning up this mess right now."

The room was dark and smoke was still present from the explosion, which had been extinguished by the overhead sprinklers. The monitors that still remained in places were black. Others were cracked and broken, laying in the piles of electronic carnage. "Hank, I want contractors and repairmen out here immediately," Pig instructed. He walked through the mass of bodies and rubble toward what was left of the front entrance. Several police units were parked in the drive. Ambulance services and fire department workers were there, ready to enter the building, but had been detained. The police had checked the outside perimeter of the mansion. Pig's guards who'd survived were not allowing them to enter the building.

"We need to get inside, Pig, tell your men to stand down. We need to carry out the dead and take care of the injured. The fire department needs to make sure there isn't any further danger of a fire breaking out. It could burn the rest of this place down. What the hell happened here, Pig?"

Pig motioned for his men to put down their guns. "You may enter my home only to take out the dead bodies and help those who are hurt. My sprinkler system has taken care of the fire." Pig sat down on what was left of a concrete banister that once held several potted plants, now strewn over the steps and driveway from the blast of the explosives. "Officer Kingman, my home has been under attack. My men have eliminated the threat at great cost of life, most of whom, you will find were intruders." Just as he spoke, an unmarked police car arrived. "Ah, your boss, Chief Ryan has arrived. I believe he'll explain to you your authority on my property."

The driver of the tinted, four-door sedan exited the driver's seat of the vehicle. He opened the rear door, allowing a thin, blue-suited, grey-haired man to emerge. "Chief Ryan, how nice of you to drop by for a visit. I was just explaining to your man here that he'll not be allowed into my home. He seems to feel otherwise. Perhaps you can explain to him our arrangement."

Chief Ryan looked at Kingman, giving him a nod backwards. Without a word, the officer had his men holster their weapons, moving them back away from the entrance of the mansion.

"Thank you, Chief Ryan. I was afraid there was going to be another firefight."

Chief Ryan made his way up several steps. He stood eye-to-eye with Pig who was still seated on the banister. In a low voice he said, "Pig, I can only protect you from the rule of local law to a certain point. This little escapade is well beyond those boundaries. What the hell happened here? It looks more like a war zone."

Pig threw up his arms with a laugh. "My party was crashed by the LA Bad Boys. I know you are familiar with them. They invited themselves to my ball and attempted to take over my business while we were dancing. My men did what they had to do to protect my property, my guests, and me. Your mayor and his wife were here; I'm sure they can vouch for what happened tonight."

"Why do you think I'm here, Pig? The mayor called and asked me to check on things. We are trying hard to keep our relationship with you out of the public eye, but these kinds of activities are hard to hide. People are going to start asking questions and someone may even notify the FBI if we aren't careful. Once the Feds are involved, there is nothing more we can do to protect you."

"Don't forget the amount of money I pay you people every year. I pay you to stay out of my business and keep your people quiet. Use that money to keep them quiet. If I fall, all of you will go down too. It is in your best interest to protect me."

The medics had entered the mansion and were hauling out the injured people while Pig and Chief Ryan continued their conversation.

Several firemen were removing dead bodies on stretchers. Harry's body soon emerged. Pig stopped the men who were taking Harry to a waiting van. "This man was my personal assistant. I want his body well taken care of. I'll come for it later. He'll be buried here."

The police chief informed his men that Pig's security would be handling the investigation and that they could return to their duties.

"Seriously, sir, you're not going to call in the FBI or anything? There have been some serious crimes committed here. With all due respect, sir, I don't think leaving the investigation up to a group of modern day gangsters is the right thing to do. You know they are going to cover up any involvement they may have had in the incident."

"Sergeant Kingman, I am well aware of your concerns. I have talked with Mr. Pig and I believe that he has everything under control at this point. He has assured me that he'll handle everything and let me know if we can be of any assistance."

Kingman knew he wasn't going to get anywhere with his boss. "Yes, sir." He motioned for his men to return to their police units and leave the property. "Let's go, men. There is nothing for us to do here." Once in his patrol unit, Kingman decided that he was going to call the FBI himself when he was at home.

When the police were gone, Hank approached Pig. "The contractors and electricians will be out in the morning, sir. I don't believe that the second floor has had much damage. Would you like for me to walk with you to your room?"

Pig got up slowly from his seat. "No, Hank, I can manage on my own. I want you to keep an eye on these people coming into my home. I want you to locate my computer and cell phone. I believe I left them somewhere in the ballroom. I need to get a hold of Tito and several of my other friends that attended tonight. I need to make sure they made it home okay and assure them that I'll be up and running again in a few days. I don't want to lose any of my business over this fiasco. Also, I want you to get in touch with the new leader of the LA Bad Boys. I think that's Lizard. I want him to know that his attempt to overtake me only netted him a whole lot of dead people."

"Yes, sir. Your computer and phone are right here. I carried them out of the ballroom with me." Hank handed them to Pig.

Pig took them without a word of thanks. "I'll be in my room. Don't disturb me unless it's necessary." Pig walked slowly to the stairs and to the entrance that led to the second level. Everything was in shambles, broken from the blasts of the bombs. He continued on through the destruction until he reached the steps to the upper levels located in the kitchen area. He stopped for a few moments and looked out the back windows of the mansion. Several trucks were missing from the line. He had no idea which ones at this point. He also noticed that several of his warehouse doors were open. He wanted to check on what was missing, but he was exhausted. There was nothing he would be able to do about any of it until morning.

◊◊◊

Lizard hung up his cell phone and looked around the clubhouse. He had just lost half of his men without successfully taking over Pig's empire. He thought about how he was going to tell his members' families. He leaned back in his chair.

Time Bomb entered the room. "They're dead, aren't they, Lizard?"

Lizard sat up in his chair. "Time Bomb what are you doing here?"

Time Bomb moved across from Lizard. "I've been doing some checking on things, Lizard. I made a little visit to Bullets' widow. I found out that Bullets' medallion ended up at his house after he was dead. How do you suppose that happened?"

"What's this all about, Time Bomb? I don't want to play these stupid, conspiracy theory games with you. Lethal just told me that the takeover of Pig's empire failed. Half our club members are dead."

Tine Bomb's face turned red. He put his hand on the knife in his belt holster. "It's your fault they're dead. Just like it's your fault Bullets is dead. You killed him, didn't you? You'll never be the leader Bullets was, Lizard."

"Get out of here, Time Bomb, you're an idiot. You have no idea what you're talking about."

"Liar! Several of the men who saw Bullets before the job in Socorro saw him with the medallion. Most of them can't even remember seeing you during the firefight. Those who did see you only saw you going away from Socorro. You would have had to have run into Bullets going that direction."

Lizard pulled out his own knife. "Like I said, Time Bomb, you're an idiot and don't have a clue what you're talking about." He brandished his knife towards Time Bomb. "Now, I'm not going to say this again. Leave!"

Time Bomb lunged at Lizard. Lizard pushed Time Bomb away. Time Bomb swung his knife at Lizard, leaving a long gash across his arm.

"This isn't going to turn out good, Time Bomb." The two men circled around each other, looking for openings to attack their opponent. "We have already lost half of our club today. You want to be added to that list?"

"I'm not the one who's going to be added to that list, Lizard, you are."

The men swung their knives at each other, then fell, wrestling like bears as each tried to stab the other. "You killed him, Lizard, admit it."

Lizard broke away and stood. Time Bomb had managed to stab him several times in different parts of his body. He had complimented each stab from Time Bomb with a stab of his own. Both men were soaked with blood. Lizard took several deep breaths before replying, "Yes, I killed that fucking, cokehead. He was destroying this club. He would have gotten all us of killed in Socorro if I hadn't taken him out and you know it."

Time Bomb jumped on Lizard taking him to the ground. "I knew it! I knew you killed him." Lizard blocked several of the stabs that Time Bomb had forced toward him, but one finally landed in his side. The pain rang through his body. Lizard knew he had to get Time Bomb off of him or he was going to die. With all his might Lizard threw Time Bomb off his body.

Once Time Bomb was on his back, Lizard jumped on top of him. He plunged his knife deep into the center of Time Bomb's chest. Time Bomb yelled out in pain but with one last thrust of energy, stabbed his knife deep into Lizard's chest. "Now we will leave this earth together, Lizard."

Lizard fell to the side of Time Bomb's body. Both men took their last breaths together, drenched in blood, on the cold floor of their once beloved clubhouse.

CHAPTER TWENTY-SEVEN

Rex had taken over the driving and they were now as far as El Paso. Angelica had fallen asleep in the sleeper and Jack was asleep in the passenger seat. Jack's phone rang. Still half-asleep, he forced himself to concentrate on the phone call.

"Jack, this is Shift Gears. I'm coming through El Paso right now with several of my buddies. I contacted several of Barbie's trucker friends and they're ready to help out. Some of them are eastbound on the 8 and 10. I didn't know where you wanted to meet up but I was thinking Benson."

Jack jerked out of his seat and hunted for the map on the dash of the truck. "Okay, Shifty, but we were thinking that since the call I got from her was near some town called Pitiquito, that she might be headed to Douglas. Nogales is closer, but Douglas is smaller and less monitored by the cartel."

"Okay, it will be a little further down the 10 from the cut off road we take just inside the Arizona line. Benson will be a good place for everyone to meet, there are roads leading to both Douglas and Nogales out of Benson. We really need to get together and make some plans."

"You're right, Shifty. I need to get a hold of Bones, my biker buddy, and let him know we're headed there. From there we can figure out how to find her and get her out."

"We'll see you there."

Jack looked at Rex. "Where are we?"

Rex pointed to the green sign on the side of the road.

"We're twenty-six miles from the state line," Jack told Shifty.

"Great, we're just outside El Paso."

Jack hung up and called his biker buddy. "Hey Bones, this is Jack. We're going to meet up with the truckers in Benson."

Rex and Angelica had been listening. "Angelica, I'm going to pull over the next chance I get so you can take over driving. I need to make a few calls to some of my contacts and see if we can get some local intelligence on Tito and his men."

◊◊◊

Tito's cell phone rang. "Yes?"

"Tito, the shopkeeper in Pitiquito said she was headed toward Santa Ana. The closest border is Nogales."

"Go to Santa Ana and look in every rat hole you find. I'll check out Nogales. Uncle Jesse will go with his men to Douglas, after he gets his foot wrapped up. He owes me. I don't really care about this bitch, but no one, no one escapes from me."

"Yes, sir. What about the tunnels in Juarez?"

"I doubt she's going to make it that far without help. It's going to be hard for her to find anyone who will help her here in Mexico, especially if they want to keep their heads. Let me know what you find out in Santa Ana."

◊◊◊

The sun pushed light through the holes in the metal building where Shelby had found shelter for the night. She tried to pull herself up off the cardboard bed she'd made for herself. "Oh God, my head hurts." It had been days since she'd bathed and every bone in her body ached as she tried again to get up off the ground. She remained on the cardboard. Shelby sobbed as she curled up in the fetal position; she had no more strength. "God, please help me. Please help Jack find me. Protect me from the men who are looking for me, please!"

"Well, the government isn't going to be any help. I did, however, find some agents who I worked with some years ago. They've been inside Tito's gang for years. According to one of the agents, Tito's been occupied over the last couple days with finding a woman who escaped from his custody in Hermosillo. His men are searching for her in both Nogales and Douglas.

They're also looking for her in Santa Ana. Apparently, they believe that she is hiding there."

Jack looked at his map. "That's exactly where we suspected that she would be headed. We have to go get to her before those killers find her." Jack waved the map frantically.

"Calm down, Jack, there are a lot of places she can hide and she's smart. We need to try and get those agents on the inside to help us locate her. If they can give us some idea of where she's at, then we can take our trucks and go in after her."

"What if they can't find her and Tito finds her first? How will they be able to keep Tito from hurting her?"

"Tito finding her might not be that big of a problem. In fact, if he has her, it will be easier to get her away from him than trying to find her. She could be anywhere, and without her being able to contact us, it's going to be really hard to find her."

"No. If he gets a hold of her, he might kill her."

"I really doubt Tito has any intentions of killing Shelby, at least right away. She is a pawn in a game that he and Pig are playing."

"I don't want my wife to be a pawn in anybody's game."

"I know. Let's get to Benson. Maybe by then one of the agents down there will know something. Trust me, it will be a whole lot easier once we have her located."

◊◊◊

Tito's men reached Santa Ana. Agent Rojo had been undercover in Tito's gang for several years and had earned Tito's trust. He was now one of Tito's top leaders. Rojo received a text from Agent Martinez, another agent who had infiltrated Tito's gang. Martinez let Rojo know that he and Tito were in Nogales. Martinez also let Rojo know that he had received a message from Glenn his handler, saying that Rex, a friend of theirs, was on the U.S. side looking for the same package they had been ordered to find. Rojo was to let Martinez know if he found the package. Rex and others were standing by in Benson to come in with lots of power to retrieve the package. Rojo wondered who this woman was that all hell was about to break loose for. Rojo texted back that he would let him know if they found the package.

Rojo and his men had entered Santa Ana on the road that led from the little town of Pitiquito. They had checked all along the roads on their way into Santa Ana, but had found no signs of Shelby. Once inside the town, Rojo wanted to separate himself from the others in case he was lucky enough to find Shelby first. "Let's get busy, Tito wants us to check every abandoned building in this town."

The three vehicles full of men who had come with Rojo to Santa Ana pulled together for a meeting once they entered the town. Rojo pointed toward the north. "Omar you and your men head in that direction. Juan, you and your men head in that direction. Leo and Markus, you guys take the truck and head up that way. I'm going to go out here on foot and check out these buildings. I'll meet you up there about two miles away. You start checking everything from there back to me. If you locate her, do not capture her. Just keep her in your sights and let me know where you are. Tito wants her alive. If you scare her, she might try to run, which will cause trouble with the locals." The men followed Rojo's orders without question.

◊◊◊

As they pulled into the parking lot of the truck stop in Benson for the meeting Angelica's phone rang. She looked at the caller ID. "Where the hell are you, Lethal?"

"I'm rolling along I-10 toward the California state line, where you at, baby girl?"

"Well, I'm in Benson with a few of my trucker friends. I was wondering what happened to you. I thought maybe you got hurt or something at that ball of Pig's."

"Hell no, I got out of there as fast as I could when that bomb went off and bullets started to fly."

"Yeah, Rex and I left too. In fact, we left with Jack, Shelby's husband. Have you had seen Shelby lately?"

"I haven't seen Shelby in days. Why? What's going on?"

"Shelby is missing, and from what we know, Pig apparently had her kidnapped and taken into Mexico. Jack got a brief call from her from somewhere in Mexico. Tito is behind it. We're trying to get her out before Tito has her killed."

"Tito's a really bad player too and one of Pig's biggest customers."

Angelica was curious how Lethal knew so much about Tito's and Pig's relationship, but she let it slide. There were more important things on her mind at the moment. "Well, if you decide you want to help, we're meeting here in Benson."

Lethal was actually closer to Benson than he was to California. He decided he'd stop by if for no other reason than to see what was happening. "Well, let me turn this rig around and head that way. I was going to head home, but I think I'll see if I can help. Why was Shelby kidnapped?"

"There's a lot of speculation, but we think it was because she saw something she wasn't supposed to."

"Not good. I'll be there as soon as I can."

"Great. We can use all the help we can get. See you soon."

The small truck stop in Benson was beginning to fill up with big rigs, many there to help rescue Shelby. Jack, Rex, and Angelica were devising a plan. But without knowing where to look, any operation was going to be difficult to execute.

◊◊◊

Rojo had searched several buildings along the road without any sight of Shelby. He was beginning to doubt she was on the road he had selected to search. He decided to keep checking the rough and dilapidated buildings until his men reached him. He entered the wide opening of a metal structure filled with piles of old machinery parts. Rojo stopped in his path when he noticed fresh, small shoe prints in the dirt.

He pulled his pistol from his belt as his detective's instincts kicked in. He reconnoitered through each of the rooms. When he came to the room with the pile of parts in the middle, Rojo spotted Shelby's golden blonde hair lying across the cardboard. He holstered his gun and quietly approached her from behind. He placed his hand over her mouth causing Shelby to wake with a start. She instantly went into fight mode.

With his hand still over her mouth and his arm around her body, Rojo wrestled with the scared Shelby. He spoke quietly into Shelby's ear, "Don't scream, my name is Detective Rojo and I am an American, undercover agent with the DEA. You have to trust me and don't make any noise if I let my hand go from your mouth. There are hundreds of men looking for you, I can get you out of here, but you have to trust me."

Shelby stopped struggling as Detective Rojo removed his hand from her mouth. She grabbed hold of Rojo and broke out in tears. "Oh, thank God. I was almost ready to give up. Please get me out of here."

Rojo extricated himself from her and cautiously moved to the door of the room. He looked around it to see if any of his men were around. "Shhh! I don't have much time. I'm here with a bunch of Tito's men looking for you."

"Please get me out of here." Shelby sobbed.

Rojo reached into his pocket and pulled out several pesos. He handed the money to Shelby. "I can't take you with me. There is a huge fleet of people on the American side making their way to Mexico to get you. I think the best thing for you to do is to stay right here and wait for them to come for you. Use this money to buy some water and food. I'll get word to your people about where you are."

"Oh, no. I can't stay here. What if they come back here?"

"You have to stay here. If I take you out of here with me, you will be in Tito's hands again. There is no telling what will happen to you if he gets a hold of you again. Look, I don't have time to argue with you. Stay put. There are a few small stores back toward the west. Don't let anyone follow you and don't draw attention to yourself. I'll get word to Rex and Angelica of your location."

Rojo's cell phone rang and he put it on speaker so Shelby could hear the caller "Rojo! Where are you? We haven't found the bitch? How about you?"

Shelby took the money from Rojo and hid behind the pile of metal.

"I'm here, señor." Rojo walked calmly out of the metal building. "Nothing in there but a bunch of dusty old mechanical parts and some rats." Rojo's men helped their leader into the pickup. "Let's go see if any of the others have located her. This is a lot of trouble over some woman." Rojo laughed and his men laughed in agreement.

◊◊◊

"This is terrific news. I just received a text that our undercover agent spotted Shelby in Santa Ana. He sent me the location. Right now, she's safe but we don't have much time to get to her. Jack, you round up everyone that you got here and head them to Nogales. There is a truck stop off the 19, we'll all meet there. Make sure everyone maintains radio silence until I give the all clear. Tito himself is in Nogales. We don't want to give him any heads-up. I hate going into Mexico through Nogales, but that's going to be the quickest entrance."

"Is she okay?" Jack asked.

"She's alive and hiding in a building in Santa Ana. She's been instructed to stay where she is until we can get to her."

Jack shook his head in disbelief.

"Angelica, I need you to get on the phone and notify Border Patrol that we'll be coming through their border. Tell them not to notify the Mexican authorities. It is hard to know exactly who is on the take on that side of the line. There may be some who owe Tito favors.

Just as the group of truckers and bikers were leaving out of the truck stop in Benson, Angelica noticed a PIGT truck pull into the parking lot and pulled up next to it. "Lethal, glad you could make it. We're headed down to Nogales. Care to join us?"

"Sounds like a plan. You guys have any idea where Barbie might be?"

"We got word just a little while ago that she's somewhere in Santa Ana. That's where we're headed."

"How're you going to get her out of there?"

Angelica pointed toward the two men in her truck. "Well, Rex and Jack are conjuring up a plan. I'm pretty sure it's going to be a doozy."

Rex spoke up, "I think we can get her out. We've got plenty of men and vehicles, but I sure wish I had more fire power."

Lethal thought about the secret he had hidden in his trailer. He'd wanted to save it for his gang members. Most of them were dead now anyway and starting the club all over was going to be hard. "I got something you might want to see. Come on, it's in my trailer."

Angelica put on her air brakes. Jack and Rex piled out of the truck and went to the back of Lethal's truck. Lethal opened it up. The men laughed as they climbed into the trailer with Lethal. "Where the hell did you get all this fire power?"

Angelica knew where it came from the minute she saw it. She stood at the bottom of the trailer. "Well, is someone going to help me up or what?" Rex and Lethal reached for Angelica's hands.

"After all hell broke loose at the estate, I kind of found my way to the warehouses in the back," Lethal explained. "I wasn't sure what I was going to find in those buildings, but to tell you the truth, I wasn't too surprised. I was going to take this stuff back to California and sell it, but after finding out about Barbie, I figured you guys could use it more. Besides, if Pig survives and gets his tracking system back online again, it won't be long before he hunts down this truck. Of course, if he doesn't survive, I can always have the truck painted and sell it in Mexico for a little money."

"There's enough ammo, guns, and explosives here to handle a small war," Rex said.

The thoughts of her time as a Marine flooded Angelica's mind. "Well, if our intelligence on Tito is right, he's going to hand us a small war. Not because of Shelby, but because we are on his turf. Look, Rex, aren't those boxes of ammonium nitrate?"

"Yeah, and that looks like thermite, tubing, and some pressure plating. This gives me some ideas. Let's get to Nogales. I have work to do."

Lethal was confused. "Intelligence? How did you guys get intelligence on Tito?"

Angelica stopped handling an AK she had picked up. "Lethal, I've got something to tell you. I'm an undercover DEA agent and this is my partner, Rex."

"Seriously, DEA?"

Angelica put the AK's strap over her neck and swung it to her back. Then she picked up a couple of handguns and placed them in her belt. Rex and Jack were doing the same. With boxes of extra ammo in her hands, Angelica sat on the end of the trailer. "Yep, we've had Pig, Tito, and most of their customers under surveillance for quite some time now. It's time to take them all down. Including that gang out of LA that's been a real pain in the ass."

Jack and Rex jumped out of the trailer with Lethal. All of them were loaded down with firearms. Rex helped Angelica jump off the trailer bed. "What gang in LA? I'm from LA, maybe I know who you're looking for."

"They call themselves the LA Bad Boys. We have mug shots of most of the members. Some haven't been identified, but I'm sure that's coming soon. That chaos at Pig's place wasn't some random intrusion. I don't have proof yet, but I think it was the LA Bad Boys. After we get Shelby back, that's the first place we're headed. Only this time, we're taking a fully armed unit of DEA and FBI agents. I'm sure the body count on Pig's ball is going to be made up of a lot of the Bad Boys." Angelica walked over to her truck. "From what I saw, they were getting the hell kicked out of them. Guess they aren't the Bad Boys they thought they were."

Lethal was stunned. "Yeah, I guess you're right, it was a real blood bath." Lethal walked toward his truck. "I'll follow you guys."

Angelica waved that she heard him as she pushed in on her air brakes and moved the truck forward.

As they headed out, Lethal wondered if Angelica knew he was a Bad Boy. *Nah, she would have said something.* He decided that he'd help get Barbie out of Mexico and then disappear. *That way, when she does get a chance to look at the mug shots, if she sees me, I'll be long gone.*

Rex's voice came over the CB. "All right, when we get to Nogales we'll meet in the truck stop off Highway 19. I want to keep radio silence until after we go in for the package. The channel we will run on will be Angelica's age. If you don't know it, you'll be informed when we meet up."

The radio sung with the 10-4 replies.

◊◊◊

Shelby had not moved from her spot since Rojo had made contact with her. The money he had given to her was clutched in her hand. The day had turned to night but she had continued to sleep. She was too weak to go anywhere. She knew food and water would help her to gain strength, but she didn't care. She fell back to sleep.

CHAPTER TWENTY-EIGHT

Rojo made contact with the other men in Santa Ana. "We didn't find anything, how about you guys?

"No. Maybe we should go back toward that store where she was spotted."

"No, I think we need to head toward Douglas. Maybe we'll locate her going that way. I'll contact Tito and let him know we're headed toward Jessie."

Rojo pointed his men in the direction of Douglas. He knew he had to get them out of Santa Ana. *The further away before the cavalry arrived the better.* He made a call before heading out, "Martinez, it's Rojo, she's not in Santa Ana. Tell Tito we are going to head toward Douglas."

Martinez informed Tito who had Martinez put the phone on speaker. "Fine, but if they don't find her there, I want them all to head here. I believe she's here somewhere. Reach out to the locals and tell them they'll be doing me a favor if they find her for me."

"I heard him, Martinez. We will head that way if we don't find her."

◊◊◊

Pig and Hank walked through the mansion. All of the bodies had been removed from the estate. A large percentage of Pig's guards had been either killed or were recuperating from their injuries. The command center was down, but technicians had been working for hours to get his business back online.

"Hank, make sure that everything gets replaced. When do you expect the contractors back to repair the structural damage? How about the warehouses? What is missing, do you know that yet?"

"Contractors are due back in the morning. After they've finished all the exterior work, your interior design specialist will arrive to replicate the look you had before. The electricians have advised me that you should be back online by tomorrow. I have taken inventory of the warehouses. Several hundred weapons, grenades, and most of the ammo are missing. The ammonium nitrate, thermite, and a lot of the tubing and pressure plates are also missing."

"So what you are telling me is that my customers' entire cache, is gone." Pig was livid.

"I also have to mention, sir, that two trucks are also missing from the truck line. Angelica's truck and Lethal's trucks and trailers are both gone. There were several others who were on jobs during the ball, but I've been able to track down most of them. But Lethal and Angelica's trucks are definitely gone without notice. There is, of course, Shelby's truck, which is still at the warehouse in Mexico."

"How about Harry? Did you make the arrangements to have him buried here on the estate?"

"Yes. That will take place right after the cleanup. Sir, I hate to bring this up but the Chief of Police has called several times. Tito has called you several times, too. What do you want me to tell them?"

"Tell the chief I'm busy and tell Tito to do whatever he wants with that blonde bitch. I should have never let my guard down, especially when it came to a woman."

◊◊◊

In Nogales, Rex and Jack congregated with the twenty-seven truck drivers and fifty bikers who had shown up to help. "Okay, I think the best thing for us to do tonight, since it's so late, is to get some rest. We have some things we need to do in the morning to prepare for our entrance through that border tomorrow night."

"Why don't we just ram the SOBs and get her out of there? There are plenty of trucks and riders here. We can do it," a biker said.

"That might work if we were in familiar territory. I want to get Barbie out of there, but I don't want to get all of you killed in the process. We have plenty of firepower to do this rescue quickly, without losing a lot of life," Rex replied.

"Okay, but how do we know she'll still be there when we go in tomorrow?"

"We have some men on the inside with eyes on her. If she moves or Tito moves her, they'll let us know. Right now she's safe and not in Tito's hands. What I need all of you to do is get some rest, fuel up your trucks and bikes. I need truckers who have room in their trailers to open them up so these bikers can load their bikes. We'll be using them, but not until we get inside. You bikers can bed down in the back of those trucks tonight. We'll meet here by Angelica's truck at 7:00 a.m. We have a lot of prep work to do before we ram that border."

"Rex, are you sure we need to wait until tomorrow night to go in? I'm really worried about Shelby," Jack said.

"Me too, Jack, but we can't take all these trucks and people in there without being somewhat prepared. Tito isn't an idiot; he hasn't been the top cartel king all these years for nothing. Martinez told me that he, Tito, and a bunch Tito's men are in Nogales right now. They are looking for Shelby, but they aren't expecting a small army coming in to get her out. We need an element of surprise since we will obviously be outmanned. I'm going to get you up earlier so we can do some recon on the Mexican border patrol. I want to know where they park and what they drive. Tomorrow, Martinez will let us know where Tito and his men are at in Nogales. I'm going to get these men to help me make some thermite bricks and some burlap bags of ammonium nitrate for IEDs. We can use diesel fuel for an igniter and detonate them with those .308 rifles."

"Sounds like we really are going to war."

"Trust me, Tito isn't going to take kindly to an invasion of his territory. He kills other cartel kings just for talking about coming into his space. He's not going to give Shelby up without a fight."

"I don't like it, but you guys are the experts. I'll have to trust you." Jack grabbed a pillow and a blanket. "I'm going to crawl into the back with Bones and some of my biker friends. Just wake me up when you're ready to go in the morning."

"Okay, Jack, go get some rest. Try not to worry; Shelby's going to be okay. This time tomorrow night we'll be busting out of Mexico near Douglas."

Angelica and Rex crawled into the sleeper. "You really think she's going to be okay, Rex?"

"Yes, Rojo wouldn't have left her if he didn't think she would be extractable."

"Have you figured out how you're going to get her out?"

"Yes, I have a really good plan running through my head." Rex snuggled up with Angelica. It had been the first time they had ever slept together, but it seemed so comfortable and normal. "I'll tell you all about it in the morning."

◊◊◊

"Why the hell can't you idiots find one little, blonde-haired woman?" Tito asked and then chugged his beer.

Martinez sipped at his beer, while holding the phone that was on speaker. "Tito, we have searched everywhere. We have searched every building. We have put out rewards to everyone in all the surrounding cities. No one has come forward so far with any information or knowledge about where she might be hiding. Maybe she's already across the border?"

"We are right here at the border, stupid. There is no way she got all the way from Pitiquito to Nogales this quickly without help. And trust me, if anyone helped her and I find out about it, they are dead. Now, go back and check everywhere again. Rojo and his men will be headed here tomorrow. The rest of you will head back toward Santa Ana tomorrow night. I still think she's hiding somewhere along that road from Pitiquito to Santa Ana."

"Yes, sir. We'll check everywhere in Douglas again."

Do it right this time, Jessie. You might be my father's brother, but next time it won't be just your foot if you let me down."

◊◊◊

Shelby moved around on her cardboard bed. "I need to find something to drink." Rojo's money was still in her hand. It was pitch black in the building.

Shelby slowly made her body get up off the ground. "Damn, every bone in my body hurts." At the opening of the building, Shelby carefully checked to see if anyone was around. She hugged the corner of the building and slid along the backside of it, away from the road. Rojo had mentioned stores to the west of her hiding place. It was late so she wasn't sure that they would be open, but she was thirsty and hungry. She had to at least try and find something. "Where the hell are you, Jack? Hurry up and come get me before they come back and find me."

Avoiding the streets, Shelby continued to slink along the walls of buildings and houses. Within two blocks, Shelby found a liquor store on the corner that was open. She entered the store, which was occupied by several men. Some were buying liquor, others were playing cards and a board game. Shelby wasted no time in finding two large bottles of water, a bag of chips, some cookies, and two large oranges from a basket by the cashier.

The storekeeper began to bag Shelby's items and told her the total in Spanish. Shelby had no idea what the man said and handed him two of the bills. The man put his hand forward for more. Shelby handed him two more bills. The man put it into his register without giving her any change. Shelby decided to make the man believe she knew what he had said. She put her hand out. The man smiled and opened her drawer. In Spanish, he apologized while handing her several coins and a bill. Shelby grabbed her bag and left the store.

Not wanting to draw attention or allow anyone to see where she was headed, Shelby quickly slipped behind the building. She put her bag on the ground after taking out one of the bottles of water. She drank the water so quickly that it made her cough. After getting her cough under control, Shelby put the lid back on her water, slipped it into her bag, and then checked to make sure no one was paying attention to her.

Slowly, Shelby moved back to her hiding place. When she finally was able to sit down on the only thing that she felt was hers, she took a deep breath. The first bites of food she had in days gave her a new found appreciation for things she had always taken for granted.

Rays from the sun came through the holes in the metal, just as Shelby took the last drink of her first bottle of water. She had eaten the chips, cookies, and one of the oranges. She carefully placed all of her trash in the paper bag. She slipped the orange that was left into the pocket of her hoodie. She crushed the trash that was in the bag into a ball, and put it inside the zipper of her jacket. Shelby laid down on the cardboard again in the fetal position, holding onto her last bottle of water. It wouldn't be safe to be out in daylight. "Come on, Jack, I'm waiting."

◊◊◊

"See, over there, Jack? Rex pointed at a group of uniformed men. Those are the Border Patrol for the Mexican side. See where they park some of their vehicles? Over there is the van that brings some of the Border Patrol to work. Over there are some of the local police vehicles. I came up here a few hours ago and those police units came to the border, apparently when things got slow in town. I guess they were getting together for a bullshit session or something."

Jack pointed toward a blacked out vehicle near the border patrol office. "Look over there."

Rex took his binoculars back from Jack. He looked toward the direction that Jack had been pointing out. "Hot damn, that's got to be one of Tito's vehicles. There are several vehicles around him that are loaded with men. I bet you fifty bucks that Tito is in that vehicle. They must be checking with the night shift to see if anyone saw Shelby trying to cross."

Rex motioned for Jack to move away from their concealed spot. "Let's get back to the trucks. We need to create some surprises for our friend Tito. I also want to make sure everyone understands what they need to do. I want to break through this border around 2:00 a.m. Not everyone will be asleep yet, but hopefully a good bunch of them will be intoxicated since it's a Friday night."

◊◊◊

Tito slammed his fist down on the seat. Martinez was sitting in the front seat with Tito's driver. "This is bullshit! How does a little white girl evade all of the men in my army? Even the cops haven't seen her."

Martinez tried to get Tito to focus other things. "I just got word from Juan in Mexico City. Mando has been moving stuff through our turf over the last couple months. The Federales have been taking a lot of our stuff out of the hands of the locals too. Juan says that it looks like Mando and the feds are trying to take down our section of the city. Should we go down there and check it out?"

"Shit, I guess we better but I want to wait until tomorrow. I want one more day to try and find that little bitch."

"Okay, I'll text Juan and let him know. Rojo and his boys should be arriving here soon. They are in Santa Ana right now."

"Tell Rojo I want him and his boys to check that town again. Have them check with the storekeepers and as many of the locals as they can. She didn't just disappear, she's got to be out here somewhere."

Martinez sent a text to Rojo letting him know that Tito wanted him to check out Santa Ana again. He also let him know that Rex and his boys would be coming through the border tonight. He had tried to get Tito out of town but couldn't, so Rojo needed to be ready for possible warfare.

◊◊◊

Rex had gathered most of the drivers and bikers into the back of his trailer. "Make sure that every driver has at least one gunman. I'll need six bikers and two trucks to go down into Santa Ana with Angelica and Jack. I'm going to ride with Lethal and we'll bring up the rear."

Angelica took over the meeting with a paper diagram. "I have drawn up twenty of these maps and our intended execution for this extraction. Now, this is only a plan; we have no idea how strong a force we'll be facing. Once we get into the theater, we have to be flexible."

"You sound like military. What branch?"

"Marines. Now, back to the task at hand. Once we're in the theater, we'll charge through the border here with six of the trucks. These trucks will, without doubt, draw a lot of fire. We will lose two trucks here. They'll be used as explosive deterrents, no bikes or gunmen will be riding in these two trucks. Drivers will exit their vehicles, hide as best they can and be picked up by trucks in the second wave."

"What if they don't make it to the trucks?"

"They will," Rex said. There will be so much chaos, that Border Patrol will be unable to handle the situation. But if for some reason if any of you don't catch your rides, go directly to the United States Border Patrol."

"We'll bring in the second wave of ten trucks. These trucks will include the two trucks with bikers, one being my truck. Then we will go straight into Santa Ana to retrieve the package. The trucks left over from the first and second wave will move quickly to our point of confrontation. Please allow the trucks heading to Santa Ana to pass and protect them as much as possible. Our point of confrontation will be the intersection of Highways 16 and 2. The third wave of ten trucks will blow through the border, bringing up the flank. This diagram will give you some idea of our plan. I have made one for every truck."

Rex stepped in again. "Now, this is only a possible scenario of what we hope will happen. This is our entrance, and from the diagram you can see how we plan to get out through Douglas. It is important that when we get to the point of confrontation, we set up quickly the already discussed plans for the explosives. Tito, his men, the local police, and the Federales will engage us. How we handle those engagements will determine how well this thing goes off. When you go to make shots at pursuing vehicles, make those shots count. Use the automatic weapons we have handed out for the confrontation point. Those who are going to bring up the rear will be receiving the strongest force of this conflict. After we have broken into their world and they gather their faculties, they will come at us with everything they have."

Jack interjected this time. "Our goal in this fight is to get Barbie out and all of y'all home. We are not here to fight with Tito and his men; we are only fighting to survive. Don't be heroes and please listen to Rex and Angelica. They are the experts here and they will get all of us out of this mess if we follow their lead."

"Jack's right," Rex said. We want to get in and get out. Now, let's load up. Radio silence until I give the go. Once I give the go for the first wave, we will communicate fully over the CB, channel 22. Bikers, only those that we have assigned will be taking their bikes off the trucks at the confrontation point."

Rojo was doing his best to keep the men that were with him from checking out the row of buildings where he'd found Shelby. "Tito wants us to go over Santa Ana again. He wants us to talk to the local people and check out the stores."

"Really? We have been over every inch of that town, Rojo. She's not there."

"I know, but Tito wants it done. We will all go back to the areas that we searched yesterday and check them out again. This time check with as many locals as you can and ask storekeepers."

Rojo passed most of the buildings he had checked until he came to the building Shelby was occupying. He once again snuck into the building. He found Shelby sleeping. He didn't wake her up this time. He only wanted to make sure that she was secure. He left the building, moving away from the warehouse as quickly as possible.

Just as he was about to check out the two stores on the corner, one of Rojo's men came running toward him. "Rojo, the storekeeper in that store over there saw a blonde female in here early this morning. He didn't see exactly where she went but she was here. Tito is going to be pissed if he finds out we missed her."

"We didn't miss her, Miguel. She wasn't here when we came through the first time. Maybe she just passed through here this morning and is headed to Nogales. We didn't see her on the way from Douglas. Chances are we will spot her on our way to Nogales. Did the shopkeeper say if she looked like she was running?"

"He said she was dirty and nervous. No one saw where she went so maybe you're right. Maybe we better check these buildings around here again?"

"I just checked all these buildings along here. She's not in any of them, maybe she's in some of those." Rojo pointed toward several buildings in the opposite direction of Shelby's hideout. "Well, I just checked those and Pablo is checking along that other side."

"She's not here, Miguel. Maybe one of the others found her in their area. Come on, let's go help Pablo. We need to get to Nogales."

Rojo and his men left Santa Ana. Rojo texted Martinez to let him know that a shopkeeper had identified Shelby but that she was still safe.

Martinez decided not to relay that information to Tito. He realized that their time under cover with Tito was coming to an end. *The minute Tito finds out that Shelby was rescued in Santa Ana, he'll know that someone on the inside helped with that rescue.* Martinez sent a text to Rojo letting him know that they would extract out with the rescue team. Rojo agreed.

Martinez sent a text to Rex, letting him know where Tito and his men were holed up for the evening. He told him that Rojo's team and the men who were with Tito were in excess of over one hundred and fifty men. Not including the local police, Federales, and Border Patrol. Firepower was limited except for the Federales. If they engaged, there would be the danger of RPGs and helicopter usage. Rex acknowledged the text.

CHAPTER TWENTY-NINE

The smell of diesel fuel, exhaust smoke, and burnt oil filled the air in the parking lot of the truck stop. The silence of the CB was suddenly broken. "Go!"

Truck engines whined into high gears as the first wave rolled at unstoppable speeds toward the border. The American Border Patrol knew the trucks were coming, leaving one lane empty. "Hit that open gate and haul ass, Blue Devil."

"The left lane is open, boys. Oops, looks like someone forgot to notify Mexico we were coming. Mexico's center lane is clear, I'm taking down the gate." The smashing of wood, flying metal pieces, and shouts from shocked Border Patrol rang out into the dark, cool morning air.

"Yee haw! Now this is what I call a road trip. Watch out for those border boys, my brothers, they are pulling out their side arms. Going to be some bullets flying. How many of you guys have made it through the gates?"

"This is Comanche Joe, truck two. I'm through. They noticed us."

"This is Lucky, truck three, and I'm through."

"Panda, truck four, I'm through."

"Big Purple, five, I'm gone. I think they want us to stop, but I don't understand Spanish. Guess I should have paid more attention in class."

"Cowdog, six, I'm through."

"T-bone, truck seven, I'm through, but they're laying down some heavy gun shots."

"Truck eight, Biggy, my partner is giving it back to them, but we are through."

"Cueball, truck nine, heading through now. Taking fire."

"Gear Jammer, truck ten, just cleared the gate. Plowing through the bullets and the smoke. Looks like the Patrol are headed to their vehicles. Hope you guys disabled as many as you could. They sure look mad. Boy, I wish I was in my truck instead of this piece of crap PIGT truck. Just kidding, Angelica."

Several patrolmen went for their vehicles. Rex had several of the bikers and truckers pull plugs, flatten tires, cut fuel lines, and place small amounts of thermite on top of engine blocks.

"Shit, my tires are flat," a Mexican border patrolman reported.

"My truck is smoking and Carlos can't get his started. We better call in the birds and back up."

"I'll call Tito. He has a lot of his men in the area. Oh, shit! There are more trucks coming through. What is going on? Call the Federales now!"

"Wave two, time to go!"

"Cover Girl, truck eleven, I'm through. Some shots at my truck but they seem busy with their vehicles. Good job, Rex."

"Mexican, truck twelve, I'm on her bumper. They look like they are using their phones, going to have company real soon I suspect."

"Little Chicken, truck thirteen, I'm through."

"Shakespeare, truck fourteen, in my rear view mirror.

"Short Stack, truck fifteen, taking fire, I'm gone."

"Grumpy, truck sixteen, they are shooting rifles now. I'm through."

Rex interrupted, "Keep moving, drivers, and don't stop for anything or anyone. Front trucks move over enough to let Cover Girl and Mexican through. The rest of you continue on to our confrontation point. Wave three move out!"

Big T was the first truck to go through in wave three. "Hey guys, they are attempting to put a car in the center lane. Rex, what do you want me to do?"

"Ram the car, Big T, we're right behind you."

"Big T, truck seventeen, just rammed a little white car. Come on through drivers, you're all invited to the fireworks just down the road a little ways."

Seven more trucks reported they'd made it through.

"I think we got company, Rex, disco lights coming from all directions," Lethal reported.

"Ram that gate, drivers, and get on our bumpers. We'll deal with them on the road. They have too much cover under the gate."

"Cupcake, taking a whole lot of fire, cops everywhere. Truck twenty-five pushing through. Just took fire to the windshield. We are through, but we've got lots of damage."

"Rooster on your bumper. Truck twenty-six blowing them up with little surprise grenades. That should slow them down a little bit. Oh, shit! I think that carload of boys is going home in body bags." We are through, Rex, but they are on our ass. Should we have the rear end opened up and drop them a little shit?"

"Not yet, Rooster, we need to get down the road a little further. Truck one, keep going, I'm switching you out with truck twenty-five since they are damaged. Truck ten, truck twenty-five, you remember what I told you about hanging back and blocking the road with your trucks? Ten you hold up in about twenty miles. The rest of you drivers move on through. Truck twenty-five, when you reach Lethal and Gear Jammer's trucks, prepare to use your truck for a blockade."

"Alright, Rex, headed at you."

"We got company all over the place Rex. They are coming at us from everywhere."

"We got them trying to come up our sides, Rex."

"Take the fuckers out, we can't use Rooster's surprise until we get at least ten to fifteen miles in the theater. Knock them off and keep moving."

Some of the truck drivers were using their trailers to fishtail the vehicles that were attempting to get around them. The bikers that were riding in the trucks were firing at as many intruders as they could. "We really need some help back here, Rex, they're gaining on us. We don't have enough firepower. We need to open up the rear and let the shit fly."

"Hang in there, Rooster, just a few more miles. Lethal and I are holding back. You trucks pass us and let us reach the back. Use a block and swing maneuver with Cupcake, Rooster. Put your trucks side by side. Let them get up close and then let Cupcake move up on you. Let them follow Cupcake to your side, then swing out wide, put those bastards in the ditch."

"Where are you, trucks eleven and one?"

"We are headed to the front, Rex. There are a few lights coming up on us from the south, but most of the lights are well behind us."

"Wow, Rex, that worked great, those sorry pricks are in the ditch. We still have lights behind us but they seem to be falling back."

"Okay everyone, we're coming up on our fifteen-mile point. Rooster, you ready to pull them in and drop that surprise in your trunk?"

"I got the pin and I'm ready to pop this balloon."

"Bring them in close, Rooster, get as many of those assholes as you can following you. Make sure Wes can get a good shot at those bags when they drop, then open that lid and spill that hot stuff."

"They are closer, closer, closer. Yes, baby, the pin just sent that hot balloon to the ground. Those bitches won't be following us for a while. Those ammonium nitrate burlap bags dipped in diesel fuel went off like fireworks, with just one shot from Wes' rifle."

"Good job, Rooster and Wes, you have bought us some time. Cupcake, hang in there, Lethal and I and truck ten will be with you in just a few minutes. Hurry up, drivers, and get by us. We have ten miles to set up the blockade. Cupcake, you and your driver will hitch a ride with us. Gear Jammer, just do what I told you to do earlier today. Cupcake doesn't have an explosive device, but I have an idea that will send his truck up in flames with yours."

"Okay, truck twenty-six just passed us, Cupcake and truck ten is just in front of us. On my signal we'll slow down and put your trucks side by side. Once they're together we will slow down even further, almost to a stop. Once we are almost to a complete stop, I want you to angle your trucks out, but keep your trailers together."

"We're in position, Rex."

"Carefully exit your trucks and head this way. Lethal, I'll be right back." Rex grabbed a long strip of ignition tape from the floor.

Gear Jammer stopped to help Rex with the rig-up. Rex took the cap off the fuel tank of the truck. Gear Jammer saw what Rex was doing and took the other end of the ignition tape, dragging it to the fuel cap of Cupcake's truck. Each man placed the end of the tape they held into their respective tanks and then they both replaced the caps.

"Okay, Jammer, head to the truck. Tell Lethal to move the truck up at least a mile. I'll be right behind you. I need to make sure the shot hits the target."

Jammer ran toward Lethal's truck and boarded it with the other drivers. "Rex says to move the truck up about a mile. He's going to hit the ammonium nitrate we put on that truck earlier today. Once everything goes up, he'll make it for the truck."

"Fine, but I'm not leaving him out there without cover. Once we get up about half a mile, I'm getting out, Cupcake, you drive the truck further up. I'm going to back his ass up."

"I'm armed, I'm coming with you."

Rex positioned himself on the ground so that he could take cover once the explosion occurred. He took one shot. Before Lethal and Gear Jammer could hit the ground, Jammer's truck went up in an earth-shaking explosion. Jammer and Lethal tried to stand up and move toward Rex, but the tape ignited the tank on Cupcake's truck, putting them flat on the ground again.

Once Rex knew the trucks were in full blaze, he picked up his weapon and ran toward the truck that was parked down the road. Half way back to the truck, Jammer and Lethal were dusting themselves off. "What the hell are you guys doing? I was about ready to shoot both your dumb asses."

"We were trying to back your ass up."

"Well, come on, that should hold them while we set up at the confrontation point. You guys hear whether the others have made it to the crossroads?"

"All I heard was Angelica and Mexican were still a few miles out. She did say there were disco lights still coming toward them. She didn't sound worried, so I'm thinking there probably weren't enough for concern."

"Let's get to the crossroads before Tito and his men get to us. I'm sure that Federales birds and firepower will be joining the party before long. We need to get set up so that we can get not only Shelby out of here, but us too."

◊◊◊

"Fucking assholes!" The handle of Tito's rifle slammed into the belly of one of the Border Patrol officers standing in front of him. "I pay you thousands of dollars every year to protect my interests on this border. You dumb sons-of-bitches let a bunch of worthless truckers through my border." He turned the rifle around and put a bullet in the heart of the other patrolman standing there. Tito looked at Martinez. "What the fuck is that noise?"

Martinez looked at the window of the border patrol office. "It's the Federales. They have two birds in the air. I see several units headed this way."

"Fuck, who called the feds?" Tito looked at the last patrolman in the building.

"We did, Tito; they disabled some of our vehicles. We figured the birds would be useful in finding the criminals."

Tito shot the man in the head with his pistol. "Let's go. Let the feds figure out what happened here. I want those assholes and I want them now." On the way to the vehicles, Tito looked at Martinez. "Did they give you any information about who these intruders are or what they want?"

"No, the only thing was that one of them remembered seeing a PIGT truck. A couple of them, in fact. No one seemed to know what they were doing here or why."

Tito put his rifle in his other hand as he entered the back seat of his car. "I think I know what they are here for, I'm just not sure why they know where she is and I don't…Where is Rojo?"

"They are at the hotel, sir, they got in a couple of hours ago."

"Have him and his men meet us out on Highway 19. We'll take this fight to them. They think they can run from me, but they can't hide, not for long. I want to know where those trucks are headed and how many there are."

Just as the cartel gang was about to leave the parking lot, the feds stopped them. "Where are you going, Tito? Is this some more of your trouble you're bringing into our country from the U.S.?"

"Fuck you, Rodriguez, you and your boys need to go back to bed. You couldn't handle this if you wanted to."

"That's not very nice, Tito, we are the law here. I think you need to stand down and let us deal with these intruders."

Tito motioned for his driver to go around the Federales' vehicles. "Do what you want, Rodriguez, just don't get in my way."

"I don't suppose that we will, Tito. You may think you run this country but you are sadly mistaken."

Tito flipped the bird to the officer and they drove off.

Martinez finished his phone call to Rojo. "They are on their way. They will meet us out on the 19."

"Call Jesse and have him move his men toward Santa Ana and up this way. Omar and his brothers can come in from Hermosillo, Pitiquito, and Guaymas. I want these bastards' heads; I'll hang them on the light poles, for everyone to see. Then they will know who rules Mexico."

Martinez made the phone calls. He also sent a text to Rojo letting him know that Tito was pissed. *We have to get out tonight Rojo. If he finds out we had a hand in this, our heads will be on the poles he's planning to use for those drivers he captures.*

CHAPTER THIRTY

Rojo knew Rex wouldn't use civilians for something like this unless he had a good plan. So he wasn't surprised when he came across border patrol officers on Highway 19. They were attempting to put out the fires that were engulfing their vehicles. Tito and his men had already been there.

The patrolman waved Rojo and his men on by. "Tito is that way."

Rojo and his men went on down the highway. The Federales' helicopters were overhead. Rojo knew Tito was not going to be happy with the interference from the feds. Within a few miles, Rojo and his men found Tito. His men were attempting to move the trucks that were on fire from the middle of the road. One of the men came to Rojo's vehicle. "I've tried to tell Tito we can't move them. We need to go around, maybe you can talk to him."

Rojo approached Tito's vehicle. "Tito, I think we should go around. We can take some of the side roads and come back to the highway. It won't take as long as trying to move these trucks."

"So you think you know better?" Tito asked.

Rojo backed away not wanting to get shot. "No, Tito, you always know better. But it's going to take some time to even get to those trucks with the heat coming off them. I just figured you would want to get around quickly."

Tito yelled for Martinez and his driver to come back to the vehicle. "Tell those idiots that we will go around. Rojo, you lead the way."

"Yes, sir, I'll get you to the other side of this road quickly. Where are we headed?"

"Wherever those bastards that left these piles of shit are headed."

Rojo got back in his vehicle with his driver and another man. It only took Rojo a few minutes to explain where he wanted the driver to go.

Martinez sent a text to Rex, letting him know that the blockades had worked to delay Tito and his men, but that they were going around the blockades and that the Federales' birds were in the air, headed right at them.

"Rex, this is Cover Girl. Mexican and I have broken off from the other drivers. They are waiting for you at the confrontation point. The bikers have been unloaded out of our trucks and when we left, the other bikers were rolling off the backs of the other trucks. We have the location of the package. I'll text you and let you know when we have it safely in our hands."

With only three trucks and a dozen bikers, Angelica hoped that they would be able to find Shelby quickly and get out of Santa Ana without too much trouble. Unfortunately, the flashing lights she had seen a few miles back were now almost right in front of her. "Rex, we got company."

The bikers that were riding in front of her truck could see the trouble approaching. "Okay, Mexican and Blue Devil, I know you can see what's coming. Let's keep rolling just like we planned. Let the bikers try and deter them if they can. We only have a few more miles. Once we are in the city, we will raise hell while the bikers we assigned to go in and get Barbie."

"You got it, Cover Girl. I'm ready to blow up and tear up some shit."

The vehicles that Angelica thought were approaching her and the others quickly turned their vehicles around, following the trucks. There were still flashing lights in front of Angelica. "This is a trap, boys. They are trying to block us in. I'm going to go around the bikes, Mexican. I'll use my truck to smash through the blockade. I want you and Blue Devil to flash the bikers to the right side of our trucks. Let's put our baby boys in the cradle. I've flashed for them to let me pass. The bikes are moving over, I hope they do what we want."

Angelica rolled down her window as Jack yelled at Bones, "We are going to ram the blockade. Get in the cradle so we can protect you!"

Bones nodded his head that he understood. He motioned for the bikers to move to the right and form a small cluster.

Angelica put her foot deep into the accelerator. Mexican moved to the left of Angelica's rear trailer side, blocking all oncoming traffic. Blue Devil, moved to the right side of Mexican's rear trailer side, forming a three-sided box around the bikers. "Here we go, boys, these bastards want to play? We'll show them how American truckers like it."

The police who had formed the blockade quickly moved out of the way once they realized that Angelica was not going to stop. Angelica saluted the Mexican police as she pushed and smashed their vehicles out of the way.

"No wonder my wife liked you. You're one scary, tough lady," Jack said.

The three trucks and the bikers easily made it through the blockade. "Everybody made it, Cover Girl, but we still got two police cars on our bumper."

"Blue Devil, can you fishtail them in the ditches?"

"No, I don't think so, Cover Girl, they're staying center to my truck."

"Mexican, drop back a little, side by side with Blue Devil while I get all these bikers in front of me again. Once we have them up front, we'll slow down enough to get them to come up on our sides. Once they're on our sides, we'll slowly move over on them, making them either take the ditch or eat our metal. They'll choose the ditch."

The three trucks would be entering Santa Ana in a few minutes. Angelica knew they had to get rid of the pests on their backside fast. The bikers were already ahead of them about a half-mile. They would break off and find Shelby once they made the town's city limits. "Let's get rid of these guys, boys."

Bones had the exact location of Shelby's whereabouts. He took two riders with him while the others raced through the town, breaking the silence of the night with their loud mufflers. Several local police attempted to make contact with the rowdy bikers, but the bikers raced away in all directions, flashing lights in fast pursuit.

Bones sorted through the streets until he came to the one Shelby occupied. He took no time in locating the dilapidated warehouse. "There, it's over there, follow me." The bikers quickly pulled up next to the building. "You guys stay here in case the cops show up. If they do, take off and give me a chance to get Barbie out. Once I have her on my bike, you guys head back toward the highway just like we planned."

Angelica keyed up her CB. "Those guys didn't give us too much trouble but now that we're in town, I suspect this isn't going to be as easy. The bikers are doing a good job of distracting the locals; you guys raise a little hell too. Jack and I are going to see if Bones found our package."

"Got it, Cover Girl, we'll do our best to keep the locals busy. Meet you back at the city limits in thirty."

"Look over there, Jack. Looks like those local cops are headed down the street toward where Shelby is held up. Let's give them something else to do instead."

Angelica put her foot into the accelerator, she found an old, almost falling down building. "Come and get us." Angelica put her truck right through the middle of the building. Wood and dust flew everywhere. The cops that were headed toward Shelby turned their vehicles around.

"Here we go! Hang on, Jack. We need to play cat and mouse for a little while."

The police chased Angelica all over the city. Angelica went through several other buildings while Jack threw a few grenades. Mexican, Blue Devil, and the bikers were doing the same thing all over the city.

Bones entered the dark building while Pee Wee remained with the bikes. He searched each room until he found Shelby asleep on her cardboard bed. As he moved to picked her up off the ground, Shelby screamed out, the water bottle she'd been clutching quickly became a weapon. "Let me go! Let me go!"

"Stop, Shelby, its Bones. I'm here with Jack and Angelica. We're here to get you out. Can you ride with me?"

"Yeah, I think so. Where is Jack?"

Bones lifted Shelby off the ground, ran out, and put her on his bike. She was weak and unsteady. Bones pointed to Pee Wee. "Hold her up while I get on. She's not in good shape. She won't make it on the back of this bike all the way to the crossroads."

"We've only got about five minutes before everyone is supposed to meet at the city limits. Can you hear them in the distance, giving the city hell? We need to get out of here before the feds show up as reinforcement."

The three riders headed toward the city limits. "Watch out, Bones, we got two cops coming at us. Shit, they're chasing Mexican."

"Come on, let's get out of here."

◊◊◊

"Rex, we have everything set up just like you wanted. These trucks and bikers will be ready to haul ass once they bring Shelby out of Santa Ana. The trucks here will be used as shields. The RPGs are set up in case the birds decide to return and fight. The explosives are set."

"Good, Martinez says we have company coming from the Douglas direction, but it's a small group. Tito and his men are headed at us from Nogales. The Federales have already flown over us, but have not engaged. There's no telling if they will or not. Has anyone heard whether the package has been picked up?"

"Not yet, but we've just now reached the time they're supposed to be at the city limits."

"Okay, stay close to the radio and let me know when they're headed this way. Things are going to go fast once all the players in this game enter the theater."

I'll keep you posted."

◊◊◊

"Rojo, Tito wants to know how much further before we reach the highway?"

"We just pulled onto it, Martinez."

Tito was talking on his phone. "Omar, head toward Santa Ana—sounds like they're tearing the town apart. I think I know why. Find out what's going on and then head toward me on 19. I'm headed toward Santa Ana now. He turned to Martinez. "Ask Rojo why our intruders are tearing apart Santa Ana?" Martinez relayed the message. When Rojo said he had no idea, Tito replied, "He better hope that all this shit isn't going down because of that bitch. If I find out that she was in Santa Ana and that this is her rescue, he's a dead man."

"Maybe it's the LA Bad Boys trying to show you they have some balls?" Martinez suggested.

"I'll cut every single one of their heads off and torch their bodies if it is."

◊◊◊

"It's time to go, Mexican. You hold back a bit, then you and the bikers head out of town first. Blue Devil, you hold back too and let your bikers get out. Has anyone seen Bones?"

"They're right in front of me," Blue Devil said.

"Does he have the package?"

"Yes, but he is flagging me down."

"I'm right behind you. Flash him to pull over. Mexican, it's time to use the surprise in your trunk. Blue Devil, you pull back with Mexican to give him fire cover. I'll make contact with Bones."

Angelica drove up slowly beside Bones. "She's in bad shape, Jack. She won't make it much further on the back of this bike."

"Go on a little further. We can't stop here. Mexican and Blue Devil are about to let go of their hot load. I'll meet you in about a mile and put her on board with us."

"Rex, we're taking fire from the helicopters, what do you want us to do?"

"T-bone, get those RPGs out of the back of your truck. We only have about a dozen rounds so don't use them unless you can hit them. Lucky, Cueball, Big T, Shilo, and Bomb-fire, take those automatics I gave you earlier. Find places in those trucks blocking the road where you can fire on anything that moves."

"Hey, Rex." Grumpy walked up behind the agent. "Angelica just came across the radio. They have the package and they are headed for us. Mexican and Blue Devil dumped their loads to keep the Santa Ana locals busy. As far as she knows, everyone has made it out."

"Good, one less thing to worry about. Is everything set up for us to evacuate toward Douglas?"

"Yes, but we're going to have to do something about the helicopters. They are going to bring in a whole lot of military we can't handle."

"I know; T-bone needs to take them down."

"Rex, Tito and his men are here. We're already taking a lot of fire from them."

"Okay, it's time to get down to business."

◇◇◇

Tito looked from the back seat through the windshield. "What the fuck is that?" Tito's driver slowed down behind the group of vehicles in front of them.

"Not sure; it looks like a wreck or something. The Federales' birds are flying; it must be something bad."

The vehicles came to a complete stop. One of Rojo's men came running back to Tito's vehicle. "We got trouble up there, Tito!"

BOOM! Flames flew in every direction, illuminating the outline of a helicopter as it fell to the ground.

"Shit, Tito! The truckers that busted through the border station are out there. We are taking on fire. Rojo and some of the men are already up there giving them hell. The feds are laying down some fire. The truckers took out that bird with what looks like an RPG."

"RPGs? You're crazy. No one has those but the military and me."

"They've got them and are using them. We've already lost several of our men."

Tito got out of his vehicle. "Go tell those idiots to get back here. Martinez, go back there and tell all those fools to get up here." Once most of the men had congregated, Tito asked Rojo, "What's going on up there?"

"They have a blockade of about five or six trucks, maybe more. We can't get through there unless we fight."

Tito's phone rang. He threw it at Martinez. "Tell whoever it is I'm busy."

Martinez answered the phone while walking away from Tito's explanation of what he wanted his men to do. "This is Martinez, Tito is…"

"Look asshole, this is Omar. Tell Tito we're in Santa Ana but this place is a fucking mess. We can't even get out of town. They left two piles of flaming shit in the roadway. The fire department is trying to put it out but it's eating through the road. I think it's thermite."

"I'll tell him. At least we have everything under control here." Martinez went back to Tito. "That was Omar, I conveyed your message. He said they're almost to Santa Ana."

"Good, we can use them for a flank attack. Pull these vehicles up there, load your weapons, and let's kill these bastards."

Rojo looked at Martinez; he knew they were soon going to have to make a break for it. Martinez grabbed his phone and sent a text to Rex and Rojo. *We'll make a run for it ASAP. We'll come on the right side of your blockade. Don't shoot us.*

◊◊◊

Jack helped Shelby off Bones' bike. "Hey baby, come on, we need to hurry." He picked Shelby up in his arms and kissed her forehead before lifting her into the passenger's seat. Angelica helped her to get into the sleeper before letting go of the brake. Jack hadn't got all the way into the truck before they were headed down the road. Once he slammed the door, he checked on Shelby.

"She's going to be okay. You need to get ready; this fight isn't even close to being over. Big Purple let me know that they're all set up at the crossroads. But we have lots of company there; this isn't going to be an easy shutdown."

"I'm ready." Jack looked back at Shelby. "I'm just glad she's okay."

◊◊◊

"Go around the trucks," Tito yelled.

Gunfire rang out all over the area. The Feds decided after they lost one of their helicopters to fall back and regroup. They had also got a call for help in Santa Ana. The Federales didn't want to fight Tito's wars for him anyway. They were more than happy to let Tito and his men fight the battle.

"Rex, Angelica just radioed. They're about three miles out."

"Good, when they break through that opening, I want everything up in flames. The bikers will be standing by to pick up the strays after the fireworks go off."

"Hey, those two men you told me about are here."

Rex spotted Martinez and Rojo as they came around the corner and motioned them over. "You okay?"

"Yeah, I'm fine it's just a scrape."

"Good, we have held them off pretty good so far. Angelica and the other trucks will be blowing through here in a few minutes. Once they clear the area, we'll blow this mother up and head toward Douglas."

"Sounds good. You've managed to take out a bunch of Tito's crew. But, Tito has men coming from both Douglas and Santa Ana. I hope you guys are ready for a hundred miles of hell."

"With these truckers and bikers, we can handle anything Tito throws at us. We have a few injuries, but we haven't lost anyone."

"Just remember, Tito isn't dead and he won't give up until we are."

Just then, Angelica, Mexican, Blue Devil, and all the bikers that had been in Santa Ana blew through the crossroads. "Maybe so, but they haven't met Angelica. I doubted going through with this extraction without the agency, but she said she'd go with or without me."

"Good for her. Let's give Tito a one-way ticket to Hell!" The men gathered up their weapons, positioned themselves behind the trucks, and joined the fight. Rojo picked up a grenade and lobbed it toward the vehicle that Tito had been hiding behind. The car went up in flames but he couldn't tell if he got Tito.

The trucks and motorcycles stopped several hundred yards away from the firefight. Angelica jumped up. "I'm going to help them get things set so we can get the hell out of this place. You take care of Shelby. There's some water and food in the fridge. If I'm not back by the time those motorcycles in front of you take off, put this baby into high gear."

Angelica jumped down from her truck and ran over to the others. "Where do you want me?"

Rex looked at her in disbelief. "I want you in your truck. We're about done here. Take Rojo and Martinez with you."

Several bullets whizzed past nearly hitting Rex. He quickly pulled Angelica down to the ground. "Get the hell out of here."

Angelica gave Rex's cheek a quick kiss. "See you in Douglas. Come on, boys, let's get out of here."

"Light this thing up, boys!" Rex pointed to the men he had put in charge of setting the explosives off. "The rest of you, find a ride. Bikers, you'll have ten seconds to evacuate after the first truck goes up. The rest will follow simultaneously and if you don't get out you'll go with them. Fall back!"

Each person fled to his or her respective rides. Rex pointed to the explosive men and the riders who would get them out of there. "Blow this bitch!" Rex took off with Lethal toward their truck.

The bikes in front of Jack started to move out and just as Jack readied himself to move out, Angelica suddenly opened the driver's side door. "Glad you made it."

"Yeah, and I brought a couple of riders." The men entered the truck.

Once inside, Angelica took over the wheel, pushed in on the air brakes, put the truck in gear, and moved the truck as fast as she could down the road toward Douglas just as the explosions detonated.

CHAPTER THIRTY-ONE

The truck shook with each explosion. "That will keep whatever is left of Tito's men busy for a while." Rex said on the radio. "Good job everyone. But we aren't out of the woods yet. Tito has a group of men coming this direction from Douglas and another from Santa Ana. I'm sure we'll run into the Douglas group soon. Santa Ana won't be far behind. We need to be ready for whatever happens."

"Aren't those bikes going to be too exposed?"

"Yes, but they aren't going to stay on the main road for long. I'm sending some of them out to scout the group coming at us. I'm also having some of them hide for an ambush on those that might come in behind us."

Rojo was with Jack and Shelby in the sleeper. Martinez was in the passenger's seat. "Thank you for helping to get Shelby out," Jack said.

Shelby was awake and holding onto Jack's arm. "You're the man who gave me the money and told me they were coming to get me out. Thank you."

"It's my job, ma'am, to protect the innocent. I'm glad to see you're okay."

Martinez overheard his partner. "I'm glad you're okay, ma'am, but we just blew a three-year undercover operation because of you."

"I'm sorry." Shelby put her head on Jack's shoulder.

"Don't worry about him," Rojo said. "He knew we were going to have to take Tito down in a week or two anyway along with Pig and his circle. He just wanted to collar Tito ourselves. He'll get over it."

Martinez warmed. "Pig's been on our watch list for a long time. Angelica here has given us more than enough info to make sure Pig either sees the inside of a jail cell or a coffin. That will be his choice when we go in. She's quite the undercover agent."

Shelby lifted up her head. "I want to be there when that fat son-of-a-bitch hits the ground."

Rojo shook his head. "I'm not sure about that."

"I don't see why not, she helped me nail that bastard too."

"Hell no! She'll just get in the way."

"No she won't. She wouldn't have been in Mexico if it wasn't for Pig. She didn't get kidnapped on purpose. Pig had her taken, we're lucky she's alive. Look, I'll take responsibility for her, but she's coming with us when Pig goes down."

◊◊◊

"Where is Martinez?" Tito yelled as he wrapped his bleeding hand in the shirt of a dead man lying next to him. The bullets taken by the men around him had been fatal. "Find me a phone. Bring me a car," he bellowed. "Where the fuck is Martinez?" A small man with a ruddy complexion approached the cartel leader. "We can't find him; he must have been shot when he and Rojo tried to get around those trucks."

The man noticed Tito's cell phone a few yards away and went to retrieve it. Tito pulled if from the man's hand and called Omar.

"Tito, where are you? We finally got around that mess in Santa Ana and are headed toward Nogales."

"What mess in Santa Ana? Martinez told me you were almost in Santa Ana a while ago. He said you were headed this way."

"I told Martinez we were detained because of the fires here."

"I'll kill that bastard when I find him."

"What's going on?"

"Never mind, just get here. There's a fucking mess at the crossroads. When you get here, pick me up. I'm going to find some way to get around this shit. We're headed to Douglas. I'm not sure who these bastards are or why they have entered my territory, but they are dead now."

Just as Tito hung up his phone, it rang again. "What do you want, Pig? I'm rather busy."

"I was just wondering if you located our little friend yet? When my security system came back up I noticed two of my trucks were in Mexico, but both of them seemed to have just vanished off the screen a little while ago. They were at the intersection of 19 and 2. You don't know anything about them, do you? One of them was loaded with a lot of fire power."

"Pig I don't have time for your shit. I haven't located that little bitch yet. I'm certain your trucks are part of this blaze in front of me. Do you have any idea how these bastards got into my territory? It looks like we've been infiltrated by the DEA. Weren't those weapons some of mine that you were supposed to be protecting?"

"No, they belonged to another client. Yours are still safe in my warehouse."

"They'd better be."

"Everything is fine, Tito. Perhaps, we should meet in Cancun next week."

"I'll be in touch, Pig—very soon."

Pig was nervous. If Tito had been infiltrated, then he had been as well.

◊◊◊

Angelia noticed that several of the riders ahead were breaking off. She looked in her rear view mirror and noticed that several of the motorcycles were getting off the main road as well. "Won't be long now, everybody. I suspect that in a few miles we'll be making contact with Tito's crew from Douglas." One of the bikers from the front soon returned to the convoy of trucks headed toward Douglas. He waved the trucks in front of Rex's on by. He turned around quickly and pulled up close to Rex's truck. "They are about fifteen miles up the road."

"How many?

"I think about six or seven car loads. We'll take out what we can."

Rex motioned with his hand to the biker that he understood. The biker took off down the road.

"Truckers, we got company headed at us, about six or seven car loads," Rex said over the CB. "The bikers are going to take out what they can, but be prepared to take evasive measure against the ones that will be coming at us."

◊◊◊

The man who had found Tito's phone found a Jeep with its windshield blown out. He was also able to drive Tito and the five other survivors around the multiple fires.

Tito and the six men climbed up the last sand dune, before reaching Omar. Omar had ten carloads of men with him. "What the fuck is going on, Tito?"

"I'm not sure, but the bastards responsible for all of this are headed toward Douglas. I want them dead." He got into Omar's vehicle. "Let's go, they couldn't have gotten that far."

Omar led the posse of eleven vehicles down Highway 2 toward Douglas. "Who are these people, Tito? Some of the local officers told me that there were motorcycle riders and three big rigs in Santa Ana. They said they tore up a lot of the city, but they didn't do anything else. One of the cops said they did see one motorcycle rider with a blonde passenger but the others were single riders. It's strange they'd come into our territory just to blow things up for fun. Are they just trying to piss you off or what?"

"I have no idea, but whoever they are, they won't get away with this. This is Mexico. Did you say there was a biker with a blonde female with him?"

"Yes, he said it was strange that she was the only female rider with the bikers. They said she didn't seem like a gang woman, more like they were protecting her."

"I see. They came to get that bitch Pig sent me because she saw too much at PIGT. And…they knew where to find her because of Rojo. He and Martinez must be undercover. I want to catch those bastards before they get out of Mexico. I'll use them as examples of what happens when you mess with Tito."

◊◊◊

"Angelica, look out!"

Four vehicles headed straight at Angelica's truck. She turned the truck to the right and put the eighteen wheels in the ditch. "Hang on everyone, this isn't going to be pretty." She slowed the vehicle down and put the vehicle back up onto the road before bringing it to a complete stop.

Some of the trucks behind her took the ditch as well to stop their trucks, but one of the trucks had to take one of the vehicles straight on. The car exploded on impact, leaving the truck with a ball of fire molded into its bumper. Smoke poured from the rig's engine, the driver and passengers jumped from the now immobile truck. The last car made several circles on the road, after being hit on the back quarter panel by a truck that was swerving to avoid the wreckage.

Without making contact, the car came to rest within inches of Angelica's truck. Angelica grabbed her rifle, opened her door, and jumped from her truck. Martinez, Rojo, and Jack followed suit. "Go around the back with Jack, Martinez. Watch yourself, these guys are armed. Take out anything that moves."

Most of the men in the vehicle that had ended up next to Angelica's truck had already exited their seats. They ran toward the other vehicles that were now in the ditch. Rojo hit several of the men as they ran. Angelica held her rifle on the only man left in the vehicle. "Get out."

The man limped as he exited the vehicle. The bandages around his foot were soaked with bright red blood. He held his foot off the ground and put his hands in the air. "Please, don't shoot."

Angelica looked at the man's face, it was familiar.

"Mamacita, Angelica. It's me, Jesse. Your friend from Mexico." Jesse was the man who had befriended her on her first trip undercover into Mexico.

"Jesse, what the hell are you doing here? What happened to your foot?"

Rojo looked at Angelica. "You know this man? We don't have time for this Angelica. Shoot him or cut him loose. We have to go. We have company coming from the south. We have to get out of here and get to the border."

"Yeah, okay!" Angelica pointed her gun to the car. "Get back in the car and lay down. Don't move until we are gone."

Jesse got back into the back seat of the vehicle and did as Angelica had instructed.

Rojo yelled, "Get back to your trucks, we have to get out of here," and then got back in the truck. "Who the hell was that?"

"He was a man who was kind to me and protected me when Tito forced me to have dinner with him one time when I brought a load to El Centro."

Dust from Omar's vehicles blew over the armed bikers as they rose from their hiding spots in the ditches. Their bullets ripped through the clouds of dust and shrapnel rained down on the unsuspecting cartel members.

"Move, Omar, we've been ambushed. "

Omar looked in the rear view mirror as he sped up. "They've taken out half my crew, Tito. We need to go back."

"No! Keep going; we need to get to those truckers. That is just another distraction to slow us down. We'll come back after we take out the truckers and their allies."

"There will be no one left when we return. I bet it's the bikers from Santa Ana."

"We'll take care of them later. We must be gaining on that convoy of trucks by now. Where the fuck is Jesse and his crew? They should have already made contact with them. I guess he could be dead, too. Move, Omar, move!"

Bones contacted Rex after the ambush. "We took out as many as we could, but they still have several vehicles headed your way. The boys and I'll come in from the rear—get as close to the border as you can. I'm sure we'll have to stop the trucks somewhere along the way to confront these bastards, but let's get as close as we can to home before that happens."

"I hear you. We just put the crews coming at us from Douglas out of business. I think you're right about confronting them again but for now, we're headed to the border. I'll let you know when we make contact with the leftover crew members."

Rex radioed Angelica. "Bones just told me they took care of several of the predators, but more are out there. Once they catch up to us we'll have the last five trucks in line to stand and fight against them. The rest of you head to the border."

Angelica was not one of the last five trucks. "I'm not going to the border without you Rex. We will all stand and fight together."

"No, Angelica! Go to the border."

Rojo, who was now occupying the passenger seat, grabbed the CB mic. "We will all fight Rex. We're all in this together. I suggest, since we know that they are coming, we pull over and get ready for them. They won't be expecting another showdown. They'll run right into us. We still have a few good weapons left. Let's take these son-of-a-bitches out!"

"Okay, maybe Rojo is right. Drivers let's pull over up here in another mile. We'll put some of the trucks on the right side of the road and some on the left to block the road as much as possible."

Angelica pulled her truck to the left side of the road. "Shelby, you stay in here, we will be back soon." She and the men grabbed their weapons and exited the truck.

Rex spent several minutes setting up the men and weapons to create an element of surprise. "Put those RPGs up there, one on each of the back trailers of those two trucks. I want those with automatic weapons along those ditches and some behind the sides of the trailers. Rifle and Pistol Holder will hang back to take out any leftovers that might get through. Keep yourselves covered and safe. We're about twenty miles or so from the border. Let's all get out of here alive."

Omar was doing his best to maneuver his vehicle around the wreckage. "This must have been where Jesse and his men met up with the truckers." He scanned the road. "Look over there, Tito, in that car—someone is moving inside!"

Jesse slowly emerged. Tito lifted his gun and shot Jesse in the head. "I should have shot him the first time he let me down. It's always family that keeps me from acting in my best interests."

◊◊◊

Shelby sat in the passenger seat of the truck and watched as her friends and husband waited for their final confrontation with Tito. They had done all of this for her. Shelby noticed a pistol still sitting on the dash. She picked it up, opened the passenger side door, and slipped out into the cool of the morning.

CHAPTER THIRTY-TWO

Pig entered the modified command center. Hank was still busy with the contractors and electricians. Pig looked at the monitors that had been placed in the once central hub of his empire. A few red dots moved on the screen but the lack of the red was a clear indication that his life's work was almost at a complete halt. "When are things going to be completely up and running? Every day we aren't up and running means I'm losing money."

Hank excused himself and went to his boss. "Yes, sir, I understand. But it is going to take some time to get all this damage repaired. I have sent some trucks out to pick up some things in Florida, but Black Jack is still in the hospital, and we lost a lot of drivers. It's going to take some time to get back on track. Perhaps you might want to take a few weeks off, go on vacation, maybe."

"Hurry things along, Hank, time is money."

Pig had attempted to contact many of his clients, but most didn't answer or return his phone calls. *Maybe it is time to head for the Bahamas.* He turned back to Hank. "You may be right, maybe a vacation is warranted."

◊◊◊

"What the fuck! Omar, what is that?"

The two men holding the RPGs found their targets and pulled the triggers. Within seconds, several cars in the line that were headed toward the trucks exploded, turning somersaults in the air. One car landed in front of Omar's car. Omar ran straight into the mess of flaming metal. One vehicle landed on top of another, causing the vehicle it landed on to burst into flames. The Jeep with Tito's men crashed into the rear of a vehicle that had taken an RPG head on. Both vehicles were ablaze.

Screams were heard from men still alive, but trapped after the initial impacts. Omar's car was on fire and Tito leaped out and limped as quickly as he could behind the wreckage. He tried to dodge the bullets coming from the automatic weapons hellbent on finding any trace of life still among the flames.

Omar's badly burning body was slumped over the steering wheel. One of the men in the back seat climbed from the wreckage with his pistol in hand. In Spanish, he shouted contempt and profanities as he aimed toward the trucks. He got in a few unsuccessful shots before taking several rounds from a sniper rifle, strategically hidden beneath one of the parked trucks.

A few men from the back had been hurt but not killed ran from their vehicles toward the ditches. Tito screamed at them, "Get them, you cowardly bastards! Get them!"

Not one of Tito's men moved toward him or from out of their hiding places. "I'll kill all of you myself when this is over!"

Shelby held the gun in both hands as she emerged from beneath the truck and focused on the man who had taken her.

Tito saw her and laughed.

Jack also saw her and said to Rex, "Make them stop firing, Shelby is out there."

"What?"

Jack pointed toward the place they knew Tito was pinned down at. "There!"

Rex spotted her. "How the fuck?" He then shouted at the gunmen, "Stop! Stand down!" The gunfire ceased. "What the hell is she doing?"

Jack slowly moved toward his wife.

Tito laughed harder. "What? You're going to shoot me? You're just a woman, you don't have the balls."

One shot rang out. Tito lay dead on the ground with one single bullet hole in his head. "Wanna bet? Never underestimate a female truck driver, you bastard."

Jack grabbed Shelby and ran with her toward the cover of the trucks. He placed his hands around her tear-filled face. "Are you crazy? Baby, what were you thinking?"

Shelby buried her face in Jack's shirt. "I'm so sorry. I'm just so tired. I just wanted it all to end." As Jack smoothed Shelby's hair with his hand, her sobs subsided as she realized what she had done. "Jack, I just shot that man."

"It's going to be okay."

Rex, Angelica, Martinez, and Rojo led a few of the civilians through the wreckage. Many of Tito's men had run from the battle and they now stood up from their hiding spots in the ditches, threw down their weapons, and took off running through the dirt. Some of the civilian gunmen raised their guns to fire on the defectors but Rex ordered, "Let them go! We're done here. Let's go home."

After checking to make sure there wasn't anyone hiding in the wrecked vehicles, the warriors headed back to what was left of their convoy. Just as they reached the trucks, several of the bikers from the rear flank, rode up through the carnage and pulled in behind them. "Well, looks like we just missed the battle."

Rex threw his gun into the back of one of the trucks. "Yeah, I feel like I just got back to base after dealing with a bunch of Iraqi insurgents. I'm tired, let's get the fuck out of here."

Angelica reached for Rex's arm. "We aren't done yet, babe."

Rex turned toward Angelica, then he turned back and walked toward the cab of the truck. "We'll make it just fine through that border. Even if I have to ram it too."

"No, you don't understand. We still have to take down Pig."

"I know, Angelica, but we are three days away from Pig's estate. The ATF, DEA, and the FBI are already coordinating a bust there as we speak. They'll probably have him in cuffs before we get there."

Shelby overheard them talking. She ran to Rex and pulled on his arm, stopping him in his tracks. "Please, Rex, I want to see that fat bastard go down. After all he's done to me, to all of us, we should be there."

Rex looked at both women. He put his hands over his head. "I must be out of my mind. What the fuck am I thinking? I'll call the agency and make sure that they don't take him down until we get there. Load up. We've got a long way to go and not a lot of time to get there."

The bikers and the truckers headed across the border without incident. The American Border Patrolmen saluted the trucks and bikers as they passed by. Word had come down from both the Mexican and American governments that this team of renegades not only saved the life of one innocent woman, but took down one of the worst cartel drug lords in Mexico.

◊◊◊

It took a few days for Shelby, Jack, Rex, and Angelica to reach Pig's estate. They had said their goodbyes to most of their trucker and biker friends at a truck stop shortly after crossing the Arizona and New Mexico state lines. Agents Martinez and Rojo had been returned to their DEA headquarters in El Paso. A handful had decided to run with the foursome all the way to Louisiana.

Rex had kept his word to Shelby and Angelica. Angelica drove the SUV they had borrowed from Rojo in El Paso through the now FBI-controlled gate, and by the time she brought it to a stop near the mansion's entrance Pig, Hank, Black Jack, and several others were being escorted from the building.

Angelica and Shelby looked on with pleasure as Pig's massive body was forcibly placed into the back seat of a patrol car. Pig glanced from the rear window as the car pulled away from his mansion and saw Shelby and Angelica standing near their SUV. "Well, I'll bet Pig wishes he had never hired us now."

"You're right. We both know that women are great at what they do, but don't fuck with us."

"Maybe you should consider a job with the DEA, Shelby."

"No! Hell no!" Jack said.

Shelby and Angelica laughed as the couples headed out for a night at one of the local casinos.

"I think I'll stick to driving trucks."

ACKNOWLEDGMENTS

I would like to thank Danielle H. Acee, Mindy Reed, Douglas Brown, and all those involved in editing and perfecting the text. Their guidance made the book release possible.

I also can't forget all of the individuals who supported me with their encouragement—my daughter-in-law, Cydney and my friends, Tina, Tamra, and Tammy. To so many others (truckers, friends, family members) who helped me in this endeavor, sometimes without even knowing it, thank you.

I will always remember all those who helped make this dream a reality.

With all my heart forever.
—Robyn Mitchell
robynmitchellauthor.com

ABOUT THE AUTHOR

Robyn Mitchell left the comforts of teaching in a classroom to explore the open road in an 18-wheel sandhauler. Her experiences and time on the road birthed Mother Trucker, a series of suspenseful thrillers based on the trouble and happiness Shelby Mathews—a well-educated, gorgeous blonde, wife, and mother of three grown men—finds while trucking.

Read More
Mother Trucker Book Series
Mother Trucker
Trucktress
Outlaws
Jumpers
Terror West